THE
HONEYMOON

KATE GRAY

WELBECK

First published in 2023 by Welbeck Fiction Limited,
an imprint of Welbeck Publishing Group
Offices in: **London** – 20 Mortimer Street, London W1T 3JW &
Sydney – Level 17, 207 Kent St, Sydney NSW 2000 Australia
www.welbeckpublishing.com

Copyright © Kate Gray, 2023
Cover design by Simon Michele

Kate Gray has asserted their moral rights to be identified as the author of this
Work in accordance with the Copyright Designs and Patents Act 1988.

A CIP catalogue record for this book is available from the British Library

Hardback ISBN: 978-1-80279-372-7
Trade paperback ISBN: 978-1-80279-373-4
Ebook ISBN: 978-1-80279-374-1

Printed and bound by CPI Group (UK) Ltd., Croydon, CR0 4YY

FSC
www.fsc.org
MIX
Paper | Supporting
responsible forestry
FSC® C171272

10 9 8 7 6 5 4 3 2 1

To my wonderful mum, for everything

PROLOGUE

A heavy storm rolled in last night – a month's worth of rain in two hours, unheard of outside of the rainy season. The soaking wet steps leading down from the remote viewing platform would have been lethal.

The sudden change in weather caught everyone off guard, including the man whose body now lies at the foot of the rough concrete steps – splayed out on his back, body twisted to the ground, as if he had plummeted from the raised structure. His gaping mouth is crusted with dried blood; his slackened, tanned skin already slowly mottling in the morning heat appears more severe due to the spread of bluish-purple bruises.

He probably came here for the view. After all, the Indian Ocean is just metres away, over the edge of the limestone cliffs. But, this high up, the sea breeze does little to slow the pace of decomposition. The body is already rotting under the glare of the bright sun.

Hundreds of tiny leaves and colourful petals from over-hanging trees have been blown across the corpse by the warm wind, but the floral confetti crown does little to soften the man's haunting expression.

Then, you take a step closer.

The fresh grazes on his thick knuckles. The marbled bruises spread across his exposed forearms. The muddy brown half-moons of dirt in his nails, evidence of a desperate grapple to stop him hurtling towards death.

A fresh gust of salty sea air is all it takes to reveal the truth, the petals covering his neck now dancing away in the breeze.

Suddenly, everything is a little clearer.

This is no accident.

1

Erin

Monday 12 September

As soon as I see her, I know that we will never be friends. Not back in normal life. And I don't mean that in a bad way. But fate is clearly about to bring us together – so who am I to complain?

I try not to make it too obvious that I'm looking as she pads over in her Chloé sliders, the rose gold lettering sparkling in the sun. Her blonde hair is pulled up into a neat topknot. She seems like someone who invests in herself and takes care of things. Nothing like me.

'Is this bed taken?' she asks. She has the voice of a radio presenter, full of energy and warmth. I detect a London accent.

I pretend to look up. 'Sorry?'

She points to the sun lounger next to me, her nails a pretty pale pink. That's when I see the ring. It catches the light and makes me blink, despite the very large black sunglasses I'm wearing. It completely overshadows my single stone solitaire.

'No, it's all yours,' I say, as casually as I can. 'My husband is having a siesta.'

The novelty of calling him my husband hasn't worn off; I don't think it ever will. I picture Jamie spread naked across the bed under the chill of the air-conditioning, on top of sheets that still hold the scent of our lovemaking from this morning.

'Well, it's hard work, relaxing in paradise.' She smiles and sinks on to the thick, squishy pad.

Within seconds a member of staff is by her side. 'Would you like a drink, Mrs Spencer?'

'No, thank you, Ketut.' She smiles, shielding her eyes with the side of her hand.

I see a name badge pinned to his pressed linen uniform. Ketut clasps his palms and bows his head; he vanishes as quickly as he appeared.

'Hot, isn't it?' She removes her thin ombré-shaded sundress in one seamless movement, exposing a slender, tanned figure that immediately makes me wish she'd sat anywhere but next to me. 'They're saying there's going to be a thunderstorm later. It makes sense. Something needs to clear the air.' She fans her face. 'I like it hot, but not this hot.'

'They're supposed to be pretty epic out here,' I say, then cringe. Who uses the word *epic* at my age? 'You here on your honeymoon?' I nod to her left hand, the glinting engagement ring nestled next to a thick gold band. It's amazing she's able to lift her arm with the weight of all that diamond and metal. It clearly cost an absolute fortune.

'Guilty.' She laughs. She has this charming, husky chuckle. My own laugh is too loud. It makes people in the street turn in a start when they hear it.

'Snap,' I say, but keep my hand by the side of my thigh. I wouldn't say I was embarrassed by my rings, just that they aren't quite to my taste. Both my wedding and engagement rings used to belong to Jamie's grandmother, and I love the sentimentality, but they're not what I would have chosen. Not that I could ever dare say this aloud to anyone. I'm still getting used to wearing them; perhaps they'll grow on me.

'I'm Sophia, by the way,' she says.

'Erin.'

Sophia. I couldn't picture a more perfect name. The way the final syllable rolls off the tongue like slipping into a warm bath on a cold evening. She reclines on the lounger and stretches out her long, slim legs. Of course, she must be thinking what I'm thinking, comparing our bodies, my burnt skin next to her olive tones. I self-consciously rearrange my faded black T-shirt that covers my plain and slightly too snug swimming costume. Chilled beach club music carries across from the infinity pool, all plinky repetitive beats and soulful vocals coming from the DJ booth in a bamboo cabana.

'Where's your husband?' I ask.

'Mark? Oh, he's gone to the local market, but I wanted to have a lazy day before we fly home. We've been doing all sorts of activities all week, but today is our last full day. I couldn't face trawling around packed stalls, not in this heat.'

The hotel is up on the cliffs but today the air is unbearably close. Cloying. Without a fresh breeze wafting through the rattan parasol every so often, the heat feels suffocating. My pale English skin has protested enough during this honeymoon, hence the T-shirt cover-up.

'We're leaving tomorrow too. First thing.'

'Ah, we're tomorrow evening.' She lets out a heavy sigh. 'God, I really don't want to go.'

I nod in agreement, but I don't mean it – this tropical heat is wearing me out.

Sophia rummages in the woven beach bag resting by her bare feet. Her neat toes are the same colour as her fingernails. She pulls out some sun cream and squeezes a dollop on to her hand and starts massaging it into her shoulders. Her arm twists into a funny angle as she tries to get to the part in between her shoulderblades.

'Do you want me to do it?' I offer.

'Oh. Thanks. I just can't get this bit here. I don't know why they haven't invented anything that lets you put it on without needing help.' She laughs again and I notice the awkwardness in her voice.

I take the sun cream. The heavy scent of coconut rushes up my nose. It's not the type I use – you can tell straight away that it's expensive: it doesn't drip like the cheap one I picked up in Boots. This feels more like a luxurious body soufflé. She flinches at the coolness of the cream against her warm skin that heats my palms.

I make sure to be as gentle as I can.

The next few hours pass by quickly. I'm taken aback by how effortless the conversation is considering we are two complete strangers. It's not deep and meaningful by any means, we mostly chat about our weddings, but she doesn't make any excuse to leave.

'I mean, I would give anything to relive it all but this time really enjoy it. Less stress, you know? I know everyone says planning a wedding is stressful but I had no idea how exhausting it would be!'

I gather that they had a big day, lots of guests, a detailed schedule, a seating plan military leaders would be proud of, made up of hundreds of tiny decisions which all fell to her. 'I can't believe I got so worked up over such small things. Seems a bit silly now. I just wanted it all to be perfect.'

I nod in agreement but, in all honesty, I never cared about the pointless details of the day itself. No wonder she has so much tension in her back.

'What is it you do?' I ask, expecting her to say she works in fashion or PR.

'I'm sort of in between jobs at the moment. I worked in the City but the long hours got too much,' she says, adjusting her bikini straps. 'Mark works as a mortgage adviser. What about you?'

'Jamie owns his own security system business and I used to be at Red Bees, it's this sort of youth facility which takes care of challenging teenagers – the ones that no one else wants to deal with.'

'Wow, stressful but rewarding, I bet?'

'Just like planning a wedding.' I swat a buzzing insect away.

She laughs. 'Exactly!'

I flush; not many people think I'm particularly funny.

At one point she goes for a swim, does several powerful lengths then rejoins me. There is still no sign of Jamie, or of her husband, Mark.

'So, what are you doing for your last night? Anything nice planned?' she asks, sliding off her hair elastic and combing her fingers through her wet hair.

'We've got a table booked at the Blue Fin.'

Her eyes widen, as I knew they would. We were lucky to get in; Jamie booked it ages ago as a treat for our final night.

'Oh, wow. I've heard amazing things about that place.'

'You should come!'

The offer spills out of my mouth. I expect her to turn it down immediately but she pauses. Her green eyes crinkle.

'Really?'

'Yeah.' I waft a hand to pretend it's no big deal. As though we go to places like the Blue Fin all the time, which is a lie. I've looked up images online; even our wedding venue wasn't as fancy as this place. It's a little further along the cliffs, nestled against the limestone rocks, with its own viewing platform suspended over the vast ocean. The kitchen staff actually go down to one of the sandy coves and fish while you wait.

'No.' She shakes her head. Droplets of water sprinkle on her flat stomach as she does. 'Thank you, but I don't want to intrude on your last night.'

'You wouldn't be, honestly. It'd be nice to have some company. I've had ten full days, twenty-four seven, with Jamie, I think we've almost run out of things to say to one another!'

I don't know why I say that. It's supposed to be a joke but she doesn't laugh. Instead, she chews her bottom lip. 'Are you sure? Really?'

I nod, and push my feet into my flip-flops. 'I'll go and ask reception to call and add two more chairs. I'm sure it'll be no problem.'

'Don't you want to check with your husband first?'

'Jamie's so laid-back about things like this.' I swipe my hand and dash off, buoyed by my sudden spontaneity.

Despite him telling me it's fine, I can tell that Jamie isn't enchanted by the idea. I probably shouldn't have woken him from his siesta, but he must see how excited I am. So, to keep his new wife happy, he doesn't dampen my spirits and tell me it's ridiculous having dinner with a couple we've only just met. I feel a thrill when asking the receptionist to amend our reservation, telling her that it's now a table of four, not two.

2

Sophia

'Don't you think it's weird to make friends on our honey-moon?' Mark asks as we walk into the clifftop restaurant.

'I already tried to get us in here and there was a waiting list,' I say, shifting in my silk jumpsuit, hoping it's smart enough for a place like this. Up close, the Blue Fin looks even better than it did online. A petite waitress leads us past a DJ playing ambient house music, his decks under low-hanging chandeliers made from driftwood that sway in the air-conditioned breeze. Sun-bleached drapes hang on either side of the doors, framing the view. Flickering candles in glass lanterns light our way across the large terrace that juts out across the Indian Ocean.

Mark flashes a winning smile and shakes his head. 'I wouldn't expect anything less from you.'

'Well, there's still time to turn around.'

'It's fine. Let's just hope they're a nice couple.'

'If not, the food will make up for it,' I say behind my hand, spotting Erin waving at us. They are sitting side by side, waiting for us to take our positions. A spectacular spray of delicate white orchids and vibrant lotus flowers takes up the centre of the table.

'Sorry we're late!' I give an awkward wave, unsure whether to kiss her hello or not.

Erin is wearing a sleeveless dress covered in wide, dark green palm leaves. She flicks her hair back and I try not to wince at how sore her burnt shoulders look.

'I'm Sophia, and this is my husband, Mark.'

'Hey! I'm Jamie.' The men shake hands across the table. I guess they're around the same age as us – early thirties.

Jamie is one of those people who smile with their whole face. He welcomes us and gestures for us to sit down. A waft of expensive oaky aftershave fills my nose as he goes to sit back in his chair. He looks nothing like I imagined. Dark wavy hair, a hint of stubble across his tanned jaw, and the most piercing blue-green eyes. I'm ashamed to say I'm surprised – Erin is so . . . plain.

'I still find it strange introducing you as my husband,' I say to Mark, laughing, feeling flushed. 'Wow, this place! Thank you so much for inviting us,' I continue, pressing my hands to my cheeks.

'No problem,' Jamie says warmly.

'Our pleasure!' Erin grins.

Just then a waitress appears and hands out drinks menus. I focus on the extensive list of fresh fruit cocktails and try to get a grip. Of course Mark is handsome too, in a cuddly, honest, salt-of-the-earth kind of way. When you've been together for as long as we have, it's easy to overlook this. I give his thigh a stroke under the tablecloth, grateful that he can't read my thoughts.

I choose a lemongrass-infused mojito. The men have gone for spiced rum cocktails.

'Oh, hang on,' Erin says, as the waitress is about to leave. 'Please can I change my order? I'd like the same as Sophia.' She gives me a wink.

'So, whereabouts do you live in England?' Jamie asks.

'London. How about you?' I say, picking up a complimentary spiced rice cracker.

'Same, well, I used to live in Battersea but recently moved out to the country,' Jamie says.

'I was so used to living in small flats, I couldn't believe it when we first went to see the house in Sussex,' Erin adds.

'Sussex? My sister is over in Harrow End,' Mark says.

'Really? We're in East Fern. We only just moved there, literally a week or so before the wedding.' Erin smiles.

I sit back. 'You moved house, got married and planned a honeymoon? Wow.'

'Makes sense to get the stresses in life out of the way in one go,' Jamie says casually, shrugging. I imagine he's downplaying how hard it's been.

'If you're ever nearby then let us know,' Erin says. 'The house has plenty of room for guests.'

At first, when Erin invited us tonight, I was only thinking about being able to say we've dined at the Blue Fin. Now I feel mean for taking this couple's hospitality for granted. They're clearly just very generous and friendly people.

'Sophia told us you went to the market today?' Erin asks Mark, fanning her face with the menu. 'Was it full on? I don't know how you coped in this heat.'

'Yeah, it wasn't too bad.'

'I've never been a fan of markets,' she says. 'All the pressure of haggling and having to make decisions on the spot. I get all flustered. Then add in the heat. God, I would have been useless!'

Jamie lets out a warm laugh. 'You're not that bad.'

'You just have a much better poker face than I do,' she says to Jamie, who pours cucumber-infused ice-cold water into our glasses as we wait for our cocktails.

'The moment you hesitate, that's when you've lost. You can't let them see any sign of weakness, right, Mark?' Jamie replies.

'Exactly, mate.' Mark nods in agreement. 'Nerves of steel is what you need. It's all about willpower, really.'

'Willpower? That's never been my strong suit.' Erin pats her round stomach and laughs a little self-consciously. I watch as Jamie leans across and plants a kiss on her forehead.

'Well, clearly I could do with some advice from you, Jamie, as I didn't get any bargains,' Mark says with a smile.

He had returned from the market in a mood, annoyed at himself for getting confused or misunderstanding the price or something and ending up spending more than he wanted to. I told him not to beat himself up: it's easy to do. The Indonesian rupiah has felt like Monopoly money, especially as neither of us ever carries much cash back home. Thankfully it wasn't a vast sum and, apart from hurting his pride, it could have been a lot worse.

I sit back in my wicker chair as the waitress brings over our elaborately decorated cocktails.

With the sea air, the relaxing music and the scent of the tropical flowers, I can't help but sigh with happiness, but it's not long before thoughts of returning to drizzly grey England overtake this moment of gratitude. It's more than just holiday blues kicking in early. Much more. Being thousands of miles away from our lives and our problems is about to come to an end. I try to blink the anxious thoughts away. I can't change anything – tomorrow is happening whether I like it or not, so I just need to concentrate on enjoying this last night.

Erin is gesticulating wildly; I try to tune back in to whatever story she's telling.

In an instant, a gust of salty wind snuffs out the candle in the centre of our table. The terrace lights flicker. There's a ripple of awkward laughter across the busy restaurant. The storm is on its way. All of a sudden, the restaurant lights cut out completely, plunging us into near darkness. Panic unfurls in my chest. There's no time to say a word. My mind is trying to work out what's happening when I hear a sound that makes my back prickle with fear. I sit bolt upright as my ears ring with an ear-piercing scream.

3

Sophia

A woman at the next table is giggling at her over-the-top reaction to the power cut, while her friends tease her for being so dramatic. In a matter of seconds, the lights come back on and normal chatter resumes.

'I guess this storm is going to cause a few problems. You OK, Sophia?' Jamie asks, his piercing eyes fixed in a look of concern.

My heart is still racing at the interruption. I pick up a napkin and dab it against my forehead, my breath shaky. 'Fine, yeah. It just made me jump.' I try to let out a light laugh but even I can hear it's forced. 'Let's hope our flights are all delayed and we get to stay.'

Erin smiles and looks down at her menu, but it takes Jamie a second or two before he takes his eyes off me. 'Sure,' he says. 'An extra few days would be ideal!'

'Hard agree,' Mark says, clinking his glass with Jamie's.

I shift in my seat. I've never liked storms. The change in the weather just adds to the nerves about going back home. A smiling waitress rushes over to relight the candles on our table.

'So, Mark.' Jamie clears his throat after we order. 'Erin tells me you're a mortgage adviser?'

'Yeah,' Mark says with a tight smile. He hates his job. It was only supposed to be a temporary thing but somehow, ten years later, he's still there, trapped by the perks of a decent pension and sick pay – the sexy things in life.

Erin nods politely. 'That sounds interesting.'

'Nah, it's pretty boring really. What about you two?'

'I'm about to start project-managing our house renovation and Jamie has his own security business, installing residential and commercial alarm systems,' Erin says.

'See, now that sounds boring!' Jamie lets out a warm laugh, leaning back in his chair. 'Basically, my company fits and monitors smart alarms, app-based stuff.'

'But soon they'll be launching a brand new model to the market. They've just got the final investor on board!' Erin adds, rubbing Jamie's arm proudly.

I know this will get Mark interested. He's obsessed with gadgets. As predicted, he sits forward and taps his phone, which is on the table in front of him.

'Well, you can monitor your surroundings so much more easily nowadays.'

'You've got one fitted, have you, mate?' Jamie asks.

'Yeah, monitoring only. I wanted the bells and whistles but . . .' Mark rubs his forefingers together.

Erin looks at me and I raise a smile but I hate it. I never wanted to live in a place where I was being watched, yet needs must. Mark told me he hasn't been checking the live feed while we've been away but I wouldn't be surprised if he has.

16

'I mean, the image quality's a little grainy, but the main reason we wanted it was as a deterrent.'

Mark shrugs, and Jamie nods. 'Sometimes the grander the system, the more it's like pointing a flashing neon sign alerting criminals that there's something valuable worth robbing. What I've been working on with my team is far more covert: cameras the size of pinheads, that sort of thing.'

Erin beams at him as he speaks. I wonder how long they've been together – they look very much in the first flush of love.

'Excuse me.' A waitress appears by the side of our table holding a tray full of dishes. A waft of aromatic spices fills the air and soon the table is heaving. Seared, blackened tuna and scallops with a hot chilli paste, plump chicken skewers with lemongrass, grilled prawns in a rich coconut broth, beer-battered shrimp with green papaya slaw, and smaller bowls of rice and carved vegetables seem to fill every inch of space.

'Wow.' I shake my head, overwhelmed. 'I hope you're hungry!'

'I know, right? We *have* to take a photo,' Erin says, nudging Jamie. 'Can you do it? I left my phone charging in the room.'

'Hang on.' Jamie pulls his out of his pocket and pulls a face. 'Ah, sorry. Mine's dead.'

'Let me get one.' I angle my phone high above the food and take a snap. My mouth is watering at the smells filling my nose. 'Now one of you two?' I offer.

Erin lets out a small protest, saying something about not being photogenic, but they move closer together and smile for the camera. It's suddenly a lot busier on the terrace, bodies jostling about in the space, spilling over from the bar area.

'Say cheese!'

'Oh! I wasn't ready! Can you do one more? Hang on, let me . . .' Erin lifts her arm to place it around Jamie, at the exact same time that a man walks behind her carrying a pint of lager. Her arm knocks into his drink and frothy golden liquid spills over both of them.

'Oh, my God! I'm so sorry! I didn't see you!' Erin squeals.

His pale blue short-sleeved shirt is drenched. 'Bloody hell!' he barks, creasing his sweaty brow.

'I'm so sorry, I honestly didn't know you were there. It was an accident,' Erin says, quickly dabbing her dress with a napkin. Liquid glistens on her burnt cleavage.

'An accident?'

You can tell he's had a drink. His narrowed bloodshot eyes scan our table. I sense his gaze resting on me for a fraction too long. Mark's whole body has gone rigid beside me; he hates any sort of confrontation.

'Mate, she said sorry. Let us buy you another drink.' Jamie tries to call for a waitress but it's too busy to find one. 'Here.' He passes a business card and the man takes it sharply. 'Just get in touch and we'll sort the dry cleaning out too.'

'You better believe I'll be in touch. Do you know how much this cost?'

The many greys in his short back and sides put him around my dad's age – possibly early sixties – but it's hard to age him because of the heavy tan. His thin mouth is pinched in a line surrounded by a neat goatee.

Erin is fanning her cheeks. She looks as if she wants to cry.

'Listen, we're sorry, but don't let it ruin the night, yeah?' You can tell Jamie's sympathy is waning. The man still isn't leaving.

He glances at the table full of food then at Erin, pointedly. 'You sure you should be eating all that?'

'What?' Jamie slowly stands up. The tendons in his neck taut. 'What's that supposed to mean?'

'Jamie, please, ignore him.' Erin looks mortified. I have this awful vision of him throwing a punch to defend her honour.

Mark has gone mute, as expected. The man still won't leave.

'They've said sorry. It was an accident. You don't need to be rude. Now please leave us alone,' I say sharply, catching Erin's eyes widening.

The man glances my way. There is a flicker of something unreadable on his face. 'All right, sweetheart,' he says. Then winks.

Before I can say anything else he flashes a wry smile, turns and is soon lost in the crowd.

I let out a ripple of awkward laughter. 'Jesus.'

'Excuse me.' Erin gets to her feet, pushing past people to rush towards the bathroom.

'You OK?' I ask Mark, who's gone pale.

He nods and picks up his cutlery. 'Yeah, er, this is going cold. We should probably get stuck in.'

'So sorry about that, guys. Some people really can't handle their drink,' Jamie says with forced brightness. His cheeks are flushed with colour but I notice his jaw is still taut with tension. I'm surprised by a sudden tug of envy: Mark would never be as protective over me.

'It's fine,' I say, picking up my drink and finishing it in one.

I'm about to ask Jamie if I should go and check on Erin when she reappears, her mascara smudged as if she's been

19

crying. Before I can ask if she's OK, a flustered waiter rushes over, apologising for the interruption to our meal. We're all given a drink on the house to make up for it, but the mood's changed and we struggle to pick the conversation back up.

It's no one's fault, but the incident has put a real dampener on things. Erin seems to retreat into her shell and picks at her food. I want to tell her she shouldn't listen to what that drunk man said, but I don't want to bring it all back up again. I'm beyond grateful when Mark complains of a 'blinding headache' as soon as our plates are taken away, giving us an excuse to leave early.

4

Erin

'Are you OK, babe?' Jamie asks, finishing his drink.

I nod, too upset to speak. The night wasn't supposed to end like this. It was no surprise how quickly Mark's mystery headache came on. Sophia fussed over him, telling him he should probably head back to the hotel. At first I thought she meant for him to go alone, but they both stood up and said their goodbyes. I can still taste her heavy night-time perfume at the back of my throat from her kiss goodbye. They put down some notes for their half of the meal and rushed out of the restaurant, whispering to one another.

We'd got there a little early. I had wanted to make sure everything was OK with the last-minute additions. From the moment they'd arrived, Sophia had commanded the attention of the terrace and she didn't even seem to notice. Mark is nowhere near as good-looking as she is, I noticed smugly – he's certainly not as handsome, as tall and muscular, as my Jamie. In fact, it's a bit of a strange match.

Despite us not knowing each other, I had thought it was going well. I wanted to ask why they needed a house alarm – from what

Jamie tells me about his clients, people only install one because something has happened, but I didn't want to pry so soon.

I probably shouldn't have invited them to pop in if they were ever nearby. Of course we're never going to see them again. Our lives are too different. As soon as I suggested it, I saw the look on Sophia's face. I had braced myself for a quick but polite excuse, but it never came.

'Erin?' Jamie says, breaking my train of thought. 'Do you want dessert?'

I shake my head. I've completely lost my appetite.

'It's a shame they don't live closer – you and Sophia could be friends.'

I nod. Sophia is far too glamorous to hang out with someone like me, but I appreciate him trying to cheer me up.

A waiter brings over the bill and four shot glasses of clear liquid on a small tray. Jamie slowly runs his finger down the piece of paper. I know I shouldn't, but I find this irritating. I neck the shot of fermented rice wine that's in front of me, tempted to ask for another, before he drops his debit card on the table and swipes the notes that Sophia and Mark left behind, tucking them into his wallet.

Now we've left the busy restaurant I can feel the storm growing closer. A strong wind has picked up, sending litter and leaves skittering across the road. A bird squawks from high in the dancing palms.

'Let's go for a walk first.' Jamie places his arms around my waist as I head in the direction of our hotel.

'Really? I'm not sure . . .' I stop and nod at the threatening clouds. Other restaurants along the small strip are pulling down their wooden shutters, preparing for the rain to hit. We're on borrowed time. I want to get back before the rain starts, take off my ruined dress and try to forget how the meal ended.

'Come on. It's our last night!'

I guess he's right. Soon I'll be wrapped up in jumpers and jeans complaining of how cold autumn is in England. So, we walk away from the line of tuk-tuks and taxis, away from the house music coming from the Blue Fin, and down through a tree-lined path, his hand laced through mine. Perhaps a walk will help me get over the disappointment of the evening, but with every step I can smell that man's yeasty beer rising off my dress.

'Do you know where you're going?' I ask.

'Trust me.'

I hold his hand tight as the light from the streetlights ends and we move forward in the growing darkness. Without our phones, we haven't got a way to illuminate our path. I don't know how close to the edge we are, but I hear the roar of the ocean and feel the salty sea-spray on my face. I'm about to tell Jamie to turn back, that it's too dark, we might have an accident, when he pushes away low-hanging branches and wide palms and I gasp. We've found ourselves in a secret viewing spot, looking out on to the edge of the world. The ocean stretches out before us, lit by the bright glow of the moon.

I peer over the edge at the swell of the agitated waves, the white tide marks rolling in and out, crashing on the rocks down below. A sudden rush of vertigo makes my leg shake.

Behind us, facing the ocean, is a whitewashed stone structure that has long been left to the elements. This shell of a building offers the most amazing vantage point. Jamie takes my hand and leads me towards it.

'Are you sure?' I pull back slightly, my eyes still adjusting to the gloomy light.

'Come on, I'm here. Nothing will go wrong.'

A cool wind rustles through the leaves as we move past. He leads us up the exposed stone steps that cling to the exterior walls. The breeze brings with it a gorgeous heady scent from the flower offerings that I've seen everywhere during this trip: square baskets made from braided palm leaves containing dried petals doused in holy water, fresh flowers, rice and incense sticks. A gift for the gods left by locals outside temples, hotels, shops, you name it, to signify respect and ward off demons. A couple of these gifts have been left on the steps here too.

From the stone platform, the lights from the Blue Fin terrace are just visible lower down the cliffs. I stand still, close my eyes and take in deep lungfuls of fresh air, grateful for the heightened breeze. Jamie comes up and leans against me. I relax into him.

'Pretty cool, hey?' he whispers in my ear.

'Very.' I kiss him on the cheek, inhaling his aftershave. 'But look at those clouds.' The sky has changed to a sort of violet hue – it's beautiful but ominous, with heavy blackened clouds gathering pace.

He steps in front of me. 'Stop worrying. We wanted to have an adventure!'

He trails his fingers up my bare arms then slides them under the straps of my dress. My body reacts instinctively – the familiar pull of desire to make love to my handsome husband. I feel him harden as he presses against my thighs.

'People might see,' I whisper.

'Babe, there's no one around.' He tips my chin up and kisses me hard on the lips, then he takes my hand and leads me to one of the stone benches in the centre of the raised platform.

We've never had sex outdoors before. I would never do this back home. I don't know whether it's the alcohol, the tropical heat or the fact that we're still in a sort of altered reality on our honeymoon, but I don't stop him. I'm flushed with the excitement at the person I'm becoming. Is this who I am now that I'm married?

He tastes of alcohol, the warmth of the liquor still on his tongue as he roams my mouth. He hitches up my dress. His fingers curl under the edge of my knickers, the elastic resisting for a second. I pull at the button of his dark jeans, the fabric too tough to do with one hand. He helps as I fumble with the button and guides me on to his lap on the bench.

There is a low rumble of thunder from further down the cliff; I pull myself closer towards him, holding on to his firm arms and kissing him with renewed passion. This feels incredible. I forget the angry red mosquito bites and my obvious pink sunburn lines. I even forget what that horrible man said in the restaurant. My body is strong and powerful. I don't know if it's the wild roar of the ocean, the hungry yearning for one another or the thrill that anyone could spot us, but I blank everything else out and lose myself in the moment. My breathing is getting faster and faster, I'm getting so close. It's as if I can see dancing lights in my vision.

Then he stops.

I feel Jamie's whole body change before I see what's caused this interruption. He pulls away from me and zips his jeans quickly, shoulders tense.

There's a flash of light across the stone floor. I blink but I wasn't imagining it. Someone else is here.

I tug at the hem of my dress and let out an awkward laugh. All my bravado has vanished. Jamie turns away from me, blocking me from seeing who it is.

I pull his arm to try and see where the torchlight is coming from. As I do, my heart skips a beat.

It's the man from the restaurant. The one I accidentally spilt a drink over, his pale shirt now dry. He starts laughing as he sees us – the harsh, raspy laugh of a smoker. It sends a chill down my spine. Why is he here? Has he come to find us on purpose, for some sort of revenge? Did he see us making love?

Funny the things that will later seem so insignificant.

5

Erin

I don't know how long he's been standing there, watching us. Nausea rises from my stomach. I grab Jamie's hand, wanting to lead him away, when the unwanted stranger lurches closer, bringing with him an offensive blast of fresh alcohol.

'You know sex in public is illegal over here, right?' he drawls. I'm too distracted by the bright light moving across the concrete slabs. It's coming from his phone, which he's holding at a funny angle.

A splitting headache claws underneath my skull, the pressure of the brooding sky making it hard to concentrate. A loud rumble of thunder comes from nowhere, as if the heavens are being flattened. The approaching storm doesn't scare me as much as what I can see on his phone screen. My mouth rushes with saliva.

'Don't let me spoil the show,' he sneers, tapping at his phone.

'Come on, let's go.' Jamie ignores him, taking my hand and leading us away.

He hasn't realised our al fresco session has been recorded.

A dart of lightning flashes across the sky, making me jump. 'I think he's been filming us . . .' I hiss.

Jamie's eyes darken as they lock with mine. I don't need to say any more. He turns to the drunk. 'Give me your phone, mate.'

'What?' the man scoffs. I blink as he waves his arms dramatically. 'You want this?'

'I said give me your fucking phone!'

'Now, now, calm down, don't want the wife to get worked up. It's not good for someone her siz—' He doesn't finish his sentence, as the next thing I know, Jamie punches him.

His neck snaps back with the force of it.

'Jamie!' I scream, tugging his arm, shocked by the sudden escalation. He's like a caged animal, his chest vibrating with tension, every inch of him alive.

The man is holding his face with his left hand, blood trickling through his fingers. A splash of crimson blooms under his nose. Perhaps it's the adrenaline but he lets out a brittle laugh. The pain hasn't registered yet. It's going to sting in the morning.

Jamie shrugs me off and spits on the ground just as the rain starts to fall. Warm, fat, cleansing drops that feel a relief to begin with, but, in a matter of seconds, it really begins to pour.

'You want my phone? It's yours.'

I let out a breath but the relief is short-lived.

'For a price,' he taunts. 'Yeah, I googled you.'

I try to keep up with what he's saying. The business card. The offer to pay for his dry cleaning.

'I bet plenty of people would love to see this.'

'What the – are you bribing us?' Jamie snaps.

28

'What's your price? Everyone's got one.' A bloody trail of saliva drips from his busted lips, staining his grey goatee as he speaks.

'Jamie?' I'm gripping his shirt.

I barely register the rain falling on my face. I think of what he's caught on camera. Illegal. What if he's right? What if he takes that to the police? I've seen documentaries of the terrifying-looking prisons over here. My stomach flips. The footage could end up online; there's no control over a leaked sex tape on the internet.

'We have to pay him. If this gets out, your business, the investors . . .' I'm trying to work out how much cash we have left. It's mostly small change at this point of the holiday.

Jamie doesn't let me finish. 'Fuck this. Give me the phone. Now!'

I jump as he bellows. Finally, Jamie's tone registers on the man's face. We're not here to barter. He turns and staggers towards the steps down to the ground, trying to run away, the phone still in his hand. We need to get it back. Both Jamie and I move towards him.

'Stop! I'll pay!' I yell.

Instinctively he turns at my shout. That's when I realise how precarious and slick the concrete steps have become in the rain. Glassy puddles like polished mirrors fill the many gaps in the uneven concrete. This sudden twist sends him off balance. His ankles sway and his portly stomach tilts forward. His arms dart to one side like a startled newborn.

There's a moment, a brief second, where I expect him to right himself and grab hold of the handrail, but the metal's slippery – it's too wet. He pitches forward, moving too fast to get a proper grip. The rail glides between his fingertips as if it's wrapped in silk. He seems to move in slow motion. With nothing to grab hold of, he drops towards the ground.

This can't be happening. Everything tenses inside me, as if I'm the one falling. He keeps tumbling. The steps seem never-ending. All I can do is stare in helpless horror as his limbs slam against the concrete. If I make a sound, I'm not aware of it; even the crashing waves being whipped by the storm are immediately drowned out, as my racing heartbeat fills my ears. I hold my breath, bracing myself for the inevitable impact.

I don't want to watch. I want to pull myself away but there's no time. Before I can close my eyes, there's an ear-splitting crack, followed by a heavy exhale of breath that's not quite a scream but not far from it. The sudden silence is unbearable. A rush of vertigo forces me to steady myself. My trembling hand grasps the dripping wet rail as if my life depends on it.

'Shit!' I feel Jamie move past me, swearing as he tears down the steps to the still figure at the bottom. I desperately want to warn him to take care, but any sound is lodged in my throat.

I try to swallow, remembering to breathe again.

What the fuck just happened?

'Is he OK?' I shout over the wind, still gripping the rail, frozen with shock.

Jamie looks up at me from the crumpled body at the foot of the stairs – a look that I won't ever forget for as long as I live, his eyes wide with fear.

'Erin, I think he's . . . dead.'

6

Sophia

At first I thought Mark was making up the migraine as an excuse to leave – he never used to get such bad headaches. But, as we quickly walk from the Blue Fin back to the hotel, I can see how pale and quiet he is.

'Poor Erin. It really was just an accident with that guy's drink. I thought at one point Jamie might actually swing for him,' I say, filling the silence.

'I'd have done the same for you, babe,' Mark says in a quiet voice.

'Really?' I pull a face. 'You hate confrontation.'

'Well . . . sometimes doing nothing is the best thing.'

He must sense this has hit a nerve. We had so many arguments during the week from hell because I expected him to stand up for me more, to have the courage to fight back at the men who made our lives miserable.

'Sorry, Soph. Ignore me. My head is pounding, I'm just going to take some sleeping pills and crash out.'

I'm surprised he still has them; I thought he'd left them at home. I glance at my watch. It's not even eleven o'clock;

31

it's too early to be going to bed on our last night, but I say nothing.

'You stay out, though?' Mark suggests.

'No, I can't just leave you like this.'

'It's fine. Don't worry. I probably just need a good sleep. Anyway, I'll be dead to the world soon.' He dips his head to give me a firm kiss goodnight. 'Love you.'

'Love you too.'

There's a pang of uncertainty as I watch him head towards the lifts in the hotel lobby. Perhaps I should call it a night too, but I'm not the least bit tired and he needs to lie still in a dark room without me tossing and turning beside him. He'll be fine. I'm sure it's the pressure in the sky. The air is fizzing with tension, needing to crack and allow us all to breathe a bit more easily.

'Another drink, please, sir. Same again,' Leroy, another hotel guest who is here with his wife, Angie, asks the barman in his strong Mancunian accent. We met a few days ago. They're in their sixties, recently retired secondary school teachers, originally from Jamaica but they've lived in Trafford for most of their lives. They are here to celebrate their silver wedding anniversary.

Ketut, the friendly barman, winks and flamboyantly pours tequila into a silver cocktail shaker. There's a soft glow from the strings of colourful bulbs wrapped around palm trees. Faint reggae beats play from hidden speakers. Finally I feel as if I can breathe, away from the cramped, noisy terrace of the Blue Fin. Here, there's only a handful of guests at the bar, the brooding storm discouraging others from coming for a drink.

'What are you having, Sophia?' Leroy asks, running a hand over his short greying afro.

'I should probably call it a night soon,' I reply.

'Go on. One more won't hurt.' Angie places a warm arm across my shoulder. She's wearing a busy floral-print dress. Chains of multicoloured necklaces sit crumpled in the wrinkles across her chest. 'Come and join us! How come you're all alone?'

'We were having dinner with another couple who are staying here, but we had to leave early – Mark wasn't feeling so well.'

'Too much sun?' she asks.

'Something like that.'

Maybe I should check he's OK, but I'm not finished drinking yet. I'm still not ready to face up to the fact that we're leaving tomorrow. Going back home means going back to a reality I'm not ready to be part of. I know I'm safe here. It's a silly reason to stay away, but it's true.

All of a sudden there's an almighty roar of thunder. I flinch.

'Someone's jumpy!' Leroy says.

I try to smile as I unclench my hands and take a big gulp of my drink. 'I'm not a big fan of storms. It's a childhood fear that I've not managed to outgrow.'

'Aww. A bit of thunder can't hurt you, darling,' Angie says.

There's a flash of brilliant white lighting. Someone makes an oohing noise. Angie gets up to go to the bathroom, stumbling a little.

Leroy places his arms across his broad stomach, tight in his United football shirt, and chuckles. 'This is going to be quite the show!' He offers me a rice cracker from the glass bowl in front of him. I shake my head.

I wish I were as relaxed as him. Instead, my eyes roam the flimsy structure we're sitting under. My hand begins to feel clammy under my bouncing knee. I cross my legs and try to wipe my palms on my dress under the table.

'So, Sophia . . .'

I'm struggling to listen to what he's saying. There is a painful screech from beside us as a member of staff drags the empty chairs across the floor to a store cupboard. The sound is like nails down a blackboard. I glance round, expecting to see Ketut, but he's nowhere to be seen.

'S-sorry?' My mouth has run dry.

Other guests get up and say goodnight. I want to do the same but I'm pinned to the chair.

'I was just saying that . . . whoa! Did you see that one?' Leroy laughs again as another dart shoots across our heads. He picks up his phone and starts filming, tilting the camera towards the brooding grey sky.

Then, the first drops of warm rain fall. Within seconds it grows heavier, bringing a chill that hasn't been there all holiday.

'I bet Angie's fallen asleep.' Leroy laughs.

'Y-yeah, I'm going to finish this and head to bed myself.'

He starts to say something.

'Sorry?' I have to strain to hear what he's saying over the sound of the rain.

'I was asking if you like photography? I've just got into it, "learning as I go"-type thing. I don't want to beat my own drum but I've taken some pretty great shots since we've been here. Mostly scenery and the odd close-up of a monkey when we visited Uluwatu Temple. Cheeky buggers, they are!' He's scrolling through the colourful images in his phone's photo album. 'I mean, you wouldn't think you could get such cracking shots with just a phone camera, would you?'

'Oh. Er . . . yeah, they're lovely.'

Another beat of thunder. My jaw tightens. 'I'm actually going to call it a night,' I say decisively.

'Oh?' He finally glances up from his phone as I scrape my chair back. 'All right, then, love. I think I'll go for a wander, see if I can capture this storm.' He shakes his phone at me.

'You're going out in this weather to take photos? You'll get soaked!'

'It's only a light shower, it'll pass soon.' He gives a shrug. 'If Angie has fallen asleep then it'll be nice to show her some pics of what she's missed.'

'Well, please be careful,' I say, finishing my drink, knocking the table and jostling empty glasses as I walk away.

7

Erin

It's as if the world has stopped spinning.

'We need to get help!' I pant, moving closer to the lifeless man. Blood is oozing from his head on to the wet steps beside us, trickling closer to my toes.

'Erin, no, it's too late . . . he's dead.' Jamie has dropped to his haunches, his head in his hands. 'Fuck! What do we do now?'

'No. He can't be . . .'

I reach out a trembling hand to his neck the way they do in films, pretending I have a clue what I'm doing, needing to search for a pulse. His skin is rough where he shaved this morning.

I can't feel a heartbeat.

Jamie shoots his head up and steps in front of me. His heart thumps in his chest, pressed against mine. Sweat clings to his skin. 'Don't touch him.'

'P-p-perhaps he's just passed out!' Even as I'm saying it, I know I'm clutching at straws.

My breath is coming out too fast. A strong gust of wind sends a sickly-sweet scent up my nose. He must have knocked one of the flower offerings as he fell – dried petals and grains

36

of rice are scattered like confetti around us. The rain is driving down now, dripping in my eyes and mixing with the mascara I applied earlier, stinging my burnt shoulders like needles through my skin.

'Oh, my God. Oh, my God.' I can't think straight. I gulp and press my trembling fingers to my temples.

Jamie is saying something to me but I can't hear over the sound of the rain and the pulse in my ears. He has his arm outstretched. I follow where he's pointing.

The man's phone lies on the hard ground. The camera is still on, the flashlight pointing up at the dark sky, the cracked screen glistening with raindrops. Just seconds ago, he was taunting us with it. Now, the stillness is terrifying.

Jamie turns the phone over in his shaking hands. I don't know how he doesn't drop it.

'He *was* filming us. You were right. Fuck. Imagine if this had got out!'

Without hesitation, he casts his arm back and launches the phone as far as it will go over the cliff edge into the dark ocean. The sight sends my head into a spin. I can't hold it together for much longer. I dash away towards a cluster of trees and vomit. Uncontrollable waves of nausea roll across my body, adrenaline the only thing keeping me upright. The rain has almost stopped. Heavy drips fall off the glossy palms and on to my head.

He's dead. He's dead. He's dead.

Maybe Jamie got it wrong – perhaps he's still alive, and we can still save him.

I wipe my mouth and walk back towards the lifeless body, swallowing deeply as I move closer. His left foot is bent into an eye-wateringly unnatural position. Jamie has his back to the man, facing the ocean with his eyes closed. I can see him trying to slow his breathing; he looks as if he's dry-heaving.

'We need to call for help,' I pant.

'How? Your phone's at the hotel and mine's run out of battery.'

We're both thinking the same thing, wishing he hadn't impulsively thrown the man's phone away. The terrifying darkness presses against us. Without the light from his camera, we're dependent on the moonlight.

'Then we need to go and tell someone, ask someone to help, get them to call an ambulance!' My voice is high and shrill. I blindly twist my wedding ring around my finger.

'No, Erin.' He quickly shakes his head, drops of water flicking in the air. 'We need to get as far away as possible.'

'What?' Despite myself, I turn to look at the bloodied body. I keep expecting him to get up, to shout and swear at us. 'But—'

'Erin, we can't help him. It's too late.'

Both of us are shaking like frightened animals.

'He's dead.' Jamie's voice cracks, as he pulls me close. 'I'm sure of it.'

He'll never move again. My stomach clenches with the finality of it all.

Fuck.

'What do we do now?' My voice is a whisper against his racing chest. I'm horribly aware of how loud we were. The shouting, crying. Did I scream? Did he? I try to speak. 'The police . . .'

'If we call the police then we'll both be arrested. Haven't you seen what Indonesian prisons are like? Cockroach-infested cells, or worse – face a firing squad. They still have the death penalty here.'

'B-b-but it was an accident. A silly fight. The rain, the steps were wet . . .' My voice is wavering. Uncertainty dances on every syllable. 'It wasn't anyone's fault, just an accident.'

'I know. But who's going to believe us? We're standing next to a body with blood on our hands. They would have seen the commotion in the restaurant, knowing you tipped a drink over him. People could easily recognise us from the Blue Fin.' He lets out a shaky breath and looks around. 'Here there's no witnesses. No CCTV. We're leaving tomorrow morning, in a matter of hours. There's nothing we can do—'

He stops suddenly, freezing mid-sentence. I stop breathing.

'Do you hear that?' He narrows his gaze, trying to make the sound out.

'What? What is it?'

Jamie darts his head to the side and drops his voice to a hiss. 'I thought I heard something . . . We have to get out of here.'

'What!' I gasp, light-headed with fear.

'It sounded like footsteps . . .'

I strain, trying to hear what Jamie thinks he's heard. My eyes are unable to focus in the gloom, grisly shapes playing tricks on me.

'I-it must be the rain.' There are no lights or voices coming towards us.

He frowns and swiftly shakes his head. 'Maybe I imagined it.'

He's taking me by the hand and tugging me away. It's as though I'm hovering above my body, watching this all play out. Surely this isn't happening? I resist. I need a moment to think but there's no time. I glance back at the man we've left behind, my whole body trembling with shock.

Wait – is that . . .? I squint, certain that I can make out a silhouette.

A terrifying sense of light-headedness crashes over me.

Jamie's right – someone else is here.

I can't tell if it's a man or a woman, just a hazy figure. I expect to hear a scream as the macabre discovery is made but there's no sound other than the thrashing waves, the wind rushing in the trees and my wild, racing heart.

'Erin! Move!' Jamie hisses, panic-stricken.

We shoot into the bushes, tripping on vines, down a narrow overgrown path leading away from the cliffs. We lurch towards real life as if emerging from a nightmare.

My brain can't keep up. An hour ago, we were sitting having a leisurely dinner with Sophia and Mark. Now we're sprinting away from a dead body.

8

Erin

Our pace is unnaturally fast, hands gripped as we make our way back to the hotel as quickly as possible. I can't stop shaking. How the hell has the last night of our dream honeymoon ended like this? Panic sends my mind into freefall.

'We didn't find out his name,' I say, breaking the silence.

'What?' Jamie leans closer.

'The man.' I swallow. 'We don't know his name. We should have checked his pockets, found some ID, looked for something that might have, I don't know, helped.'

Jamie's eyes flick to a tuk-tuk driver sheltering from the rain, eyes glued to his phone screen. He hasn't noticed us rush past. 'We'll talk when we get back, I promise.'

Maybe it's better this way, him staying nameless. It keeps it feeling more like a horrific nightmare than reality.

The odd car drives past in a sea of spray. The streets are eerily deserted. Restaurants have pulled down their awnings, a faint beat of music playing for those hardy customers sitting inside. The storm has forced other places to close early.

As we approach the hotel's grand entrance, I need to say something. Speak up.

'Jamie . . .' I swallow.

'Hang on.' He rummages in his pocket for his keycard, swearing under his breath as he drops it to the floor.

'Jamie,' I try again. 'I've changed my mind. We have to go back. We can't just leave him there.'

It's the right thing to do. Going back proves we're good people. But, as a voice inside my mind reminds me, we already know we're not.

'Jamie? Did you hear me?'

'Erin, please.' He snaps. 'Just give me a minute to think.'

He manages to open the doors to the lobby. I barely notice the chill of the air-con because I'm trembling so much. I keep my head low as we walk past the curved reception desk. Thankfully the place is pretty much deserted, aside from a cleaner moving a mop and bucket against the marble floor. He doesn't glance up as we squelch our way towards the lift.

Suddenly, I hear an English voice.

'Evening!'

It's the older woman that I saw having drinks with Sophia and Mark a few nights ago. Angela, Angie, I think her name is. I watched them from our balcony, all sitting together, lifting their glasses to toast one another, and felt a pang of jealousy. Sophia makes socialising look so effortless.

She's wobbling through the doors that lead from the pool bar, coming towards us. Her husband, a man who is far too old to wear football shirts, is nowhere to be seen. My heartbeat quickens.

'I can't do this,' I whimper, wanting to fold myself into Jamie or drag him behind one of the oversized plant pots dotted around the lobby and hide until she passes.

'Just wave, babe. Act normal,' he breathes.

All I can do is keep linking my shaking arm with his, hoping he'll hold us both up. I lift a hand and give what I hope passes as a wave. It feels more like a cry for help. She waves back and thankfully keeps on walking.

We double-bolt the door once we're inside the room. Our suitcases are already packed, lined up by the wall. We're leaving in five hours. Jamie strips off his clothes and puts on the hotel bathrobe, passing one to me and telling me to do the same. Now we're alone, my thoughts explode.

'We shouldn't have left. Running away makes us look guilty!'

'We had no choice but to leave.' He paces the room. 'We're not guilty. We did nothing wrong.' He stops moving and exhales heavily.

'We could have paid him for the footage. Why did you have to punch him?' I spin to face him. 'What the hell got into you?'

He holds his hands up; they're still trembling. 'Look, I'm sorry. I know I lost my temper but he was threatening us, bribing us. There was no way we could have agreed on a price with a guy like him. It's bullshit! I never expected this to happen! The weather, the steps . . . You saw how drunk he was! He fell and it was an accident, a horrible, scary accident.'

He lets out a shaky breath. I've never seen him look so deathly ill.

'But—'

'Babe, just think of what my investors would make of this, let alone what it might look like after everything that happened with Claire.'

I shiver. He's right. If this gets out, it could cost us everything.

'We need to strip off. Get rid of these clothes. There'll be DNA all over them.'

'DNA . . .' I stutter.

'I know, it's hard to think straight and it sounds mental, but . . . just to be on the safe side.' He presses his fingers to the bridge of his nose. 'There's nothing to place us at the scene, no other evidence that we were there.'

My brain can't comprehend all of this – crime scene, DNA, dead bodies – this is supposed to be our honeymoon . . .

As he's thinking aloud, I tug off my dress and stand shivering in my underwear. He picks up a roll of plastic laundry bags and puts the wet clothes inside one, wrapping it up tightly.

A sudden thought hits me. 'We didn't get your business card back. You gave it to him in the restaurant! When they find his body, they'll see it and then people will remember us arguing with him and—'

Jamie holds me tightly. He shushes me into my damp hair. 'It's OK. I got it back.'

'What? When?'

'When you were being sick.' He runs a hand over my goose-bumped skin.

'But—' I start. My head is a jumble of unanswered questions.

He talks over me. 'Get a shower, warm yourself up. I don't want you to get ill.'

I am so desperately cold, I don't argue. I run the hot water and turn off the fan, letting the steam fill up the bathroom. I take long, deep breaths as my reflection soon becomes hidden. I steady myself with a hand against the cool glass of the mirror. Condensation drips down my palm.

I go through the motions, squeezing out a dollop of coconut shower gel, flinching as it touches my sunburnt shoulders. Mud washes from my legs. Another man's blood runs down the plughole.

When I get out, wrapping a towel around me, Jamie's sitting in the armchair beside the window, looking out over the pool bar. The sky is murky black but the air does feel a little less close.

His voice makes me jump. 'I know it's frightening, but we had no other choice. It was a horrible, scary accident. No one is to blame.' I'm about to say something when he holds up a hand. 'Listen, the transfer bus is coming in a few hours. You need to get some sleep, babe.'

'Sleep?' I say this as if it's the most incredulous thing he's ever suggested.

He rummages in one of the bags and pulls out a box of Nytol. 'Trust me. Here. I'm going to get a shower.'

I don't usually take anything like this but, right now, I'm so grateful I'd swallow the whole packet if I could. I take double the recommended dose. When I close my eyes, all I see are images of the man's bloodied, grimacing face imprinted on the other side. Should we have found someone to call us an ambulance, stayed with him, even if he was already dead? We could have given our version of events to the police, made them understand it was a horrible accident. That's what I would have done back home.

Or at least, what I hope I'd have done if I had found myself in this situation.

But out here, in a country where we don't speak the language, when we're leaving in a matter of hours and there's no evidence of the fact we were even there . . . everything feels much less certain.

9

Sophia

The bedroom door closes behind me with a gentle click. It takes my eyes a second to adjust after the brightness of the hotel corridor. I don't want to put the main light on in case I wake Mark; I can just about make out his shape under the covers. The room is silent, bar the hum of the air-conditioning. He must have set it lower than normal, as my arms have broken out into goosebumps. I fumble my way to the bathroom but it's too dark and I'm a little unsteady and I crack my shin against the side of the bed. A dart of pain shoots up my leg. Somehow I manage to suppress a yelp, knowing it's going to leave a bruise.

Once inside, I turn on the light above the bathroom mirror. I look terrible. My jaw aches from clenching it so tightly as I tried to hide how scared I was in front of Leroy. I can't believe he's actually gone off to chase the storm; no doubt he'll be showing off the shots he's captured when we bump into them by the pool tomorrow. I wonder where Angie got to. I thought she would have come and said goodnight.

I wash my face, brush my teeth then slip into my pyjamas, a silky vest-and-shorts set that I bought especially for our honeymoon. We got a late checkout so at least we can put off packing until tomorrow. It's as though I'm doing everything possible to stick my fingers in my ears and pretend it's not happening. I even researched staying for an extra week and moving our flights, but Mark looked as if he might pass out when I told him the astronomical cost.

I sit on the closed toilet seat and unlock my phone. My fingers move to my email app. I agreed with Mark to spend less time on our phones while we're away – be in the moment and all that – so I've had to take sneaky 'long walks' to check my work emails. It's been so tricky keeping this from him but it's only a small white lie. He just wouldn't understand if I told him why I need to know the second her email lands in my inbox.

I reload the page, my tired eyes scanning past the spam and wedding-related offers.

Nothing.

With a sigh, I minimise the app and prepare to go to bed. I need to stay positive. There's still time to hear from her and everything be OK again. My old boss will take me back and my record will be wiped. A blip in my career, that's all. I have to hold on to hope.

I turn off the bathroom light, and am easing open the door and preparing to feel my way in the dark to my side of the bed when I hear a low creak coming from behind me. My eyes dart to the door of our room.

The silver handle is moving slowly.

I must have forgotten to lock it when I came in; I was too focused on being quiet. A wave of panic grips my throat. Someone is breaking into our room as we sleep.

I'm frozen to the spot, eyes on the door as it opens. A scrape of wood across tiles. A rush of air. The bright corridor lights cast a ghostly glow around a silhouette of a man.

He's coming closer. Into our room.

I scream.

'Sophia! What's the matter?'

'Mark? You scared me.' My heart is hammering in my chest as my husband steps towards me. 'What the hell? I thought you were asleep!'

He hits the main light and I see that the mound in the bed was just a tangle of bedsheets and pillows.

'The storm kept me awake. I know how much you hate them so I wanted to check that you were OK,' he says quickly. 'But I took a wrong turn and ended up locked out of the fire escape and I've been waiting forever to be let back in.'

'What? How long have you been out there? Why didn't you call me?'

'The sleeping tablets messed with my head. I left my phone—'

His reply is cut off by a sudden trilling sound in the room. I swear. My heart is thumping in my chest – I'm still trying to get over the shock of thinking a strange man was breaking into our room.

'I'll get it. You get ready for bed,' I say, leaning across the messy bed and picking up the ringing telephone.

Mark nods then goes into the bathroom.

'Hello?'

'Oh, hello, madam, I'm calling from reception. This is a courtesy call to check everything is OK? Another guest reported hearing some sort of commotion.'

A rush of heat washes over me. Someone must have heard me scream. I tell them everything is fine, I'm just a little jittery because of the storm. The receptionist tries to hide her amusement, but I'm embarrassed at having to admit I'm a grown woman who is still scared of thunderstorms.

I hang up, then pad over to the balcony. The bedroom is filled with the scent of Mark's damp clothes. I pull the double doors open to bring in some fresh air. Filling my lungs with the warm breeze, I thank God that the storm has finally passed.

10

Erin

Tuesday 13 September

I dreamt I killed a man. It was real. So real. My ears rang with his tortured cries, his mouth twisted in a horrifying frozen scream. The nightmare wasn't just that I'd taken his life but that I was about to be caught and face my limited last days in a cockroach-infested prison cell shared with thirteen other desperate women. Being told in broken English that my name was on the death penalty list. Execution by firing squad. All because of a single horrific mistake. The police were getting closer, their sirens increasing in volume, nearer and nearer. I had nowhere to hide. Until . . .

'. . . Erin, my love? It's time to go.' Jamie's voice filters through the heavy fog of artificially induced sleep. The siren I can hear is his phone beeping with the alarm he set last night.

My eyes flash open, scanning the darkness of the bedroom, trying to make out the familiar shapes of objects to prove that I'm safe, that it's all in my head. There's no stern-faced translator reading me my rights. I'm drenched in sweat. Jamie's too busy getting ready to notice the state of me.

I tug on the outfit I left out. Neither of us speaks. Making conversation is too difficult right now.

It's only when we get to the airport, stepping into the air-conditioned terminal, that it hits me. Soon we'll be boarding a plane as if nothing happened. But still, with every minute that passes I can't help wondering if they've found him yet, the nameless older man dead at the bottom of the slippery stone steps.

Our flight is delayed, and it feels like a sign. An omen. Disgruntled passengers around us grumble and moan. We look at one another in horror. I ask him to go and queue for a slip for complimentary coffee, like the rest of our flight. I don't need any caffeine, there's enough adrenaline coursing through me as it is, but we need to blend in. Act like everyone else.

Somehow, we manage to hold it together and follow the signs to our gate as if on autopilot, flashing our boarding passes and manoeuvring past the crowds craning their necks at the departures board. As we walk, I squeeze Jamie's hand. I'm so grateful that he's here with me; there's no way I could do this without him. He leans over and plants a heavy, comforting kiss on my forehead. He knows. This ability to speak without speaking is still there. No matter what happened yesterday, we still have each other. No doubt his mind is racing with catastrophic thoughts too.

We find an empty row of seats. I can't bear to be among normal people clustered under the bright lights shopping and eating.

'Do you think they've found him yet?' I ask, the moment we sit down on the hard plastic chairs.

There's silence. I think he hasn't heard me and am about to speak again when he gives a little shake of his head. 'I don't know. Maybe.'

I lower my voice. Something is on my mind. 'When you took your business card back . . .' I take a breath. 'Was it in his wallet?'

'What? I . . . I'm not sure. No. It was just in the pocket of his shirt. Why?' He frowns.

'I just thought if it was in his wallet then you might have been able to see his name. He was English, wasn't he? I wonder if he was here on holiday. Maybe he was an ex-pat.'

I'm aware I'm speaking of this man in the past tense.

'Keep your voice down, babe,' he says through clenched teeth despite there being no one around us.

I wish he'd checked the man's name. I don't know why, but it feels important.

'Try to think about something else.'

My legs twitch with restlessness. I can't sit still. I go and find the nearest bathroom to splash water on my face. I should probably try to eat something but the thought makes me feel nauseous.

Finally a tannoy announcement calls for our flight to begin boarding. I remember the last time I was in an airport about to leave, feeling equally empty and scared but, that time, for very different reasons.

The memory comes flooding back.

At first, I had cursed my luck at getting my period on our first trip away. A long weekend in the sunny town of Girona. We'd only been at our hotel for one night when the headache started. I was overcome by a wave of heat, as if I'd stood up too quickly. A vicious pounding in my skull quickly followed. I remember seeing Jamie's mouth moving and the slant of his concerned eyes but I tried to play it down. I didn't want to alarm him.

Then I went to the toilet and felt a dampness between my legs. Naïvely, I wondered how you asked for a tampon in Spanish. Then the cramps started, but beyond anything I'd ever experienced before: breathtaking waves that grew in severity.

At first I joked, embarrassed by this unromantic set-up – we didn't know each other that well and I was sending the poor man out to buy sanitary towels. He returned with three different kinds, to be on the safe side, and my heart bloomed with love, momentarily overtaking the pain. I woke hours later, sticky from a deep, dreamless sleep. Jamie was by my side in seconds, watching me, his wide eyes full of concern.

'Erin! How are you feeling?'

'I'll be OK,' I lied.

A sudden shock of pain ripped through my groin as I stepped towards the bathroom. My legs gave way and Jamie launched from his chair to catch me, but he wasn't quick enough. I was hit by a new torrent of pain when my head caught the sharp corner of the desk. Stars momentarily clouded my vision, distracting me from what was happening between my legs.

'We need to take you to a hospital.'

Because it was so late, the doctors had wanted me to spend the night, but Jamie wasn't allowed to stay. At first, they were more concerned with the cut to my temple than the miscarriage. It was just one of those things. Very early days.

No one to blame. Still, they put me in a bed on a ward with new mothers. Perhaps there was a mix-up with the language barrier or perhaps they just really hate English tourists. It was unimaginable. Sleep was impossible; I lay there hearing the mewling call of a newborn fresh out of the womb and knew I had to discharge myself.

The painkillers they gave me were strong enough to forget the cramps. Desperate to keep moving, I swallowed another pill and kept walking. As well as wanting to let Jamie sleep, I needed to be by myself for a while. The amber glow of a string of lights tacked to the door of a small tapas bar drew me in like a moth to a flame. One drink, to help with the shock. And another after that.

When I got back to the hotel Jamie was asleep in his clothes, lying on top of the sheets, mud all over his trainers from pacing, my blood still clinging to his shirt. He woke with a start. I lied and told him they'd let me leave early and I hadn't wanted to wake him. The tears in his eyes shocked me. For the first time in my life, I had someone who was really fucking worried about me. I fell even more in love with him right then and there.

Everything changed after that trip. A baby hadn't been on the cards. Not yet. The question hadn't even been brought up. We'd only been dating for six weeks, but things had shifted. After that, we had known we wanted to have a family together more than anything.

The tannoy slices through the memories and into the airport bathroom, announcing that our flight is ready to board. I find Jamie fidgeting on the seats where I left him, the colour drained from his face. He leaps up when he sees me. A rapidly moving queue snakes behind him.

'There you are!' he says, pulling me close to his tense body. He laces a clammy hand through mine. His face is flushed and there's a rash across his neck, as if he's been scratching it. I'm about to ask him what's going on when a member of staff calls out.

'Passports and tickets, please!'

That's when I catch what's spooked Jamie.

My stomach clenches.

'Breathe. Try to breathe,' he says quietly. I'm not sure if he's telling me or himself.

At the door of the gate, behind the flight attendants who are welcoming passengers, are two police officers. And they are both staring directly at us.

11

Sophia

Tuesday 13 September

I push myself out of the pool and pad over to the nearby sun lounger, feeling the heat from the sun-warmed stone slabs under my bare feet. I had to get out of our stuffy bedroom and go for a swim; it felt as if I'd barely slept a wink last night. I left Mark packing the last few bits into our suitcases, telling him I'd be quick.

I pick my phone up off my beach towel. I promised Mark I wouldn't be late for our extravagant floating breakfast – a treat he'd booked for our last morning here. It's a bit of Insta fodder, a reed basket containing plump pastries, freshly squeezed orange juice and smoothie bowls, all adorned with delicate tropical flowers, floating on the top of a lagoon pool over on the other side of the hotel.

My phone almost slips out of my grip.

Not only is it a lot later than I thought, but there's finally an alert on the home screen that I've been waiting for. I quickly dry my hands on the soft towel, my fingers tingling in anticipation, and try to remember to breathe.

I hold up the screen to my face, removing my sunglasses to unlock it.

It's from her. For a moment I worry my eyes are playing tricks on me. The subject line is blank but it's her email address.

Hi Sophia,

Your previous message went into spam. Sorry for the late reply. If you're serious about exposing Rupert for who he really is, then you need the full picture of what he's capable of. There's too much to say in one email. And I don't trust that it won't fall into the wrong hands. Let's meet.

Lou

A fire is lit inside me.

Her evidence could be just the thing to get the story back in front of the news editor. I tap 'reply', just as I hear my name being called.

'Sophia!'

It's Angie, shuffling her way towards me in bejewelled flip-flops.

'Morning,' I say distractedly.

'Looking at this beautiful blue sky, you just couldn't imagine that there was such a terrible storm last night, could you?'

'Mmm. Crazy.'

Thoughts are rattling around my brain. Being able to interview Lou on the record is literally what I need to get the story to print. She knows Rupert better than anyone.

Angie is still talking to me. 'I just came to see if Mark's feeling better?'

'I think he'll be all right, although he still looked a little pale to me. I told him he should just stay in bed and rest, but he insisted he was OK.'

'Don't tell me he's got food poisoning from that fancy place you went to?'

'The Blue Fin? No, I don't think so. I ate the same as him.'

I think of Erin and Jamie. They must be in the sky as we speak. My stomach pulls at the thought that that will be us later.

'Where did you go last night? I thought you were going to rejoin us,' I ask.

'I was! I went to the loo but then decided I just had to get into my comfy sandals, I've got terrible corns from those other ones, so I went back to the room but I needed some plasters and . . .' I half tune out her explanation of how she ended up falling asleep by accident. All I can think about is hurrying to meet Mark *and* replying to Lou. 'God knows what time Leroy made it to bed. He's still asleep now. Did you two stay up late, then?'

I shake my head. 'He went off to take photos of the storm.'

Angie lets out a bark of a laugh that makes me jump. 'What's he like! Fancying himself as some sort of David Bailey.' She swats a buzzing insect away. 'Well, I'll love you and leave you. I'm off for a massage, although I'm not sure being pummelled is the best way to cope with a hangover.' She clutches her head and winces. 'When I see Ketut I'm going to be putting in a complaint: those cocktails are lethal. I've sent you a friend request on Facebook, so stay in touch. Have a safe journey back!'

'Thanks, I will.'

Angie waves and shuffles towards the spa.

I check the time. Shit, I'm going to have to run. My fingers dance across my screen as I type out a short reply to Lou.

Name a time and place and I'll be there. I promise.

I press send and throw my phone into my beach bag. Instinctively I want to rush and tell Mark about the email but I know I need to keep this to myself, at least for the time being. Mark will only worry if he knows I'm back in contact with Lou; he'd warn me about dragging up the past. But this time things will be different.

I jog through the ornately carved wooden doors to the hotel's secret pool. It's an oasis inside an oasis. Tinkling water fountains, sweet-smelling hibiscus and jasmine fill the air, while relaxing music plays through speakers hidden behind rocks surrounding the man-made lagoon. The sheer white drapes of a cabana to our right move in the warm breeze. Mark is already in the water, waiting for me. I notice the glimmer of irritation at how late I am. You book this experience by the hour.

'Sorry! I got held up by Angie. Then I had to walk the long way round because of some storm damage to one of the villas and, anyway, I'm here now!' I say, hands held wide.

'That woman can talk for England. Wait, what are you laughing at?' He self-consciously pushes his hair back. He looks as if he's posing for a ridiculous perfume advert.

'Nothing! You just look cute, that's all.' It's hard to keep a straight apologetic face when he's surrounded by a dizzying number of bright flower petals bobbing on the water around him. 'Pink really is your colour, did anyone ever tell you that?'

'Oi, pipe down and get in.' He grins. 'I hope your coffee is still warm.'

'I'm sure it's perfect. Thank you.' I drop my beach dress to the ground and ease myself into the water. It's like sinking into a warm bath. 'God, how nice is this!' I press myself against him and kiss him hard. 'Are you feeling OK?'

'Loads better now.' He runs his hands around my waist, and effortlessly lifts me closer. 'We're all packed.'

'Do we really have to leave?' I jut out my lip.

'What about your new job?'

'It's not a job,' I correct him, 'it's a trial.'

'Well, either way, you can't miss it.'

'And we need the money.' I say what we're both thinking. The honeymoon has been a complete luxury from start to finish, funded by credit cards.

'Fingers crossed John gives me that promotion he's been hinting at.' He smiles, but even from behind his sunglasses I can tell it doesn't meet his eyes. 'Chin up, though. I know it's not ideal but it won't be forever.'

I give a slight shrug and pick up a petal that's stuck to my damp shoulders. I'll never forget the day my news editor, Peter, called me into his office. It would have been better if he'd done it publicly rather than pretend it was only between us. He explained that he had to let me go. I didn't say a word to anyone on my way out. Not that I had to worry: everyone had watched the grim-faced lawyers march down the corridors, past my desk and into his office. Everyone had held their breath that it wasn't their fuck-up. It was mine.

Mark had to take a day off work to look after me. I was a mess, my whole career hanging by a thread because of one moment of carelessness. The prospect of being out of work, of losing the job that I'd trained for since I was sixteen years old making terrible cups of tea at my local newspaper, was unimaginable. All I'd ever wanted was to be a journalist. I didn't want to work in features or write about fashion or events. It was crime that drew me in. The lure of working with the police, to serve in the public interest and bring those to justice, was what got me out of bed every morning.

But then I flew too close to the flame.

The wedding was a week away. The honeymoon was waiting for us. I never expected to start married life unemployed and I could only blame myself. When I was offered a trial place at the *Islington Post*, calling in a favour, I knew it was beneath me. But beggars can't be choosers.

'Check this out, Soph.' Mark's eyes light up as he glides the large reed basket containing our sumptuous breakfast towards me. 'I'm going to see if I can find someone to bring hot coffee. I'll be two secs.'

I watch as he gets out of the water, smiling at his attempt to suck in his stomach. I know he's conscious of his dad bod, but I love him exactly the way he is.

Grateful for the chance to be alone for a bit, I push myself under the shade of an overhanging palm tree. Reporting from a local paper *is* below me – it's many paces back from being a senior crime correspondent for a national tabloid – but it will have to do for now. I just need to get some money, keep my hand in the game and stay under the radar for a bit.

I replay Lou's email in my mind. I have no intention of giving up on my career. I just need to figure out how to claw it back.

12

Erin

I freeze at the sight of the Indonesian police officers in their uniforms, their perfectly ironed pale blue shirts, the polished metal badges fastened to their chests, the leather holster around their waists holding loaded guns.

'Jamie,' I whimper, acutely aware of the pounding thuds of my racing heartbeat. It's all I can do to say his name.

We keep walking, shuffling closer, carried by the sea of passengers. I try to fight the tide but it's no use.

'It's going to be OK.' I can hear the trepidation in his voice, yet he continues to place one foot in front of the other.

Oh, God. This is it. Our terrible choices coming back to haunt us. Can they see how riddled with guilt we are? We're going to be pulled aside. Interrogated. Arrested. Locked up. Possibly even sentenced to death. My hands start to sweat; I rub them across my stomach. I feel light-headed with fear. This actually can't be happening; surely I'll wake up and this will all have been a horrific nightmare?

Jamie is slightly in front of me, as if shielding me, letting them take him first. I want to grab his hand, pull him back – we're in this together – but my limbs have turned leaden.

I have to try to stay calm. Panicking won't help us. I have to think rationally. We haven't done anything wrong; the man was bribing us; it was his fault he tragically fell down the steps to his death. Yes, we should have stayed and called for help, but hindsight is a wonderful thing. When we explain this to the police, they'll understand. I push my shoulders back and swallow. But it won't be that simple. Despite our best intentions of explaining what actually happened, they may put two and two together and come up with five. There will be a language barrier, confusion; we'll have to explain that we were making love outdoors without knowing it was illegal; people in the Blue Fin might say they saw a disturbance between us and the man . . .

Oh, God.

Terrified thoughts go round and round in circles.

My throat runs dry. I need some water but I can't open my mouth to ask Jamie to pass me the bottle. There's not enough air. A sweat breaks out at my temples, behind my knees, in between my breasts.

Someone has stopped up ahead. They can't find their boarding pass; they swear they had it on them a moment ago. The police officers glance over at the hold-up. One pair of eyes lock directly on mine and I'm sure I'm going to pass out. I clench my jaw and shoot my gaze to the ground, acting as if I'm assisting in the search for the missing boarding card. Tears press at the back of my tired eyes.

'Found it! It was in my pocket all along.' The man laughs, followed by a ripple of polite laughter and a couple of groans.

We move closer. Only a few more steps to go. Two flight attendants are speaking to the couple in front of us. Their matching sing-song voices are bright and chirpy despite the early start. One is apologising for the delay as if she is personally responsible. I can't bear to bring myself to make eye contact with either of them.

Jamie and I are entwined, glued together by the sweat pressed in our clasped hands. Why have the police not pulled us out of the line yet? We're not going to be able to leave, surely. Someone will take one look at us and—

'Miss? Excuse me?'

My heart freezes in my chest. It's one of the police officers; his deep accent seems to travel all the way up my skin and into my bones.

'You dropped this.'

He's holding up a scarf. It's pretty, the sort you'd drape over your shoulders on a chilly evening. Then I spot the tiny embossed rosebuds printed on the soft-looking fabric. Little flashes of blood-red and green thorns.

The police officer is holding it out for me to take. 'Miss?'

It's not mine. The scarf isn't mine.

'Thanks.' Jamie reaches across and takes it, placing it around my neck.

Why is he giving me a scarf and not arresting us?

I can't speak to tell Jamie it doesn't belong to me, that I've never seen it before, that someone else must have dropped it. Then I realise he's saving me. The longer I stand there dumbstruck and trembling at the sight of a fucking pashmina, the longer the crew will have suspicions about my ability to board this flight. Strong floral perfume hits my nostrils. This is another woman's scarf, yet I can't take it off. The thin fabric feels like a noose around my neck.

'Good morning. Can I see your boarding passes and passports, please?' the brunette flight attendant asks.

This is it. She's going to check our names and that's when everything is going to come crashing down. Jamie fumbles for the passes.

'Have a wonderful flight.' She hands the documents back and flashes a bright smile. There's a tiny smudge of ruby-red red lipstick on her front teeth.

I grip a handful of Jamie's T-shirt, feeling his clammy back as he leads the way past the policemen, avoiding eye contact. Down the narrow, airless tunnel towards the plane. The fabric of the scarf is tight around my dry throat.

Every step takes us closer to leaving Bali and the hell of what happened last night. Not that I'll ever be able to forget – small things keep coming to me, like the fact that he got dressed yesterday morning not knowing it would be for the last time, or that he went to the Blue Fin not knowing how his night would end.

So many what-ifs. What if our paths had never crossed? What if I hadn't spilt his drink over him? What if he hadn't gone to the cliffs? I still don't know where he was heading when he saw us. What was he even doing there?

What if it hadn't been raining and the steps were dry? Would he still have plummeted down them? My stomach lurches when I think of his blood-soaked, rain-slicked grey hair. The heavy thump of breath knocked out of his lungs as he tried desperately to hold on to the concrete wall. The oozing crimson stain where he cracked his skull.

'Here we are,' Jamie says, interrupting my sickening thoughts.

We've reached our row. There's a backpacker against the window who gives us both a polite nod as we slip in next to him. Jamie on the aisle. Me trapped in the middle. I let him buckle my seatbelt and sit rigid, watching everyone else casually prepare for the flight. The backpacker's put headphones in, bobbing his head in time to the beat only he can hear.

'Are you OK?' Jamie asks quietly.

'I think so,' I lie. My breath is coming out in starts. 'Are you?'

He nods, then leans over and kisses the top of my head, the familiar scent of his aftershave bringing forward a rush of emotion. I want to nestle into him and block the rest of the world out.

'I love you.'

'I love you too.'

The aircraft doors close.

'Everything's going to be all right, I promise.' He's trying to sound authoritative but even he must hear the slight wobble in his voice.

I can't help but cry into this stranger's pashmina, wishing I could believe him.

13

Erin

Wednesday 14 September

The world is still spinning. People are going about their business and we're playing the role of tired honeymooners. Our paleness could be passed off as exhaustion. Somehow, we've survived two flights and five painfully long hours in transit in Dubai. Another place where they have the death penalty, my brain helpfully reminded me over and over again.

We did nothing wrong; we did nothing wrong. I repeat it like a mantra.

Yes, leaving him was probably not the most humane decision but it's not as though we pushed him. The wet steps, the sudden turn. He fell and we couldn't save him. We could only save ourselves, by getting back to England and carrying on as normal, as if nothing terrible and tragic happened on the last night of our idyllic honeymoon.

I don't let go of Jamie's hand as we follow the throng of weary passengers off the plane and through immigration and pick up our suitcases. I only begin to breathe properly again

68

when we go through customs and wheel our cases through the main doors, out into the buzz of Heathrow's arrivals hall. Incredibly, I fall asleep in the car the moment Jamie starts the engine, exhausted by the sheer relief.

Ten days we've been away, yet everything has changed.

Before the honeymoon, life was fun in that chaotic kind of way. Going from a small one-bedroom flat in the city to a spacious, detached three-bed in the countryside was a no-brainer. Of course, Jamie told me Renhold House needed a bit of work, hence why he got it for a bargain at auction just before we met, but I wasn't prepared for how much. I think I romanticised it all, as people have told me I have a habit of doing.

When we'd officially moved in in August, just two weeks before the wedding, a heatwave was gripping the UK and all the windows were flung open, bringing in smells of the honest, fresh country air. But now, in the middle of September, the house is dark, cold and uninviting.

It has potential. This word sticks in my mouth like hard toffee. It's also not that close to anything. We have to drive everywhere; the closest village is a good forty-minute walk away. The nearest neighbour is a farmer's cottage that you can only get to over a boggy field. But the view over the patchwork landscape is pretty spectacular and there are lots of original features in the house that have been unloved for too long. In the hallway is a beautiful original parquet floor that I'm determined to bring back to life, along with the stained glass above the front door that will shine again. With a lot of hard work and a little patience, it's easy to imagine how this house will become a perfect family home. The life I've always dreamt of is within touching distance.

It'll be nice to have a project. I think the reason we've crammed so much into the past few months is to keep me busy, to not dwell on what happened in Girona or think of the ache in my womb that only I can feel. We've both earmarked the box room overlooking the garden as a nursery. Not that Jamie is rushing things – he's been amazing, insisting I take things at my own pace. When I said I wanted us to start trying for a family on honeymoon – in a fun, relaxed, no-pressure sort of way – he was very happy to get on board. This house needs a beating heart once more; it deserves a happy family to live here. Maybe we can get a dog or two.

Not that I can think about any of that right now.

Jamie is pulling the suitcases from the boot, shutting it with a heavy thump that makes me jump. I use the sleeve of my crumpled hoodie to wipe away the tears that have appeared from nowhere. I didn't think I had any left to shed.

I follow him as he walks through to the kitchen and drops the bags next to the washing machine. This is the most modern room in the house. It's a farmhouse style, with charcoal-grey granite floor tiles that send a chill through you the moment you set foot on them. There's a double patio door at the far end that leads on to a large garden. The grass needs to be cut. Wild flowers and weeds cover the space. I don't actually know how far back it goes.

In the centre of the room is an island with an ugly low-hanging light. The bulb must be an eco-saving one, as it never seems to give off enough light. Even now, I have to squint as I turn the fridge back on. I run the hot water tap and flinch. It's ice-cold. I forgot that we need to wait for the boiler to heat it up. I took for granted in my old place just how simple it was to jump in the shower whenever I wanted. I'm immediately annoyed, with no one to blame.

He watches me and pulls a face. 'Ah, I was going to run you a bath . . .'

'It's fine,' I sigh. 'Thanks, though.'

I'm too tired anyway. If I sank into a hot bath now, I'd probably never get out. I flick the kettle on.

'Damn. We forgot to get milk at the airport,' I say, shocked at how normal it is for this to come out of my mouth. We watched a man plummet to his death and did nothing to help him. Then we fled the country in fear, but *darling, there's no milk*.

'I'll pick some up in the morning. There should be some long-life stuff in the pantry,' he replies.

I have a pantry now. I bet Sophia Spencer has a pantry. Or would she call it a larder? I don't know the difference but I bet she does.

Jamie yawns. 'Listen, my love, I'm going to grab a couple of hours' sleep. I've got to go to the office later.'

I twist around in shock. 'You're going to work?'

'We need to carry on as normal, Erin.'

'But—'

'Remember what we spoke about.' He takes hold of my hands. His tired eyes focus on mine. 'It was an accident. We can't let ourselves go mad with what-ifs for the rest of our lives. We have to just keep calm and carry on.'

I don't know what to say. I'd presumed we would at least have a few days together first. We need some time to let everything sink in. It's not just the tragic end to our honeymoon that's overwhelming. There's still so much that needs to be unpacked: boxes piled in every room dumped by the removal men who ignored my neat handwriting detailing what needed to go where. That all feels like a past life, one where the only thing I stressed over was bubble wrap and cardboard boxes.

Jamie's on his phone – he's moved nearer to the router that he must have switched back on. His eyebrows are knotted as he taps at the screen.

'Is there any news?' I ask, biting my bottom lip.

What I want to ask is *Have the Indonesian police put out a wanted poster for our arrest?* A shiver passes through me every time I think of how simply we ran away.

'No.' He clears his throat and puts his phone in his pocket. 'I'll look again when I wake up.' He lets out another yawn. 'I'm shattered. You must be too. Come to bed soon, babe.' With that, he kisses me on the cheek and leaves me alone in the cold, gloomy kitchen.

14

Sophia

Wednesday 14 September

The yellow-gold of autumn appeared while we were away. Our terrace-lined street is a beautiful display of crisp orange leaves. Mark pays the taxi driver and I let out a sigh at being back home. Real life has to start now – no more pretending or putting things off. But right now, all I want is a takeaway, a hot bath and an early night.

'Chinese or pizza?' I offer as he lugs our cases in.

'What were you saying about tightening our belts?' he teases.

'This can be the last supper. It's on me,' I promise.

'In that case I'll have whatever comes soonest. I'm starving.'

I head to the kitchen to find the stain-splattered paper menus, despite always picking the same thing every time. I decide on Chinese, with a sudden yearning for some duck spring rolls.

I go to ask what he wants, expecting him to be unpacking in the bedroom. Instead, I find him hunched over his laptop, the view of our street whooshing past at triple speed.

'Anything good on there?' I ask.

'Jesus, Soph! You made me jump! I didn't hear you come in.'

The screen shows the standard goings-on of our plain, normal street – the occasional car, motorbike or pedestrian strolling down the pavement. Nothing out of the ordinary. The light changes as the days rise and fall. In the near-darkness the camera turns infra-red, making a passing fox glow and the white lace threads of a spider's web ethereal.

'What are you doing?' I ask, despite it being obvious.

'I just thought I'd make sure everything was OK since we've been gone.'

He shouldn't be living like this.

'Mark, it's fine. Nothing has happened in weeks now.'

'I know, but you just can't be too careful. I mean, I spent all that money on this system. I may as well keep using it.'

Peace of mind comes at a price. I hated the day he got it installed. The whole routine of locking the doors and windows and triple-checking the cameras before he can think about winding down for bedtime makes me so sad – it's because of what I did that we live like this now.

'I think it's time to think about getting rid of the cameras,' I say as tactfully as I can. 'They're making you paranoid.'

'No, they're not. I'm fine, I promise.' He looks back at the screen. 'Anyway, you'll be pleased to know nothing ominous happened on here since we've been away.'

He expects me to breathe a sigh of relief but I just lean across and kiss his forehead, telling him I'm going to run a bath while he orders the food, handing him my purse. With the water running, I sit on the closed toilet seat and look at the envelopes I picked up. I managed to scoop up the post while Mark was distracted turning off the alarm. I used to do this as a way of protecting him. I'm painfully aware of how he still checks the CCTV and I still check the mail – both of our habits forever changed because of what I've done.

I flick through the post. A dull brown envelope with a utility stamp on it, a couple of flyers for local plumbers and Domino's Pizza. There is a postcard from my parents, who are currently on holiday in Morocco, and two credit card bills. I can't face opening them and being given more bad news, not right now. I exhale. There is nothing else here. No handwritten note, no newspaper cuttings of my face, eyes poked out with the tip of a sharp pencil; no printed photographs of me walking alone down the street, oblivious to the fact that I was being watched.

Mark is always saying how I remind him of a terrapin, my exterior is so hard. I tell him that it's a hazard of the newsroom, that there's no way I could do my job if I let everything get to me. I'd never last a day. And it's true, I have a heart of stone – but I still feel things. And I felt fear.

I was terrified when the death threats started arriving at our house, not just the newspaper office. Peter wanted us to have an unmarked police car on our street as a precaution. Mark almost moved out then. He didn't feel safe in his own home. I explained that the paper was just being extra-cautious. It was all linked to the story that cost me my job.

The one that I know I can claw back if Lou tells me her side of things – and allows it to go to print.

'Food is on the way,' Mark shouts through the closed bathroom door, pulling me from the spell I've fallen into.

'Everything OK in there, Soph? You've been running that for ages.'

Shit. The bath is almost overflowing. I leap up and turn the taps off. The hot water hasn't heated up. Just a bath of icy-cold water.

'Sophia?'

'Everything's fine,' I call back, pulling the plug.

15

Sophia

Friday 16 September

From the outside it looks more like a job centre than a newspaper office. Inside, it smells of cheap coffee and a faint whiff of bleach. I'm handed a lanyard, the scratched plastic shell holding a scribbled piece of paper with my name incorrectly spelled, highlighting that this is a trial run.

Mark reminded me last night as I picked out my outfit – a pair of charcoal-grey trousers and a plum-coloured blouse that looks like Whistles but is actually Zara – that I don't need to do this. I could find another job, something in a totally different industry. I had to bite my tongue. He doesn't understand: I can't do any other job. In some ways it would be easier if I could. His desire to move to the countryside, where property is cheaper, is a pipe dream, one he likes to bring up with growing frequency, but my home is here in London.

Despite what happened, I am a good journalist. I just got caught up in the wrong story.

I think of Lou's email. I've read it so many times now. I'm sure that after we meet – not that she's given me a time or place yet – I will be able to set the record straight. I do feel slightly guilty about the fact that I've kept it quiet from Mark, but I just don't want him worrying that I'm picking at an old wound. Or, worse, that I'm getting my hopes up for nothing.

It was near-impossible to tear myself away from his tanned body nestled into our duvet this morning. He isn't back in the office until Monday so he's going to catch up on sleep and laundry. I wished I'd not been so hasty to accept this offer at the *Islington Post* and given myself more than just one day at home to recover from the long journey home and the jet lag.

Claudia, the editor, a big-boned woman with ebony curls and a gobstopper necklace, breezes down the office, pointing out with a jiggle of an arm the stationery cupboard, the meeting room and the communal kitchen. I'm briefly introduced to other tired-looking members of staff.

'. . . And here you are.'

We stop at a desk next to a window, beside grubby blinds that sit haphazardly on their rails. Claudia raps a hand on top of the ageing desktop computer. There's a curled-up Post-it with log-in details beside the keyboard.

'It might look old but it still works. Ha, the same could be said for me!'

I try and lift up the corners of my mouth in a matching smile.

'To get you started, could you go through the inbox and check what emails have come in over the week, please?'

There's a central email system that's full of general enquiries, PR requests and spam. It's usually the job of the work experience kid to empty it. I nod. What else am I supposed to do?

'Then, once you're settled in, it would be great for us to have a little chat about your ideas!' She pushes her lipstick-red plastic glasses back up her nose with a matching painted fingernail.

'Of course.'

'Welcome to the team, Sophia. I hope this is the start of a beautiful relationship.' She waddles off across the stained carpet tiles, her shoulders juddering as if she's laughing.

I rummage in the stationery cupboard, which is little more than a disorganised pile of plastic wallets, brown envelopes and loose highlighter pens, to find a notepad and working biro. I can feel a headache coming on as I scroll and delete unimportant emails. This inbox hasn't been emptied in months.

An hour or so in, I need a coffee.

'It's Sophia, isn't it?' a woman in her early twenties wearing a light grey hijab asks as we stand in the cramped communal kitchen, shared with the IT company down the hall, waiting for the kettle to boil. In the *Sunday News* offices, we had a professional barista-style coffee machine.

'Yes, hi . . .'

'Amira.' She looks like someone you'd find hidden among the bookshelves of an old library. Earnest and a little bit startled. Her dark brown eyes flutter around my face, trying to make eye contact. 'I couldn't believe it when Claudia announced that you'd be starting here! You've just come back from your honeymoon, haven't you?'

A zip of adrenaline rushes up my legs. 'How did you know . . .?'

'Oh, er, Claudia mentioned it. The tan also gives it away.'

'Sorry, I've clearly not had enough of this yet today,' I say, nodding at the jar of cheap coffee, making a mental note to bring my own tomorrow, and not to be so guarded. Not everyone is out to get me.

Amira flashes a small smile. 'I just have to tell you how much I loved your piece on the Lancashire police corruption trial. I made sure to share it on all my socials.'

'Thanks, yeah, that one took some work.'

Tears unexpectedly press against my eyes and the suddenness of the emotion takes me aback. It's the jet lag. The tiredness. The sudden shock of going from the balmy Bali dream to this cramped, slightly smelly kitchen. And the realisation of how far I've fallen. Will I ever work on undercover exposés again?

Amira doesn't seem to have noticed. She's sniffing the milk and pulling an unimpressed face. 'I'm working on a few things myself that I'd love to share with you some time? I mean, Claudia is really kind, she's been good to me, but it would be amazing to work with the actual Sophia Spencer!'

I swallow the lump in my throat and tear off a piece of patterned kitchen roll hanging limply on a half-empty tube, to dab my eyes.

'Are you OK?' She shifts awkwardly on her heels.

'Yeah, just a bit tired. Still adjusting to things. Sorry.'

'Er, well, just let me know when you've got some free time. I'd better get back to work.' She hesitates for a second, as if she wants to say something more, before darting off down the corridor.

I sit down at my desk. At first I'd thought I was the one doing Claudia a favour, coming to help out in her skeleton-staffed newspaper – I strode in here thinking I would be the one in charge – but now I realise, as I repeatedly scroll and delete, that she is the one doing me a favour. There's not enough work here for all of us, but by giving me the crap jobs, in the corner of the room, she knows no one will ask questions and I'm still getting paid. I decide to do another hour of this and then go and have a proper chat with Amira, apologise for earlier. This is not who I am. Sophia Spencer doesn't just burst into tears in public.

I look back at my computer screen. It's a habit of my old job to scan the news wires. There's one subject line that catches my eye.

British Man Found with Fatal Injuries in Southwest Bali.

I sit closer to the dusty screen.

JAKARTA, September 14 (AP)
A BRITISH man has died following extensive storms across Bali. Police said the man's body was discovered at Tebing Terjal viewing point, near Uluwatu beach, on Tuesday (September 13). Indonesian police are appealing for witnesses. A spokesman said that consular officials had been informed.

I frown. If they found his body on Tuesday morning, then he must have died when we were at the Blue Fin the evening before. Uluwatu beach was right near our hotel. I'm about to google and double-check the location when I hear footsteps approaching.

'It's Sophia, isn't it?' A scrawny guy in his mid-thirties, with a camera around his neck and an unkempt beard, comes up to my desk, jolting me from my thoughts. 'I'm Brad, and today is your lucky day.'

'Oh?'

'Claudia has asked me to take you with me to visit Ethel, a one-hundred-year-old great-grandma who is doing a charity knit-off to raise money for the local children's hospital.' He taps at his chunky camera. 'I'll sort the pics if you sort the words.'

Lucky me. 'Oh, right. Hang on.'

He peers closer to my screen. 'Bali? You're not on your honeymoon now.'

'I just thought it was an interesting story . . .' I trail off, feeling this guy's eyes on me as I scramble to put my notepad and pen in my bag, slightly concerned at how everyone in this office seems to know so much about my life.

'Hmm. Well. Tick-tock. We don't know how long this old dear's got left.'

'Sure. Coming.'

Instead of deleting the news wire, I forward it to my personal email, then I grab my coat and follow him out of the building.

16

Erin

Saturday 17 September

Surely someone has found him by now.

I wish I could remember more details of the person I saw when we were hiding in the bushes. I don't even know if it was a man or a woman. In all honesty, I'm not even sure if anyone was even there; perhaps it was just shadows and light. My overwhelmed brain playing tricks on me. Surely we'd have heard a scream of discovery or some commotion as we hurried away?

I'm cold all the time. I'm sure it's the lack of sleep. The change in temperature from the balmy days of Bali to the autumnal English chill has been a big shock. Frost seems to have settled in my bones. It doesn't help that this house is so draughty. So many times, I've gone to close a window only to find it's already shut. I need to work out how the heating works – I must be doing something wrong, because every time I go to turn the thermostat up, I see that it's somehow switched itself off. Faulty electrics is just one thing on the list of what we need to fix in this house.

Apart from the kitchen, none of the other rooms has been touched in decades. I don't know what the previous owners were thinking. It's such a mishmash of styles. From seventies chic in the avocado bathroom, to fifties chintz in the bedroom, full of headache-inducing floral-patterned wallpaper and clashing carpets, and an eighties lounge that's got two enormous, ugly green leather sofas that Jamie said came with the house and he hasn't got around to taking to the tip. I had planned to come back from our honeymoon and create pinboards and lists, visit bathroom showrooms, traipse around furniture shops, but I haven't got the brain space. It all seems so trivial now. Who cares about the style of door handles or the finish on a skirting board after what we did?

The jet lag doesn't help.

My brain is unable to focus on the smallest of tasks. Each box I start on overwhelms me – I didn't realise we had so much stuff. I started, then gave up on, the cleaning. It seems that as soon as I polish one mirror it's clouded with dust the next moment.

Jamie's gone in to the office and I've got the news on my laptop. I've been checking it on the hour, every hour, alternating between the BBC, Sky, Twitter and the Bali newspaper sites. Nothing has made the headlines yet. There's not even been a mention of anything matching the man's description. I wish we knew his name so I could be more specific in my search terms.

I glance at the clock. Time's up. I haven't got time to do any more digging right now – I have to get ready for my best friend Kat's baby shower at a local hotel.

I try to ignore the swish of my stomach as I'm getting dressed. I never told Kat what happened in Girona. How could I? Not when she was so caught up in her own life-changing news. For some reason, it felt as if it needed to stay private. Like fire with no air – the smaller the amount of oxygen, the less damage can be done.

Soon I hear the tyres of the taxi I ordered pull up on the gravel drive. I thought about driving but there's no way I can get through trying to act normal without the help of alcohol.

I'm looking for my handbag when there's a knock at the door. The sudden sound makes me jump.

Another knock. This time it's firmer, more authoritative. My body reacts before my mind does, my skin immediately prickling.

Spiralling thoughts barge over one another. It's not the taxi I've ordered. The police. We must have been followed home. There's no way I can deal with this on my own. Oh, my God.

I crouch down and try peering through the fussy net curtain without being seen. Before I can make anything out there's another commanding knock. I swallow and force my shaking legs to walk towards the heavy front door.

I open it ever so slowly.

A man is standing there. But it's not a policeman. It's a delivery guy. My relief is short-lived and a new wave of nausea washes over me when I see what he's holding. In his arms is an enormous bouquet of tropical flowers. A spray of vibrant yellows, burnt oranges and creamy-white foliage surrounded by deep, glossy palm leaves.

'I've got a delivery for . . . Erin Steele?'

All I can see is the churned-up petals of the flower offering scattered over the wet ground, trailing on a river of the dead man's blood.

'Shall I leave them here or . . .?'

I mumble a thank you and take the surprisingly heavy bouquet from him. The heady perfume rushes up my nose. I try to blink back the tears.

'Can you sign here, please?'

My hand leaves a trembling, shaky signature. There is a crisp white envelope tucked into the edge of the bouquet with my name on. My heart is racing, the tang of bile leaping to the back of my mouth as I tear it open.

Welcome home, my darling wife. Love J x

My husband has sent me flowers and I want to vomit.

I pick up my phone, jabbing his number in, cursing that it always takes him so long to pick up.

'You've reached Jamie, leave me a message and—'

I bunch a fist towards my scrunched-up eyes, waiting impatiently for his voicemail to click in.

'What the hell, Jamie?' That's all I can get out before my throat thickens and heavy repressed sobs erupt. I swipe at my eyes and try to catch my breath. 'The . . . flowers. You sent me sodding flowers, but . . .' How do I tell him that his thoughtful gift has thrust me back to Bali, without sounding completely deranged? I can't explain that the clashing colours and strong scent take me back to the aftermath of the rain-soaked steps. Panic. Disbelief. Another shaky breath. 'Jesus. Just call me back!'

I hang up. My legs give way as the adrenaline evaporates and I fall on to two unopened cardboard boxes in the hallway. All I can smell is sickly jasmine and frangipani trapped in the musty air. Vibrant petals have fallen on the dusty parquet. My phone buzzes again. This time it's a diary reminder. The baby shower is starting in fifteen minutes.

Where the hell is that taxi? Maybe it's a good thing it's not turned up. There's no way I can see Kat like this. I glance at my reflection in the hallway mirror that's yet to be put on the wall. The angle of it makes me look grotesque. My eyes are puffy, cheeks blotchy, and my limp hair is a mess where I've tugged at strands without realising.

I open up my messages app. *I'm so sorry but I'm sick, I'm going to have to take a rain check*, I type, my fingers trembling over the keys, autocorrect mistaking the words.

I'm about to press send when I close my eyes and force myself to breathe slowly. What did Jamie say about acting normal? I can't cancel on my best friend, not when she's already waiting for me. It will raise alarm bells. I'll be late, but late is better than letting her down completely.

There's the sound of another car pulling on to the gravel. I turn to see the taxi sweeping up to the house, and delete the text. With a forceful shove, I dump the bouquet in the wheelie bin by the side of the house and get into the back of the car. The driver says a cheerful hello, asks me how my day has been so far. I tell him curtly that it's been shit, then give him directions and close my eyes. I can still smell the sickening sweet scent on my fingertips as he reverses off the drive.

17

Erin

What the hell am I doing here? I'm sitting under an arch of pastel-pink balloons, among a bunch of women I hardly know all clucking about babies and birth stories. I try to stop fidgeting in my seat. The woman next to me keeps giving me a tight but annoyed smile. There are seven of us in total. Each one is nearly identical to the next. None of them looks like me.

I rushed in, just as they began the games, apologising to Kat for being late. It's amazing how quickly she seems to have grown since I last saw her. I know that she's pissed off with me, I've caught the looks she's given her sister across the room, but she's clearly trying to do her best not to let it ruin the day.

'Someone's got a nice tan,' one of Kat's university friends pipes up.

'Who, me? Oh, it's probably more sunburn than suntan,' I say, feeling warm under their eyes. 'I've just come back from my honeymoon.'

'Ooh. Where did you go?'

I clasp my hands together until my knuckles turn white. If Jamie can go to work, putting in overtime at the weekend, and pretend nothing happened, then I can do this.

'Bali.'

There's a wistful sigh in near-unison. 'Was it amazing?'

I have a sudden craving for a cigarette, despite having given up in my early twenties. Pairs of interested eyes are fixed on me. 'It was . . .'

How can I even begin to describe the honeymoon? Explain how it felt seeing his skull crack against the rough concrete; watching the dark pool of blood rush out towards my feet. Hyperventilating in my vomit-flecked, beer-soaked dress.

'. . . magical.'

Kat frowns. My heartbeat quickens at this look. She's my best friend; of course she can tell that I'm lying.

'Don't cry.' A hand pats my shoulder.

'Holiday blues,' another woman murmurs sympathetically. 'Do you know what you need to do?'

I shake my head, sniffing away the sudden tears.

'Book another one.' She laughs.

If only it were that simple.

A second later, a young waiter appears, carefully holding a tray of free prosecco. He moves around the circle, handing out flutes, and Kat and another lady, who's breast-feeding her chubby baby, perform an over-the-top refusal. The bubbles taste acidic but I need something to get through the next couple of hours.

Suddenly, there's a loud BANG! and I leap up from my seat, spilling prosecco on the plush carpet. One of the balloons has burst.

'You OK?' the woman to my right asks gently, clearly wishing she'd sat somewhere else.

I want to cry again. I'm trapped in a nightmare, but I nod and fix a tight smile on my face. My heart is racing and I have an overwhelming urge to leap from my chair and sprint out of this room, but I can't. I have to sit and suffer this. Is this what my life is going to be like for evermore? This exhausting permanent state of pure panic?

'Right, new game!' Kat's older sister, Victoria, announces, clapping her hands, oblivious to how close I am to cracking. 'This one is Truth or Dare. Lucie?'

'Dare.'

'Awesome! This is called "tinkle in the potty". You have to put this balloon up your top and a ping-pong ball between your knees to waddle to the toilet without dropping the ball,' Victoria explains.

I can't believe it when Lucie leaps up to take part. The women squawk their approval. I stare at Kat, expecting her to roll her eyes, but she is clapping along with the rest of them. Soon, it's my turn to pick. After watching that horrific performance, I have no doubt what I'm going to go for.

'Truth,' I say firmly.

'OK.' Victoria passes an unsubtle look to her sister, then scrunches up her nose. 'What's the biggest secret you've never told anyone?'

The circle goes quiet. Everyone is looking at me expectantly.

I accidentally killed a man.

If I hadn't shouted, then he wouldn't have turned and lost his balance. But if Jamie hadn't punched him then he wouldn't have been so dizzy. If it hadn't been raining and the steps had been dry, if he had just given us his phone, if hadn't been film-ing us in the first place, if we hadn't had sex and had just gone back to the room after the meal . . .

'Erin?' Kat stares at me.

Someone gasps.

I pull the flute from my lips and realise what I've done. I said it out loud.

'Ha. Your faces!' I stammer. Trying to push it back on them for being so gullible, while all the time my heart is pounding and my palms are sweating. Jesus. I've had too much to drink. It's far too warm in here.

My phone buzzes against my legs. I shift to the edge of my seat. What if it's a Google alert I set up? A breaking news announcement linked to our man? Victoria made such a big deal about no phones, wanting everyone to be 'present', but I'm desperate. I need to see what it says.

The woman beside me laughs. 'Oh, my God. You had me for a second then.'

'Er, I guess my biggest secret is that when I was dating Jamie, I pretended to be ticklish because I liked him touching me, but really I'm not.'

Am I talking too fast? Too slowly? Every second feels as if I'm under the microscope. I surreptitiously pick up a pastel pink *Baby Girl!* serviette to wipe my upper lip that has beaded with sweat. I need to get to the toilet so I can check my phone. Kat is still staring at me, a hand pressed against her chest.

Miraculously, they all breathe a sigh of relief and giggle. Someone actually coos at my lie.

The next round of fun is the 'smell the nappy' game.

My phone buzzes again. I can't cope with not knowing any longer. I stand up on wobbly legs and head to the bathroom. On the way, there's a small table with champagne flutes. I hesitate for a moment before stretching over and picking up another glass.

'Erin? Are you OK?' Kat intercepts me in the corridor. I hadn't heard her waddle up behind me.

'I'm great!' I say, a little too eagerly.

I don't want to stand here talking, I need to check what's on my phone.

'I didn't expect you to be here,' she says, rubbing a hand over her stomach. I bite down a sudden pang of envy at the sight.

'Why? Because group activities aren't exactly my thing?' I force a laugh. She knows I've never been great in a crowd. 'Did you think we were still away? Well, we only got back a couple of days ago, but of course I wasn't going to let you down!'

I'm talking too much. I can't help it. I told Jamie I'd keep an eye out for any news, and I'm letting him down. I can catch up with Kat properly later. Right now I need to see what's pinged on my phone, in private.

'No, I just—' She stops, as something catches her eye behind me. I turn and look and see my husband standing there.

18

Erin

Just one look at Jamie standing in the hotel lobby makes the room spin. Immediately, I fear the worst. Why is he here? What's happened? Is this linked to my phone buzzing? If only I'd been able to check it in time, I wouldn't feel so blindsided right now. To the outside world, it seems nothing is wrong, but I know. It's the way he's standing.

'Erin?' Kat is staring at me.

'I'll be back in a sec!' I say, walking as fast as I can to join him. A tight smile is fixed to my dry mouth.

'Hey! There you are.' He leans in to give me a kiss. I catch the receptionist peeling her eyes off him and picking up a ringing phone.

I'm about to ask him what he's doing here when I see something. A scratch down the length of his arm.

'Jamie, your arm . . .' I couldn't finish the sentence even if he let me. Snapshots of rushing through the branches away from the lifeless bloodied body flood back.

'I did it this morning. Caught it on the door as I moved our suitcases to the loft,' he replies quickly, tugging down his sleeve. I don't know if I believe him.

93

I blink and catch myself.

Of course I believe him. Why would he lie to me?

'W-w-what are you doing here? My phone has been going but I haven't had the chance to check it.'

He moves closer, his voice barely a whisper. 'OK, don't panic, but there has been some news.'

The floor tilts.

Jamie smiles politely at a member of staff who walks past, waits for her to leave, then leads me towards an empty meeting room.

'Oh, God. What?'

He pulls his phone out and shows me a screen grab of an English-speaking Balinese news site. It's only small, a paragraph or so. I blink. The letters jumble together. It takes me a second or two to focus on the words. The article is a few days old.

A man's body has been found near Uluwatu beach.

Our man.

They are appealing for witnesses to try to piece together what happened.

My stomach drops. I feel faint and hot and sick all at the same time. Jamie gently pulls me to sit down in a plush velvet chair, taking his phone away from me, his hands tight around mine. He has had longer to digest this but still, he isn't able to hide the sheen of sweat glistening on his pale forehead.

'It's fine,' he tries to say with some assertiveness.

'It's not fine!' Seeing it printed in black and white makes it all seem even more real. We may be almost eight thousand miles away but we're never going to be able to escape this. 'Not only did we leave him, we threw away evidence.'

'What?'

'His phone. You threw it into the ocean. That was the only thing that would prove he was filming us having sex, that he tried to use that to bribe us, and that's why you punched him. Without that, it just becomes our word.'

'Erin.' Jamie gently takes my face in his warm hands. 'No one suspects us. We weren't to blame for the accident. Nothing could have stopped it from happening, it was just a horrible misfortune. Tragic accidents happen every day, all over the world, but eventually people move on. You just have to stay calm, babe.'

I can hear the quiver in his voice, even if he thinks he's playing it cool.

He gives me a firm kiss on the lips. I hear a whoop from the baby shower party as a waiter appears with another tray of prosecco.

'How's it going in there, anyway?' he asks.

'It's hell – wait, how did you know I was here?'

He frowns for a split second. 'You told me.'

I'm confused. I'm sure I didn't tell him about the baby shower. I thought that if I did then he might be worried about me coming here, after what happened in Girona.

'Anyway, I got your voicemail and I wanted to check you were OK.' His eyes widen. 'I'm so sorry, babe. I had no idea the flowers would upset you so much. What did I do wrong? Why didn't you like them?'

His face breaks into such a genuine look of worry that I swallow. How could he forget the delicate petals churned in the mud and a dead man's blood? 'Do you not remember? The smell, the colours, the same flowers that were there that night on the cliff . . .'

Out of all the bouquets to order, he had to go for that one. You couldn't make it up.

'What? Oh, no, I'm sorry. It honestly wasn't on purpose! I literally ordered them ages ago, like before the wedding, as a nice surprise for when we got back. I can speak to the florists and see if they'll swap them?' He pauses. 'I just want you to be happy, Erin.'

My heart clenches with guilt at flying off the handle over such a stupid thing. Why am I like this? I feel terrible for such an overreaction to a very sweet gesture.

'No, I'm sorry. Thank you. That was really kind of you. I'm sorry for leaving such a shouty message.' He must have thought something serious had happened when he picked up my voicemail.

'I think we've both lost our heads a little,' he says, wrapping an arm around me. 'Listen, if you're not enjoying the party, then I can give you a lift back if you like?'

'Yes, please.' I need to lie in a dark room and take something to help me sleep.

Jamie places a firm hand at the small of my back.

'What would I do without you?' I say, suddenly feeling choked up.

He presses his lips against the crown of my head and gently tells me I'm the strong one.

He's wrong. He's my knight in shining armour.

19

Sophia

Saturday 17 September

The bright lights of high-rises wink at us from the thirty-second floor. From this high up the whole city is spread before us – ours for the taking. The bar is heaving with a fun Saturday-night atmosphere. The chilled house music the DJ is playing reminds me of the sultry, sun-kissed evenings of our honeymoon. If I close my eyes I could be back there, sipping a frozen mango daiquiri under swaying palms. Instead, we're in a busy London bar with fading tans and precious memories. I know we said we were supposed to be saving money but the thought of coming here has kept me going all week.

'I should wait until we've got our drinks before I say a toast.' Mark grins. 'But I wanted to say well done for getting through your first day, yesterday. I know it's not your dream career move.'

'You can say that again.'

I haven't told him about the pitying looks from my new colleagues, the frozen whispers every time I enter a meeting room or step into the shuddering old lift. Everyone apart from Amira.

'I know it won't have been easy but I'm proud of you. I just want you to be happy again.'

'Thank you.' I lean over the high table, wobbling on my stool, and kiss him.

He's wearing the aftershave he bought specially for our wedding day. The fresh citrus scent takes me back to our first dance. Holding one another, utterly exhausted but high on adrenaline.

'So, has work been OK? Really?'

'Yeah, as you say, it's not ideal but it's fine.' I pick up my phone. 'Oh, I forgot to tell you about this.' I search for the email about the guy who died in the storm. 'Check this out.' I hand him my phone just as a waitress appears.

'Do you want to share a bottle?' I ask Mark, quickly opening the velvet folder containing an extensive wine list.

'Sorry?' He glances up. 'Uh. No. Remember we're seeing Oakley for his birthday tomorrow.'

'Shit, I forgot.' My spirits fall. A hangover and our exuberant five-year-old nephew is not a good idea. 'In that case, I'd love an espresso martini, please. I'll just have the one.' I promise Mark. 'What would you like?'

'Oh, erm, just a gin and tonic, please. Thanks.'

'Can you believe it?' I say once the waitress has taken our order.

'Hmm?'

'The guy in the storm!' I nod to my phone that he's placed in between us. 'It was on the last night of our honeymoon, right near where we went for dinner.'

'Really?'

'See, I told you it was a bad storm,' I say. 'I wonder what exactly happened to him.'

'God knows. Poor guy.' Mark gives a small shrug then glances out at the view. There's a beat of silence. 'So, speaking of Oakley's party, I said we'd get to Jules's about four-ish – that OK?'

I smile at the change in subject. Mark has never truly understood my interest in the macabre. He believes people are inherently good and, although he has always supported my career, I'm mindful of sharing too much about what I get up to every day, especially as he's so squeamish. I always play down any horrific court cases I've covered, to spare him the gory details. I rarely dwell on things, whereas he's an overthinker.

I nod. 'Fine by me. It'll be nice to see them all again.'

'You know she'd love to see more of us. It'd be nice to be part of the kids' lives while they're growing up.'

I knew this conversation was coming.

We used to joke about getting out of the city. Being able to afford to buy our own place felt like such a momentous achievement, and it is, but our cosy terraced house in London is the size of a postage stamp compared to what you could get in the countryside. His sister and her growing brood have all the space they need. She keeps bees and chickens and has soil embedded in her fingernails. This was a woman who, for her own wedding, refused to have any alcohol that wasn't clear in case it dripped on her designer dress. I think it's just a phase, that the *Country Living* magazines will soon be replaced with copies of *Vogue*.

He continues, 'I've been looking into it. We could sell our house and get our money back, more if we were savvy. Or we could rent it out and see how we get on first?'

I sigh. 'Our life is in London. We've worked hard to get what we've got. You want to just throw that away?'

'No, not throw it away. I guess what I'm trying to say is that we're married now. Maybe that place was perfect for us in our twenties and early thirties but now we're a bit older, more responsible. We're not those partying kids any more. Maybe, Sophia, it's time to grow up.'

The memory of him hunched over his laptop engrossed in the CCTV footage, double-checking there was nothing he'd missed while we'd been away, rushes back. It's not normal to come back from holiday and immediately check your home hasn't been compromised in any way. Out in the sticks, he would relax. The cameras could be binned. No one would want to hurt us.

The thought is tempting, for my husband's peace of mind. It's just not something I want.

'Mark, I don't want to move. Our jobs are here.'

'We'll find new ones. I mean, Soph, you're on probation at the moment. Perhaps there's no better time to move than now? I just don't understand what it is you're chasing. Would it really be the worst thing in the world to give it up?'

I feel as if I've been slapped.

Moving would be an admission that it's over. That my career ended on a failure. There's a moment of silence, punctuated by the shrill laughter from the table next to us as they take numerous selfies.

I'm too hurt to speak, so I absently look at a notification that's popped up on my home screen and push a stray hair from my face. I keep expecting to hear from Lou with a plan of where to meet, but the message isn't from her. I need to tell Mark about the fact that she's back on the scene. If she agrees to talk on the record then the *Islington Post* won't be a long-term career move. I'll be back at the *News*, where I belong.

I take a deep breath. 'So, I've been thinking.'

'Uh-oh, dangerous.'

I give him a playful shove.

'Just kidding. Go on, tell me.'

I take a breath.

'When we were away, I had an email from Lou.'

'Lou. From Rupert's gang? That Lou?'

I nod. My stomach clenches at the look he's giving me.

'Sophia, no . . .'

'It's fine.' At the mention of these names, it's like PTSD. I don't know how long I'll have Mark's attention before he shuts down. 'Listen, if I can get her to give me her side of events, then it'll back up what I have and the story can be printed properly!'

'But what if they find out you're planning this?' He drops his voice, wide eyes darting around the busy bar as if Rupert himself were here.

'We'll be OK. I'll be careful. I promise.'

The waitress returns with our drinks, perfectly balanced on a rose gold tray, served with tiny black serviettes. Mark takes his drink and gulps a mouthful before she's even lifted mine from her tray.

'I'll just leave this here.'

She places the bill on the table. Mark leans forward to pick it up.

'I'll get it,' I say decisively, already pulling my purse out.

He doesn't argue. It's the least I can do.

20

Erin

Sunday 18 September

I spent another fitful night tossing and turning, feeling as though I was lying in a coffin of sheets, swaddling me so tightly I couldn't breathe. God only knows how much sleep I managed.

'What have you got planned for today?' Jamie asks, pulling me from my thoughts.

I'm still lying in bed, while he's got up, showered, dressed and is about to leave for work. Despite it being a Sunday, he has a trade show he needs to be at – he spent all of yesterday preparing for it. He tried to get out of it, but it's all about visibility with the investors. I bit my lip when he told me it was going to be an all-day thing.

'Er . . . I was thinking about dusting off my CV.'

It's the last thing I want to do, but maybe it would be good for me to have a reason to get up in the morning. I need to keep busy.

Jamie turns to face the mirror. 'I told you, you don't need to work right now. I can cover us both. Plus, the house will take up so much of your time.'

And then we'll be filling it with children, I imagine he's thinking.

I originally felt honoured that he trusted me enough to oversee the renovations, despite my total lack of experience. But since the honeymoon, being alone in the house with just my spiralling thoughts has shown me that I need to do something else. I'll go mad otherwise.

'I'm only looking at getting something small, a part-time thing, just until work properly starts here and then I can try and do both.'

He gives me a look that I'm not sure how to interpret. He's said many times how he wants to look after me, provide for us.

'But, you know, I might just take it easy instead.'

In all honesty, I'll probably spend all day glued to my phone.

I'm also waiting to hear back from Kat. She must be sulking that I left the baby shower without saying goodbye, as she's not replied to me since I asked if she liked her present. I got it delivered to her – it may have been late, but I bet none of the others sent her such a thoughtful gift.

'I think that's a much better idea.' He straightens his tie. 'I'm getting worried about you. You know it's not good for you to get too overwhelmed.' He leans across the crumpled bed and gives me a firm kiss. 'Right, do you need anything from me before I go?'

I shake my head, wishing I could pull him into the covers and stay with me.

It's only when I hear the front door close behind him that I realise I forgot to ask him about the heating again.

It takes me a while but eventually I'm showered and dressed. I smile to myself as I pad into the chilly kitchen and see Jamie has left me some breakfast out on the worktop. I pour milk over the cereal, despite it being nowhere near breakfast time, and make a mug of strong coffee. Jamie said not to spend hours down a rabbit hole searching for news, but I can't help myself. I settle at the kitchen island and pull open my laptop.

There are no updates from Bali. I pull my cardigan tighter and stare out of the grubby patio windows, warming my hands against my mug as I return to that night. I keep going over and over what happened, retracing our steps in my head. Torturing myself, as if I'm somehow able to change the ending.

I wonder if Mark and Sophia have heard what happened during the storm. No. Of course not. Why would they? They will be going about their business in blissful ignorance of the horror we endured on that last night.

A wave of sudden jealousy tears through me. Why did this have to happen to us? I bet nothing terrible has ever happened to a woman like Sophia Spencer.

Absently, I type her name into Google. Usually, by now, I would have performed a deep dive into the online world of a new acquaintance, especially one as glamorous and perfect as Sophia.

I hit search. The moment the results flash up, I wish I hadn't.

The kitchen suddenly feels extremely warm.

She's a journalist.

Until very recently, she worked as a senior crime reporter for a national newspaper, the *Sunday News*. I swallow and shift in my seat. When she told me she 'worked in the City' I assumed she meant she worked in finance or something. Why would she be so secretive? I take a couple of screenshots. Her name is on a number of different high-profile crime stories. According to numerous online comments, she is utterly ruthless in her pursuit of a story.

My mind is whirring; what will Jamie make of this? I try and take a breath. What would he say to me if he were here? Stay calm. Stop overthinking. But, despite this imaginary pep talk from my stoic husband, my mind continues to race. I wonder if she covers foreign crimes. Surely she will have contacts. What if she's somehow able to place us at the scene?

I feel the walls of the kitchen closing in.

I hurriedly try different search options in order to dig a little deeper but, annoyingly, I can't find any reference to where she works now. She told me she was between jobs; perhaps that means she's left the industry altogether. I have to cross everything that that's the case.

I'm about to send the screen grabs to Jamie when my phone chimes to life. The chirpy ringtone makes me jump out of my seat.

'I was just about to message you!' I say.

'Erin? Are you OK?'

'Sophia's a journalist!' I blurt. There is a moment of silence. I hear him apologise to whoever he's with, then the sound of footsteps and a door creaking open.

'Are you there? Jamie?'

106

'I'm here.' He exhales slowly. He must have moved outside as I can hear a siren in the distance.

'She worked as a senior *crime* reporter.'

'OK . . .'

OK? What does he mean, OK?

He coughs. 'It's not ideal but, listen, this is why I was calling you. They're coming to ours later.'

I steady myself on the work surface.

'Mark contacted me at work as he wants to upgrade his security. I said I'd sort him out with a mates' rate. That's when he suggested today – they're visiting his sister nearby. Listen, they clearly don't know anything about the accident or they wouldn't be coming round for dinner.'

'Dinner!'

'Well, I couldn't just invite them in for a coffee and then tell them to leave.'

I press my thumb between my eyes until fuzzy spots appear. Utterly blindsided. A ruthless crime reporter wants to come to dinner with us. Us. A newlywed couple who watched a man fall to his death on the last night of our honeymoon, then didn't tell a soul and ran away. You couldn't make this up.

'We need to cancel. Tell them you're sick, or—'

'I can't cancel, it'll look too—'

'Jamie?' someone calls his name. I can hear people talking in the background.

He lowers his voice to a whisper. 'It'll look too suspicious if we cancel on them, babe. We just have to act normal. Life carries on. We did nothing wrong, remember? Trust me. Maybe give the house a quick tidy. They'll be here at seven. I'm sorry, but I have to go.'

'Wait! But what will we cook—'

He hangs up before I can say another word. I place my phone on the kitchen surface with trembling fingers. *We did nothing wrong.* I repeat the words, my new mantra, and wonder if I'll ever end up fully believing them.

21

Sophia

Sunday 18 September

'Barney! Watch that sword! I've told you, you'll take the twins' eyes out!' a harassed mother calls.

My ears ring with the sound of high-pitched excitable shrieks and up-tempo music that echoes around the enormous soft play warehouse. We thought we'd time our arrival to catch the tail end of the party. The plan was to show our faces before enjoying a nice evening meal with Mark's sister, Juliet, and her husband.

'Ah, there you are!' Jules drapes a skinny arm across my shoulders. I can tell by her eyes that she's had a drink. I don't blame her. She's already surviving on zero sleep with the baby, and this is how she spends her Sundays. 'So pleased you could make it. Oakley is thrilled!'

Right on cue, Oakley, the birthday boy, leaps past wearing a superhero cape and an oversized 'five' badge stuck on his chest.

'So, tell me all! You're both glowing. Gosh, I bet the weather was glorious! And when I say glowing, I mean . . .' She gives me a very unsubtle wink.

Ever since announcing our engagement, it seems the world is desperate to know the ins and outs of our procreative desires.

'It was great. Very relaxing.'

'I want to hear all about it! I'll try not to be offended that you're not joining us for dinner. How you had the time to leave the bedroom to make friends, I have no idea. Surely it was non-stop shagging. Whoops! Hang on. Melody is getting tangled in the rope swing.'

I frown as she dashes off.

Mark puts down an inflatable guitar he's picked up from somewhere. 'You OK? What's that face for?'

'Jules just said that we're *not* going for dinner with them?'

'Ah. I forgot to mention it but,' Mark scratches his neck, 'I've told Erin and Jamie we'd pop in.'

'What? The couple from our honeymoon?'

'Yeah. I was messaging him about something in the week, and he invited us for dinner as I said we're down here for this party. Sorry, I thought you'd actually prefer that to hanging around, helping to clean up and all that.'

I think back to the meal in the Blue Fin. The spilt drink. The awkward tension and rushed goodbye.

'Fine, I guess.' It's not ideal, but it's better than sitting through the aftermath of the sugar comedown Oakley and his friends are going to experience later. 'Hang on – what were you messaging Jamie about? I didn't even know you two swapped numbers?'

'He said he'd sort us out with an upgrade for the alarm system.'

'An upgrade?' I stare at him. 'I'd hoped we'd be getting rid of the cameras soon, not upgrading them.'

Colour rushes to Mark's cheeks. 'He's doing it for barely anything, if that helps!'

He flashes an apologetic smile just as Mark's brother-in-law strides into the room with an enormous birthday cake and starts a powerful rendition of 'Happy Birthday', which makes a nearby toddler burst into tears.

The bellowing, out-of-tune singing is giving me a headache. I'm hot, uncomfortable and keep getting pungent wafts of unwashed feet every so often. Perhaps if I were dressed a little more casually then it might not be as bad. My chiffon leopard midi dress with laced leather boots isn't practical. I've already clocked the unimpressed looks from the cluster of mums seated around an indoor picnic bench in their uniforms of Breton-striped tops and stretchy leggings.

'Sorry, potential trip to A&E averted.' Jules is back at my side. She blows her long blonde fringe out of her eyes. 'So, where were we? What's been going on with you?'

I tell her that I'm working at the *Post*, trying to keep the disappointment out of my voice. She responds with over-the-top enthusiasm that I know is for my benefit. 'What's the maternity leave situation like?'

I grit my teeth. 'I don't know. It's only a trial at the moment.'

Thankfully she must pick up on my mood, as she changes the subject, not before hollering at her son to stop eating Haribo rings off the floor.

'I thought of you last week: there's a place not far from here that's just come on to the market. It would be ideal for you two. You could probably sell your place and live mortgage-free.'

She passes her phone over, and Mark's eyes light up as he flicks through the images of a respectable three-bed semi with a neat garden and an opportunity for an extension. It is so cheap compared to London prices. Suddenly there's an ear-piercing shriek from the ball pit. One child has pushed another and caused a nosebleed. All the Breton-top mums bolt into action, wet wipes are thrown in the air and harassed calls are made to seal off the bloodied play equipment.

We leave not long after.

I fiddle with the dial on the radio. My ears still haven't adjusted to the sudden change in volume since leaving the soft play venue. I'm grateful Mark is the one driving up the winding track.

I peer at Google Maps. 'Er, left, I think. God, it's remote here, isn't it?' We've already had to stop to let a couple of sheep wander past.

We drive for another five minutes down a narrow and very bumpy road with farmers' fields on either side. There's the faint hum of a hidden tractor. Lines of blackbirds sit atop a telephone pole before they all take flight at once.

'Hang on.' I shift in the passenger seat as a lone grey house comes into view. 'Is that it?'

'Yep. It looks like we're here.'

'Whoa,' I gasp, getting out of the car.

A full sky greets us just as daylight is leaking away. No smog, no planes, no sirens. The scents of damp earth and fresh manure from the fields carry on the cool wind.

I look up at the imposing grey building in front of me. The house is nothing like I imagined. Roof tiles are misplaced, ivy has claimed half of one side and the chimney has a bird's nest in it. The roof appears to be sinking in the middle; each end looks as if it's been pulled up by invisible rope. They weren't lying when they said there was work to be done.

The strong breeze whips my hair as I walk along the uneven gravel drive. Tufts of hardy weeds poke through, sharp and snagging at my chiffon dress. The land around is entirely flat and uninspiring. They could be the only two people left in the world and they wouldn't know. A chill dances up my arms.

Judging by his face, this is hardly the rural dream Mark had pictured either.

'Well, I wasn't expecting this,' he says, craning his neck to take it all in.

The silence is deafening. I have no idea how they cope, being so remote. I would feel suffocated in a place as quiet as this.

'Do you reckon they can still get a Deliveroo?' Mark grins, pressing the doorbell. A traditional ringing chimes from somewhere over our heads.

I clutch the bottle of nice wine we picked up on the way here closer to my chest but there's no time to worry about how awkward this reunion might be, as there's an ominous scrape of a lock and the sound of a chain being pulled back. Then the door starts to open.

22

Erin

It was pretty much non-stop scrubbing, spraying, wiping and dusting the moment I got off the phone with Jamie. I then had to go to three different farm shops to get everything I needed – only the best-quality ingredients for our guests – including driving to the Pig & Pepper, a fancy deli in Somerford, a forty-minute round trip, just before it closed. It was a frantic dash to grab sourdough bread, pots of olives, a selection of dips and some cured organic meats that I've artfully arranged on a platter for the starter, then a couple of artisan pies for the main. My fingers still smell of chorizo and caramelised onions.

Sophia on the other hand smells like a summer meadow. It still doesn't feel real that she's in my house. Her leopard-print dress is so chic. Her hair is tied in a low fishtail plait that drapes across one shoulder, strands of honey-blonde hair teased loose, framing her face. I wish I were a bit more casual. The dress I picked out would look more suited to a beach bar. Even Mark commented on how I was bringing the holiday vibes, until Sophia nudged him and told him not to tease me. I wasn't aware that he was.

We've done the polite small talk about their journey (not as long as you'd think, actually) and the weather (how different from what we're used to in Bali, ha ha). Soon the men are talking about football. Sophia pulls out one of the bar stools and wraps her long legs around the frame.

'So, how are things?' I ask, pouring her a glass of the white wine they brought. Even though it looks fancier than anything we would normally drink, I'm sticking with tap water; I mustn't miss a thing.

'Fine. Back to reality.' She clinks her glass to mine. 'Thanks for having us, it's lovely seeing you again.'

'No problem,' I stutter under her gaze, trying not to blush at her bright smile. She really is so beautiful. I can't stop looking at her handbag, a classic black quilted Chanel on a silver chain strap, which she tucks beside her feet. Nothing in my wardrobe is a designer label but if I did own anything as fancy as that, I certainly wouldn't be shoving it on the floor.

'So,' I take a deep breath. 'Are you back at work?'

The smile drops. She picks at her nail polish. 'Yeah.'

'It must be hard, going back after the holiday.'

'Yeah. It's been a bit of a shock to the system.'

'What is it you do again?'

'I'm freelancing at my local paper at the moment.'

'Oh? You're a journalist?' I ask, screwing the bottle cap back on, trying to act as casual as possible. 'What sort of stories do you write?'

'I cover all sorts, really. Before this I was a crime reporter on a national but . . . I fancied a change.'

'So you don't write crime stories any more?'

'Last week I wrote a feature on Ethel, a great-grandma who has launched a charity appeal for others to start knitting, and an in-depth double-page spread on how the cladding crisis is affecting a block of flats near the tube station.' She rolls her eyes. 'But my passion is crime.' She moves a touch closer; her inviting scent fills my nose. 'Between us, in the background, I'm working on a few things.'

I nod, trying not to freeze mid-smile. Inside I'm screaming, desperate for more details, but I stay silent, wary of pushing it too far. I don't want it to look as though I'm taking too much of an interest in her job.

'Erin. Are you OK?' she asks, looking at my arms, at the goosebumps which have appeared across my bare skin. I excuse myself to go and throw on a cardigan. An ugly mohair thing that itches.

When I return, Jamie has seated them at the kitchen table – not in the places I would have chosen, but I don't mention it.

'What have I missed?' I ask as brightly as I can.

'I was just showing Mark the app, giving him a quick run-through.' Jamie glances up from his phone, his fingers scrolling the activity feed, the HD playback feature, the intuitive interface and voice control options.

'Have you had it long?' I ask Sophia. 'Your alarm, I mean.'

'Mmm, I hate it. It gives me the creeps,' she says. 'Sorry, Jamie – no offence.'

Jamie laughs. 'None taken.'

'We got it when Soph was getting a bit of attention because of one of the stories she was working on,' Mark explains. 'As I said to you before, it's more of a deterrent.'

Jamie has his tongue out in concentration, syncing Mark's phone to some piece of upgraded kit. 'I'll give you a sixty-day free set-up. Will that be long enough?'

'Nice one, cheers, man,' Mark clinks his beer bottle. 'Hear that, Soph?'

Sophia dips her eyes to the table and then finishes the rest of her glass in one long gulp.

23

Erin

Intrigued to see more of the house, Sophia and Mark have gone off on a self-guided tour. I rush to help Jamie dish up the starter.

'You OK?' he asks, passing me a serving spoon.

'I was about to ask you the same thing. What do we do about Sophia? She's a journalist. She'll know something's up!'

He gives a firm shake of his head. 'She *was* a journalist. Now she works at the *Islington Daily Bugle* or some bollocks. It's not like she's dominating Fleet Street. Trust me, you're worrying too much.' He leans over the counter and gives me a reassuring kiss. 'Thanks for sorting this. I didn't expect you to go all the way to the Pig & Pepper.'

I turn the dial on the oven to 180 degrees. Pie and mash may not be exotic but it's tasty – and foolproof.

'It's fine.' Then I pause. 'I didn't think I'd told you that I went there.'

He gives me a look I can't quite read. 'Are you OK, babe?'

I'm about to say something when I hear Mark and Sophia's voices from the hallway.

'Come on, let's get this over with,' I say, giving him a peck on the cheek.

We're all seated around the table once more.

'This is delicious, thank you,' Sophia says. 'Even better than the Blue Fin.'

I know she's being polite, but hearing that name again is like a twist of a knife in my stomach.

'God, that was some crazy weather that night.' Mark shakes his head.

I'm standing at the edge of a diving board, trying to will myself to leap off, not knowing if anything will catch me. Sophia and Mark are both sitting back casually in their chairs. There's no interrogation, no inkling that anything is off.

'You left for your flight and missed the aftermath!' Sophia says, grinding black pepper over her food.

The noise grates through me.

'Yeah, there was quite a bit of damage to the hotel. One of the main offices got flooded and the bar was a bit mangled,' Mark explains.

'And a man died,' Sophia adds.

'I knew you'd bring that up.' Mark wipes his mouth on a napkin.

Dread twists in my gut.

'Really?' Jamie asks, going to top up their wine glasses. Only I can see the slight tremble in his hand.

I hold on to the edge of my chair, needing to touch something solid. Needing to feel anchored. 'H-h-how did you see that?'

'It came through on the news wires.' Sophia wafts her hand as if she can't really remember. 'I only clocked it as it was near where we went for dinner, literally down from the Blue Fin, on that same night.' She shudders. 'I mean, what he was doing out near the cliffs during the storm, I have no idea. It's like some people have a death wish.'

There is a scrape of cutlery. The sound pierces through my bones.

'Are you writing a story on this?' I ask boldly. A bolt of anxiety pounds in my chest. I've overstepped the mark.

Sophia points to her full mouth and smiles. I wait for her to finish chewing. It feels like a lifetime.

'I doubt the *Islington Post* would be interested,' Mark replies, scoffing into his glass, replying for her.

She finally swallows. 'Well, actually . . .' She stops and scrunches up her nose and sniffs. 'Is something burning?'

'The pies!' Jamie leaps from his chair and pulls open the oven door. Suddenly the kitchen is filled with acrid black smoke.

'Get the extractor fan on!' I splutter. My eyes are watering. I can feel it burning at the back of my throat.

'It doesn't work,' Jamie says, coughing into his arm.

Mark gets to his feet and pushes the patio doors open, bringing in a gust of cool autumnal air. Tea towels are wafted. We all laugh awkwardly as Jamie pulls out a large sad-looking pie with a charcoal lid. Inside, I'm mortified.

'I think you might need a new smoke alarm.' Mark grins, pointing to the one that's fixed to the ceiling. The red light is flashing but it's completely silent.

'Yeah.' Jamie shakes his head. 'Batteries probably need replacing, like everything else in this house. Babe, what temperature did you set this at?'

'One hundred and eighty.'

'Are you sure?'

'I cook pretty much everything at one hundred and eighty!' I say, seeing the look on Sophia's face at how snappy that sounded. 'I mean, yes, I'm sure.'

Jamie doesn't seem to pick up on my sudden outburst. Instead, he looks worried. He drops his voice. 'Then why is it on max?'

I can feel Sophia and Mark's eyes on me, as they fan their faces, coughing.

I can't get rid of the acrid taste of burning coating the back of my throat.

'Excuse me.'

I almost knock my glass over in my haste to push my chair back and get out of the room, tears falling down my flushed cheeks. I only just make it to the downstairs bathroom before I throw up.

24

Sophia

Monday 19 September

To keep busy this morning I've already made two rounds of tea for everyone, ignoring the comment from Brad, who said loudly for all to hear how he never expected Sophia Spencer to be making him a hot drink. I gritted my teeth and willed myself not to give into the temptation of accidentally spilling the rest of the contents of the stained plastic tray over him.

'Do you need me to do anything else?' I ask Claudia.

She shakes her head, praising me for working so fast on the small selection of articles I fired off before she'd even turned her laptop on.

Back at my desk, I pick up my phone. I still haven't heard from Erin after I thanked her for having us. I wanted to check that she was feeling better after dashing off so suddenly. Jamie managed to scrape the burnt crusts off and salvage the dinner but she didn't rejoin us, complaining of a dodgy tummy.

Curiosity makes me open Facebook and look the couple up, but both their profiles are set to private and I can't find them on any other social media sites. I rap my fingers against my desk then decide to message Lou again to see if she's ready to confirm a time and date to meet. I really thought that we'd have pinned the logistics down by now. My previous messages have been read but ignored. I know that I need to tread carefully.

I return to the inbox and see a new email has come through.

JAKARTA, Sept 16 (AP)
Police Appeal over British Man Found with Fatal Injuries in Bali
A BRITISH man found dead during storms in Bali is named as George Kingsley, 62.

Mr Kingsley, from Portsmouth, was discovered at the Tebing Terjal viewing point near Uluwatu beach on Tuesday (Sept 13) following a suspected fatal fall. In a statement, Indonesian police said Mr Kingsley was a retired butcher who had lived in Bali for a number of years. He leaves behind a wife and two children. He had recently become a grandfather for the first time. Appealing for witnesses, detectives released an image of Mr Kingsley. Mr Kingsley was last seen wearing a royal blue short-sleeved button-down shirt, brown chino pants and a brown pair of sandals.

I press print just as my phone pings.

See you tonight. 8pm outside Supper Club. Lou.

My heartbeat quickens. I re-read the message. Supper Club is a restaurant in Soho, a well-known haunt of those who work in the media industry and the occasional celebrity, who usually gets papped as they leave looking the worse for wear.

Yes! Tonight is fine.

Mark's words of concern ring in my ears after I press send. Am I really ready to open this story again? My husband could be right: if Rupert finds out that I'm planning on going down another angle to publish the piece that lost me my job, then he could suddenly reappear in our lives.

And do everything in his power to stop me.

The more I think about it, the more it makes sense that Mark wanted Jamie to upgrade our security. It gives him some reassurance that we're safe. Now I understand his motive, I feel a pull in the pit of my stomach – he's always looking out for me, for us. And here I am, focused solely on my career and my wants.

'Is this yours?' Amira is at my desk, pulling me from my thoughts. She's holding a printout. It's the story about George Kingsley.

'Ah, yeah. Thanks.' I take it sheepishly. Mark is right: what would the *Islington Post* want to do with this?

'I came to tell you that there's a team meeting starting in five. I was just about to put the kettle on.' She turns to walk away. 'Just a word of advice: be careful printing off personal things. There's a lot of prying eyes here,' she says, with a kind wink. 'I made sure Claudia didn't see.'

I pick up my half-empty mug, about to join Amira in the kitchen. My arms are pressed against the desk, pulling myself up from my chair, when I catch a glimpse of the printout she gave me. There's a photo at the bottom of the email that I didn't see on my computer screen.

George Kingsley.

There's something about him that looks familiar. I pick up the paper and bring it closer to my eyes. My head is whirring with memories trying to rush back to the surface. The same neat goatee, the silvery hair, the deep tan.

No, surely it can't be . . .

'Sophia?' I hear my name being called across the office.

I peer at the photo. It looks like him, but . . .

The photocopier noisily whirs. Someone lets out a bark of a cough. I sense movement around me but I can't pull my eyes from the photograph.

'Are you joining us any time today, Sophia?' Claudia snaps.

I leap to my feet as it suddenly comes back to me.

I've met George before. Erin accidentally spilt his drink over him at the Blue Fin. He's the one who made some mean comment about her weight. He must have died only hours after that happened.

There's a crackle of tension in my skull. What are the chances?

25

Erin

Monday 19 September

I didn't expect it to be like this. The nightmares. I never imagined my mind capable of creating something so visceral. Every night it's slightly different, as if my subconscious is scrolling through an album of horrific scenarios. Sometimes his skull is caved in, crawling with maggots, and there's the audible clicking of cockroaches feasting on his head wound that is so severe, a black, tar-like liquid is oozing out. Other times he looks peaceful, as if he's napping in the lazy afternoon sun. I get closer, building the courage to jab him with a finger to check if he's alive or dead. The second my skin makes contact, he blinks his eyes wide open and launches for my neck.

I leapt to the bathroom to splash cold water on my face, always cold, so cold, which helped snap me awake and catch my breath. Despite wearing two jumpers, I made sure to open every single window as wide as it would go, hoping the fresh air would somehow make a difference – blow away our sins, carry them across the fields. I can hardly concentrate because

I'm shivering so much, but it's worth it. The house now just smells cold, the mustiness finally dissipating.

I've had to turn my phone off. Sophia has called a couple of times this morning – her messages, wanting to check in, so light and friendly, are waiting for a reply. I just don't know what to say to her. I'm no good at pretending everything is OK when it's not.

And today, things are definitely not OK.

I've joined a bunch of English-speaking Balinese Facebook groups full of gossiping ex-pats and locals. That's how I see the news. More to the point, that's where I see his face again, on the Uluwatu ExPats page, circa 1k members.

The bedroom tilts and I'm forced to concentrate on slowing my breathing.

Some of you may have seen the news about regular poster and fellow ex-pat George Kingsley. He was known to the locals and was a familiar face to many in our district.

My stomach is in knots as I read what someone has posted.

I don't know him personally but here is a link to the GoFundMe page set up to help his wife with the funeral costs.

There's a flurry of likes, sad face emojis and love hearts. #RIPGeorge. People are tagging others, all leaving messages of sympathy and shock. I keep reading and discover he was a retired butcher from Portsmouth who moved to Bali to start a guest house with his wife a few years ago. He had just become a grandfather for the first time.

Further down, there's a request for anyone with information to contact an emergency phone number or the nearest police station. There's an accompanying photo of George Kingsley, full of life, standing proudly beside his wife. *Together forever.* I don't know how I manage to keep the rush of vomit down. I think about the missed calls from Sophia. Is she calling because she's seen this too? Does she somehow know we were there?

No. Surely not.

Like Jamie says, there's nothing to pin us to the scene. I try to imagine what my husband would be telling me to do right now. *Stop overthinking. It was an accident. These things happen every day.* You just normally don't watch them with your own eyes. Scarred with guilt that you could have somehow stopped it from happening. That, in a way, you were to blame.

I close my laptop and blow on my chilly fingers. Suddenly I hear the front door open and slam shut. I'm confused. Jamie can't be home already.

'Erin?' he calls, the thud of his work bag dropping to the floor.

'Jamie? You're back early.'

He runs up the stairs, saying something that I can't quite hear. The bedroom door flies open.

'Oh. Why are you not ready?' He stops still and frowns. 'Did you not get my message?'

'Ready for what?' I turn to face him.

A mixture of relief and panic washes over me, imagining him suggesting we go to the police. If we were to give our statement, our side of events, then perhaps I would finally get some sleep. We could calmly explain that we found ourselves out of our depth. We panicked and did what we thought was right at the time. I can try to get them to understand that we acted out of fear but that our hearts were in the right place. I can't see any other way that I can clear my mind from the guilt over leaving him like that.

We need to speak up before someone else does.

I've been going over and over that night and the more I think about it, the more I'm certain someone else was there. What if that person saw everything that happened? What if they could identify us? Jamie was the one to say he heard footsteps, and then I'm sure I saw a figure heading towards the man. Towards *George*, I correct myself. He now has a name. It makes it feel much worse now that he's been identified. He didn't look like a George.

Jamie's still talking, giving me a confused look.

'Erin? Did you hear me? I thought you'd be ready to go to the Plaza by now.'

He rushes around the bedroom, opening the wardrobe doors, sticking his head inside rummaging for his navy suit. I blink. I don't have a clue what he's talking about.

'W-w-what? Hang on. You haven't seen the news? I was just about to call you. The man on the steps, the one who . . . His name is – was – George Kingsley. The police are appealing for witnesses!'

It's as if he's not heard me.

'We need to get ready, Erin,' he says, clearly exasperated. 'Did you forget? All the investors will be there. I can't be late.'

I stare at him. I swear on my life that he's never told me about this work event.

'Jamie!' This time my shrieks reach an ear-piercing level. 'I can't do this. We have to tell them!'

'Tell who?'

'The police! We have to tell them that we were there, that it was raining and George slipped. We saw this tragic accident happen, but that's all it was. An accident, pure and simple.'

He takes a breath before coming to sit next to me on the unmade bed. 'Erin, please, babe, you need to calm down.'

'I thought that was what you meant, the reason you're home early. I thought you were going to say it's time we speak to the police.' I wipe the tears from my eyes. 'Maybe if we can just explain and—'

'There's nothing to explain.' His voice is soft and low. 'We did nothing wrong. Going to the police isn't going to change anything.'

'But they want witnesses to come forward.'

'It's protocol.' He waves a hand. 'The police need to rule out any foul play, but once the post-mortem's been done, they'll see that he tripped. His injuries will show he fell by accident. Nothing suspicious. They just need to go through the processes.'

'You really think so?'

He gives a firm nod. 'The louder we shout, the more attention we'll get. We can't be linked to this tragedy, not with the investors watching me so intently. We need it to blow over.'

I know he's trying to reassure me but it's not working. How can he possibly be so calm?

'Listen, sweetheart. There'll be a lot of people I have to impress tonight. Guests will be expecting me to be top of my game.' He exhales slowly. 'If it's all too much then I understand if you want to stay here instead.'

I bite my thumbnail. He's giving me a choice.

'Of course, you could just quickly get dressed and come with me. I really would love you to be by my side . . .'

I don't want to go. However, it's not fair if I abandon him, force him to get through this alone. 'Give me ten minutes?'

He smiles and kisses me firmly on the crown of my head. That was the right answer.

'Just throw anything on, you always look gorgeous. Just try and be as quick as you can. We're late.' He leaves the room and the shower starts running immediately.

I catch my reflection in the mirror opposite the bed. My tan has almost disappeared, the sun-lightened strands of hair that frame my face the only hint of a recent holiday. Jamie's wrong: I look as tired as I feel. My eyes are dull and my skin is flaky. I'm left staring at the reflection, without a clue who I'm looking at.

26

Erin

I manage to put on make-up – smearing thick foundation over the blotches on my cheeks – and tie my hair, which could do with a wash, back into a simple plait. I pull on a long-sleeved navy dress; Sophia would never wear anything like this. It's too tight around my stomach and the lace collar itches my neck.

'You look nice,' Jamie says after I'm finally dressed.

He looks so smart and handsome in his suit, I can't help but feel I'm letting him down.

He's on a work call for most of the drive to the hotel. I stay silent in the background, my anxiety rising at leaving the house. He's driving too fast, taking the bends without his usual caution. I grip the seat and breathe ever so slowly, forming a tight pinprick for air to squeeze through. It's too late to ask him to turn back. Pull yourself together, Erin.

My stomach swishes at the sight of two security officers standing outside the Plaza hotel. Their black leather boots remind me of the uniforms of the Indonesian police.

'Evening.' One nods hello. 'Can we take a quick look inside your bag?'

I've sweated all over the fabric. What was once a sheer satin now looks discoloured. Behind us, a car alarm screams and the clutch bag tumbles from my grip at the sudden, ear-piercing noise. I squat down and scrape my belongings together as quickly as I can. A large tattooed hand passes me my lipstick, which has rolled to a stop beside his boots.

My cheeks flush under the security guard's focused gaze.

'Have you got everything?' Jamie helps me up to my feet and checks there's nothing I've missed. He starts talking too fast, telling them we need to hurry.

Anxiety is prickling all over my body as we walk into the busy conference room. I want to be here to support my husband but I'm terrified that someone will bring up our wedding or ask about our honeymoon and I don't know if I can manage to keep it together. I'm beyond exhausted. However, if normal life is to resume, then these are the things I need to get used to – I can't keep dwelling on what happened; it's not going to change it.

Jamie squeezes my waist as if reading my mind.

As long as I stay by his side, then I'll be OK.

I'm introduced to beautiful women and names are reeled off as I shake their hands, apologising for mine being so clammy, blaming the heat. They pull away politely and I see them subtly wiping their palms on the nearest chair cover. I'm in awe of how Jamie holds it together so well in the spotlight of everyone's adoration when inside, I imagine, he feels as frantic as I do.

I try to follow conversations, smile when spoken to, laugh at the right moment. The real world hasn't stopped. It's amazing how we can act as if nothing has happened. As long as I don't think about George Kingsley.

When a waiter in a smart shirt and denim apron approaches with a tray of champagne flutes, I don't hesitate to accept.

I turn around just as Jamie is being pulled away to greet someone. An older man has his arm around his back, steering him in the opposite direction. He gives me an apologetic look and I smile, but tears press at the backs of my eyes. I tuck myself against a cold wall, suddenly feeling very exposed in this enormous noisy room. The chatter around me is overwhelming.

When Jamie glances over to check I'm OK, I give him a thumbs-up, internally hating myself, and accept another glass of the prosecco that's going past on a silver tray. In fact, at one stage I'm holding a glass in each hand. A gentleman with white fluffy eyebrows notices and comments how it's *good to be prepared* or some other quip that I don't fully understand but smile at nonetheless. I let him believe I'm holding one for my husband; every second he's networking alone is killing me.

A woman glides past with the same honey-blonde hair as Sophia and for a split second I do a double take. It's not her – but I then wonder what she would do if she were here. She wouldn't be pressed against the wall, willing herself to turn invisible. She would be as charming as Jamie is. Working the room.

I remember how she held her own with George Kingsley in the Blue Fin. When he refused to leave us alone, despite my apologies and Jamie offering to pay for his ruined shirt, Sophia had sat tall, locked eyes with him, and calmly but forcefully told him to piss off. Or words to that effect. Sophia didn't cower in her chair. She found her voice.

Something fires up inside me and, inspired by her energy, I decide to channel this fake confidence. I stand up taller and smile hello at a woman wearing a shiny sequined jacket. Amazingly, she smiles back. Soon we're having a polite, if dull, conversation about the choice of canapés, when Jamie finally comes over. He rubs the small of my back and a glow spreads throughout my body. He's visibly relieved that I've found someone to talk to.

As long as I keep this act up, it'll be like nothing happened in Bali. We are the exact same people.

It gives me hope that maybe, one day, we can be those people again.

27

Sophia

George Kingsley is running through my mind as I jog to the Supper Club to meet Lou. It looks as though it's going to rain. Exhaust fumes hang in the gloomy air. I quickly cross the road, moving out of the way as a double-decker bus wheezes to a stop. The grumbling driver is drowned out by loud grime music. A pack of squealing girls wearing tight Lycra dresses saunter past, followed by the smell of stale cigarette smoke.

I pray I don't see anyone I know. A lot of the *Sunday News* team like to hang out here after work to swap insalubrious industry gossip with other tabloid journalists. I'm hoping that a Monday night means less of a risk of running into anyone from the past.

My stomach rumbles. I skipped lunch so I could get through my to-do list. I was finally able to slip into an empty meeting room to make a call to the British Embassy in Bali, curiosity getting the better of me. As I waited to speak to a human being, tuning out from the repetitive lift music playing, I looked back at the photo of George Kingsley, his bright smile caught mid-laugh.

An embassy officer confirmed, over a shuffle of papers, that they were providing consular assistance to the family of Mr Kingsley.

'Incidents like this aren't common,' the officer explained, in a nasal voice, leaping into a well-worded script explaining the importance of tourism to a place like Bali.

'Is there anything else you can give me?' I asked, when he took a breath.

'No, miss, just that investigations are under way and that authorities will be retracing Mr Kingsley's final movements to establish what happened.'

I can help with that, I thought. George's final movements involved leaving the Blue Fin and then a short while later ending up dead. I couldn't stop thinking about the crazy and tragic coincidence that we interacted with this man on the very night he died.

'Can you at least confirm if his death is being treated as suspicious or not?'

There was a beat of silence.

'Sorry, miss, I have told you all I know—'

'Ah, well, I might have some information that can help . . .' I took a breath. 'If you're willing to give me something else? Whatever you say can stay completely off the record. I just need to know if George's death is looking like an accident or not.'

It was a gamble. I didn't want to drag myself and Mark into a police investigation – we'd gone through enough recently – but if I wanted to tease some more details from this guy then I needed to offer something in return. I told the embassy officer what I remembered from the night. I could hear the clicking of a keyboard as he noted it down. When I'd finished, I reminded him that I'd kept up my side of the deal.

The typing stopped. He paused. I imagined him weighing up what he was allowed to tell me.

'Fine. But this is not for print.' He cleared his throat. 'From the looks of things, George Kingsley's death was no accident.'

The line crackled. I had to ask him to repeat himself.

'Of course, this isn't fully confirmed until a complete autopsy has taken place but, from what I hear, there are other marks on his body which don't add up with the injuries sustained from the fall.'

I felt the familiar buzz of adrenaline that grows when I know I'm on to a story.

'So you think he was murdered?'

'The police have different lines of inquiry at the moment.' Another cough. 'That is all – I've probably said too much.'

Despite pressing him once more, it was clear he didn't have anything else he was willing to tell me. I thanked the officer for his honesty, promising it would stay between us.

George is the victim of a crime.

I shudder at the thought of him in the restaurant – how oblivious he was to his impending doom.

As juicy as this reveal is, I have to get my head in the game for meeting Lou. Diners keep walking past and throwing me odd looks. I'm not dressed for dinner at the Supper Club but, despite this, the doorman has already asked me if I'd prefer to wait inside. I shake my head. Lou explicitly said to meet outside, so I tuck myself into the small alcove of an empty shop doorway.

A gust of wind makes my skin break out in goosebumps. The fierce heat of Bali is a distant memory. I blow on my fingertips to try to keep warm, cursing myself for not wearing something thicker. As the first raindrops begin to fall, I tuck myself further inside the doorway, so I don't get wet.

A few moments later I hear a familiar voice.

'Sophia?'

My stomach drops. 'Peter.'

My old news editor has walked out of the restaurant under a black golf umbrella, looking as puzzled to see me as I am to see him. He says something to his wife, Diana, and escorts her to a waiting taxi. She flashes a polite but tight smile in my direction, then hunches over her phone as she climbs into the back seat. I wonder if she remembers having me and Mark round for dinner. The apple crumble she made for us, the famous family recipe she wrote down for me because I loved it so much. The planned short break we had spoken about at length over end-of-the-night coffee and peppermint chocolates. I try to bite down the sadness that all I get now is a vague wave.

Peter tells the driver he'll just be a minute then walks over to me. 'Sophia, what are you doing here?'

'Me? Oh, I'm just waiting for someone.' I make a point of peering down the road expectantly. Wiping away the raindrops that hit my forehead.

'Mark wouldn't leave you standing out here, would he?'

'It's not Mark. It's a source,' I swallow. 'The whistle-blower who tipped us off about Rupert has been back in touch. But this time I know she will have enough proof for us to nail him.'

I immediately regret blurting this out.

He raises his silver eyebrows, a flash of something on his face that vanishes in an instant. He's probably caught between concern for me and wanting to follow a killer story. I know that delicate seesaw pull of emotions – the guilt I feel when my career makes my husband unhappy versus the desire to hold those who are corrupt accountable.

'Really?'

I nod, buoyed by his curiosity. 'She was one of Rupert's team. She had intel on everything the gang were up to. She can identify exactly who was responsible and it's even bigger than we thought. She just went silent when it got too hot but, with a bit of space, she's now decided to speak out.' I pause for breath.

'And she's meeting you here?'

'Yeah, she's running a bit late. I'm sure she'll be here soon.'

The door to the restaurant opens. A woman on her phone strides out and dashes to a cab. There's a rush of heat and a snapshot of chatter and laughter before the door closes again.

'Listen, if you want my advice . . .' Judging by the way he's looking at me, I'm not sure I do. 'Just leave this alone, let someone else pick it up. Enjoy time with your new husband, get a new hobby or simply take some time off.'

He may as well tell me not to be a journalist any more, and that's like telling me to stop breathing. It's all I've ever known, all I'm good at. Well, I thought I was.

'I know there's something here,' I say, 'and if I can prove it to you then you'd have to have me back.'

'Sophia.' He slowly brings his eyes to meet mine. 'You know we could only take you back if it was truly exceptional.'

'What about a murder?'

He frowns, confused. 'Sorry. Rupert murdered someone?'

I shake my head. 'No. Not him, not that we know . . .'

He lets out a slow exhausted sigh and taps at his Apple watch, which has lit up. 'I'd better go.'

'Hang on! It's not the Rupert story, but there's something else I'm working on. I've just come back from my honeymoon in Bali and on the last night there was this terrible storm and an ex-pat died. It happened literally five minutes down the road from our hotel.'

'Right. It's not exactly ground-breaking. Sorry, I thought you said something about a murder?'

I exhale. 'Yes. I don't think the storm had anything to do with him dying. A source confided that the police are treating it as suspicious, something to do with unusual marks on his body.' I'm pinning everything on what the guy at the embassy told me. 'And I have my suspicions about who did it.'

It's a complete lie. I haven't got a clue. For all I know the guy at the embassy could be spinning me a line, but I need to grab Peter's attention. I'm desperate.

He brings a hand up to cup his chin, running his index finger over the stubble of his moustache. 'Can you get me a list line by conference tomorrow and I'll see what I can do?'

Conference is at ten, where all the editors pitch their stories for the paper.

'Erm, that might be tricky. There's a few more threads I need to work on first.'

'Fine. Wednesday, then.'

That's only an extra day, but this time I don't argue. 'Sure. No problem.' I pause. 'And then you'll look at having me back?'

'Sophia, I can't promise you anything. Let's not run before we can walk, eh?'

I don't know if it's the rain or the fact that I'm shivering in a graffiti-stained doorway, but he clears his throat.

'I'm probably not supposed to say this, but we miss having you around the office.'

A lump suddenly appears in my throat. He doesn't know how much that means. I sniff and bite the inside of my cheek. I know he's not good with emotion; I have to keep it together.

Peter straightens up. 'But look, drop the Rupert line. There's nothing this source can give you that we don't already know. We've moved on, the conversation has moved on and you need to too.' The beep of a taxi pulls him away. 'I've really got to go.'

I nod. A wave of exhaustion rolls over me.

He turns to leave then pauses, offering me his black golf umbrella. 'Do you want it?'

Despite the fact that I'm not even wearing a coat, I shake my head. 'I'll be fine.'

He shakes his head with a sad smile. 'Of course you will, Sophia.'

I watch him jog around a puddle, see his wife mouthing something as they pull away. I check my phone again but I already know the screen will be empty. No apology or anything.

Lou's not coming.

Of course she's not coming. She probably never was. The realisation is like swallowing a shard of glass.

And now I've promised Peter an exclusive news story that's completely fabricated. I step out into the night, unable to feel the cold raindrops falling on my hot face.

Why am I like this? What's wrong with me?

28

Erin

I'm still buzzing on the drive home from the Plaza. Jamie hasn't stopped complimenting me, telling me how everyone loved meeting me. I bask in his pride and turn up the dance song playing on the radio, shimmying to make him laugh. The sound lights me up; I hadn't realised how long it's been since I'd heard his rich, deep laughter.

It was fun to step into someone else's shoes for a while. It makes me wonder what else I could do to be more Sophia. Maybe I'll get a tattoo. I wonder if Sophia has anything inked on her body. I doubt it; I can't imagine her flawless olive skin being graffitied with globs of ink. Jamie has one. I hate it. His ex had a matching design – two pieces of a jigsaw slotting together. I have no idea what he was thinking.

The song changes and I sit back to watch the busy streets fade away to woods and then into fields towards our house.

A flicker of jealousy erupts whenever I think of Jamie's past relationships. Stupid, really – he's married to me, for God's sake – but it's hard to dampen the envious flames. I know he's out of my league – not that he would for one second believe this, but it's true. All I have to do is think of the women at the Plaza and their hungry, lustful eyes whenever Jamie spoke. He really does light up a room with this magnetic appeal, one he isn't even aware of. My light mood suddenly falls away. I appreciate his compliments, but his colleagues only loved me because I was playing a role. I was being Sophia.

'You OK?' Jamie asks.

A yawn escapes. 'I didn't realise how tiring it is, socialising.'

I need to sleep tonight. Please God. My body aches, muscles braced in fight-or-flight mode, but that's nothing a hot bath won't ease. Instead, it's my mind that I can't seem to turn off.

Firs on either side of the dark road kiss in the middle, creating a tunnel of pine needles above our heads. There's not a streetlight in sight.

I twist my wedding ring around my finger and take a deep breath. 'Have you thought any more about telling the police what happened in Bali?'

He groans and scratches his cheek. 'Erin . . .'

'I know you don't think we should, but if we can clear our consciences, we might start to feel better.'

'Erin, listen, I . . . Shit!'

A deer is standing in the centre of the empty road. A solid roadblock of tawny coat and spindly legs. Its bright hazel eyes are fixed on the car's headlights, completely frozen. My breath is trapped in my throat. Time simultaneously slows down and speeds up. It's a blink of an eye but also the longest few seconds of my life. I think I scream but I can't be sure.

Jamie swerves.

The severe jolt sends shock waves through me.

A flash of russet shoots past, away into the undergrowth. Incredibly, we've managed to avoid the deer.

But the relief is short-lived. Suddenly there's an oak tree in front of us, far too close. My eyes widen at the looming trunk hurtling towards us.

I shoot my palms out, slapping them against the dashboard, elbows locked. My fingernails dig into the plastic. My seatbelt is taut, cutting into my flesh. I brace myself for impact.

We're going to hit the tree. It's too close. So close that I can see tufts of moss sprouting from the cracked bark, the thin threads of a cobweb quivering in the beam of the headlights.

Jamie's left arm reaches out across me. There's a deafening roar as the car veers dangerously, the back tyres screeching in resistance. A painful bump then a scrape as we miraculously slide into a ditch and finally come to a complete stop. The tree is parallel to us.

'Are you OK?' he asks, panting. Sweat is beaded across his hairline.

Amber lights are flashing on the dashboard. My own racing heartbeat fills my ears, blocking out the hum of the dying engine. All I can do is nod and unclip my seatbelt, leaning across to hold him. We could have slammed into that tree; we could both be dead now. The deer is nowhere to be seen.

'I love you.' My face is wet with tears.

'I love you too.' Jamie tenderly wipes my forehead with the pad of his thumb, concern in his eyes. 'Shit, you're bleeding.'

I must have knocked my head against the door as we were violently jolted about. I glance in the mirror; thankfully it's just a scratch. Everything inside me is lit with adrenaline. I pull myself closer to him. A primal need to be held takes over.

I manage to move across the gearstick and on to his lap. Jamie's face washes with a mixture of emotions. We start to kiss. The faint taste of whisky on his tongue. Soft at first, then it builds to a frantic, heavy pace. Rough. I need it like this.

He tugs on my bottom lip with his teeth, slaps a hand across my exposed thighs. It stings but gives me a thrill. I'm fired with a boldness I've never known before. Is this how Sophia and Mark have sex? Subconsciously, am I still channelling her confidence? There's no way they're a vanilla couple. I assertively pull up my dress. He tugs my knickers to one side. His fingers know what I like. I press myself closer to him.

Suddenly, something outside catches my eye.

I peer out of the window. Dark woods surround us; branches sway as the wind moves through the trees. The car's headlights illuminate the empty country road. There's nothing there, I tell myself. Just leaves in the wind – movement in the corner of my eye.

I steadily exhale, trying to lose myself in the moment. But I can't shake off this awful sense that we're not alone. That we're being watched. Jamie is oblivious and I want to ignore it too, but I can't. I have to look again. This time a scream gets trapped in my mouth.

There's a face through the dark windscreen.

George's face.

Watching us as he was back then.

An icy hand touches the back of my neck. I'm not in a steamed-up car down a remote darkened lane any more. All I can think about is George hiding in the shadows as we made love on the stone bench. I imagine his drunken eyes. His cocky taunts. The arrogance that he thought he could blackmail us and get away with it. Then the sudden horrific realisation as it dawned on him that he was plummeting to his death.

I blink away tears and look out of the window once more.

Moths flutter in the beam of the headlights. There's no one there. No one is watching us. Only dark pines and thick hedges surround the car.

Jamie lets out a soft moan, his breath hot in my ear, unaware of my pure panic. I don't want to alarm him. If I tell him I'm now hallucinating, he'll only worry about how badly I'm dealing with everything. So I take his hands from in between my legs and focus on pleasuring him instead.

He comes with a satisfied groan and grins at me. 'I should crash the car more often.'

My heart rate is slowly returning to normal – not through passion but from fear.

Every time my husband touches me from now on, will I think of that night?

This is a far cry from our early days. We've always had such great chemistry. Every weekday, before we moved in together, he would leave at the crack of dawn and endure a lengthy commute just so we could share the same bed each night. I remember how effortlessly we made love before falling asleep with our naked bodies pressed together. In the morning, hours after he'd left for work, I would discover scruffy handwritten notes propped up against a mug in the kitchen alongside two bowls, the cereal already poured out so I didn't feel alone as I ate my breakfast. He would patiently listen as I admitted I was struggling hearing all about Kat's blossoming pregnancy. I'd felt like I wasn't being a loyal friend, but he told me to cut myself some slack.

We talked about having children in the way you do when you're dating. Coming up with funny made-up first names, creating amusing narratives about what they would be like. He said he pictured two little girls who looked identical to me. It was only after the trip to Girona that we spoke about it more seriously. It shocked me how difficult it was to move on from what had happened – I'd never even considered my fertility being an issue before. I spent hours every evening looking at online parenting forums, searching for advice from other women who felt the same as I did. Shocked by the stats of how common miscarriage is, relieved at how normal my doubts and worries were.

So when Jamie proposed, not long afterwards, I said yes. To the outside world it might seem like a cheesy proposal – one morning he left a ring on top of the bowl of cornflakes and a note beside it telling me to turn around, then I spun in shock to find him on one knee – but it was special to me. I never wanted or expected anything more.

Everyone from Red Bees, even Kat, did a terrible job at hiding their surprise at our announcement. I'd not told any-one about what had happened in Spain. They had no idea how that dreadful experience had cemented just how wonder-ful and caring this man could be, despite us moving so fast. I knew that he was a decent human being, one who would be there for me when I was at my most vulnerable. When I needed him the most.

'If you really want to talk to the police, then we can.' His words hang in the stuffy warmth of the car.

'I'll think about it,' I reply. Suddenly, doing the right thing doesn't seem as important as it was before.

He squeezes my hand then pulls out his phone, miraculously managing to find one bar of signal to call a tow truck to come and rescue us.

I can't imagine being apart from him. What we've got is too special, for better or for worse.

29

Erin

Tuesday 20 September

Everything aches. The muscles across my shoulders and arms pulled taut from when I braced for impact, convinced we would hit that tree. It's a miracle we're both OK, yet I don't feel in any way invincible. I've spent most of the day moving around like an old woman, worrying about delayed whiplash, massaging my aching neck and downing painkillers.

The AA was able to fix Jamie's car last night – it was mostly body damage – so he went to work on time this morning. Before he left, he ran me a hot bath – it was bliss to soak my tense muscles, watching the steam curl towards the cracked plaster on the bathroom ceiling. He won't be back until late. I told him it was fine; I was planning an early night anyway. I've only just finished dinner – reheated jacket potato and beans – when the doorbell chimes.

My head snaps up and I instantly regret the sudden movement. I'm certainly not expecting visitors. A creeping dread washes over me. What if it's the police, finally pulling us in for questioning? They said in their statement that they wanted to speak to witnesses.

The doorbell rings again. Despite my trepidation, I force myself to take hold of the metal latch and open the door. A cold gust of air hits my face. A shiver runs the whole way through me.

'Sophia?'

'Hey! I tried calling you!' She's holding up a box of expensive-looking chocolates with a wide, easy smile.

'What are you doing here?'

'I just thought I'd pop over. Why should the boys have all the fun?'

She looks great. Her tight-fitting monochrome jumper is obviously designer. I'd love to know where she buys her clothes; there's no way she picks things up on the spur of the moment during a Tesco shop. In my scruffy jeans and bobbled cardigan, I feel as if I've crawled out of a gutter compared to her.

'Sorry?' I stick my head out to look for Mark.

'Mark's out with Jamie,' she says, with a quizzical look. 'They've gone to see D.R.U.M.? Did he not tell you? I think it was all a bit last-minute. Mark couldn't believe it when Jamie invited him. Apparently the tickets sold out ages ago.'

I rearrange my face to look as if I knew this. I'm sure he didn't tell me he was going to a gig, and he definitely didn't tell me he was meeting Mark. Maybe he kept it from me so I wouldn't spend the whole evening in a panic that something from the night on the cliffs would come out. Which, of course, now I will.

Sophia is still talking.

'. . . so I thought I'd surprise you. I got a taxi here from the station.'

She came all this way just to hang out with me? I think of the missed calls from her. This was what she wanted to talk about. Plan a girls' night in.

I pull myself together and open the door wide. 'Come in!'

She moves past me in a cloud of sweet perfume. 'Oh, God, what did you do to your head? It looks sore.'

My fingers move to the cut on my forehead. 'I banged it on the kitchen cupboard.'

I'm quite proud of how fast the lie springs from my lips. I need to keep my life as boring and mundane as possible. If I tell her that we had a car crash then it will only make her ask more questions. I'm already in a spiral of lies and deception as it is; one more won't hurt.

'Tea or coffee?' I offer, once she's sat at the kitchen table.

She rummages in her large handbag and pulls out a bottle of sauvignon blanc. 'Up for something stronger?'

I hesitate for a second then fetch two glasses, telling myself that this is what friends do. For the first time since she's arrived, I dare to relax a little. As she pours the wine, I catch her looking at the scratches on my forearm. I self-consciously pull my sleeve down and raise my glass to cheers.

She asks me what I've been up to. I tell her about going to the Plaza, playing the role of a proud wife, but all the while my mind is elsewhere. I wish I were a fly on the wall at the gig so I could hear what Jamie and Mark are talking about. I spin my wedding ring around my finger. Jamie's not going to let the team down. I have to trust him.

153

There's a lull in the conversation before she goes to the bathroom. I use this as a chance to pull out my phone and text Jamie, ask him when the gig finishes and tell him we have company. I hope he doesn't mention the car crash to Mark. I don't want them to compare stories at the end of the night and for Sophia to realise I lied to her.

'Oh, listen! Remember the last night of the honeymoon?' she asks, coming back from the toilet and picking up her phone.

I sit up in my seat, eyes trained on her as she taps open the photos.

'I can't believe I forgot to send this to you! Hang on, let me find it.'

She scrolls through until her fingers pause on a shot. It's the photo she took of Jamie and me at the Blue Fin, the many plates of food in front of us. There's not a care in the world on my sunburnt face. Just seconds later I spill a drink over George and the nightmare begins.

'Hang on.' She pinches her fingers together to zoom in. Her eyebrows knot in concentration. Her smile falters. I blink at how still she's become. The temperature in the kitchen drops.

'That's the man who died in the storm.' She hands the phone to me.

I don't want to see but I can't look away. George Kingsley fills the screen; he was in the background of the photo. She's enlarged it so all I can see is his face; he must have looked over just as she took the first shot, capturing his face that's angled towards the camera. The smiling jovial grin, the neat grey goatee, the relaxed posture. Not the bloodied skull, contorted mouth and painfully twisted, lifeless body that I remember.

'I told you about it on Sunday, didn't I?'

I can barely contain myself. Everything is clenched. I grip my wine glass. 'Oh, yeah . . .' I try to sound as relaxed as I can. 'So sad.'

'Mmm.' She swipes again and his face vanishes. 'Can you believe that you knocked a drink over him, of all people!'

I attempt to look shocked, as if this is the first time I'm hearing this information. 'Yeah . . . I guess he looks sort of familiar. Are you sure it was him?'

She nods. 'I mean, we might have been the last people he ever spoke to. Well, shouted at. He was pretty pissed off, wasn't he?'

I take a gulp of wine. It tastes acidic.

'Mmm, it's crazy.' I clumsily put down my glass and wipe my clammy hands on my jeans.

She sits a little closer. 'The worst part is that they're saying it wasn't the storm that killed him – the police are treating it as suspicious.'

Everything goes still.

'What do you mean, suspicious?' The final word is barely a whisper.

'Well, that it wasn't an accident.' She delicately nibbles one of the chocolates that she's brought. 'Someone killed him.'

I take a gulp of my wine, coughing as it goes down the wrong way. My mind is overtaken by a deluge of panic.

'You can't imagine that happening so close to where we were, can you?'

I shake my head. I need some air. The walls are closing in on me. She must be able to see my heart pounding in my chest. Am I sweating? It's much too hot in here.

'Did you see anything strange when you left the restaurant?' she asks.

There's a tightening at the base of my skull, the warning sign of a migraine.

'I just wondered who George was with and where he went.'

'No. We had to get back to get ready for our flight, remember?' I manage, weakly.

'Oh, yes. Did you go anywhere after the meal? For a drink or anything?'

'Nope. It wasn't exactly the weather to stay out!'

Am I talking too fast? I'm horribly aware of how fidgety I feel. I need to get up and thrust open the back door, flood the kitchen with cool air.

She slowly sips her wine. 'Yeah, the storm would have started around then.' She runs her forefingers up and down the stem of her glass. There's a pause. 'So you went straight back to the hotel? You didn't see George Kingsley again?'

'Sophia, I'm starting to feel like this is some sort of interrogation,' I snap.

I know this outburst shocks her. Immediately I regret not holding my tongue better, as Jamie does.

Suddenly there's a bang – the wind must have slammed an open door. Sophia's whole body seems to jolt. Her eyes widen. 'I was only making conversation, Erin.'

'Sorry,' I mumble into my glass, furious with myself.

30

Sophia

Erin looks shocked to see me standing on her doorstep. My spontaneous visit is partly so I don't have to sit at home alone, and partly in desperation to do some digging. I still can't believe I've foolishly pitched the honeymoon murder story to Peter without any concrete details.

I need to give him something, especially as Lou didn't show up. She's since gone underground, ignoring my emails and her number just ringing out. I'm clutching at straws to make this Bali story stand up but I hope that, having also met George, sort of, Erin may have something to share from that night. She and Jamie stayed out later than we did. Perhaps she saw George leave with someone. Or might remember something from that night that I could work with.

It's weak, but it's a start.

'Hey! I tried calling you!' I say when she answers the door. 'Why should the boys have all the fun?'

She looks a bit dazed for a moment. Hesitating, before inviting me into the house that gives me the creeps. I can't put my finger on what it is – the dated, mismatched furniture, the musty smell, the chilly air? I honestly don't know how she copes here. The cut on her head looks sore, as do the scratches up the inside of her arm. She notices me looking and pulls her sleeve down over her wrist, telling me quickly that she 'caught it on a cupboard'.

It's when I pull out the photos from my phone and go through my camera roll that things definitely shift. Subconsciously or not, she flicks her eyes to the left, and her neck flushes when I start talking about George Kingsley. From her reaction it's obvious she knows more than she's letting on.

I don't get the chance to press her as I jump out of my skin at the sound of a slamming door. The next thing I know, Jamie strides in, a fleeting look crossing his face at the half-empty bottle of wine.

'Hey! Well, this seems like a bit of a party.'

His tone is light and friendly but Erin leaps to her feet, clearing away our glasses as if she's been caught doing something she shouldn't be. 'Sophia just turned up,' she blurts, her back to us both, leaning over the large white basin.

'I thought it wasn't fair that you men had all the fun,' I say as he gives me a light kiss on the cheek. His smart polo shirt shows off the tan he's held on to, but his blue eyes don't have the brightness they did in Bali.

'How was the gig? Is it over already?' I ask.

'Yeah, it was decent. I think Mark enjoyed himself. He might have a sore head tomorrow.' A playful smile appears on his lips as I let out a groan. 'Sadly I couldn't stay out as I've got to be in early for work, or else I'd have joined him for the beers too. Anyway, what have you two been up to?'

'We've just been catching up about the honeymoon,' I say.

Erin turns to face us. 'Sophia was just telling me she thinks the guy who died in the storm was the same man I spilt the drink over at the Blue Fin.'

'Seriously?' Jamie turns to look at her.

'Yeah, but that's not all,' Erin continues. 'The police think someone killed him.'

Jamie lets out a sort of slow whistle. 'No way. That's mad . . . Anything to eat? I'm starving!' He starts rummaging in the kitchen cupboards. 'Sophia, can I get you anything?'

'No, thanks.' I look at the time. 'In fact, I should probably be making a move. Thanks so much for the company though, Erin.'

'No problem! Do you want me to call you a taxi to the station?' Erin asks.

'I'll take you,' Jamie says, looking up from a drawer.

'It's fine, I don't mind calling one,' I say, pulling out my phone.

'I insist. Maybe I can stop by the chippy on the way back,' he says with a jingle of his car keys, a bright smile on his face.

The car radio is set to a classical station that keeps dipping in and out of frequency, the crackle interrupting the low bass of an oboe playing an ominous tune. Jamie doesn't seem aware of the irritating pauses in the symphony.

'Thanks again for taking me. You didn't have to,' I say.

'It's honestly not a problem. Don't want anything to happen to you, do we?' He smiles, taking his eyes off the road for a second. The winding lane has widened out a little as we pass through the woods, the canopy of trees above us blocking out the moonlight. There's an eeriness with no streetlamps, as if anything could be lying in the darkness behind the beam of his headlights. I wish I'd brought a thick coat. My arms are covered in goosebumps.

'I said to Mark we'll have to arrange another dinner soon. He suggested maybe we could come over to you guys?' Jamie says. 'I'm often in London for work things.'

'Yeah, definitely.' I pull my phone out. 'In fact, I should tell him I'm on my way back.'

'There's no signal down here.'

He's right. There are no bars on my phone screen – 'no service' where 4G should be. Before I can say another thing, the car suddenly jerks to the right. My phone tumbles out of my grip and falls into the shadows of the footwell. He's pulled into a lay-by and turned off the engine. Ever so slowly he turns to face me.

'I've been meaning to get you alone,' he says. 'I think maybe we should have a chat.'

31

Sophia

There's a crackle of leather as Jamie shifts in his seat. He runs a hand through his hair, looking out of the windscreen at the shadow of trees and trunks surrounding us.

'Is everything OK?' I ask tentatively. There's something about his tense posture that unnerves me.

He doesn't say anything, then slowly turns his head to face me. The relaxed, playful Jamie I thought I knew has vanished in an instant.

My pulse quickens. 'Jamie? Are you OK? What did you want to speak about?'

Why has he stopped for a chat but isn't saying a word? The longer the silence drags on, the more unnerved I feel. Terrifying scenarios suddenly shoot through my mind. I used to carry hairspray whenever I went out on particularly testing jobs for the *Sunday News*. A small can was tucked in my purse next to my ID and shorthand notebook, in lieu of pepper spray – the next best thing. I've never used it, but the tiny makeshift weapon gave me slight peace of mind. But I don't carry it around with me any more.

I bend forward to run a hand around the footwell, scrabbling around for my phone. It's too dark to see a thing.

I'm about to lean across and press the central light above the gearstick when Jamie lets out a deep sigh.

'Erin's going through a bit of a hard time at the moment. A period of . . . change.'

'What?'

'You're probably not the right person to talk to about this. I know you don't know her very well but . . .' He trails off, looking as if he doesn't know how to finish his sentence.

'What do you mean?' I ask.

Another sigh. 'Sophia, I've got a favour to ask.'

'A favour?'

He finally turns to look at me with big, sad eyes. 'I know it might sound strange but, well, I know you'll understand.'

'Understand what?'

'Erin's jealous of you.'

I blink. A bubble of laughter is trapped in my throat. What is wrong with me? Why do I always leap to the most extreme scenarios? Jamie isn't a threat. He's concerned for his wife. I'm embarrassed at how quickly I leapt to the wrong conclusion. He's simply stopped the car for a heart-to-heart.

'And it brings out an ugly side to her that badly affects her moods, so I'd really appreciate it if you gave her some space. She's a very anxious person and your visits leave her extremely depressed, even self-harming. That's why it's so hard for me to tell you – I know she'd be mortified if you knew this but I had to say something. For all our sakes.'

I think of how long it took her to close the front door as we left this evening, watching our every movement. The scratches down her arm could easily be self-harm marks, not to mention how she's changed compared to the bright, bubbly woman I met at the poolside in Bali.

Jamie rubs his chin. 'Her mood swings can be pretty unimaginable. Her bipolar disorder comes out in different ways.'

'Bipolar? I had no idea . . .'

'Yeah. She'll be cross with me telling you, as she doesn't want it to be a *thing*, you know? But I had to make you aware of what she's going through. For her own good.'

I nod, trying to keep up.

'She was diagnosed in her teens. Since then, she's sat in front of different psychiatrists all trying to help her but the medication she's on is the only thing that seems to do anything. Well, *when* she's on it. Her old GP has messed up sending her prescription over to her new doctors.' He lets out a deep sigh. 'I'm sure when they manage to sort this out she'll begin to feel a lot better. It's just one of those things we sadly have to learn to live with.'

I've written a couple of stories about people with bipolar disorder, defined by their radical shifts in mood and behaviour. I think of her previous job, working at the place for challenging teenagers, helping them through tough times too. She does have an energy about her that I've never seen before, but this confession still comes as a surprise.

'I'm just grateful that she coped OK on our honeymoon. Thankfully, a change of scene and slower pace of life really seemed to help, but since coming home it's been tough. Really tough. Her head is somewhere else most of the time. I just wanted to give you a heads-up in case you thought she seemed off. It's not you, trust me.'

He's right. I think of how she reacted to burning those pies when we came for dinner and how exhausted she looks.

'Will she be OK?' I ask. 'Without this medication, I mean.'

'Yeah, I hope so. I've spent most of the day chasing her GP, so fingers crossed it'll be sorted soonish. I'm just asking that you give her some space, at least until she gets her meds and they start to kick in.'

'Of course.' I blink. 'I hope she starts to feel better soon.'

The thud of my heart lessens but for some reason I'm still uneasy at the look he's giving me.

'Thanks, Sophia. I really appreciate it.' He places a hand on my upper arm for a moment. The warmth of his skin and the unexpected movement shocks me. 'You're freezing! I'll turn the heating up. I didn't realise you were so cold. You should have said something.'

Just as suddenly as he pulled over, he turns the engine back on and continues down the wooded track. He fiddles with the dials and soon wonderful warm air is blasting from the heaters. He turns the radio station up, a sonata full of moving strings filling the car.

I try to match his cheerful wave as he drops me at the train station.

I sit down in the practically empty carriage and pull out my phone. Fields stream past the window, a blur of dark greens and the occasional amber streetlight. That's one reason I'm not in a hurry to move anywhere rural – you don't know what's lurking in the shadows.

I dial Mark's number, wanting to let him know what time I'll be back, and to see how his night was. I'd love to find out what he thinks of our new friends – something is bugging me about Jamie's abrupt confession in the car but I can't work out what.

His phone rings for ages. When he eventually picks up, he sounds upbeat and happy. And drunk.

'Here she is, wifey for lifey! I was literally just thinking of you. I miss you. Where are you?' The slight slur in his voice is unmistakable.

'Hey, well, it sounds like someone's had a good night.' I smile. 'I'm just on the train now. I've been to see Erin.'

'Erin? You've been to see Erin?' He repeats. 'Do you know what? I like her. She's different from your other mates but that's cool. Different is good.'

'How much have you drunk tonight?'

'Barely anything . . . All right. Maybe a little. Jamie's just super-generous! He was driving but I made the most of it. The gig was amazing, by the way, you'd have loved it!'

'Yeah, er, speaking of Jamie . . .' I take a breath. 'What do you think of him? Did you think anything seemed up with him tonight?'

'No. Why? Should I have done?'

'Something strange just happened. In the car, on the way to the station.' I take a breath, feeling a little guilty about confessing this so soon, but I need to talk to someone about it. 'Jamie told me Erin's bipolar but I don't know if I believe him.'

Mark thinks for a second. 'What? I mean, I guess she could be. I don't know much about the condition – but, hang on, why don't you believe him?'

'Don't know. Something feels off.' My gut is telling me something that I can't quite put my finger on.

'Soph. The last time you followed your instinct, look where it left you.'

'Hmm.' I bite down the flash of irritation. He's drunk, and unaware how hurtful that sounds. 'Well, she doesn't seem like the Erin we met on holiday, that's for sure.'

'Everyone acts differently on holiday, though. I mean, swapping the sun for that haunted house—'

'It's not haunted.'

'You know what I mean. Once the holiday is over, it's back to reality.'

'I guess.' I pick at my nails.

'I think you're reading way too much into this, Soph. They're a nice couple. Maybe a bit keen, but that's no bad thing.' He lets out a yawn. 'God, I really can't hack it like I used to . . . So, what time will you be home?'

'Probably just before eleven, but don't wait up, I'm going to be working late.'

He lets out an unsubtle groan. 'Working on what? Something for the *Post*? I didn't think they'd be making you pull all-nighters.'

'No, it's not for them. Peter has asked me to do something for him. I have to get it to him early.'

'Peter? Your old boss Peter?'

I nod then realise he can't see me. 'Yep, he wants me to look into the guy who died on our honeymoon. I think there's more to it.'

At least, that's what I've told him. Somehow, I need to make this story stand up.

'Oh. Right.'

I sense a tone. 'What?'

'Nothing.'

'Go on, there's clearly something.'

'It's just . . . well . . . you said on honeymoon you were going to get a better work-life balance, and since coming home all you've done is work. You've not even properly unpacked your suitcase.'

I'm about to argue back but he does have a point. I did promise him I would try to change. I just had no idea how difficult it would be.

32

Erin

I watch Jamie out of the window. His car pulls on to our drive but he doesn't move. He must sit like that for a good ten minutes. My own legs are growing pins and needles from trying to keep an eye on him.

'Everything go OK with Sophia?' I ask as casually as possible when he finally walks in.

'Fine,' he says.

I follow him to the kitchen. 'That was nice of you, to drive her to the station.' I start running the hot water tap. 'Was there a problem?' I ask, squeezing lemon-scented washing-up liquid into the sink. 'You took a while to get back.'

It took a long time, longer than it should have, even if he waited at the station with her until she was safely on the train. I googled her train times.

'Roadworks,' he says, moving over to the drinks cabinet.

'Oh. So, did she say anything else about George?' I grip the scourer. 'I can't believe the police are treating it as suspicious. You know what this means . . . they think someone murdered him, Jamie.'

168

Saying it out loud makes me want to be sick. Sophia's got it wrong. This is a mistake. Someone's lying. I wanted to tell her all of this when she was here but I couldn't, not without confessing that we had some part to play.

I hold my breath, waiting for him to react.

Jamie pulls out a bottle of whisky. I shake my head when he asks if I want a glass.

'There are bound to be rumours. Until there's been a post-mortem then people are going to talk. Don't worry about it.' He pours out a large measure, and despite how calm he's acting I can spot the slight tremble in his wrist. 'Is that why Sophia was really here?'

'I'm not sure – she said she just wanted to hang out,' I say slowly. I turn off the hot tap and face him. I don't like the look he's giving me. Have I been completely naïve?

'It's a bit odd, don't you think?' He sits at the kitchen table. 'You said she was talking about the honeymoon.'

I pick at the skin on my thumb. 'She just wanted to know if I saw anything when we left the restaurant. Who George was with or where he went, that sort of thing.'

'So she *is* planning on writing about him.' He rubs his eyes with the heel of his hand.

'But, as you said, why would she bother when she works for a local paper now?'

'A story is a story. It doesn't matter where she works – she still has contacts, doesn't she? So what did you say? To all these questions?'

'Nothing! Don't worry. I underplayed it all. I didn't tell her what we did, if that's what you're worried about.'

I immediately regret being so offhand. I dig my nails into the flesh of my arm.

'It's not a joke, Erin.'

'I know. Sorry. I just thought you might be worried about me blabbing. You always say I talk too much, that's all.'

There's a stretched-out silence. I can hear him slowly sipping his drink. I quickly wash the empty wine glasses, rubbing a thumb over the imprint of Sophia's lipstick, and rest them on the draining board.

'How was your night?' I ask, trying to change tack. 'How come you didn't tell me you were going to a gig?'

'Hmm? I thought I told you. It's no big deal. Someone in my office had spare tickets.'

No, he didn't tell me. He doesn't even like indie music. I bet if I asked him to name one of D.R.U.M.'s hits he wouldn't be able to tell me. But I bite my tongue. There's no point starting an argument for no reason.

'Oh. Well, it would have been nice to know, that's all. I felt like an idiot in front of Sophia when she turned up, not knowing you and Mark were hanging out together.'

'Am I not allowed to have friends, Erin?'

'Course! Sorry, I didn't mean it like that.'

Another beat of silence. I dry my hands on a tea towel and let out a yawn. 'I think I'm going to call it a night.'

Jamie asks if I'll pass him the bottle of whisky. He's finished his large glass already. I have to bite my tongue to stop myself from nagging that he's drinking too much. I find a clean glass, then lean over and give him a kiss goodnight. I need to get some painkillers for the headache that's not budged since Sophia's visit. My brain feels as if it's been on a spin cycle in a washing machine with all the new information I've learned this evening.

'I need to come clean. There weren't really any roadworks,' he says as I turn to leave the room.

'What?'

He lets out a deep sigh. 'I only said that because I knew you would get annoyed by the real reason I was late.'

I hold my breath at the look on his face.

'Which is what?'

'Sophia tried it on with me in the car.'

I steady myself against the doorframe. Somewhere, deep down, I knew he was going to say this. I mean, I'm not an idiot. I know my husband is attractive and so is she. No matter what he's about to say to me, it can't be worse than the images my mind immediately conjures up.

'What happened?' I swallow and try not to let this light-headedness submerge me.

'It was honestly nothing, don't worry.'

Why is he trying to shrug this off? Doesn't he know that I need Every. Single. Detail.? There's no way I'm going to sleep tonight, not that I sleep any more anyway. But this will become my new nightmare.

'Go on. Clearly it was something or else you wouldn't have mentioned it.'

Tell me everything.

'She completely took me by surprise. She asks me to pull over, so I do, thinking perhaps something is wrong. Then, as soon as the car stops, she launches herself over the seats at me, trying to kiss me.'

'Oh, my God!' I blink. 'Are you going to tell Mark?'

Jamie gives a pathetic sort of shrug. 'What good will that do? Clearly they're not right for each other if she's lost interest in him already. They've only been married for three minutes.'

As long as us.

'So . . . what did you do?'

'I told her it was inappropriate and that I didn't want to see her again. It's up to you if you keep in touch but . . . I personally don't want to have anything to do with them.'

I take my phone out of my pocket.

'What are you doing?' he asks.

'I'm going to call her. She can't pretend to be my friend and then try to kiss you behind my back!'

'No.' He scrapes his chair back and comes towards me, reaching his hand out as I bring my arm forward. The movement surprises me. My phone tumbles to the kitchen tiles as if in slow motion. I wince as I hear a crack.

'Oh, God, see! She's trouble!' He bends down to pick my phone up. I'm holding my breath, crossing everything that it's not as damaged as I fear. Thankfully the screen is still in place but there are hairline cracks all down it, cutting across our smiling faces on the home screen.

I know it was an accident, but I have to bite down shouting at him for making me jump. It's not Jamie I'm annoyed at, not really. It's Sophia who's to blame for this.

'Erin, listen. Please don't get involved, my love. We've got enough to deal with without any more drama.'

'I just can't believe she tried it on with you. How could she do that to me?'

There's a sudden squawk from a couple of gulls outside the window.

'Is there something you're not telling me?' I push.

He takes a long, slow sip of his whisky. 'You don't trust me.'

His voice is so low, I think I've misheard him at first. 'Sorry?'

Out of nowhere, he launches his whisky glass at the wall behind me. It shatters immediately. I leap out of my skin, my heart hammering as he thunders towards me.

'Have I ever given you a reason not to trust me?' A blast of alcohol hits me.

My body is pinned to the spot, pressed against the cold wall. 'I do trust you!'

He ignores me. His hands clasp the sides of my face, cupping my jaw. They move down my throat, the pressure increasing ever so slightly. Imperceptibly at first until he's digging his nails into my skin. Tears spring in my eyes. I blink at the hurt and anger that's marked on his reddened face.

His hands are only held there for a second or two but it feels like forever. Suddenly, they release and fly from my throat as if he's been pulled from a trance. He thumps a fist against the wall. Before I can say anything, he storms out of the room, slamming the door shut behind him, where it vibrates in the wooden frame.

My breath is jumping in my chest. Tears spill down my hot cheeks. I want to tip my head back and scream until my lungs ache. I finally loosen my grip on my arm. When I look down, there's blood on my fingernails. I've broken the skin without realising.

33

Sophia

Wednesday 21 September

I'm surrounded by terrifying dogs. They strain on leashes, globs of saliva splattering to the ground with every tight jerk from a masked handler. Their aggressively loud growls are trying to warn me of something; I just can't figure out what it is. The barking won't stop.

I wake with a start.

My hair is clammy at the back of my neck, the duvet tangled around my sweating limbs. Heart thumping, jaw aching as I unclench my teeth. The sky is dark, with thick navy light stamped around the edges of the curtains. The barking has stopped. Was it just a bad dream? I strain my ears but all I hear is the heavy exhaust of a bus from outside.

I fumble with my phone on the bedside table to see what time it is and inwardly groan. It's only half past four. I'm about to put my phone back when I see the security app, the one Jamie upgraded for us. At a touch of a button, I can check our CCTV and see if those dogs were really there or not. It felt too real for it to be just a nightmare.

I tap open the app, trying to hide the glow from the screen that lights up the bedroom. Mark is fast asleep beside me. I can smell a faint scent of booze on his breath as he steadily exhales. At least I don't have to wake him to get the log-ins – it's all automatically saved.

I brush off the damp hair stuck to my neck and swipe a finger along the horizontal bar at the bottom of the screen – speeding up and slowing down time in our London street. There's something hypnotic about putting life on fast forward and being able to rewind. It's grainy in the twilight hours but apart from the bus that goes past, which was actually a delivery lorry, there isn't any movement. According to this, the last time anyone walked a dog down our street was seven hours ago and, even then, it looks like a scruffy white terrier, not the ferocious hunting dogs I was remembering.

It was just a nightmare.

Everything is fine – only my subconscious playing tricks on me. Being ghosted by Lou is clearly playing on my mind.

Eventually my heart rate returns to normal. I minimise the app and place my phone back on charge. I need to be up in two hours to do some more digging for Peter – I can't remember what time I stumbled into bed after being glued to my laptop once I got back from Erin's, but the promise of another chunk of sleep is too enticing, especially now I know that I'm safe.

I roll over, pressing myself into Mark's warm, bare back, his rhythmic heartbeat calming me down. In the morning I should probably confess that maybe he was right to install those cameras: being able to quickly scan our surroundings without leaving the bed is priceless. I was too hard on him. In fact, I don't tell him often enough how lucky I am to have him looking out for us. I snuggle in closer. The sleepy scent of his skin is enough for me to drift off again. Safe in the knowledge that nothing is going to harm us.

The bedroom is bathed in light when I next open my eyes and stretch with a glorious sigh. Outside, the traffic has picked up and there's a rumble of roadworks from further down the street. Mark is snoring next to me. I spot the packet of sleeping pills on his bedside cabinet. How has he become so reliant on these without me noticing?

I tug my phone from the charger where I plugged it in last night. The screen is blank. My stomach lurches. The disorientated start suddenly snaps into clarity. I need to know what time it is. I set my alarm for six. A slow, sickening realisation washes over me.

My phone hasn't charged. The alarm never went off.

I sit bolt upright, tugging back the covers to let in a shock of cold air, which wakes Mark. 'Hey. What's going on? You OK?' he asks, his voice heavy with sleep and confusion.

I stumble to the kitchen, my legs not fully engaged with my brain as I clatter about. The blinking red light on the oven says it's half past nine.

'Shit! Mark! Get up. We're both so late!'

He swears and is soon on his feet.

'Why didn't you set your alarm?' I pant.

'I could ask you the same thing.' He rushes past and turns the shower on.

'I thought I did!'

176

The charger must be broken or perhaps I didn't plug it in properly. Snippets of the dog nightmare pierce my mind. I haven't got time to get into a fight with Mark.

How could I have overslept? I need to get a shower but there's no time. Peter said he wanted to meet for a coffee before the morning conference. He can't just rely on my word any more.

Perhaps I can still make it. I tear around the flat. I'll use dry shampoo. A can of deodorant. Grab an Uber. Do my make-up in the back of the car. Skip coffee. If I'm quick, I can be out of the door in ten minutes.

I stop. What sort of impression is that going to give?

There's no way I'll be able to get ready and make it across town in time. I slam my palm against the worktop, wincing at the slap of cold marble.

With a heaviness inside my chest, I open my laptop, preparing to send Peter a grovelling email apologising for letting him down.

Again.

34

Sophia

I slope to my desk, feeling my colleagues' eyes on me. Claudia has given me a loud ticking-off about my timekeeping, or lack thereof, making it clear how disappointed she is. I try to block out the stares and ignore the hushed voices and instead focus on my inbox. There's already a reply from Peter. In one short line, he tells me to only get back in touch when, and if, I have something newsworthy for him.

'How's the George Kingsley story going?' Amira asks, pulling her desk chair over to mine, bringing the fresh scent of her washing powder.

'Sorry?'

'I saw the printout on Monday,' she explains, colour flushing her cheeks. 'I knew that if you were interested in it, then it was going to be a great story.'

I smile, taken aback by her belief in me. I'm not sure what to tell her as, despite searching online last night, I feel like I've hit a bit of a brick wall. However, her curiosity could be invaluable. If I want to get to the bottom of this, then I could do with some help. I quickly check no other colleagues are listening and I begin to fill her in.

'So you were there? You met him?' Her eyes widen behind her glasses.

'Sort of.'

'And what do you think happened?'

'I have no idea. I just don't know why George would be there at that time of night. It's not like he got lost, he lived there. I've asked the police for another update but it's taking a while. I've also contacted his family to see if they might speak to me.' I let out a sigh. 'Whatever he was doing up at the cliffs on a stormy night, well, someone must have seen or heard something. I can't help but wonder if the couple we met on our honeymoon could somehow be involved . . . It sounds a bit strange, but just something isn't sitting quite right with them.'

Amira leans forward. 'Go on.'

'Well, they stayed out later than we did, so I wondered if perhaps they'd seen anything, especially as, just a few hours before he died, Erin accidentally spilt a drink all over him. But then, when I asked her about it, she went pale and snapped at me, saying she felt I was interrogating her, but I genuinely wasn't. I'd literally just shown her George's photo and asked if she could remember anything about the night.'

'Weird.'

'It was just strange how quickly she shut down my innocent questions about what they did after the meal. Like she had something to hide.'

I think of what Jamie said to me in the car about his wife suffering with her mental health. I have to tread carefully. Her change in behaviour may not be suspicious; it could all be linked to her condition.

'Amira?' Brad's voice booms across the office.

'I'd better go,' Amira says, quickly getting to her feet. 'I'm guessing you've already done a location search on socials?'

I inwardly kick myself for not doing this already. 'On it now. Thanks.'

I open Instagram and search for the name of the cliffs. #TebingTerjal. I filter the results to the twelfth of September. A few hardy tourists took arm-stretched-out selfies or artfully captured the sunset, but they're all hours before the storm. Hours before George died.

I sigh, tapping a biro against my shorthand notebook.

Another search. #TheBlueFinBali. Images of colourful Balinese food, beaming couples tilting their wine glasses together and the view from the lantern-covered terrace all fill my screen. I scroll and scroll, looking in the background of each shot, trying to catch a glimpse of George's blue shirt or his short silver hair that shimmered against his deep-set tan. It's impossible.

I'm about to give up when something catches my eye.

Not all the photographs using this hashtag are taken inside the restaurant. Some users have captured themselves beside the Blue Fin logo at the entrance, wanting to make sure followers know exactly where they are.

I lean closer to my screen.

A pretty Australian travel influencer, judging by her blue tick and thousands of followers, has posted a reel from the very same night. She's standing outside the restaurant and enthusiastically waving to the camera. She must own a built-in ring light as everything is perfectly lit up in flawless definition. The shot slowly pans around 360 degrees to return to her climbing into a colourful tuk-tuk.

The reel lasts for ten seconds or so, but it's enough. Just as the shot returns to the wholesome blonde, you get a clear look at the path towards the Tebing Terjal cliffs – in the direction George must have gone.

My office chair groans as I shift my weight closer to my screen, playing the clip again and again.

There's someone in the background.

I press repeat. It's time-stamped. Half an hour or so before George died.

There, heading away from the restaurant, away from the taxi rank, is a couple moving towards the cliffs, hand in hand. The man is wearing a nondescript dark shirt and chinos, but it's the woman, in a bold palm print sundress, that makes me sit up.

I blink, unease growing in the pit of my stomach.

I've seen this outfit before.

I have to watch it a couple more times to be sure. Each time I do it, I see them even more clearly.

Erin and Jamie didn't walk straight back to the hotel, as she said. They headed in the direction of the cliffs.

35

Erin

Wednesday 21 September

Jamie holds the door open to the Italian bistro. Glossy ivy climbs across the brick façade. It's busier than I expected for a midweek lunchtime. He asked the manager for his best table after they greeted one another like old friends.

I slide into the padded booth seat, taking care to place my new handbag next to me. He came home with the exact same Chanel bag that Sophia has. Of course, Jamie wouldn't have picked up on this coincidence. It's a timeless classic: chain strap, diamond-stitched quilting, burgundy interior trim. It smells of money and success. I've never owned anything so beautiful but, despite the extravagant apology gift, the effects of the other night still sting. Jamie has apologised profusely, blaming the demon drink and promising that it will never happen again.

He leans towards me now, fixing his honest blue eyes on me. 'I want you to know how sorry I am, babe. Work has been manic and with everything else going on – well, you know, it all just got too much.'

'It's fine.' It's not fine, but I don't know what else to say.

'You know that I'd never hurt you, don't you?'

I nod. I didn't marry a monster.

I gaze around the busy bistro full of glamorous-looking clientele. It reminds me of the place we went to on our first date when he picked me up in his fancy car, so low that whenever I wore a skirt it would ride up inappropriately as I got out. I didn't realise then that the restaurant's speciality was seafood. I've never been very good with things like that – my palate isn't as sophisticated as Jamie's. He made me pick lobster and I wasn't sure if he was showing off or trying to be kind, feeling the usual pity that most people show me, wanting to broaden my horizons.

'You know the screams are just steam escaping from the shell? They feel nothing,' he explained, nodding to the murky tank containing the lobsters, their claws bound by tight blue elastic bands.

I wanted to ask him how he knew this. I didn't particularly like the taste but he had gone to all that trouble and expense for me, so I tried to stomach as much of it as I could. The rich, decadent dinner was unlike anything I'd ever had on a date before – I'd never felt so spoilt and special. He's always been so good to me. What happened the other night wasn't my husband, and I believe him when he says it won't happen again.

'So . . .' Jamie accepts a menu passed by a smiling waitress '. . . have you thought any more about finding work?'

I shake my head.

'Good. I just don't think now is the right time for change, my love.'

Every so often I can hear the telltale buzz of his phone from his suit jacket. It pleases me that he's not responding to it; I'm enjoying having his full attention. As nice as the setting is – there's not a lobster tank to be seen – I'm still uneasy. Loitering waiting staff have been watching us intently, earwigging probably. It's the same when we walk through the street. I find myself gripping his hand tighter whenever we pass people. Are they spying on us? Are they listening to us?

'Do you feel like people keep looking at us?' I ask him. I just can't shrug off this sense of being watched.

'Er . . .' He glances over his shoulder. Annoyingly, right now, no one seems the slightest bit interested. 'No. And if they are, then it's probably because you're the most gorgeous woman in here.' He takes my hand and runs his thumb across it.

'Yeah, right.' I pull away, blushing at the look he's giving me. He hasn't taken his eyes off me since we sat down.

I wonder if he likes what I'm wearing. The floaty leopard midi dress I ordered online isn't as chic as the one Sophia wore when she came to ours with Mark, but the laced black ankle boots could be identical.

'It's true!' He takes a sip of his non-alcoholic beer. 'Listen, I know I messed up the other night, but I want you to know I love you. We're a good team. We need to cut ourselves some slack. I mean, bereavement, moving house, a wedding, growing a new business – in fact, we should give ourselves credit. We've been through more than what most couples go through in ten years.'

He's right. It's easy to overlook these things.

'I know we can weather whatever storm we face together.' He kisses my hand. The gesture makes me laugh. His shoulders seem to drop now he knows he's out of the doghouse.

I scan my eyes down the enticing menu as Jamie unfolds his linen napkin.

'Have you heard any more from Sophia?' he asks.

'No.'

'Good.'

'I still think you should tell Mark about her trying it on with you.'

'There's no point.' He shakes his head gently. 'I mean, yeah, I feel sorry for the guy, but we've got enough on our plate without getting involved. We just need to forget about them. They only serve as a reminder of our honeymoon. In fact, after what happened in Bali, it's probably for the best that we cut ties completely.'

Every time that place is mentioned, there's a hollowness in my chest. I sip my drink.

'What are we going to do about all that?'

'Nothing, Erin.' He takes my hand once more, his grip firm, calming. 'We do nothing.'

'But the questions she was asking—'

'Sophia won't get anywhere with this story.'

I lower my voice, glance around the restaurant once more. 'What about the footsteps? There was someone else there that night. She might find the witness and—'

'Sorry?' He looks genuinely surprised by this. 'What are you talking about, Erin? No one else was there that night.'

I blink. The bright copper lights hanging over our booth seem to flicker.

'You said you heard footsteps.' I press my palms to my eyes and try to remember that moment, as painful as it is. 'That's why we ran away from George's . . .' I can't bring myself to say 'body'. Why have we never spoken about this before?

'Footsteps? Babe, we were standing on a cliff edge in a storm. Do you really think I'd be able to hear footsteps?'

I want to say that the storm had largely passed by that time, but I'm taken aback by the look he's giving me. The tilt of his head, eyes wide and full of pity. A look I hate.

I force myself to take a breath. I'm not ready to drop this just yet.

'You definitely said you heard someone. We ran into the bushes, I looked back, and that's when I saw someone walking towards where George was.' At least, I think I did. 'I don't know who it was or how long they were there or what they saw – I mean, it was dark – but they would have heard things. I don't think we kept our voices down!' My eyes dart around his face trying to find some glimmer of a memory, but it's clear that he has no idea what I'm talking about.

'Erin, please take a breath. You're scaring me.' He glances around nervously, as if looking for help.

'Jamie.' I sit forward, jostling the heavy silver cutlery. 'You honestly don't remember? There was definitely someone else there. That was the whole reason we left him behind and ran away without calling for help!'

He shakes his head, confusion fleeting on his face, and takes a shaky sip of his drink.

'You said—'

'Listen, if I did – and I really don't remember – I got it wrong. Perhaps I thought I heard something, but I was mistaken.' A waiter is approaching our table. Jamie drops his voice so only I can hear. 'Trust me, there was no one else there. I promise you.'

36

Sophia

The smell of rich ground coffee and sweet cinnamon carries in the warm air and makes my stomach growl. I've not had anything to eat today. I think about buying something from the café but I'm against the clock already.

Amira is covering for me. It's risky, especially given the ticking-off from Claudia this morning for being late. But as soon as I found the clip of Erin and Jamie heading towards the cliffs I pulled Amira into an empty meeting room, showed her the Instagram reel, then explained that there was someone I needed to go and meet.

'Sophia,' Peter says, as he walks into the coffee shop.

Carlo's Coffee. Every day at four o'clock. For his sweet afternoon pick-me-up. Some things never change. If he's surprised to see me here, he's hiding it well.

'I was expecting you this morning for conference, you know.'

'I know, I'm sorry.' I hold my hands up.

I can't tell him that I overslept. He's already lost confidence in my professional abilities. Letting Peter down – my boss, mentor and friend – was one of the worst things that came from that terrifying week. In time, I'll forget the intimidation and threats from Rupert's gang, but I won't ever fail to remember how disappointed Peter was about what happened with the recording.

I had been preparing dinner during the week from hell when a car suddenly backfired outside. Mark and I were both so on edge, it was no surprise that the bottle of wine fell from his hand. It smashed on the tiled floor, splashing crimson liquid over the walls, the dining table – and all over my work laptop. I remember my heart being in my throat as I lifted the screen and pressed the power button. Of course, it was wishful thinking. The warped screen was a vivid blue, with crazy lines running all the way across it. I sent it to the News's tech guys to try and salvage something, anything, from the hard drive, but it was too drowned to save.

I'd been so up against it with deadlines that I hadn't had the chance to save the recording anywhere else. Without that footage, I had nothing concrete to back up my side of the story.

Of course, Mark was ashamed and very apologetic, but it wasn't his fault. We were both so highly strung and jumpy after five days solid of Rupert's campaign of intimidation. If I'd been holding the wine then I would have dropped it in fear too. I wish I had someone to blame. If anything, it was those men – they'd scared us to our wits' end. Accidents are always going to happen when you're on high alert.

I push away the memory, waiting for Peter to finish giving his order to the barista.

'So, what are you doing lurking around?' Peter asks, moving over to a high wooden ledge near the window. He rests on a stool with a heavy sigh, takes his glasses off and cleans the lenses on a napkin. 'Tell me you're dropping the Rupert story.'

'For now, yes.' I take a deep breath. I never used to get nervous in front of him, but I'm suddenly hot and uncertain. 'You know that murder in Bali I told you about? The ex-pat?'

His phone chimes from his jacket pocket, reminding me that I'm on borrowed time. He glances at the screen, then nods for me to continue.

'I think the couple we were dining with know more than they're letting on. Something is off about them. My gut . . .' I swallow. 'I've got an image placing them at the location. They lied about going to the cliffs where George died around the same time of his death and there's definitely been a change in their behaviour compared to the way they were in Bali.'

George's family have put out a statement on his daughter's Facebook page, appealing for help. They say he was the victim of a targeted attack and would never harm anyone. They claim that there is some sort of cover-up going on, tampering with evidence, that sort of thing. The Indonesian police have yet to respond to this.

'No one knows why he was there that night. His family certainly seem as puzzled as I am about what – or who – led him to the cliffs.'

Peter lets out a sigh. 'I just don't think it's strong enough, Sophia. Some local scum probably followed him then took advantage of the opportunity. They killed the guy then mugged him, or vice versa.' He shrugs.

'I know there's more here,' I say quickly. 'I need to build a picture of this couple. I want to know everything about them.'

I've still not got to the bottom of the injuries that the embassy officer tipped me off about. I'm desperate to stand this allegation up. The police still won't confirm or deny if George's injuries are suspicious or not. After numerous calls and stilted phone conversations, I discovered I could pay for a copy of George's autopsy report from the Indonesian police. I need to have it translated into English for it to make any sense, which is going to take some time as, apparently, the translator is up to her eyes in work. I used the *Islington Post*'s company account, making a note to reimburse the payment before Claudia finds out.

Peter pauses. 'A couple of newlyweds on a murder spree.'

'I never said a spree!'

He wafts a hand. 'You know what I mean. But this certainly needs more colour. If they were involved, then what did this George bloke have on them? What could push them over the edge? Takes some balls, walking away from a crime scene.'

'I will do *anything* to make it work.' I clear my throat. 'I just need log-ins for iSearch.'

iSearch is a paid-for directory. A pretty invasive website that collects the data from public records, electoral rolls, Companies House and social media sites to build a detailed record of an individual. It's the type of system that cold-calling organisations and national newspapers pay to access. Smaller, local newspapers like the *Islington Post* could only dream of having the budget to afford software like this. When I was working for Peter at the *News*, I had a log-in to access the site – a privilege I lost but could really do with getting back.

'Hmm. I can't really hand that out . . . Anyway, I could just get one of my staffers to work on this, you know?'

'I know. But they wouldn't give it the Sophia touch.' I try to look as charming as possible.

Peter just rolls his eyes. He's about to say something when my phone rings. Claudia's name flashes on my screen. He nods at it. 'Do you need to get that?'

'Yes, but please don't go anywhere. I'll be two minutes!' I rush to the ladies' toilets and answer the call.

'Sophia, where the hell are you?' Claudia snaps.

'I'm leaving for the leisure centre soon, I just got caught up in the traffic,' I lie, wincing as someone flushes the toilet in the cubicle beside me.

'The event has already ended. We've had an angry phone call from the organisers asking us why we didn't send a reporter down to cover it.'

'What? No, I'm sure that it was four-thirty.'

My stomach sinks as I check my phone calendar. She's right.

'I'm not sure what's going on but I'm afraid this arrangement isn't working out as I had hoped,' she says. 'I offered you the position as a favour, but—'

'I'm sorry! Honestly. I'll do better.' As much as I hate this job, I can't afford to lose it.

'Well, take this as a final warning, then,' she says curtly, and hangs up.

I trudge out of the toilets at the exact same time that Peter walks out of the coffee shop. My spirits fall. I don't know what I was expecting to happen – maybe for him to tell me I'm right to be suspicious, that he will take me back on the payroll as I investigate further, that he'd find the money to send me back to Bali to do a full investigation. Or, at the very least, that he would give me the details for the online directory.

A wave of exhaustion rolls over me.

I lift up the napkin Peter left behind and dab at my eyes. Then something stops me. I glance down. He must have done this when Claudia called and distracted me, as, written on the back of the white paper napkin in a shaky blue biro, are the log-in details for iSearch.

My lips curl into a smile.

He's giving me the green light to do some more digging.

37

Erin

Jamie's driving us back from our lunch date. He's already told me that he has to go back to the office after dropping me home, and I'll be left on my own again. As soon as we make our way through the woods, I feel the familiar, heavy dread in the pit of my stomach at returning to our house. It's draining being there on my own all the time. No matter which room I go into, I'm bombarded by things that need to be repaired or cleaned. A fly cemetery on the flaking windowsills. Lace threads of dusty cobwebs on the walls. Draughts coming from closed doorframes. Smells of the damp and mildew that I'm certain is spreading under the paintwork.

It's the noises, too. I'm sure I hear mice scurrying above our heads, scampering over the floorboards in the attic as we sleep. I've not seen any mouse droppings but it's to be expected being in the middle of farmers' fields – sky and land stitched together in such uninspiring flatness. A grid of straight lines and ploughed earth.

It's not just the sheer number of endless jobs that need to be completed, but the general feel of the place. I can't put

194

my finger on it. I'm not into spiritual nonsense but something doesn't feel quite right; the energy is off. There've been
moments when it feels as if I'm being observed in an empty
room – this sense that I'm being watched – but maybe that's
ridiculous. I wouldn't dare say it out loud to Jamie. He already
thinks I'm losing it a bit.

During the drive home I've been turning over and over in
my mind what he said in the restaurant. He was certain there
were no footsteps; we were all alone up on the cliffs. I should
be relieved. This means no one saw us and could potentially
identify us. On the other hand, if we do get arrested then
there's no potential witness to defend our explanation that
George simply slipped in the rain.

But if I imagined this shadowy figure, then what else have
I got wrong? I swallow. I fear I'm forgetting whole conversations. I was certain I hadn't told Jamie anything about Kat's
baby shower, but I must have. I think back to when Sophia and
Mark came for dinner and I burnt the pies – I passed it off as a
fault of the ageing oven, but what if I did put the dial on max?

Suddenly, I sit up on high alert. Those worries have no match
for what my brain conjures when our house looms into view.

We have visitors waiting for us.

'What the fuck?' Jamie's jaw is set.

A sudden shot of adrenaline blooms in my stomach. I blink
to make sure I'm not seeing things.

Just ahead of us, parked outside our house, is a police car.

Two male officers raise their hands in a formal greeting as we
approach. I expect Jamie to throw the car into reverse and
screech off the drive but he parks in his usual space, calmly

turns off the ignition and gets out. My hand trembles as I reach for the door handle.

They've found something linking us to that night.

Jamie drops his keys on to the gravel. The clatter makes me jump. I don't think my legs will work to carry me to the front door. This is it: surely our luck has run out. A heady wave of adrenaline and fear courses through me, followed by the tingle of relief. This will all be over soon. I may be able to sleep again.

'Mr Steele?' a police officer asks.

I hold my breath, waiting for my name to be uttered.

The pause seems like an eternity.

Surely they need to check who I am, but they don't even glance my way. I'm not exaggerating. The police officer, a stocky man with acne scars pitted in his thick cheeks, has his eyes fixed on Jamie, and him alone.

'Yes?' Jamie replies.

To an outsider that word might sound authoritative, as though he has a grip on the situation, but I can hear the waver in his voice.

'We'd like to speak to you,' the police officer says formally. He flicks his eyes towards me, finally acknowledging that I'm here. Frozen like a wild animal in the eye of a viewfinder. 'In private, please,' he adds.

Jamie clears his throat. 'What's this about?'

'It's better if we speak alone. We've been trying to contact you.'

I think of the number of times his phone buzzed at lunch, each call ignored. I thought it was his office complaining about his extended lunch break.

196

'Do you want to come in, or . . .' Jamie nods at our house.

It's utterly ridiculous but my first thought is that I haven't hoovered. I blink this away. Surely the police have arrested people in dirtier settings. But then, he hasn't actually said he's arresting anyone.

'I think it's best if you can join us at the station.'

Jamie pushes a hand through his hair and asks if he needs to get a solicitor, just as they do in films. To hear him say this makes it seem even more like a bad dream.

'If you would like to follow us in your car, sir,' the police officer says.

I remember to breathe. They would cuff him and bundle him into the back seat of the police car if they suspected anything really untoward. I have no idea why they need to speak to him so badly yet are giving him the freedom to go of his own free will. What can they possibly need to say to him at the station that they can't say here?

'Am I in some sort of trouble?' Jamie asks boldly.

The officer gives nothing away. 'As I said, it's easier if we speak at the station and iron a few things out there.' Then he smiles at me. I think it's meant to reassure me but it's dripping with uncertainty.

It's only when I see Jamie open his car door that I call out, reminding him that I'm standing there.

'Jamie? You've got the house keys,' I stutter.

Jamie snaps out of his trance and rummages in his pocket for the keys. He walks towards me and presses them into my hand. The cold metal is a shock against my skin. Then he leans towards me and kisses me firmly on the lips, the police officer keeping a close eye on us.

I don't know how I manage to get the key in the lock with my hand shaking the way it is. I stumble into the house without a clue what to do.

38

Sophia

I finally leave the office, long after everyone else has gone home for the day. Claudia seems to have doubled my work-load as punishment for messing up on missing the leisure centre story. I swear every task that was raised in today's team briefing ended up on my desk. Amira was kind enough to take on some of the jobs before Claudia made a point of telling her to focus on her own stories. I couldn't risk stepping out of line. But, as soon as I'm back at my desk tomorrow, I'll run Erin and Jamie's names through iSearch and see what comes up.

Every tube is rammed, the trapped heat of pressed bodies suffocating me. It's a relief when I'm pushed out with a flow of strangers at Leicester Square. I'm making my way across to the West End to meet Angie and Leroy. They're visiting London for the night and we arranged to meet up for a quick drink before they catch a show. I'm hoping there's a chance they'll remember something that will help me crack this story.

Angie gives me a bright wave the moment I walk inside the little cocktail bar. Jazz music is playing, large colourful murals take up most of the terracotta walls, and there's a smell of sickly-sweet incense in the heavy air.

Leroy pours me a glass from a bottle of rioja that they're making their way through and we quickly catch up on what we've been up to since returning home.

'I hope you don't mind me saying this, but you look a bit tired, love. Is everything OK?'

It must be the concerned look Angie's giving me, the slight tilt of her head as she pats my hand with hers, that brings a sudden rush of emotion.

'Fine! Just busy. In fact I could do with another holiday,' I say, mustering a bright smile.

I swallow the lump that's leapt to my throat. I've tried to ignore the weight pressing on my shoulders because of recent weeks. The desire to prove everyone wrong, to get back into the newsroom where I belong, has overshadowed everything. If I'm honest, I didn't imagine starting married life feeling such guilt all the time.

When I called Mark to tell him I'd be home late again, he tried but failed to hide how worried he was that I was burning the candle at both ends. I know that I need to keep the adrenaline going. I can get to the bottom of George's death, deliver the truth to Peter and become a better wife to Mark. I just need time.

The door to the bar opens, bringing in a gust of damp air. People are shaking off their coats and laughing at being caught in a sudden rainfall.

'A bit different from Bali,' Angie says, nodding out of the window on to the wet street. 'Well, apart from that terrible storm. A man died that night! It's terribly sad. He was an ex-pat, you know? I saw it on Facebook, so I joined a Bali ex-pats page. Hang on, what am I doing telling you? Of course, you probably know every detail!'

'She fancies herself as a detective,' Leroy explains with a laugh.

'I just love stuff like that. True crime. I always get it right whenever we watch those ITV dramas, don't I, Leroy? At first I thought it was just an accident but, let me tell you, the gossip is rife! You'd think the hotel would have contacted us.'

'They're not going to put it in their bloody brochure, are they, love?' Leroy says, rolling his eyes.

'You know what I mean.' She gives him a light whack on the arm.

'What gossip?' I say, needing her to backtrack. Why haven't I seen these groups myself?

'All sorts.' Angie crosses her arms. 'You don't just hang out by the cliffs in the rain on your own. Some say it was a drug deal gone wrong. Or an act of unrequited passion: perhaps he was having an affair and his mistress popped him off. Or maybe he wasn't the only one to die: another body could have been thrown in the sea. Some people's imaginations are wild. Whatever theory you believe, there's no way he was by himself. So that means someone knows what happened.'

She sits back with a satisfied smile on her round face.

'Wow, that's a lot to take in.' I take a sip of my wine. The clip of Erin and Jamie walking towards the cliff leaps to the front of my mind. It doesn't prove that they had anything to do with George's death but it does prove one thing: they lied to me. 'I still can't believe it happened so close to where we all were. This might sound a bit random but, Leroy, have you looked back at the photos you took that night when you went off to get some stormy shots? I wonder if you accidentally captured something important?'

He laughs quickly. 'Doubt it!' He pours some more wine, crimson drops falling to the tabletop.

'Can I take a look anyway?' I ask. 'I'd love to see them.'

'They're really not very good. I probably still need to edit them.' He coughs, passing a look to Angie that I can't read.

'Please?'

There's an awkward silence as he fumbles with his phone. 'Sure. Er. Hang on.'

'Speaking of what happened on that night, didn't you go to the Blue Fin with that other couple? That's not far from where George was found, is it?' Angie remarks.

'Erin and Jamie,' I reply.

'Who?' Leroy asks, wiping his forehead with a paper napkin.

'Jamie,' Angie says, nodding. 'You know, that handsome tall guy, the one whose wife stared a lot. Oh, he was lovely. Not entirely sure about her, however.'

'We came back when Mark started feeling unwell,' I remind them.

'They stayed out a bit later, didn't they? I remember seeing them in the lobby when I was on my way to ask reception for some plasters for my feet. God, I'll never wear those pink sandals again!' The smile freezes on her round cheeks. 'You don't think they had something to do with it, do you?'

'You did say there was something off about her,' Leroy replies, looking up from scrolling through his phone.

202

Angie picks up a drinks menu and wafts it at her face. 'Well, I don't want to be unkind but . . . yes. She was very intense.'

I bite my lip. 'Can you remember exactly what time you saw them?' I ask Angie, as she passes another look to her husband.

'Oh, erm, not really. It was late. Maybe eleven, something like that? I can't be certain.'

That would fit with the time frame the police suggested George died.

'Have you found the photos?' I ask Leroy.

'No.' He swallows. 'I, er, I must have deleted them by mistake.'

There is a moment of silence. Why would he delete them? My body fires with adrenaline.

'Really? Have you checked your trash folder?'

How did I not think of him before now?

He holds up his phone and quickly swipes a thick finger across the screen. It's like the images from that entire evening have vanished, as if a whole day is missing.

'But you went to the cliffs to take photos around the time that George was killed?' Photos that have now disappeared.

'Yeah.' He clicks his tongue. 'It's a bit delicate. I didn't want to say but I actually deleted them . . .' He scratches the back of his head as soon as he sees my eyes widen. 'I had the exposure on the wrong setting. Every shot was just a blur. I told you I was an amateur.' There's an awkward silence. 'Hang on a second. What exactly are you trying to suggest with these questions?' Leroy asks, the embarrassment fading.

Angie's eyes widen. 'You don't suspect us, do you?'

Leroy pulls himself taller. 'I can say, with my hand on my heart, that we had nothing to do with that poor man's death. We'd never even heard of him until Ange went on Facebook.'

Is he being defensive, or am I reading it wrong? The bashful admission of the missing photographs seems genuine. I'm about to speak but he interrupts me. 'Anyway, if we're pointing fingers, then what about your husband? Hmm?'

'What's that supposed to mean?' I ask.

Angie casts her eyes to her lace-up pumps. 'I remembered something else about that night. I must have put it to the back of my mind.' She glances at Leroy and he gives her a slight nod of the head. 'It wasn't long after coming to see about the corn plasters when I saw a man. He was acting a bit off. I don't know, I couldn't put my finger on it, but you know when something just feels . . . odd?'

I don't like the look she's giving me.

'He'd got caught in the rain and seemed a bit rattled, as if something had spooked him. At first, I didn't recognise him, but then I realised later why he looked so familiar . . . It was your Mark.'

I blink, trying to follow what she's saying.

'I was going to ask you about it the next day but then he seemed back to his normal self and I'd had a few too many of Ketut's cocktails, so I thought maybe I'd dreamt it. But then, when the news came out about that poor George fella, well, I remembered thinking how odd it was that Mark was out around the time it happened, especially when you said he was ill in bed . . .'

'What?' I feel a bubble of laughter rise up.

'Now, it might be completely innocent. We'd all had a lot to drink and I don't want to start finger-pointing. Bad things happen that way.'

'Innocent until proven guilty, isn't that right, Sophia?' Leroy shoots me a loaded look.

Angie burrows in her handbag for the theatre tickets. Leroy looks at his watch and lets out a deep sigh. 'Enlightening as this has been, we need to be making a move. The show starts soon.'

I can't ask any further questions as they're putting their coats on and calling for the bill that they insist on paying. I watch them hurry off into the gloom of the night, heads close together, talking about me and my husband.

39

Erin

After Jamie left with the police, I spent the next few hours in a daze, desperate to know what had led them to pull Jamie in for questioning. They didn't explicitly say anything about our time in Bali or mention George Kingsley's name, but there's not going to be anything else they want to speak to him about.

I open my laptop. That's when I see George's family have set up an appeal – there's a link to a post on Facebook. His daughter has gone off on one, blaming the Indonesian police for being so inept. According to her, they've either lost or stolen important evidence, as some of his personal belongings were missing. I sit up. Apart from his phone, we didn't take anything else. I wonder what other items are missing.

If it wasn't the police, then someone *must* have been there after we left him, *and* stolen something from him. Was that the shadowy figure that I thought I saw?

No. As Jamie said, there was categorically no one else there.

I try to remain rational. Perhaps George's daughter is right: maybe the police are corrupt. Clearly the investigation is flawed, or how else would Sophia find out false information about George being murdered? Someone must be feeding them lies from the inside.

I'm trying to stay calm but suddenly feel shaky with hunger. I put a slice of bread in the toaster but there's a sudden crackling noise then the lights go out. I swear aloud as I'm plunged into darkness.

Nothing happens as I flick the light switch and try to turn the oven on. The power has cut out. I knew the electrics in the house were unreliable but this is the first time there's been a total blackout. Of course, it had to happen when I was on my own – I have no idea where the fuse box is. With a heavy sigh I decide to call it an early night and wait for Jamie to come home. The light on my cracked phone guides my way up to bed.

The morning sun is emerging from behind thick grey clouds when Jamie's key finally scratches in the lock.

'Where the hell have you been?' I can't control myself. 'You stayed out all night!'

Drinking by the looks of it.

'Can we talk about it later?' he says, hoarsely.

My nails are now non-existent, bitten so much that they're bleeding. I heard noises in the house all night; I spent hours expecting the police to come back for me too. Meanwhile, he's been out getting drunk.

'No! I've been worried sick.' My voice has a hysterical lilt to it, my throat clogged with emotion. 'I called the police station. They said you left hours ago. Why haven't you answered your phone? There was a power cut here and I was alone and scared!'

'What?' He flicks the light switch and light immediately illuminates his face. I've never seen him so dishevelled. At some point during the night the power must have come back on.

'It's working again now, but still, it wasn't fun.'

He winces at the shrillness of my voice. 'I'm sorry, babe, I know I should have come home after they spoke to me but I needed to clear my head. This is getting to me too, I just don't show it like you do. I needed to let off a bit of steam but I got carried away, OK?'

'What did the police want? What happened?'

He locks the deadbolt behind him with a firm slam. 'Hang on. First I need coffee.'

'So?' I ask, the moment he flicks on the kettle. He lets out a long sigh and rubs his eyes with the heel of his palm.

'It's about work,' he says.

Work?

'What?' I don't think I've heard him right. They didn't want to talk to him about what happened in Bali, they wanted to talk to him about *work*?

'It's fine. There've been some allegations of malpractice but it's bullshit. Rumours. There's no basis to it, and nothing for you to worry about. I wasn't actually at the police station for that long – the rest of the time I was trying to square stuff up with my solicitor, then he opened the whisky and, well, I lost track of time.'

'Why didn't you call me back?'

He spoons out instant coffee with a trembling hand. Brown granules scatter on the worktop. 'I'm sorry, I thought you'd be in bed and I didn't want to disturb you. You deserve a decent night's sleep.'

'Here, let me do it.' I take the jar of coffee from him and clear up the mess.

He leans against the counter, rubbing his chin. 'I'm going to take legal action, mark my words.'

'Surely we don't need to be doing anything to draw police attention to us?'

He looks at me. 'Erin, you don't understand. This is my career we're talking about.' His jaw flickers with tension. 'I mean, it's bollocks, but I guess they have to take any sort of complaint seriously, or at least be seen to be doing something.'

'I thought . . . I thought . . .' I can barely get my words out. All the tension I'd been holding in now comes flooding out. The torturous past few hours were because of a disgruntled customer. I start to laugh and cry at the same time.

Jamie narrows his bloodshot eyes, seemingly unsure what to do with me.

'I really thought they were coming to get you.' I heave out sobs. The laughter has stopped now. I realise just how close I came to losing him, to all of this being snatched from us.

'Come here.' He pulls me into a hug and my body collapses into his. The coiled tension begins to slowly melt away as he rubs my arms and tells me it's all going to be OK. A stale odour clings to his clothes.

'I can't sleep, I can't eat. I mean, look at me, Jamie! I'm a wreck.' My face is slick with salty tears, my throat hoarse from sobbing. A wave of pure exhaustion threatens to drag me under. I could shut my eyes and sleep, curled up on him, forever. 'Are you not scared?' I ask.

There's a pause.

'Terrified.'

40

Sophia

Friday 23 September

The relentless out-of-tune singing is giving me a headache. I'm sitting on an uncomfortable plastic chair in a sports hall that smells of bare feet and reheated vegetables. Most of my morning has been tied up interviewing local schoolchildren and their head teacher about a defibrillator that's been installed in the playground. A group of eager Year Six students are giving a performance through interpretative dance on how to save a life. Brad the photographer is loving it. I try to suppress a yawn.

I've had yet another broken night's sleep, worrying about how I'm going to get this story to stand up. Angie's accusation has also been on my mind: I'm shocked that she's trying to cast doubt over Mark in some way. He was out with work last night and still asleep when I left this morning, so I didn't get the chance to bring it up with him. Not that I'd even know what to say. It makes no sense. The more I think about it, their own movements that night – Angie vanishing up to bed

211

and Leroy taking photographs on his own, which he says he deleted because the exposure wasn't right – might be innocent but they are highly questionable. She was clearly coming up with theories to take the heat off her husband. I just don't know why she then had to get so defensive and bring mine into it.

I blink back the deepening headache and rub my temples.

One thing that was clear from our meet-up is that I now have a witness placing Erin and Jamie returning to the hotel hours after Mark and I left the Blue Fin. Unless I can find out where else they went on their walk, they remain suspicious.

'Sophia?' Brad nudges me. There is a circle of grinning pre-teens in front of me, waiting to tell me their names for the article.

'Sorry, I was miles away then. Right, let me just . . .' I sit up and quickly click my ballpoint, feeling the photographer's quizzical eyes on me.

Hours later, after a full tour of the school, many questions on what it's like to be a journalist, and trying to follow along with the children's constant chatter, I'm back at my desk. The first thing I do is pop some painkillers to try to tackle the headache that's not shifting. I check my emails, but no translated autopsy report for George has been sent yet. I fire off yet another chasing email.

After a subtle glance around the newsroom, I bring up the iSearch database on my screen and carefully enter the log-in details that Peter wrote on the napkin.

I start with Erin. Their marriage has been registered and recently entered on to the site. Despite relying on this database all the time in my old job, it still gives me the creeps at how sophisticated and all-encompassing it is. Erin Steele *née* Edwards. I then search using both her married and maiden name to see what else comes up.

Annoyingly, it's sparse. Her name's not on any house deeds, her Facebook page is set to private, and I can't find any other social media accounts that could be a match. I frown. It's almost too clean.

Next, I move to Jamie.

James Steele was born in 1990 in Hoarwick, a small town on the Scottish Borders. His mother (Jill Steele *née* Dawson) died in 1999. His father (Graham Steele) worked as an engineer before he retired. No current address found for him. Property records show the purchase of Renhold House, East Fern, in August of this year. Companies House lists his name as the owner of Steele Security Services.

I chew my lips and move the cursor down the screen, double-checking that the rest of the newsroom are focused on their own screens and not looking at mine.

Along with a concise background of the business, there are a couple of links to industry news articles. One is an announcement about the firm winning a major contract at a number of luxury London apartment blocks for CCTV monitoring services. The rest of the pieces are about the upcoming launch of their latest security software.

I scroll some more.

Click here for contact details for potential relatives/spouses based largely on electoral register searches.

I follow the link.

A sudden chill enters the room, as if someone has thrust a window open. I glance up but everyone is at their desk, head down, eyes glazed.

Jamie has been married before.

According to the dates on here, his divorce was made official in June, only three months ago. His first wife was Claire Steele *née* Connelly.

I force myself to slow down, not to get carried away.

Her address is listed. I shake my head as things become clear. It's one of the luxury London apartments for which Jamie's security firm won a tendering contract. I wonder if her moving in was part of the divorce agreement. I vaguely remembered him saying at the Blue Fin how he used to live in London. I'd had no idea he was talking about living here with his ex-wife.

A quick search on Google Street View reveals a sheet of solid oak with the name of the building in matt steel. There is a rotating door leading into a glossy tiled lobby. It looks very smart indeed.

I tap open the links to her social media pages.

The most recent post on her Instagram is from 2 July. It's an arty black and white shot of a woman looking wistfully into the distance. Her plump lips are in a sort of Mona Lisa smile, her wide, expressive eyes gazing past the camera lens. She's copied some melancholy song lyrics under the image.

However, it's what's in the comments that makes me sit up. I stare at the screen. I have to re-read the information before it sinks in.

RIP Claire. A new angel got her wings today.

My brain is whirring, ten paces ahead of what my eyes are taking in. There's a pounding in my head. All my senses are firing off.

I look back at iSearch for what I've missed. Further down, the page confirms this information. Her death was registered on the fourth of July. Just a fortnight after the divorce from Jamie. The noise of the office fades away behind me as I shift closer to my screen.

My fingers race over the keyboard. I need to find out how she died. She was a young woman, a similar age to me. There's nothing mentioned in her other Instagram posts. No illness she had been living with or any hints that she was battling in private.

I discover an article from a local newspaper ahead of her funeral. Her parents, Marie and Richard Connelly, gave a brief interview with a journalist sharing how broken-hearted they were and how much their daughter would be missed.

And then I finally find what I'm looking for.

A familiar sensation trickles up my spine, that same release of adrenaline that comes from doing this job for so many years. A scent for news. Spotting a story and knowing, without doubt, that you're on to something. It's innate and tiring and exhilarating all at the same time.

Jamie's ex-wife fell to her death down a flight of stairs.

41

Erin

Friday 23 September

Our wedding photos have arrived. Jamie had thought it was unnecessary to have a professional photographer capture the day, given how small the ceremony was, so we compromised. I looked after the wedding – including booking the photographer I wanted – and Jamie looked after the honeymoon. It was his choice to go to Bali. I've spent so long wondering how different things might be if we'd gone somewhere else.

I spend the day flicking through the thick, creamy pages of the expensive photo album. My chest clenches at the shots of us standing in front of the registrar, hands clasped, immovable smiles, huge, innocent eyes fixed on one another as we vowed our lifelong commitment, oblivious to what the future held in store.

I don't recognise myself. We've both aged in such a short time. Deep wrinkles that weren't there before now mark my forehead. Jamie used to drink me up; flash his eyes in a way that made my stomach flip with heady anticipation. I was his universe. He hasn't looked at me like that for a while.

It's not just our appearance that's altered. Everything has changed. I can't sleep until every window is checked and the front door bolted shut. I'm not sure what I'm keeping out but I must follow this nightly routine if I'm to get any sleep at all. A slow, torturous *drip, drip* wakes me most nights. That, or my fractured dreams. The drips are driving me insane. Yesterday evening I went outside to see where the noise was coming from. I padded out without any shoes on, the cold, hard ground biting my toes, sure that there must be a leaking pipe, a loose tile, rainwater inching its way down the ivy-covered bricks, something that was the cause of such torment. The windows are as dark as mouths, the house looking even more ominous from this angle. Moths flutter against the thin windowpanes. I hear their tiny heads butt against the glass and think how stupid they are not to realise they're trapped. But I couldn't see anything that might be causing the noise. Jamie tells me he can't hear a thing. He looks at me as if I am losing my mind. I hear it in my sleep and now I hear it when I'm awake. All day long.

This interrupted silence accompanies me as I move from room to room.

The floorboards creak under the weight of secrets trapped there. At night, my breath is visible and the thick Indonesian heat feels like it was all a dream. Then I remind myself that it's because of our honeymoon that life has become a nightmare. Sometimes I dream about how easy it would be to tear this house apart. Take an axe or a hammer to cave in the white plaster, let the sky fall through the roof, rip the bricks from the walls with my bare, bloodied fists.

Nearly every morning I run a chilly arm across Jamie's side of the bed. He hasn't slept here for a few nights. He works late downstairs. Occasionally, I can hear the rumble of the kettle as he makes himself a late-night coffee. I see the bags under his eyes the following morning and smell the sour scent of whisky on his breath. I feel like that boiled lobster from our first date: screaming, using all the air in my lungs, knowing that no one will hear. My cries will be dismissed as hot air.

'Can you seriously not hear that dripping sound?' I ask again.

We're sitting at the kitchen table under the low light, a bland spaghetti carbonara being pushed around both of our plates.

'I think I'm going to have to call a plumber out,' I continue.

Jamie scratches his fork. 'Erin, I've looked. Every time you mention it, I look.' He chews angrily. He's come back from work in a foul mood this evening. Whenever I ask him what the matter is, he tells me it's nothing, he doesn't want to talk about it. 'I can't hear a thing.'

'What if there's a serious leak? I thought it might be coming from the boiler. I tried to check the airing cupboard but the door's locked.'

'It's not locked.' He pulls a face. 'The wood's probably just stiffened up.'

I'm about to say something when he speaks again.

'Maybe you need to go to the doctor's. Get your hearing checked, ask for some strong sleeping pills, I don't know. Do something.' He drops his cutlery with a clatter. 'Not that you ever listen to me or take my advice.'

'I do!' I protest.

But maybe he's right. I can't face this on my own; perhaps I need some chemical intervention. I can't take this insomnia. The nausea. The paranoia.

'I'll call them as soon as they open on Monday,' I reply.

Silence stretches across the table.

'Do you want to watch a film or something together tonight?' I ask hopefully. 'I hardly see you any more.'

'No. I have to work.' He doesn't bother to look at me and he scrapes his chair back. 'One of us needs to bring in an income.'

I'm stunned. He always said there wasn't any pressure for me to get a job. Why has he suddenly changed his tune? I'm about to say something but I bite my tongue. My one job was to take care of the house, and I've not even been doing that.

'Fine. I'll try harder,' I say, getting to my feet and taking the plates over to the sink.

All of a sudden, I'm caught off guard. Jamie has come up behind me and pushes me against the wall. I drop the plates with a clatter. A knife spins in the air before it falls on to the kitchen tiles.

My breath is knocked out of me. He's pressing me firmly against the wall, the cold metal radiator digging into my legs. My face is squashed to the side. One hand has leapt to my throat.

I let out a painful wheeze.

Terrifying thoughts bombard my brain. I remember how he held me by the neck when I dared to question what happened with him and Sophia in the car. How quickly his temper flared with George when he didn't give him his phone. He has so much more strength than I do. He could snap my neck if he wanted to.

The room sways.

'Don't take that tone with me.' He moves his lips close to my ear; I can smell alcohol and garlic on his hot breath.

I try to speak, tell him he's got it wrong, I wasn't being sarcastic, I was being serious, but he jolts his grip, delivering one breath-snatching squeeze against my throat.

Black blobs hover at the edges of my vision. A second or two more and then he finally releases me. I crumple to the cold floor, my trembling legs unable to hold me up any longer.

I splutter and cough. I lift a hand to my throat, feeling my racing heartbeat through my fingertips.

Jamie walks out of the room without giving me a backward glance.

42

Sophia

The flat is in complete darkness when I walk in – Mark must not be back from work yet. My thin jacket is soaked from the rain that accompanied me all the way home from the office. I shut the front door and bend down to check the doormat for post.

'I've already checked.' A voice from the lounge startles me.

'Jesus. Put a light on!' I gasp. 'You scared me.'

Mark is sitting on the sofa in the near darkness, with a bottle of beer in front of him, the label shredded in a heap on the coffee table beside it. A ghostly hue from his laptop lights up his tired face.

'You're right, it is a bit dark. I didn't realise how late it was . . .' He leans across and turns on a side lamp. 'I completely lost track of time. Er, I'd better make a start on dinner.' He gets to his feet, shutting the lid of his laptop.

'Are you OK?' I ask, giving him a kiss. His breath smells of lager. 'You look shattered.'

'Cheers. Yeah, I mean, I've not been sleeping so well since we got back, but don't worry about me. I'm fine.'

'Really? Are you feeling OK?' I press a hand against his forehead the way my mum used to do whenever I complained of being unwell.

He takes my palm away and kisses it. 'I'm not ill, I promise. Anyway, enough about me. You're back late.'

I shrug off my coat, hanging it over the radiator. 'You won't believe what I found out today.'

'Don't tell me. Some juicy gossip from the Islington parish council?' he says, as I follow him into the kitchen.

'No, actually,' I stick my tongue out. 'I've been doing some digging into the Steeles.' I purposefully ignore his eye roll. 'And guess what? It turns out that Jamie's been married before.'

'Oh?'

'They only officially divorced three months ago. Then, a fortnight after the papers came through . . .' I pause dramatically. 'His ex-wife died.'

'Shit.' He stands still. 'How did she die?'

'You won't believe it when I tell you.' Another pause. 'I don't have all the details yet but I know the police classed it as an accidental death, because . . . she fell.' I fold my arms across my chest.

'Why are you looking like that?' he asks.

'Like what?'

'Like this proves something.'

'Well, you have to admit that it looks dodgy.'

Mark gives his tired eyes a rub. 'You just said it was an accident! If it was anything more sinister then the police would be investigating.'

'Oh, come on. Jamie's first wife—'

'Ex-wife. They would have been separated for months before the divorce was formalised.'

'Fine. Jamie's *ex*-wife tragically falls to her death and then, on honeymoon with his new wife, some random man dies after falling down some steps in the exact same location where Erin and Jamie decide to take a walk.'

Mark gives me a look. 'This doesn't prove anything apart from . . .'

'From what?'

He gives his head a shake. 'Nothing.'

I tug my hair from the hair elastic and run my fingers through it. 'Go on?'

'Soph, why are you still obsessed with this?'

'I'm not exactly obsessed.'

'You know what I mean. It's just not a story that *Islington Post* readers will care about. I thought you'd have loads of other things to be working on.'

I tune out from the lecture that's about to come my way. Wondering instead if I should bring up what happened with Angie and Leroy the other night.

'Sophia?' Mark is staring at me.

'Sorry?' I blink. 'I was miles away.'

'I said I thought we'd have enchiladas for dinner – that OK?' he asks, irritation shadowing his face.

'Sure, great,' I say, watching him open the fridge and place two red peppers on a chopping board.

He takes out a sharp knife. The metal blade glints under the spotlights. I watch him effortlessly slice through the flesh, tiny white seeds leaping on to the work surface, red juice trickling out.

'Soph?'

I pull my gaze from the knife.

'I just asked you to pass me an onion.' He frowns. 'Is everything OK?'

I nod. He holds my gaze for a second before grabbing an onion himself and pulling apart the crisp outer layers.

'OK, if you're sure . . .' he says slowly. 'Do you mind sticking the TV on? The Merseyside derby is starting soon. Unless you want to carry on chatting?'

'It's fine.'

I turn on the television fixed to the wall, perfectly angled so you can watch it as you cook.

I pick at my nails. 'Mark?'

'Mmm?' He doesn't peel his eyes away from the football match. The strong scent of onion makes my eyes water.

'Why did you ask Jamie to increase our security here?'

'Because of Lou.' He puts the knife down and looks at me. 'Because I was terrified Rupert would be back to fuck up our lives again the moment he found out you were reviving this story.'

'She's ghosted me.'

'Really? Good. Sorry, that came out wrong. I mean—'

'It's fine, you don't have to pretend.'

'No, I didn't mean it like that. You know I didn't like the thought of you opening up the story again. I didn't want things to go back to how they were that week.'

'I know. Well, you don't need to worry about that now. It's over.'

The referee blows his whistle. The wild reaction from the crowd momentarily pulls Mark's attention away from me.

I take out a tin of chopped tomatoes for him.

'So, something weird happened the other night.'

'Mmm?'

'I met Angie and Leroy for a drink.'

'The Manchester couple we met in Bali?' he asks, taking the tin from me.

'Yeah. And you'll never believe what they were saying.'

'Go on.'

I fill him in on what was said.

Mark's mouth drops the more I speak. 'What? They accused me? What did you say? I hope you told them to jog on!'

'Yeah, I told them it was nonsense.'

He shakes his head with a laugh, clearly finding it more amusing than I did. 'This is just another reason why I can't stand those true crime shows you watch. Everyone thinks they're armchair detectives!' He rolls his eyes.

'Sorry, love. I don't even know why I brought it up.'

'It's fine.' He turns and gives me a kiss on the lips. 'Anyway, as you said, it sounds as if we should all be more concerned with Leroy and his night-time storm-chasing – photographic evidence or not.'

'Yeah. He's definitely going on my suspect list.'

'You have a suspect list?' He groans. 'I was only joking.'

I nudge him. 'Course. Peter wants me to get to the bottom of what happened to George Kingsley, so I have to work out who has the best possible motive.'

'Hmm. I get it, but . . .' he pauses '. . . what if you're looking for things that don't exist? I'm not sure getting so obsessed with this story is doing you any good.'

225

As much as I hate to admit this, he's right. I've let this story take over my life. It's all I think about, all I want to talk about. Yet, despite this, things still don't add up.

Maybe that's for the police to figure out, not me – a washed-up hack thousands of miles away. The fact that both Claire Steele and George Kingsley died after a fall could be nothing but a weird coincidence.

43

Erin

Monday 26 September

Jamie has agreed to drop me off at the doctor's surgery. My car is in the garage as it needs a service. I didn't think it was due already, but I'm grateful one of us is on top of things like this. He's told me it's no problem ferrying me around but his body language says otherwise: the rough way he closed the driver's door, the tug of the gears, the loud music set to a rock station I didn't even know he liked to listen to.

He's agitated.

I can't ask him what's wrong. After what happened in the kitchen the other day, I feel as though I'm treading on eggshells around him. He's apologised profusely, bringing me breakfast in bed and telling me he's going to look online for ways he can manage his temper when he's had a drink.

I didn't know what to say, apart from making sure he knows that I will walk if he ever does that to me again.

I'm not sure he believes me.

I'm not sure if I believe myself.

'I can get a taxi back if it's easier?' I suggest.

'It's fine, sorry. I've just got lots on my mind, babe. Work stuff. But please don't worry.' He leans across the gearstick and presses his lips firmly on my forehead. 'I'll pick you up here when you're done.'

I make sure to keep my arms tucked in tightly in the doctor's waiting room so as not to touch anything. Trying not to think of the millions of germs trapped in this room, carried across the stuffy air going round and round, in and out of the mouths and nostrils of the sick people who have sat here before me.

I feel as though I'm behind a wall of glass, trapped in a bubble, separate from everything going on. There's so much light and noise and chatter around me that it makes my head spin.

Out of habit, I pull out my phone to scan the news, but I can barely see the screen. The crack that happened after the night Sophia visited has spread. I wonder what she's up to right now? I think about her a lot and, every time I do, a flame-like anger bubbles inside me. She tried it on with my husband. I thought we were friends! How low can you get?

My phone chimes in my hands. I can't see who the WhatsApp message is from, as a dark splodge covers the name, but it doesn't take me long to work it out.

All ready for bubba. Not long to go now! ❤

Kat's attached a before-and-after photo of her spare room. What was once a dumping ground has now been transformed into a nursery. All feather white and marshmallow pink. A sturdy wooden crib lies under a string of fluffy clouds dangling from the ceiling. A row of picture board books – all in neutral shades – and a collection of pastel-pink teddies sit on the windowsill, keeping watch.

Seeing this makes me feel terrible for not being involved more. I've been such a crap best friend. What happened in Bali has consumed me. Kat's life is about to change very soon and I should be by her side. I'll call her later and arrange to go round with another gift, apologise for being so absent when she needs me the most.

Perhaps it's been a subconscious thing, a way to protect myself after the miscarriage in Girona. I had hoped to start trying for a family on honeymoon. I think back to when Jamie almost crashed the car in the woods after the Plaza and we failed to make love because my mind was playing tricks on me. I have to work on getting over this mental block if I'm to have a healthy love life with my husband once again. Hopefully it's a temporary blip. Once Jamie's less tied up with work and more time has passed since the fatal night on the honeymoon, then I'm sure we will get back on track in all areas of our marriage, especially the bedroom.

'Mrs Steele?'

It takes me a second to wonder why my mother-in-law's name is being called in the doctor's surgery, then I realise they're waiting for me.

'How can I help you today?' the doctor asks once we're in the consulting room. She has a kind face and straight black hair that glistens like poured oil.

I start to speak, but one glance at her expectant smile and I begin to cry.

'Are you OK, Mrs Steele?'

I shake my head.

'OK, just take your time, then you can tell me what's wrong.' She passes me a tissue from a box on her cluttered desk.

I realise something as I try to control my erratic breathing. Isn't everything you say here confidential? Doesn't she have a duty of care to keep whatever I tell her between us and these four walls?

I need someone to talk to. It's killing me holding the weight of our secret on my shoulders. Jamie never wants to talk about the honeymoon; each time I start to bring it up he tells me that I should try not to think about it, as if I'm able to forget it. How the hell could I forget it?

'Is there something that's making you feel sad?' she asks gently.

I nod. If I can just get my breath back, then I can tell her what's happened. Everything. From the beginning. She seems so nice and kind; her neat, polished nails remind me of Sophia. This could be my confessional.

'OK, and how long have you felt this way?'

'Since returning from our honeymoon,' I sniff, folding and unfolding the soft tissue into neat triangles. The calming, pale green walls, the well-cared-for pot plant on a shelf, a calendar with images of scampering kittens tacked near the window, the blinds angled for privacy. This is a safe space.

'Has anything happened to make you feel down?' she asks.

I watched a man fall to his death and I'm terrified I'm going to be caught and punished. But it wasn't my fault. My husband told us to flee. He panicked. It was the wrong decision and, with every day that passes and we don't speak up, the

230

harder it becomes to explain our innocence. Not that I have anyone I can talk to, since I've pushed away my best friend in the whole world. I'm lonely. I'm trapped in the house that was supposed to be my dream home. My marriage feels as though it's teetering on a knife edge. None of it was supposed to turn out this way.

I take a breath. It's trapped between my ribs, holding me back from admitting the truth.

'Something happened on the last night we were away and . . . now I can't sleep, I feel sick all the time, I'm constantly exhausted and my heart is like it's always racing . . .'

I need to find the right words. I can't just blurt it out or she won't understand. There is, of course, the risk that I've got this totally wrong. Is it one hundred per cent confidential? I need to be clever but my brain is too tired.

I'm about to confess when she speaks first.

'When was your last period, Mrs Steele?'

'Er . . .' I have no idea. I try to cast my mind back. It must be before the wedding. She can see me trying to do the mental maths.

'I know you say you've just got back from your honeymoon . . .' She pauses. 'Have you had unprotected sex recently? Is there a chance you might be pregnant?'

I shoot my head up. Laughter bubbling up inside me. She thinks I'm hysterical because I'm pregnant!

'Well, I mean, we didn't use condoms at all when we were away . . .'

I think of the terrible sleep. The anxiety. The feeling of going insane. Are these all symptoms? My heart beats like a fist against a locked door.

'Perhaps you should take a pregnancy test?' she suggests.

I tune out what she has to say next. I would give anything in the world to become a mother, to feel something growing inside me. I suddenly don't care that I can't sleep, that I'm going mad. A baby will fix everything. Jamie will never hurt me again. She carries on talking but I find it hard to concentrate on what she's saying. My head is spinning.

'Sorry?' I ask.

'I said, would you like me to arrange for you to do a urine sample?'

There are some clear plastic pots wrapped in sterile paper beside her desk. The disabled loo in the doctor's surgery is hardly the nicest setting for such life-changing news but there's no way I can wait.

'Yes,' I say, without a beat of hesitation.

44

Sophia

Monday 26 September

I take a deep breath and rap my knuckles against the uPVC door, crossing my fingers that someone is in.

And that they are willing to talk to me.

I lied and told Claudia I had a dentist's appointment this morning. I know Mark made it clear that he's worried about me digging into what happened to George, but I can't help myself. It's an itch I have to scratch, and I really hope that coming here will shed some light on things.

Before I left, I sent yet another email and left another voice-mail chasing George's autopsy. I desperately need clarification on exactly what his cause of death is being classed as, and what these suspicious marks on his body are.

I glance over my shoulder, unable to shake this sense of being watched. It's ridiculous. There is literally no one else around on this quiet residential street full of squat bungalows and neat patches of front lawn.

I hover on the doorstep. There's no reply so I try again, pressing my finger against the doorbell; it lets out a tight trill.

My hand is lifted in the air, poised to knock once more, when I hear a woman on the other side of the glass telling me she's coming.

There's the scratch of keys as the door's opened. Standing on the other side is Marie Connelly, Claire's mother. After reading the interview Claire's parents did with the local press, I had logged into iSearch to find their address.

'Yes? Can I help you?' she asks, with a thin, reedy voice.

Thick, coarse grey hair falls from her crown to her ears; the rest hangs limply in mousy brown down to her shoulders. She's wearing a thick jumper with embroidered flowers trailing over one shoulder. It looks as if she's been crying. For a brief moment I wobble; perhaps I should apologise for disturbing her and leave. Put this story to bed and move on.

I swallow and fix on a bright smile. Sophia Spencer doesn't give up.

'Yes, hello. It's Marie Connelly, isn't it? My name is Sophia,' I say softly. 'I'm a journalist for the *Sunday News*. I appreciate you've been through a very difficult few months but I wondered if you could spare some time to talk to me about Claire?'

There's every likelihood she'll slam the door in my face, I've had it happen enough times and been called enough names under the sun on door-knocks like this. I had debated about going in with a different tack, acting as if I personally knew Claire – we're about the same age, after all – but I decided not to. The only reason I have to hope that Marie's not going to turn me away is that, since she spoke to the press once before, she might be willing to do it again.

Marie lifts a hand to her bare lips. 'You want to talk about my Claire?'

I nod and show her my ID.

There's a moment of hesitation before the door is held open for me. 'Come on in.'

The heat hits me as I walk in, the orange imitation logs on the gas fire glowing inside the ornate marble-effect fireplace. Marie tells me to sit down and asks if I'd like a tea, wringing her hands together as if she's apologising for something.

As she bustles about in the small kitchen leading off from the dated lounge, I pad across the pistachio-green carpet that has Hoover marks running across it, to take a closer look at the shrine in the corner of the room. Every inch of space beside the flat-screen TV is filled with Claire's face. I'm looking at Erin's double. The same warm smile, plump cheeks, similar dress sense. It's unnerving.

Framed photos run up the wall next to the patio doors, which look out on to a small patch of lawn and an empty rotary washing line. They range from gap-toothed childhood grins to self-conscious smiles on her graduation day and stern-faced passport photos, that have been collaged together in a simple clip frame. A life before my eyes.

Then I see a face I recognise.

Jamie standing tall in a traditional wedding suit with a swirly-patterned waistcoat, his dark hair gelled over to one side, barely any grey, and smooth, close-shaven cheeks. Beside him his blushing bride, Claire, wearing a strapless princess dress and a veil that glistens with tiny diamanté teardrops that appear to fall mid-air. They couldn't look happier.

'Cake?' Marie asks, carefully setting down a tray holding a teapot, two china cups on saucers and slices of Victoria sponge on matching side plates, complete with shiny cake forks and serviettes folded into sharp triangles.

I steer my eyes away from the photographs and shrug off my jacket. 'Erm, sure. Thank you.'

'I only made it yesterday, so it's still fresh. I like to bake on Sundays, you see. I need to fill the time somehow. Weekends are ever so long.'

She wears her grief as heavy as her patterned sweater.

'So, you want to hear some more about my lovely Claire?' Her watery eyes blink as she pours out the steaming tea. 'So many people don't even want to say her name around me any more. They worry I can't handle it, so they change the subject, thinking it's easier.' She sniffs. 'It might be, for them.'

'I imagine people don't know what to say.'

'Saying something is better than saying nothing. They act like she never existed – let me tell you how hard that is.' Her voice is soft but there's a fierceness to it.

'Was she your only child?' I sit on the large cream leather sofa opposite her, moving a bundle of knitting to one side.

Marie nods. 'Sugar?'

'No, thank you.'

I take the cup, wincing at how sore her nails look. All of them bitten down to the quick. On her wrist is an Apple watch with a pale baby-pink strap. The screen is covered in cracks, like spider's legs spreading across the glass. She notices me looking.

'This was Claire's. It doesn't work of course but it helps me to feel a little closer to her.' She sniffs slowly. 'Sorry, back to what you were asking. Yes. Our Claire was a miracle. Richard and I had been told a baby wasn't meant to be, but then one day, out of the blue, I felt a bit off so the doctors did a test. Well, you could have knocked me over with a feather when it came back positive. I mean, I was forty-one. This might not sound like much now, but back then I certainly was the grandma at the school gates. I didn't care, though. People could talk all they wanted. We were thrilled to finally have the missing piece of the puzzle in our lives.'

My heart pulls in my chest.

'Have you got children?'

I shake my head.

'I wished she and Jamie – that's my son-in-law – had sped things up a bit, but maybe it was for the best. They ended up getting divorced.' She mouths this last word. 'Of course, a nice chap like that, it was never going to be long until someone else snapped him up.'

'Oh?'

'He recently got married again. We have to say it was a bit of a shock for us. By all accounts it was a whirlwind.'

'That must have been tough for you,' I say.

'I just hope he's happy, that's all. He's such a wonderful chap. Ever so kind. Would do anything for anyone.'

There's an order of service from Claire's funeral on the mantelpiece; she died on the fourth of July. Jamie and Erin got married on the third of September, the same date as us. He'd barely had time to deal with the loss of his ex-wife before he was saying 'I do' to a new one.

I use the delicate cake fork to break off a small piece of sponge. 'This is delicious, by the way.'

Marie smiles and pats down her trousers. 'Thank you.'

I swallow. 'I hope you don't find this an upsetting question, but can you tell me what happened to Claire?'

This is what I'm desperate to find out. As if she's reading my mind, I feel the bright eyes of the happy-go-lucky girl bear down upon me. I stutter slightly under her gaze.

'I-I read that Claire had an accidental fall—'

'Well, that depends who you talk to.'

This throws me. 'Oh . . . I thought the police were treating it as an accidental death?'

'Of course they are. Less paperwork that way.' She draws herself up. 'It may have been an accident, but that doesn't mean someone's not responsible.'

I frown. A shiver runs through me at the look on Marie's face. 'Sorry?'

'Claire was having such a run of bad luck. I know the strain of the marriage breaking up wasn't easy, no matter how brave a face she wore or how often she told us it was amicable.' Marie sniffs. 'She was made redundant, too, right at the same time. But it was losing Pepper . . . that's the name of her cat. Was. He died. It was all terribly ghastly: run over. That was the straw that broke the camel's back, as it were. I have my suspicions about who did it, too.'

I raise my eyebrows.

'I can't be one hundred per cent sure, of course. Richard, my husband, tells me off for hypothesising. But when you're retired, you have a lot more time to think. It's not always help-ful, I suppose. But someone was responsible for her downfall. She was driven to take those pills – antidepressants – and she mixed them with alcohol in order to block out all the tough things going on in her life. I wish she'd told us she was struggling so much. We could have helped.' Marie pulls out a tissue tucked inside her sleeve to wipe her nose. 'We'll never forgive them.'

'Sorry?'

'The person who did this to Claire, the one who killed her beloved Pepper. They have blood on their hands.'

A shot of adrenaline fires up inside of me. 'What do you mean? Who did this?'

Her mouth is set in a steely line. 'Claire's stalker.'

45

Erin

Every pregnancy test is positive.

A lot of things start to make sense – the headaches, dizziness, mood swings, fatigue – even my heart has been beating faster thanks to the extra hormones and sudden increase in the volume of blood circulating around my body. Not to mention my heightened senses – that would explain the dripping in the house – why I can hear it but not Jamie. It's all because I'm pregnant.

Despite being in a total daze, I decide I'm going to wait to break this life-changing news. I can't just blurt it out. I want it to be special. This is about us turning a corner, a fresh start. I know that he wants a baby just as much as I do. It will bind us together. We will be a proper little family.

'Sorry I'm late,' I say as I get into Jamie's car.

'Everything OK?' he asks, quickly putting his phone away.

I press my lips together and simply nod.

'What did the doctor say?'

'She just gave me some pills to help with my anxiety. I need to pick up the prescription in a few days' time,' I lie. It rolls off my tongue effortlessly.

He runs the steering wheel through his hands. I wish he would hold on to it properly in the ten-to-two position – we've got precious cargo on board now. For the first time in a long time there's a fire inside me and I can't help but smile.

The entire way home I stare out of the window, planning how to tell Jamie our news. It needs to be special. I'll cook a nice dinner, get dressed up. Oh, no, maybe we can go out! For the first time I think I can breathe again. Jamie must be right – we'd know if they had anything on us by now.

Back home, I stand in front of the kettle and ask him if he wants a tea or coffee, amazed at how I'm able to act so normal in front of him when all I can think is *I'm pregnant, I'm pregnant, I'm pregnant.*

When he doesn't reply, I ask him again.

He snaps his neck up from his phone screen. 'Huh? No, nothing. I need to go.'

'What? Now?' I try to bite down the disappointment.

He's distracted, fingers flying across his screen. 'Something's come up. In fact, I need to go away for a few days,' he says, before hurrying up the stairs.

'What? What do you mean, you need to go away?'

The exposed wood groans under my feet as I follow him. I've asked him before about checking the top step. He says it's fine, but to me it feels as if it's gone spongy, as though it's rotting under my bare feet. It's different from the other steps. I won't nag him about it now, though. Not today. Nothing can ruin today.

'Jamie?' I try again.

He's rifling through the chest of drawers, pulling out items of clothing. Boxers, jumpers, two pairs of jeans, a couple of polo shirts, three crumpled smart shirts. He mutters under

241

his breath that he hopes this place has an iron he can borrow, grumbling that it hasn't been done before. His tie is askew and there are sweat patches under each armpit.

The idyllic pregnancy announcement that I had in mind suddenly dissolves before my eyes.

'Jamie! What's going on?'

He huffs. 'There's a work conference in London. Someone messed up with adding my name to the list of attendees so now it's all last-minute.'

I don't believe him.

'Jamie . . .' I try again, my voice a little stronger despite the growing panic that he's hiding something, something big, something that I need to be aware of, as his wife. As the mother of his child. 'Is this linked to what the police wanted?'

He doesn't answer me.

'Jamie!' I snap. Or rather, scream. I don't realise how loud I am until he literally jumps and throws a hand to his chest.

'Erin!' His eyes meet mine. 'Don't do that!'

'I need to know where you're going. For how long? Can I come with you?' The questions tumble out.

He gives a slight shake of his head and comes to sit next to me, abandoning the messy pile of clothes strewn inside the overnight case. He glances at his watch as if this is going to take up time he doesn't have.

'It's a work thing, babe. I have to be away for four nights. It's at a hotel in Fulham. I'll leave you the address and phone number. You'll be more than fine here.'

The thought of spending four nights here, alone, feels like I'm being punished for something.

'Is this because of the police?' I ask again. 'That complaint?'

A look flashes across his face before he quickly shakes his head. 'No, that's all sorted now.' He pulls me closer and presses a kiss on to my skin. 'I told you I'd make it go away, and I have.'

46

Sophia

I can't ask Marie anything else, as the door to the lounge is suddenly flung open. A tall man with a full head of dark grey hair and rimless glasses, pushed right up against the bridge of his large nose, strides in. He holds out a veiny hand for me to shake. The grip is firm, but I'm most taken aback by how cool it is in this sauna of a house.

'This is Richard, Claire's dad,' Marie explains.

'Sorry, I was just upstairs on a call. I would have come down sooner if I'd known we had guests,' Richard says, giving his wife a look I can't quite read.

'This is Sophie. She's a journalist who wanted to talk about Claire.' Marie's eyes flick to the shrine as if Claire were standing there herself. I don't correct her for getting my name wrong.

Richard pulls himself taller. 'Hmm. Well, thanks for popping round, but if you don't mind, we've got that thing that we're running late for.' He is polite but firm. 'Don't we, darling?'

Marie looks blank for a second. 'Oh, yes, so sorry. It completely slipped my mind.' She lets out a flutter of laughter and wrings her hands together.

'I'll show you out, Sophie,' Richard says, opening the door to the wide hallway.

'Hang on! Let me get this wrapped up for you.' Marie takes my plate with the unfinished cake. She dashes off to the kitchen before I can say another word.

Richard shakes his head slightly once she's gone. 'Sorry, she's a little all over the place. She's still not come to terms with what happened.'

'Please don't apologise. I can't imagine what you've both been through.' I pause. 'Marie was telling me about Claire's stalker and I was wondering what you—'

'Claire didn't have a stalker,' he interrupts me. 'Not in the traditional sense of the word. I wish Marie wouldn't throw that term around.' He tenses his jaw. 'It was just someone who was getting a little too friendly on Claire's social media, that sort of thing. She only mentioned it in passing the last time we saw her. Even she thought it was no big deal.'

'Do you know who it was, this person?'

'No. She had a lot of . . . what do you call them? Followers. So it could have been anyone.'

'Did the police not look into it?'

'Of course we mentioned it, but the officers didn't seem the least bit concerned, and their reaction just backed up my opinion. There's nothing *to* look into. It was just a tragic accident.' Richard clears his throat. 'She was a complicated girl, our Claire. Life had a habit of getting on top of her at times.'

'But Marie said—'

'Marie is still processing everything. We all are. But trying to put the blame elsewhere isn't going to bring our Claire back.' His voice trembles as he finishes this sentence.

'Here you go!' Marie returns, handing me a cling-film-wrapped slice of cake. 'I'll only eat it otherwise,' she says, patting her stomach.

I wonder how often she used to send her own daughter off with a packed lunch. The same thought has clearly entered her mind, because she swallows, and busies herself with running a finger across the pristine hall window. 'Gosh, I need to polish in here.'

I see Richard pulling himself a little taller beside her. 'We really must be getting on now.'

'Yes, sorry, and thanks again for your time, and for the cake,' I say.

Richard walks to the front door and undoes the clasp. There is a trilling sound that I hadn't noticed when Marie invited me in.

'That's our house alarm,' Richard says with a groan as I look around to see where the sound came from. 'It shouldn't make that noise but it's acting up,' he explains. 'It was emitting the most godawful beep, so I pressed a couple of buttons but I think I've made it worse. It's a bit of an eyesore if you ask me.' He raises his tufty grey eyebrows. 'But you can never be too careful.'

I glance up just before I leave. A security camera is angled across the front door. It's slightly different from the one Mark installed in our flat – grey with sharp edges, like a beak of a bird, its flicking eye preparing to swoop down on its prey.

I feel a funny bolt of adrenaline as I realise why the logo looks so familiar. I've seen this before.

'Well, take care now,' Richard says, ushering me out.

The door is shut firmly behind me.

47

Sophia

Tuesday 27 September

The early-morning light is desperately trying to fight its way through the grey sky. My breath clouds as I pick up my pace, limbs creaking in resistance. My body is still in shock at being thrust from my warm bed and out into the slap of cold air. But I needed to get out of the house. My head is too full.

Peter's emailed asking for an update on the "Honeymoon Killers" story. What am I going to do? How do I tell him I've got nothing concrete to give him? There's still no word on George's translated autopsy, despite chasing for it. As it stands, for all my efforts at digging into the Steeles, there isn't anything rock solid that we could print, without being sued for libel. And I'm still trying to process what I learned from visiting Claire's parents. I pulled Amira into an empty meeting room as soon as I got into the office yesterday and told her where I'd been. She's certain this stinks of a cover-up.

Another message pinged as I pulled on my running jacket. It was a short apology from Lou for not turning up when we agreed, followed by a clear statement that she is retracting her offer of an interview but wishes me well.

I re-read her message. Usually, when I'm told no, it only makes me more determined to turn it into a yes. But, in fact, the initial excitement that I could try and get her to talk in the first place has dampened. If Mark is right, and Rupert knows she's considering speaking to me, then who can say what lengths he will go to shut her up? Perhaps, for her safety and ours, I should do what Peter and Mark say and leave this story well alone.

I need some time and space to make sense of it all. To make matters worse, I feel as though I can't speak to Mark about any of it – he's made his opinion very clear.

Usually a run helps me to clear my head, but this morning's jog isn't going to plan. With a teeth-clenching amount of effort, I manage to get into a sort of rhythm with my feet hitting the concrete and my brain not screaming at me to stop. I turn up the volume on my headphones playing my running playlist.

A pigeon shoots out from a bush and I swear, my heart pounding in my tight chest.

Suddenly, a piercing shock of pain zips through my abdomen. I wince at the stitch that's taken over, cursing myself for not having warmed up properly. I press both hands hard against my waist and am forced to drop back into a slow shuffle of a walk. I tap my watch, ending the fitness tracker, seeing what time it is. At this pace, I need to get back and get ready for work anyway.

There's a shortcut through an alleyway that I'd never take at night but in the mornings it's fine. But, as I turn down it, a funny sort of prickle washes over my arms as the sky darkens. The alternative is to loop round the long way, but I can't risk being late for work; I'm already on Claudia's radar as it is. I remind myself I'm not in the Bronx. Still, I take my headphones out of my ears.

Up ahead is a man walking his dog. There's something about him that unnerves me. It's the way he's struggling to hold on to the animal. A large, short-haired breed. I thought it was a Doberman at first but the all-over copper-brown colour doesn't match up. It's got the same sort of stance, though. A Vizsla. A hunting dog.

I can see the muscles straining in its chest, pulling at the fabric lead that's stretched so tight it could snap at any minute, the only thing stopping it from tearing free to launch itself at me. I try not to think how its razor-sharp jaws would have no problem biting down to the bone. This isn't a pet dog; this is one of those Terminator-style hybrid breeds, created to kill. The same sort of dogs that Rupert used that night.

A shiver runs down my spine at the sudden memory. I picture these Vizslas trailing obediently alongside him, much more intimidating than the traditional beagle used on hunts. I later learned that that was the plan.

Goosebumps spread across my arms at the sudden wind that's picked up. Dark clouds loom overhead.

Something inside me is warning me to get past this man and his dog, stitch or no stitch, as fast as possible. Call it a sixth sense. There's something seriously off about him.

I speed up. There's a sudden dart of pain in my side. We're now in the tightest part of the alleyway. Where is everyone else? I press myself towards the ivy-covered fence panels that line the side, enclosing us. I need to make myself as small as possible.

I hold my breath, as if that's going to do anything. The closer I get, the more I wish I'd turned the other way, but it's too late to suddenly spin around now. His footsteps are heavy, dragging on the gravel, tugged forward by this muscular dog.

Then, suddenly, the man does something no Londoner does. He makes eye contact. His age is hard to tell, but it's the crude tattoo of a falling tear beside his right eye that makes my insides grow cold. I see how white his knuckles have turned from the taut strap of the blood-red lead clenched in his fist.

'He's just a bit excited. Only a puppy,' the man says gruffly.

A puppy! Bullshit. That dog is fully grown and deadly. The thin tail is rigid; coppery hairs bristle along his back and the eyes are fixed in a hostile stare. A low growl escapes. His sharp teeth exposed.

I force a tight smile and nod as I keep moving forward. A heady rush of marijuana fills my nostrils as we pass each other. I want to drop back to a walk and make the pain in my side go away, but I need to put more distance between us.

There is the noisy wheeze of a train rattling out from the station, so I don't hear him at first.

''Scuse me, love.'

The man is trying to get my attention. I look back at the path in case I've dropped something that he's trying to hand over. But the ground is empty.

'Yes?'

For a split second I pray he's going to ask me the time or for some directions. Something innocent.

How naïve can I be?

'You're Sophia Spencer, right?'

I freeze at the menacing look he has on his face. His top lip curls into a snarl.

'Keep out of business that don't concern you. You hear me?'

His dog begins to bark, the sudden sound like a machine-gun fire. The rapid noise makes me almost leap in the air in fear. The man lets out a heavy smoker's laugh.

I can't speak. I stumble slightly then start to run as fast as I can, despite the white-hot pain of the stitch in my side. His booming laughter and the dog's erratic barking ring in my ears. Black spots appear in my vision but I don't stop.

I'm still panting with fear when I reach our front door.

48

Sophia

It takes me three attempts to get my keys into the lock. I sink to the floor in the hall, legs like jelly and chest burning. It can't be happening again.

The same dogs, the same menacing look, the same intimidation: Rupert's gang is back.

It all started with a phone call. A tip-off that brutal fox-hunting activities were carrying on under the cover of 'trail hunting', a dubious but legal practice, and that a prominent Tory aide had been spotted attending these clandestine pre-hunt meet-ups. Peter chose me to go undercover to see if this story had any truth.

Being chosen to lead this scoop was a real vote of confidence from my news editor at a time when there was talk of promotion. I was determined to do a decent job. It took time and patience but eventually I managed to convince Rupert, the leader of this sub-group, to meet. He believed my name was Grace Stephenson, a thirty-something huntswoman who had recently moved to the area – as passionate about the sport as he was. This lie was just the beginning. I never expected things to get out of hand the way they did.

When I had the details of the next meeting, I set up hidden cameras in a snug at the back of a country pub. I stood in the chilly car park trying to blend in, making polite conversation, hoping to spot the celebrity guest, my dictaphone recording it all in my pocket.

'Are we not going in?' I asked, blowing on my fingertips.

'We'll go and get warmed up soon.' Rupert nodded. 'We have some unfinished business first.'

It was the look in his eyes. I should have known then that it was about to escalate.

We never did make it to the snug.

'Carry this.' He dumped a heavy backpack on me and strode off, whistling for the dogs to follow.

That was when I caught sight of the politician standing on the sidelines, joking with two burly-looking men. I quickly tried to angle my phone to film him but just seconds later Rupert was by my side again yelling that we needed to get a move on. He instructed everyone to 'mask up'.

With scarves pulled over their mouths, hoods over their faces, the pack of ten or so men and a handful of women moved down a country lane away from the pub. The mood changed, voices trailing out as the group stopped outside tall wooden gates. I gripped my phone in my pocket and, as subtly as I could, opened the camera, standing back from the group slightly, the Tory politician in my line of sight.

Lou was there, of course. She was the whistle-blower who had tipped us off. I'd worked hard to encourage her to become my mentor, show me the ropes, let me into a world I knew she secretly wanted to get out of, but there was something different about her that night.

I know now that she was petrified.

'Grace?' It took me a second to respond. I looked up to see Rupert watching me quizzically. 'Open your backpack.'

The moment I unzipped it, the diesel fumes were overwhelming. All eyes were on me. I tried to hide my phone as best I could, as I reluctantly followed instructions. Petrol from everyone's bags was poured on to a dark car parked beside the gates. It happened so quickly. A snaking trail of gasoline was lit. Someone screamed at everyone to 'leg it!'

I was halfway down the lane as the car, and then a nearby outbuilding, exploded into flames.

It terrified me how insane these people were. Thankfully no one was injured, but that was when I realised the lengths they'd go to to get the message out that they were the ones in control.

The car belonged to a vocal animal rights activist who had been speaking up about trail hunting. I couldn't shake off the fact that they'd torched this guy's property because he had different beliefs. What were they going to do to me? I had evidence on their next planned attacks after they'd openly joked about who else was on their 'hit list'. I'd infiltrated the clan, seen who was part of the set-up and, no matter how cool I tried to play it, deep down I was afraid of getting caught out.

We planned to run the story on the front page of the following Sunday paper, exposing the politician for his dealings with this murky underworld, followed by opinion pieces and an in-depth interview with the activist who 'feared for his life'. The lawyers warned that I was expected to meet their rigorous standards, which made me nervous – I knew they would go in with a fine-tooth comb – but Peter told me that he'd make sure we got this over the line. He promised me he had my back.

Then came the week from hell.

Somehow Rupert and the hunters, including the politician, discovered who I was and what the *Sunday News* were planning to expose. For six days, the death threats, the trolling, the online abuse was another level. I didn't care. I held my nerve. I knew this story had to come out. I wouldn't let these people intimidate me – this was the piece of my career.

It was when they discovered my address that everything changed. The warning gifts on our doorstep, the dark handwritten notes, the reason Mark invested in surveillance.

I thought things couldn't get much worse, then the red wine was spilt all over my work laptop. I'd already sent Peter the voice recordings of them planning the stunt, but I'd purposely held back the video footage so I could edit myself out of the events before it was uploaded to the newspaper's website. However, with the laptop beyond repair, I couldn't prove what really happened that night.

I had no idea just how influential this Tory aide was, nor that he had the top brass of the newspaper in his back pocket. He insisted I had no proof and was subjecting him to harassment. The editor fell for his lies.

There were soon contrasting reports of an out-of-date boiler in the activist's property, a temperamental petrol leak and faulty electrics in the car outside, all given as evidence by Rupert's expensive, bloodthirsty lawyers. The *News*'s legal team were threatened with every libel act under the sun to spike the story. For good.

The following Sunday I read the paper and shivered in my dressing gown. Peter had lost his nerve. There was no story, just some crap about a reality TV star coming out. One of the staffers must have worked overnight to fill the gap I'd left. I knew that was it. My time at the paper was over, and my career with it. Peter had to let me go.

I was unceremoniously handed my P45. Thankfully, this was enough to make the death threats stop. The police car was taken away and the trolling eased off. Despite losing my job, I breathed a sigh of relief that I no longer had to fear for my life. But Mark was still on edge. Only once he'd checked every window and door was locked, the CCTV footage picked over and a rigorous wind-down routine complete – only then did he let himself fall asleep.

And now it's happening all over again.

I deadbolt the front door and keep the lights off until my breathing returns to normal. The cold sweat I'd broken out in makes me shiver.

I keep pacing around, unsure where to put myself. A wave of exhaustion wraps itself around me like a thick winter duvet. I could lie down and sleep for years, but I refuse to allow myself a moment of rest. I call Mark's work phone – he'll panic about what happened on my run but I desperately want to hear his voice. He doesn't answer and I don't leave a message. Perhaps it's for the best; I doubt I could even string a sentence together.

My head is spinning. Why would Rupert come back now? I haven't written a word on that story since it got spiked. Lou lost her nerve about meeting me, and it's not as though I've pursued it or chased her to change her mind. My legs tingle.

As I pace, I pull out my phone. It takes me three attempts for my trembling fingers to log into our security system. A breath of relief passes my lips when it's clear that no one has followed me home.

After a while it becomes hypnotic, watching the comings and goings of our street, seeing life outside our front door without looking out of a window. My heart starts to slow and the dizziness subsides. The sound of a heavy lorry trundling down the road suddenly jolts me back to reality. The windows rattle as the load moves past.

I need to call Claudia and see if she'll let me work from home today. I feel too shaky to face anyone right now.

I log out. Rupert won't do anything else to harm me. I've dropped the Lou story. The man and his dog were clearly a final warning, one that I've taken loud and clear. I'll delete her details. That will be the end of it all.

49

Sophia

I'm peering into the high corners of the alcove above our doorstep, flinching every time my hands touch cobweb threads. I'm still shaken up by what happened on my run this morning, jumping every time I hear a dog bark.

'Soph? Are you all right?' Mark asks, walking towards me down our path.

The dining room chair I'm standing on wobbles precariously. 'Jesus! You made me jump! What are you doing here?'

'I thought I'd pop back for some lunch as I was seeing a client nearby.' He scratches his head, staring at me. 'What are you doing? Why are you not in the office?'

'I'm working from home. Well, I was, but then I took a break.'

'And you decided to spend it examining our security camera?'

I stick my tongue out in concentration and lift up on to my tiptoes. The chair wobbles once more.

'Careful!' he calls, shooting an arm out to catch me and holding the chair legs to the tiled floor.

I lean on him as I climb down, brushing dust off my jumper, itchy from the dead flies and cobwebs I accidentally stuck my hand in.

'We really should dust up there,' I say, dragging the chair back into the house.

Mark is staring at me as if I've lost the plot. 'You going to explain what's going on, or shall I call the men in white coats?'

'There's something I can't put my finger on. For some reason it feels as if it's staring me in the face.'

'Sorry? You're literally not making any sense,' Mark says, following me into the house.

A deep sigh escapes as I slump on to the sofa. Just then a thought hits me. 'How did Jamie know you liked D.R.U.M.?'

'What? Er, I dunno. Lucky guess? Why?'

'Have you ever posted online or on your Instagram that you like their music?'

'Doubt it. That's not really my style.' He pauses. 'Are you going to tell me where this is leading to?'

I ignore the question. We have a framed D.R.U.M. band poster in our bedroom. I'm not super-keen on their music but I love the bold Warholesque colours of the print, so we decided to hang it over our bed. Of course, Jamie would never know this.

'How did it come about, you going to the gig together? I don't think you told me.'

'I thought I did. We just bumped into each other. I'd finished with a client and he was doing routine checks on security cameras in the same building. Mad, really. We got chatting and he asked if I knew anyone who would want to see the band. I was like, er, me! He wouldn't take a penny for it, either. The tickets must have cost a bomb.'

A flutter of anxiety rises in my stomach.

'You don't think that's weird? The coincidence of it all?' I'm about to explain, then stop. 'Does anyone else have access to our cameras?'

He shakes his head. 'No, only we have the log-ins.'

'But could they be hacked?'

'I guess anything that runs online could be hacked, but the system Jamie upgraded us to is like ridiculously secure – it's the type of security that commercial businesses use. Why? You think we've been hacked?' He immediately gets out his phone and taps open the smart alarm app.

'I think he's watching us. All of us,' I say, quietly.

'What? Who?'

'Jamie.'

This niggle in the back of my mind started to grow when I came back from seeing Richard and Marie. They have the same security system as us. Installed by the same company: Steele Security Solutions. Jamie's company. I think of the app he let Mark have access to for free. At the touch of a button, he could be seeing everything in our lives.

'I think we need to unplug the cameras. Something has been bothering me since visiting Claire's parents and I think—'

Mark reels backwards. 'What? You went to see Jamie's ex-wife's parents? Jesus, Sophia.'

'Their daughter fell to her death and everyone seems to think it was an accident, but something tells me Jamie had a bigger part to play.' My words tumble out. 'They said she had a stalker but nothing was ever formally reported. There has to be evidence of that somewhere.'

The only problem is how to prove any of it.

'Sophia.' His tone is a warning. 'We're not getting rid of the cameras.'

'Listen.' I bite down the irritation that he's not taking me at my word. He's become reliant on this security system and my suggesting taking his comfort blanket away is making him nervous. 'Jamie installed a similar system at Claire's parents' house. He also installed the CCTV at Claire's flat, the place where she died. Jamie's clearly been watching us, maybe even listening in. But the only place where there aren't any cameras or alarms is his own home . . . Don't you think that's odd?'

'How do you know they haven't got any?'

'I don't remember seeing any.'

Mark's hand is on mine. 'Soph, you're acting like a crazy person. Have you listened to yourself?'

I ignore him. 'The thing I can't work out is his motivation for watching us. Why is he trying to get closer to you, taking you to a gig and giving you mates' rates on things when we barely know each other? I just don't know what he has to gain. Unless . . .' I swallow. 'Unless it's all tied back to him needing control. He must be panicking that I'm getting closer to exposing him and his wife for their part in George's, and possibly his ex-wife's, death. This is just a game to him. He's trying to mess with our heads!'

Mark groans. 'Sophia, Jamie isn't watching us. Our lives aren't that interesting.'

I pull my hand away and shiver with the memory of the man on my run. Could that be linked to Jamie too? I took what he said to mean stay out of Rupert's business, but what if it was a warning to stop looking into what happened to Claire?

'OK, I need to tell you something, then you might take what I'm saying seriously.' I swallow. 'This morning, after you left for work, I went for a run.' I pause. 'There was this really threatening guy. He had a dog. A Vizsla. The same breed as Rupert. And this—'

'What?' Mark sits bolt upright. 'Shit. Why didn't you call me? Are you OK?'

'I'm fine.' I nod, trying to think straight. 'You haven't told Jamie about what happened with Rupert?'

'Course not.'

'So he wouldn't know what breed of dogs the gang used, or how hard they tried to scare us into silence?'

He looks shocked. 'What? No!'

'What about when you went to the gig? You were drunk – maybe something slipped out?'

'Soph, it's not Jamie. That fucking scumbag Rupert must have found out about you speaking to Lou. Clearly he wants to scare you and stop you looking into the story again.'

Maybe he's right. It's too much of a coincidence. Perhaps the gig tickets are completely innocent too and I'm just trying to make things add up when they don't.

'But—'

'No,' he says, assertively. 'If Rupert is back, then the cameras are definitely staying. End of.'

50

Erin

Wednesday 28 September

I've spent too long in this house feeling as if I have no control. There are plenty of jobs I can do to keep busy, especially as I'm still waiting for Jamie to call me. I hoped he would be better at staying in touch since he raced off yesterday. I rub a hand against my stomach where a bump will soon be. Now that there's a deadline to get the house renovation work done, I'm re-energised, grateful to these growing and multiplying cells for giving me a purpose now. We're still waiting for approval from the planning office, but I won't let that hold me back. There are walls to strip, carpets to rip up, floors to sand and varnish . . . the list goes on and on. As long as I'm careful with paint fumes and make sure every room is well ventilated – not difficult in this draughty place – then I shouldn't cause the baby any harm.

I have the ladder pushed against the wall up on the landing and am on the third, maybe fourth, step from the bottom. I need to try to get as much cleared in here as I can. I reach to tug a section of the ugly Paisley-print wallpaper that has given me a headache for far too long. The ladder wobbles precariously.

I reach out for something to hold on to. There's a split second when I feel like I'm falling, but the ladder rights itself and I try to calm my beating heart. Memories of George tumbling down the wet stone steps rush back and I'm there once again in the gloom of the fading storm, running away from his bloodied dead body. I've given up talking to Jamie about the possibility that someone else was there. As time has passed, even I'm unsure – I can't trust myself or my memory. Did I invent the sound of footsteps all along? If someone else was there then we would have heard them find the body; there would have been more commotion, a scream maybe. Why would anyone even head to such a remote spot on the night of a storm? It doesn't make any sense.

I climb carefully down the ladder. My nerves are shot. A thought hits me. With Jamie away, what would happen if I hurt myself and couldn't call for help? I pat my pocket. My phone must be in the kitchen. I should really keep it on me at all times when I'm here alone. I need to start thinking more clearly and making better decisions for me and the baby's safety.

I head downstairs to find my phone and make a cup of tea, promising myself to take it easy this afternoon – Rome wasn't built in a day and all that. However, something isn't right. There's a split second before my brain registers that the top, spongy step feels different under my feet. There's a huge crack down the centre of the wood. A pungent, earthy smell hits my nose. It's completely rotten.

There isn't time to think before I'm thrown off balance.

I let out a scream as my arms shoot out to grab the banister, but it slips through my grip, the force of the fall pulling me to the foot of the stairs, gravity taking over. With a heavy thump, I tumble to the parquet floor of the hallway and land in a heap. I'm paralysed with shock, my head swimming. A sharp dart of pain ricochets through me.

The baby.

Pure panic consumes me. Almost immediately, I double over with a white-hot cramp that sears through my abdomen. My breathing comes out in frightened gulps. Tears stream down my burning cheeks. With every ounce of strength, I grit my teeth, letting out a squeal of pain, and pull myself up.

I tentatively shuffle across to the downstairs bathroom, where I catch my reflection in the dusty gilt-edged mirror and do a double take. My left cheek is swollen, with a puffy, angry welt where I must have caught the edge of the bottom step. The rest of my face is ghostly pale, glistening with snot and tears. I ever so gently lower myself on to the toilet seat. My stomach is in knots, my breath trapped in my chest.

Please, please, please let my baby be OK.

With a wince I manage to tug down my jeans, the skin of my thighs tender and hot to the touch. Amazingly, nothing appears to be seriously broken; I've not even cut myself. The pain is trapped inside me. I squeeze my eyes shut, letting out a slow, forced exhale of shaky breath, before I dare to look down.

There is rust-coloured blood inside my knickers.

I wipe and wipe but the tissue stays spotted with a dark brown pattern of blood. More tears rush out. I bang a fist against the wall and scream. My petrified cries reverberate around the impossibly small bathroom, bouncing off the ugly avocado-coloured sink. A wave of dizziness overpowers me.

When I finally catch my breath, my legs numb and tingling with pins and needles, I stand on shaking legs. I flush the blood away, wash my hands and try to find where I left my phone.

The screen is so cracked, I can barely see the internet page I bring up. A voice in my mind tells me not to panic, to stay calm: there was only a small amount of blood. I google 'bleeding when pregnant'. It's hard to read the results or open the web page without getting tiny slivers of glass in my finger. Some sites say it's perfectly common, that up to one in four women experience what they call 'spotting', but another site says to notify your GP as soon as any sort of bleeding occurs.

This is where I need a woman to talk to. Someone who will hold me and tell me everything is going to be OK. For the first time in a very long time I have such an overwhelming longing for my own mum that it takes my breath away.

I roughly wipe the tears away and dial my best friend. Kat will know what to do. She's always been so calm in a crisis.

I hold the phone to my ear as it tries to connect. An ice-cold sensation washes over me: the shock is kicking in. It rings and rings, but when her voicemail kicks in I jab a shivering finger on the button to hang up. I can't leave a message. What the hell would I say? I throw my head in my hands.

I'm about to call Jamie when I stop myself. This would break him. He'd only blame himself for not looking at how dangerous the floorboards have become, when I've asked him about them so many times. It's not as though he can do anything to help from his work event.

What do I do? Should I call an ambulance? No, I'm not haemorrhaging or in severe pain, even if this does feel like life and death. Instead, I call my GP's number and am informed by a snooty receptionist that there are no more telephone appointments for today. She asks whether it is an emergency and I have to bite my tongue and say that it isn't. Remembering what the miscarriage felt like when we were in Girona, I know the pain and physical signs to look out for. This time it's just the blood, and the fear of what could happen next. There's a walk-in clinic in town that I could visit, just to get some reassurance I suppose, but I haven't got a car. It's still in the garage and I'm not sure when it's due back. What would a doctor do anyway? They couldn't save the last one once my body had decided to take charge.

All I can do is wait.

51

Sophia

Wednesday 28 September

'Where are we going to get lunch from around here?' I ask, looking around the residential street where the Uber has dropped us off.

When Amira invited me to actually use our allotted lunch hour for once, I thought she would be taking me to some hidden gem of a restaurant.

'Lunch will have to wait,' Amira winks, tapping her phone screen. 'First, we need to see Kat Broome. She lives at number forty-seven.'

'Who?' I stare at her blankly.

'You know you told me that you were struggling to find anything about Erin?'

I nod.

'Well, I used my initiative and managed to track down someone who knows her well. I'm hoping her friend might be able to shed some light on things.'

'Ha, how did you find her? Erin is like a closed book online!'

Amira proudly explains how she discovered that some of Erin's older Facebook posts weren't set to private. There were a couple of gushing birthday messages and a best-friend-iversary post tagging someone called Kat Broome, who, in her own profile, lists working at Red Bees youth facility, the same place where Erin worked. To get Kat's address, all Amira had to do was pretend to be interested in buying the sandwich-maker that Kat has listed for sale on Facebook Marketplace. Bingo.

'Come on. We have to be back at our desks in forty-five minutes. We haven't got all day.' Amira trots ahead. I smile after her.

I can't stop thinking about the frozen reel frame of them heading towards the cliffs on the night George died. Towards the scene of a crime that they lied about being anywhere near.

While Amira double-checks that we're at the right house, I pull my jacket a little tighter against the chill in the air and try to shake off the constant feeling that I'm being watched. This is ridiculous. I scan around for an imminent threat, but there is nothing untoward on this quiet terrace-lined street.

A woman who looks around my age opens the front door with a nervous smile. She's heavily pregnant, wearing a light blue jumper dress that's pulled tight around her bump over thick black tights.

'Kat Broome?' I ask.

'Yes,' she says slowly. A protective hand jumps to her stomach.

Amira's eyes are on me, waiting for me to perform.

'Hello, Kat. My name is Sophia and this is Amira. Don't worry, we're not here to sell you anything.' I smile.

Kat warily flicks her eyes between us both.

'We're both journalists who are investigating a woman that I think you might know. Is there any chance you could spare five minutes? We're not looking for you to speak out publicly or be quoted, but I really hope you might be able to help.' I quickly take a breath. 'It's about Erin Steele.'

There's a brief pause, enough time to worry that she might close the door in our faces and immediately call her best friend and tell her we're digging for information. Instead, after a moment of hesitation, she asks, 'Have you got any ID?'

We both hurry to show her our work lanyards.

After a quick inspection, she nods. 'What's she done now?'

'Perhaps we could come in and have a little chat?' I suggest.

The door opens up and we walk in.

'When are you due?' Amira asks, as we enter the tastefully decorated lounge. Plump mustard-velvet scatter cushions sit on a charcoal-grey sofa. Warm light flickers from a lit wax melt burner. The scent of vanilla is quite overwhelming.

Kat points a remote at the television to mute *Come Dine With Me*. 'Not for another four weeks, but I don't know if I can get much bigger,' she says, smiling nervously. 'So, er, take a seat.'

Kat chews an unpainted fingernail as we sit down. A cluttered coffee table holding an untouched bowl of red grapes and several empty biscuit wrappers sit between us. She doesn't offer to get us a drink.

'I'm happy to speak to you as long as I remain anonymous.'

I promise that she won't be named.

'So, what do you want to know?'

'Perhaps we could start with how you know Erin?' I click my ballpoint pen against my shorthand notepad.

'Did you meet her at a youth club, Red Bees?' Amira asks.

There is something that flickers on Kat's face. She pulls one of the velvet cushions towards her and begins wrapping a tassel around her fingers.

'Yeah.' The cotton thread is pulled taut, cutting into her skin, turning it white. 'It was called Red Bees, but it wasn't a youth club. It was more a centre for troubled teens. A place where foster parents or social workers would send difficult kids to keep them off the streets and contained in one damp and chilly room. There were some proper characters in that place. I wasn't much older than most of the people there, actually, but it was a fun, interesting job.'

'What was it like working with Erin?'

'What?' The cotton thread breaks off. Kat locks her eyes with mine. 'Erin wasn't a colleague. She was one of the teens.'

No wonder I couldn't find anything about Erin in iSearch, if she's been through the care system.

'Trouble just seems to follow her around. There were all these rumours that she was kicked out of different schools because of her temper. She had a history of obsessing over her boyfriends' ex-girlfriends. A couple of complaints were made that she was harassing them, threatening them, but that was a side to her that I never saw. She was only ever friendly and polite to me. I'm only a year or so older than her, but I think she saw me as the big sister she never had. Because I was the youngest member of staff, a lot of the other teens disrespected me, but she never did.' Kat shreds a chocolate biscuit wrapper between her fingers. 'I should never have let it get this far, but I just felt sorry for her, you know?'

'Let what get this far?'

'We were a little too friendly as teens. I suppose it's frowned upon to strike up a friendship when, at the time, I was in a position of authority. Then when my contract at Red Bees ended, I left, and that was it. Or so I thought.' She sighs. 'I mean, I was young and didn't realise the boundaries. Perhaps I did cross a line.'

I sit up.

'It must have been ten years or so with no contact. Then one day, out of the blue, Erin got back in touch with me. She sent me a message on Facebook, asking if I wanted to hang out like we did when we were teens. Except, well, I wasn't that girl any more, so I said no. But she messaged again. So, out of curiosity, I met her for a coffee but it was awkward. We had nothing in common.'

There's a long pause; Kat's eyes drop to her slippers.

'Is everything OK?' Amira asks, giving me a confused look.

There's a shift in the atmosphere of the room. I swallow the rising bubble of anticipation in my chest. The sensation when I know I'm on to a story that is turning out bigger than anyone could have originally thought. I wonder if Amira is picking up on this too.

'I just feel like an idiot.' Kat sniffs. 'It's my fault for inviting her back into my life, but I felt sorry for her. She doesn't seem to have many others who check in on her.'

'Why? What's happened?' I ask.

'It was after that coffee that she carried on messaging me. Then she invited me to be the maid of honour at her wedding. I mean, that should have rung alarm bells. But I was pregnant and hormonal and not thinking straight. We had already, thankfully, booked a holiday which clashed with the wedding

273

date, so I declined her offer. After that, though, she just became really needy. Messaging and calling more than is socially acceptable and then turning up all the time, no matter where I was, using the pretence of helping her plan her big day as if we were lifelong friends or something.'

'Sounds like a stalker . . .' Amira pipes up.

'That's what my husband says. Anyway, I should never have met her for that first coffee. She lured me in, saying it was urgent. She sounded panicked but it was all a lie.' She lets out a sigh. 'I know she gets attached easily, I guess it's because of what she's been through.'

A knot of unease is growing in my chest.

'Can you tell me about her past?' I ask.

'She transferred to Red Bees from St Catherine's. I'm not sure exactly why they expelled her but there were plenty of rumours – behavioural problems. Anyway, I stupidly chose to ignore them and believed she was just misunderstood.'

'Is that linked to her being bipolar, do you think?' I ask, dropping my voice.

'What? Who told you that?'

'Jamie, her husband.'

Kat frowns. 'Are you sure that's what he said?'

A cold prickle runs up my neck at the look she's giving me. Amira sits forward on her chair.

'One hundred per cent.' There's no way I'd forget a word of that weird moment in the car with him. The abruptness, the intensity.

'No.' Kat shakes her head. 'She had all the tests when she was younger, as part of the psychological assessment when she joined Red Bees. Nothing like that was ever flagged up.

She's just intense. Better in small doses, if you know what I mean.'

I glance at my watch. Our 'lunch break' is rapidly running out. We need to wrap this up and try to get an Uber back to the office as quickly as possible.

'When did you last hear from her?' Amira asks Kat, as I get to my feet.

'A week and a half ago – the Saturday before last. And that's the last time. I'm ignoring all her calls from now on. If she turns up again, then I'll be making an official complaint with the police.' Kat sits up resolutely. 'I mean it this time.'

There's something about the firmness in her tone.

'Why? What happened?'

'She turned up uninvited to my baby shower. I couldn't believe it. Who does that? The next day a personalised pink teddy arrived in the post wearing a Red Bees T-shirt. It was so creepy. That's when I asked my sister, who swore on her life that she never invited Erin. I didn't even know she was on the WhatsApp group either! I have no idea how she knows where to find me.' She visibly shivers. 'But that's Erin: she suffocates people.'

After saying our goodbyes, Amira and I stand outside Kat's house, waiting for the taxi. Both of us are trying to digest everything we've just learned.

Amira speaks first. 'Isn't it a mad coincidence that Jamie's first wife had a stalker and his new wife sounds like a bit of a stalker?'

'I know. There are way too many red flags springing up.' The silver taxi pulls into the road. I glance at my watch. 'In fact, change of plan. Will you cover for me? I'm going to go and see Erin.' I ask the driver to add an extra stop at the nearest train station.

'What? Are you sure? I mean, is that wise, given everything we've just found out?' Amira stares at me. 'You heard what Kat said about her losing her temper. It's not safe for you to go alone.'

I give her arm a rub. 'I'll be fine.'

She holds my gaze for a few seconds. 'If you insist. Just . . . please be careful.'

'I will. I promise. I've dealt with worse, trust me.'

52

Erin

I have to keep busy if I want to try and avoid the crippling anxiety about what's happening inside my body right now. I've been too scared to check my sanitary pad – I don't want to face the truth just yet. I don't even bother to get dressed. I've been wandering around in my pyjamas and heavy fleece dressing gown for extra warmth. Body odour and sweat clings to my unwashed skin but I don't care.

I'm about to open Facebook. There's something strangely calming about the mundane lives and trivial problems of others when everything in your own world is teetering on a knife edge. But the sound of car tyres crunching over our gravel drive distracts me.

Jamie isn't due back until Friday. A shiver darts up my spine. I'm immediately on high alert. Has he come back early? Has something happened? I push myself up from my seat at the kitchen table; every movement is a reminder of the fall. My right side has now bloomed into a delicious plum bruise that runs up over my bottom and across my hips.

I frown in confusion as I reach the hall. I can see a red car, distorted through the glass. It looks like a taxi.

There's a knock, and the tight trill of our doorbell that still manages to make me jump. Curiosity overrides confusion and I open the door a crack. A shock of fresh air hits me. There's a menacing chittering of birds taking flight over the field.

Sophia is standing on the other side.

'Erin! Oh . . . what's happened to your face?'

My hand flies to my sore cheek. 'I fell down the stairs.'

She frowns. 'Did Jamie do this to you?'

'What?' I reel backwards in shock. 'No. Of course he didn't.'

My hackles rise at the cheek of this woman coming to my front door asking me if my husband is guilty of domestic violence. The woman who tried it on with him in the first place! I subconsciously place a protective arm over my stomach, as if installing a barrier between her and us. Whenever she's around, there's trouble. It's clear to me now – she's out to get us.

'It looks painful – have you put anything on it?'

'It's fine.' I turn away. 'What are you doing here?'

'I wanted to check that everything is OK with you. Everything is OK, isn't it?'

Just as quickly as the anger arrived, I'm shocked by the suddenness of the onset of tears that appear. Bloody pregnancy hormones. I refuse to cry in front of her.

'Everything is fine.'

'Can I come in?' She places an expensive-looking chunky white trainer on our step.

'Now's not a good time . . . I'm actually getting ready for my best friend to come over.'

I don't know where that lie sprang from.

'Oh, OK. Do you mind if I just quickly use your bathroom? I'm desperate.'

I stall. I don't want her in the house, not after she came on to Jamie, but before I have the chance to say anything she's bolted past me and gone into the downstairs bathroom.

The toilet flushes and she emerges, glancing around as if looking for something. 'Thanks. So, are you sure I can't get you to postpone seeing your friend? I would really love to talk to you.'

'No. It's not a good time.' I have the front door wide open, waiting for her to take the cue.

'Maybe you could call me when you're done and we could rearrange?'

I nod but keep my teeth gritted.

She grudgingly takes a couple of steps forward, craning her neck as if looking for something on the outside of the house. 'Why don't you have security cameras here?'

'Sorry?'

'There's not even a smart doorbell,' she muses, under her breath.

I press my fingers to my temple. 'Sophia, what's going on? Why have you just shown up like this asking such weird questions?'

'I told you, I wanted to see how you were. That's what friends do: check in on one another.'

'Friends don't try it on with other people's husbands,' I spit.

She reels back as if I've slapped her. 'What? What are you talking about? I've never tried it on with Jamie!' Sophia

279

gasps. 'Erin, is that what he said to you? He's lying. I actually think he's lying about a lot of things. Don't you think he's changed, since Bali? Do you ever feel like you're being watched? Like Jamie knows things but would have no way of knowing them?'

A cold wind suddenly tears through the house. A door slams from upstairs and makes me jump. 'What?'

'Don't you find it odd how he owns a successful security business yet doesn't have any sort of security in his own home . . .?'

I wish I could tell her the things that have run through my mind as I've lain awake in bed. The coincidences that have stayed with me. I don't trust myself to speak, but she must have picked up on my hesitation.

'Erin.' She drops her voice. 'Can you tell me about Claire Connelly and what happened to her?'

The ground sways under my feet when she says that name. My head is ringing with the deep pulse of a painful memory. No. I refuse to go there.

'Claire died a few months ago. It was an accident.'

'I'm not sure it was a complete accident.'

A wash of goosebumps suddenly appears on my arms. 'Y-y-you need to leave.' I shake my head, lips sealed shut once more. 'I have to get ready for my friend.'

She's still talking as I close the door, my heart reverberating through my entire body.

'Here's my number and email again. Please contact me, Erin. We need to talk. I'm worried about you.'

A neat business card drops through the letterbox. It flutters to the dusty floor as if in slow motion. I pick it up and put it into the deep pocket of my dressing gown, rushing to sit down before my legs give way. I rock with my eyes closed, trembling with fear, my arms wrapped across my knees, wanting all of this to go away.

It is only after I hear the crunch of tyres reversing off the gravel that I begin to breathe once more.

53

Erin

Monday 4 July

I'll never forget the panic that struck me as I opened my front door to a dour-faced police officer. It was a balmy July evening and Jamie was just making a start on dinner. The windows were thrust open and smells from the neighbour's balcony barbecue wafted in. I was about to open a bottle of ice-cold beer just as the doorbell rang.

'Are you James Steele?' the officer asked.

'Yes. Is everything OK?' Jamie stuttered.

'It might be best if I come in. I've got some bad news, I'm afraid.'

We shuffled through to the lounge, not knowing where to put ourselves. I was about to ask the police officer if he wanted a cold drink – he must be boiling in his heavy uniform – when he asked us to take a seat.

'It's about your ex-wife,' he said to Jamie. 'I'm sorry to tell you that her body was discovered at her home earlier this afternoon.'

He explained, in a low, soft voice, how Claire had had a terrible fall. She'd been drinking and tripped down the stairs, smashing into the marble lobby and never getting up again. The policeman didn't say it exactly like that, but that was how I imagined it.

After leaving a few moments for the shock to sink in, the police officer cleared his throat.

'I'm very sorry, I know this is a terrible time, but I also need access to the CCTV in Ms Connelly's apartment block. I've been informed that your company is responsible for this?'

Jamie nodded.

'We will need to review the footage as part of our investigations into what happened to Claire. It's protocol, you see. I'm afraid I'm going to have to ask you to sort this as a matter of urgency.' He gave a smile drenched in sympathy.

'Of course. I'm happy to offer any help I can.' Jamie wiped his eyes.

'Thank you. Here's my card. If you can gather the footage and send it over within the next few hours, we would be very grateful.'

That was when I held my breath. Eyes darting between the two men. Sweating from the sudden rush of heat that rose all the way from my toes.

'I can't believe it,' Jamie kept repeating the moment we were alone, his head in his hands.

My stomach was in knots. I had to say something. It was now or never.

'I might have been the last person to see her alive . . .'

'Wait – what did you say?' He snapped his head towards me. 'Erin, what's going on?' The colour drained from his face. 'I think you need to start talking.'

My words tripped over one another as I tried to explain what had happened.

It all started when Jamie told me he'd been married before. I was proud of the way I acted as if it was no big deal. However, when he told me their divorce was amicable, I didn't believe him – no one escapes heartache.

As much as I tried not to give Claire a second thought, it was like an itch I had to scratch. I needed to inhale it all. Their engagement party, their extravagant wedding, the plush flat she moved into after they separated.

She liked to film short, chatty videos while walking into town. Any average sleuth could have figured out where she lived, which fancy block of flats with the heavy-looking rotating front door was hers. She took three right turns then a left before she got to her favourite coffee shop. You only needed to do that journey in reverse to work out where she started from. It was almost too easy, as if she wanted me to be part of her life.

She mustn't have liked the sudden interest from one of her followers, so she blocked me. But I found another way. A different profile. A new name. There's always ways. Each time she blocked me, the more it hurt. I only ever wanted to find out more about her. I didn't know why she didn't want to answer my questions. I guess the last few messages I sent were a little hurtful, I said things I shouldn't have, but she pushed my buttons.

Everything changed after the official warning landed on my doormat. It was after I set up the fourth fake profile. The letter explained how the police had tracked the IP address to my laptop, informing me that Claire had made a complaint and was thinking of taking it further, threatening legal action.

That was when I took it seriously. I had to back off. I also knew that, no matter how hard it was, I needed to come clean to Jamie.

It was excruciating.

I confessed how I'd lost my mind, and I laid bare all my insecurities. There's no positive spin on psycho-stalking your fiancé's ex-wife. But, in a way, coming clean was cathartic. He was disappointed I'd gone to such extreme lengths when I could have just asked him about her, but secretly I got the sense that he liked the idea of me caring so much. After that I pushed her out of my mind and toned it right back, promising myself to stay in the shadows of her social media. No commenting or liking or sending DMs. Look but don't touch.

It was fine.

Until this morning, when I viewed Claire's page and realised she hadn't posted for a few days, something which had never happened before. I made a snap decision to go and see if she was OK, despite knowing I shouldn't.

Jamie cleared his throat, bringing me back to the too-hot living room that smelt of the neighbour's barbecue. The waft of burnt meat made my stomach turn.

'Did you speak to her?' he asked, after I confessed.

I shook my head.

'What did you do, then?' He steepled his fingers on the bridge of his nose and closed his eyes, exhaling slowly.

'I left flowers.'

'Flowers? Babe! If the police find out you were there again after they issued that harassment notice . . .' He rubbed his face. 'You know you shouldn't have been there.'

'I know. I didn't go any further than the lobby. I swear! She took the flowers and told me to go, so I did. But she seemed fine! I had no idea she would be dead just hours later.'

My heart was racing in my chest. Tears dripped down my cheeks. I couldn't take the look Jamie was giving me.

OK, so she had seemed a little spooked by the flowers. I hung around after she told me to go and watched her on her balcony as she lit up a cigarette, closing her eyes as she exhaled. I never knew she was a smoker.

He lowered his voice. 'You could get into a lot of trouble for this, Erin.'

It takes me a moment to read through his fixed frown and realise what he's trying to say. A cold sweat breaks out as he starts to talk.

'What if the police suspect you of tipping her over the edge? Or, worse, that you were somehow involved in her death?'

'But . . . no . . . why would they? I mean . . .' I couldn't get my words out quickly enough. 'It's not like I killed her! The police officer just said they think it was an accident!'

'All it takes is for them to look you up on their system, find the harassment notice, work out you were there on the day, antagonising her with flowers . . .' He trailed off. You didn't need to be a genius to work it out – how simple it would be for them to put two and two together. Even if they did come up with five.

'Oh, my God!' I whimpered.

He wrapped his arms around me. 'Babe. Trust me. I won't let that happen.'

286

Jamie did what the police officer asked and sent the CCTV. He's the only person who knows I went to Claire's luxury apartments on the day she died. I know, because he was the one who wiped my visit from the security footage.

54

Sophia

Thursday 29 September

Amira is heaping coffee into a mug in the *Post*'s cramped kitchen. It's got a picture of a dog on it and says 'newshound' in small letters.

'Tell me everything!' she says, tearing open a packet of oat biscuits, fizzing with excitement. 'I know you texted last night to say it went fine but now I need all the details. I've barely slept, I'm so desperate to find out exactly what happened!'

She nibbles at a biscuit, offering me one. I shake my head then make sure no one else is around to hear us.

'Well, there is definitely something off. Her reaction when I mentioned Claire's name spoke volumes. Seriously, it was mad how quickly she shut down the rest of my questions after that.'

I picture the painful bruises on Erin's face where she told me she'd fallen down the stairs. She'd leapt to Jamie's defence when I'd asked if he had done that to her. It felt like a genuine reaction but I read people for a living. I can spot signs of lying and discomfort at a question I've asked – Erin was displaying all the classic signs of hiding something.

I tried to sow the seed about Jamie and what I believe he's capable of but it was the way her eyes widened and she practically slammed the front door in my face when I mentioned Claire's name that lit a fire in my belly.

'I knew it!' says Amira.

'She couldn't have got rid of me quicker if she'd tried.' I saw her keeping watch at the window as I waited for my taxi. The headlights lighting up her ghostly face pressed to the glass. Those dark eyes staring right through me.

'I think we need to dig a little more into what really happened to Claire and this stalker rumour. My gut is screaming that she's the missing piece in this puzzle.'

'I agree. Claire's mum seemed adamant that that was a key factor in her death.' I pick up a biscuit, thinking as I chew what else I need to tell her. 'Oh – don't you think it's odd how someone with a successful security business has zero security at his own home?'

Amira tilts her head to the side.

'I checked last night. There doesn't seem to be a single camera, security light, smart doorbell, nothing. Why? Surely his pad should be like Fort Knox, especially living somewhere so remote. A vulnerable target out in the sticks all alone like that.'

Amira shrugs. 'Maybe that's why they chose to live somewhere so rural. They probably don't even need to lock their doors. It's not like round here.'

'Hmm. Something doesn't add up. There's no way someone like Jamie would leave his home unmonitored.' I tap a pen against my lips.

'Yeah, I mean—' She stops talking as my mobile sparks into life. 'Do you need to get that?'

I look at the screen. Mark is calling. I shake my head. 'It's my husband. He'll leave a message.'

We had a bit of a row last night after I got home, this time over a bill he'd promised he'd paid. I'd absent-mindedly opened the final demand letter and things had grown heated pretty quickly. He promised to sort it out today, blaming his boss for messing up on the last payment run. But it wasn't about the bill, not really. I guess I'm holding more stress than I realised and I unleashed it on him. I just don't know who I'm supposed to trust right now – no matter what he says, he's changed since we got back from our honeymoon. Nothing major, he's just a lot more fearful, convinced something is going to go wrong. He certainly became a lot more defensive when I mentioned this sudden pessimism. His response is always that he just wishes we could move away. I got so fed up last night that I snapped and told him it was bad enough living with a grumpy man in a thriving city, let alone trapped in a rural farmhouse with only each other for company. I immediately felt bad about this and suggested going for lunch today to clear the air. We've neglected each other since returning from Bali, and I know I'm to blame for it.

Just as I'm putting the mobile down, it pings again, and this time my attention is captured. It's an email, the one I've been waiting for. I open it and start to skim the contents.

'Anything interesting?' Amira asks, pulling me back to the present.

'Yes!' I say. 'I've finally got the translated autopsy results for George Kingsley.'

'Please tell me there's something helpful in there?' Amira says, pushing her wire glasses up her nose.

'There's a lot of it to wade through.' I Bluetooth her the report on my phone. 'This is what I can make out at first glance ... um, let's see ... bruising on the back of his body is consistent with falling down the concrete stairs. But there's evidence of a punch or blow to the head, suggesting someone else was present. There's also a faint rash to his neck, a broken nose, some missing teeth and a split lip. But it was the fall that killed him. He snapped both ankles, broke a couple of ribs and shattered his pelvis. His phone and wallet are missing but nothing else seems to have been stolen. Alcohol was detected in his bloodstream. They think he was still alive for a few minutes after the fall. Police haven't released any further details.'

Amira is about to say something else when Brad wanders into the kitchen. She clamps her mouth shut. He is oblivious to the sudden silence and starts filling it by moaning that someone's finished his soya milk. I whisper to Amira that we'll pick this up later.

'Sophia!' Claudia's voice booms down the narrow corridor. Both Amira and Brad spin to look at me. 'My office. Now.'

My boss is pacing behind her messy desk. She's got a piece of paper in her hands that's being swatted through the coffee-scented air.

'I think you need to explain some things to me. What the hell is this?'

She slaps the paper on her desk on top of a stack of last week's newspapers. I step closer, trying to make sense of it. It's a bill.

Shit.

It's for the translation. I completely forgot to pay the company back. I was supposed to transfer the money across but I got sidetracked.

At my shocked silence she carries on. I can feel her sour breath on my cheeks as she rants.

'At first, I thought it was a mistake. Then I called the contact here.' She jabs a finger. 'Spoke to a nice guy who told me you had commissioned the translation for the autopsy of a man from Portsmouth who died in Bali. Now, I'm trying to give you the benefit of the doubt here, but I need you to start talking about why the hell I'm forking out such excessive costs for you to research this! I certainly never ordered you to work on this story!'

I want to bite back that it's actually not that excessive but I keep my mouth shut. I cough. I feel as if I'm back in the headmaster's office. Only this time it's worse.

As much as I hate it here, I can't lose this job. There is nothing else.

'I'm really sorry, I can pay it back, it just slipped my mi—'

'It's not just about the money.' She gives her head a firm shake. 'You knew you were on shaky ground. You've left me no choice, Sophia.'

Oh, God. I swallow. Claudia can look really fucking terrifying when she wants to. I'm waiting for her to tell me I'm fired when there's a commotion from inside the newsroom.

'What the hell is going on out there?' She slams a thick fist on the desk and the bill flutters to the bobbled navy carpet tiles, but, before she can bend to retrieve it, the door to her office bursts open.

A flustered-looking Amira is on the other side. It's the expression on her face that makes my stomach tense. A cacophony of ringing phones and rising voices rushes into the office.

'There's been a hit-and-run down by Tesco Express. It's all over Twitter!'

Claudia swears under her breath. She twists to face me. 'This conversation isn't over. But, for now, get to work.'

I rush to my desk, sweating from Claudia's terrifying stare.

For the first time since I've been here, there is real excitement in the newsroom. Chairs have been scraped back. People are on their feet and desk phones have started ringing. Everyone seems to have woken up.

Claudia calls for attention. 'Police and ambulance are at the scene. Amira – get on to them for updates. Sophia and Brad – go down and cover it – make sure to take video for the web too. Get eye-witnesses speaking.'

I finally feel that familiar buzz of adrenaline spiking through my limbs, that urge to react which comes from covering a breaking news story. The sensation was as familiar as breathing once upon a time; I didn't realise how much I'd missed it.

'We'll lead on this for tomorrow's paper, so go big. I want all the details!' Claudia calls after us. 'Oh, and Sophia, don't fuck it up.'

55

Erin

Thursday 29 September

Ever since I tripped over the rotting top step I've been pleading with a God that I'm not sure exists, praying my body won't reject this baby like the last. If he saves my baby then I will be a better person. I will do anything he wants. I know I should be obsessing over Sophia's unexpected visit yesterday, and I am, but overriding that are even deeper swirling thoughts of desperation and panic.

My prayers are answered when I go to the bathroom to check the sanitary pad I put in my knickers earlier. I hold my breath as I sit on the toilet, wanting to prolong the seconds of ignorance. I've been scratching at my arms, drawing blood under my fingernails, without even realising. My stomach is in knots with anticipation. I take a deep breath.

Then I start to cry.

Happy tears of relief. The pad is clean, not a drop of blood to be seen. This child is my saviour. A fresh start. I will do everything in my power to make sure the baby is loved and safe. I will learn from my mum's mistakes. I've even been thinking about baby names. Kat revealed at the baby shower that her daughter was going to be named after both of their grandmas. It's harder than you'd imagine. Erin isn't my name, of course. I was able to choose one. I remember being told this and feeling so excited about all the options lying before me as I flicked through a book of names. I mean, how many kids get that chance?

I'm not sure how I ended up with Erin. I wish I had a story but the truth is I just liked the sound of it, liked how short and snappy it was. I want our baby's name to have some meaning. I'm going to ask Jamie to look into his family tree; perhaps there'll be a name that stands out, that we can then attribute to a previous Steele family member. Maybe naming your kid after a grandparent isn't so bad after all.

After this moment of calm, there is a frenzied rush of anxiety. I still have to deal with Sophia. But thinking about her also means thinking about Claire.

I try calling Jamie a couple of times, needing to hear his voice, but it just rings out. A little later he messages me saying the signal at the hotel is too unreliable for a call. He asks if I'm OK. I can't tell him about the baby, nor about tripping down the stairs and the panic I've endured since. Not over WhatsApp. So I say I'm fine, just a bit bored, and that I hope that the investor meeting is going OK. The sooner this product is launched, the sooner things will get back to some sort of normal.

Sophia was right when she questioned if Jamie had changed. I still get flashbacks to how he held me by the throat in the kitchen, the terrifying panic that rushed through my helpless body under his strong hands. Not to mention the mood swings and how distant he's become since we returned from Bali.

Then she started going on about Claire. Every time she mentioned that woman's name, I felt a spasm in my gut.

It was an accident. The police say so: the evidence proved that she was on a strong cocktail of booze and pills and simply misjudged her step. But what if there was something more suspicious that went on? After all, Claire seemed fine when I saw her. What tipped her over the edge to drink so much so quickly? A prickle of goosebumps erupts over my arms but it's not the air in the cold room. What if, when wiping the CCTV, Jamie overlooked some clue? And that's what Sophia is looking into. He might have unknowingly tampered with crucial evidence.

I try and think straight. Perhaps Jamie has the master copy somewhere. I could see for myself exactly what happened that day. The unedited version.

I walk past the study. The door is ajar, revealing a mess of boxes and office furniture. A magnet-like pull in my bones calls for me to step inside and investigate more. Despite being all alone in the house, I still look over my shoulder. Something Sophia said about feeling like you were being watched all the time has stuck with me. There's a smoke alarm directly above my head. The plastic has yellowed slightly with age. A red light blinks. A thought shoots to the front of my mind.

What if there's a camera inside, watching me?

For a couple of seconds, I remain planted on the edge of the doorway. Frozen. If Jamie is watching me then he'll assume any camera feed has malfunctioned, paused for a second. It *is* odd how much he seems to know about my movements, like when he knew I was at the baby shower, or that I'd been to the deli to buy the food for the dinner party.

With a jolt, I snap back to my senses and shake my head. Ridiculous. There's no way my husband has bugged our house. Why am I letting the delusions of one woman get to me like this? If Jamie had seen anything sinister on the CCTV at Claire's apartment on the night of her death then he would have gone to the police. He didn't hold any grudge against Claire. If anything, their relationship was too amicable for my liking.

I take hold of the handle of the door to the study, pulling it shut. The click echoes in the empty house. I don't need to look for evidence that Claire's death was suspicious – the police say it wasn't. With the door closed, I carefully make my way downstairs, stepping over the broken top step.

But Sophia's words have struck a chord and, as I go about my normal business, I feel as though I'm putting on a performance for a hidden audience. There's something about the hint of observation that no one can possibly ignore. My movements are unnatural, as if I'm acting the part of the bored housewife trapped at home alone. Another part of my subconscious reminds me that, despite what Jamie says about her, Sophia has no reason to lie to me. What would be in it for her? She seemed so horrified by the suggestion of her trying it on with Jamie, her reaction so visceral, it had to be genuine.

Either way, one of them is lying to me.

I'm pulling out the dirty laundry, checking items of clothing for stray buttons or loose change so the washing machine doesn't swallow them up. There are some receipts all scrunched up in a pair of Jamie's jeans. My phone trills with a notification alert. I have to squint to make out what has just been posted to Facebook. As well as the cracks all over the screen, dark splodges have appeared under the broken glass.

Welcome to the world, baby Broome!

Kat has had her baby early, first thing this morning. A little girl. Florence Rose. It hurts that I've found out at the same time as the rest of the world. I would have expected a quick phone call at the very least. I exhale, trying not to let myself get worked up over trivial things like that any more. There'll be a good reason why she hasn't called me personally. I need to find out the hospital visiting hours. I wonder when she'll be discharged.

I throw in a washing pod and jab my fingers on the button to turn the machine on. Soon the kitchen is filled with the heavy rumble of it whirring to life, water sloshing. I grab the receipts from Jamie's pocket and am going to drop them in the bin when something catches my eye.

The kitchen tilts under my cold, bare feet.

I'm staring at an order form from the local florist for a Balinese-themed tropical bouquet. My eyes scan the creased piece of paper. Jamie told me that he ordered them *before* we went away, in advance of our wedding, as a surprise for our return. But here, written in black scratchy biro, is the order time and date.

Tuesday 13 September.

That's the day we flew home from our honeymoon. He must have ordered them on his phone when we were delayed at the airport. Just hours after we watched George die, surrounded by the sickly-sweet scent of frangipani and jasmine. A headache washes over me as a million thoughts try to battle their way into my mind.

He chose those flowers on purpose. Why would he have lied to me about that?

I'm trying to think straight, my head whirring along with the washing machine. Just then, the light above the dining table suddenly brightens, making me jump. There is a crackle of electricity followed by a pop. The bulb blows and I'm plunged into darkness.

56

Sophia

It started to rain on the walk over to the site of the incident and I didn't have time to grab an umbrella. Brad and I move closer to the supermarket, where a cordon has been set up. Debris is scattered across the road like a trail, leading to an ambulance that's parked up on the pavement just outside the Tesco Express housed at the bottom of a tall block of apartments. On the other side of the busy road is a small triangle of green ringed by black metal railings. There are two red phone boxes and a black bin that's been dented.

'It's not going to be hard to find witnesses.' Brad nods at the crowd of shoppers. Some are still wandering into the store, oblivious to what has happened.

'He was just trying to cross the road after coming out of the bookies',' I overhear a woman with braided hair telling a police officer as we walk towards the carnage. She's got an arm outstretched, pointing to the betting shop tucked beside a barber's. 'The car came out of nowhere! It then sped up that way, towards Angel tube station.'

The police officer sees me approaching, clocks my *Post* lanyard and tells me to give them some space, quickly herding the witness away. The sound of a siren drowns him out as the ambulance turns on its blue lights and heads towards the hospital.

'So, whoever it is isn't dead, then,' Brad says matter-of-factly, watching it leave.

'Do we have any more details?' I ask him. The whole way here he's been itching to find out why Claudia pulled me in for a bollocking, but I refuse to feed his appetite for gossip. As soon as we've wrapped this story up, I'm going to transfer the money across – with interest – and figure out how to apologise properly. Perhaps by the time we return to the office with some good footage and decent quotes she'll have calmed down.

'Coppers won't tell us anything. A statement is imminent, apparently. Amira is trawling Twitter, so we might be able to find out a name for who's been hit there.'

Traffic officers are diverting shoppers away from the cordon on the pavement outside the store. A bus has stopped further up the road. The destination board has changed to 'Not in service'. The driver is standing outside, frantically puffing on a chunky e-cigarette. I decide to start with him.

'Hey, my name's Sophia, I'm working with the *Islington Post* and just trying to get a sense of what happened?'

He looks at me from behind the fruity vapour cloud. A black beard speckled with grey hides a mouth set in a tight line. He looks exhausted.

'Thank God I didn't have any passengers on board. I was only just starting my shift for the day. The car shot out of nowhere. It hit a man, not much older than you, probably. The fella was minding his own business just crossing the road and then—' He makes a slapping noise with his palms. 'I don't even know if I should be telling you this. I don't want to get in trouble.'

I try to reassure him that I won't name him in the piece. 'Can you tell me what you saw?'

'A silver car, small thing. Maybe a Honda, a Fiat, I don't know. It cut me up and then ploughed straight into the poor bloke.'

'Can you remember anything about the person driving?'

He thinks for a second. 'I don't mean to be sexist, but it was a woman.' He gives a shrug as if that explains it.

'You saw the driver? Do you have any more details? How old was she?'

'No, it's a bit hazy.' He rubs at his face. 'I definitely saw long brown hair. I guess it could have been a man with long hair, but . . .' He trails off, doubting his own version of events. 'I just can't believe someone would hit a human being and not stop. Surely she'll know she's done it? I mean, half her bumper is lying across the road.'

'Do you have a dashcam or cameras on your bus that would give us some more details?'

'If you do, then we will be the ones taking that.' A stern voice comes from behind. The harassed police officer has joined us. 'Sir, I'd advise you not to say anything more to this lady – your employers may not be happy with you speaking to a member of the media without an official spokesperson present.'

The bus driver stops puffing on his vape and nods his head. He duly follows the police officer, who leads him towards the supermarket where a police tent has been quickly erected.

'I'm only doing my job,' I call as they walk off.

'Yeah, and we're trying to do ours,' he shouts back.

I swear under my breath and check my phone, swiping away the raindrops on the screen, wishing I'd brought my umbrella with me.

'Any luck?' I ask Brad, as he lollops over to me with his camera swaying around his neck.

'They've just put a statement out.' He nods to my phone. I soon have it in front of me.

Metropolitan Police officers were called to a suspected hit-and-run incident on Chelsea Road in attendance with the London Ambulance Service at 13.32 today (Thursday 29 September). A 31-year-old male was treated at the scene before being transported to a hospital in central London. His injuries are not believed to be life-threatening. The silver hatchback-type car failed to stop at the scene of the collision. Police are asking for anyone who was in the area around the time, and may have dashcam footage which could help pinpoint the vehicle, to get in touch.

Something pulses at the back of my mind but I can't grab it to make sense of it.

'May as well pick up some lunch while we're here.' Brad nods to the Tesco. 'Meal deal?'

303

Lunch. I need to call Mark and tell him I'm going to be held up. We'd arranged to meet at the *Post*'s office; he's probably already on his way. I pull out my phone and tap his number, and a cheesy photo of him wearing a daft fancy dress hat and squiffy eyes pops up as his caller ID. He set it a few years ago, telling me that if he was ever in the doghouse for anything, one look at this would get him out. It's true: I can't help but smile when I see it.

As it's ringing, I ask Brad to show me the police statement again. Thirty-one, I muse, the same age as me and Mark.

I stop. My stomach clenches.

I think back to the missed call from Mark earlier. I haven't had time to call him back. Despite telling myself I'm being paranoid, I try his number again. *The eye-witness says she saw the man leaving the betting shop. Mark doesn't gamble. It's not my husband, stop being ridiculous.* These thoughts are a stream of consciousness, zipping through my brain, with every unanswered ring.

Pick up, pick up, please pick up.

'Sophia?' Brad's waiting for me to move out of the rain and into the supermarket, but my feet are frozen to the wet ground.

When he doesn't pick up, I immediately dial his work.

'Hello, can I speak to Mark, please? It's his wife, Sophia,' I stutter, trying to sound breezy and calm.

There's a pause, a rustle of paper. 'I'm afraid he's out for lunch at the moment. Can I take a message?'

I tell the receptionist I'll try his mobile and hang up. With every second that passes the unease grows. A slow, swirling sickness that has settled in the base of my stomach. He's still not answering. I dial and redial, Mark's goofy grin on his photo now mocking me.

Come on, come on.

He's going to call me back; he's probably got it on silent or at the bottom of his work bag. He'll be worried why I've left him a gazillion missed calls. We'll joke about it later over dinner. Once this spike of anxiety has long dispersed and we're sitting with a bottle of red, catching up, grateful it's not us but some other family waiting at the bedside of a different thirty-one-year-old white man who has tragically been hit by a car. Their day spiralling after being in the wrong place at the wrong time.

But what if he doesn't?

What if this is another warning from Rupert's gang?

I break into a run, ignoring Brad calling out my name.

I just know that when I reach the police and demand that they tell me the name of the victim then my worst nightmare will come true. I barge past people in my haste. My breath is trapped in my chest. I fire frantic questions at the police officer manning the cordon. He hesitates for what feels like an eternity, unsure if this is some awful way of a journalist trying to dig for information, conflicted over what he has been allowed to reveal to the press.

'My name is Sophia Spencer. I think I'm the victim's wife!' I shove my trembling hand in front of his face. The flash of a gold band on my ring finger.

He drops his tired eyes to his scuffed black boots. This confirms what I suspected. I swallow. The whole world tilts.

It all happens so quickly after that. Another officer is instructed to take me to the hospital. People move out of our way, their pitiful glances boring into the back of my head as I'm led past the trembling bus driver. I don't know how my legs hold me up. Tears and raindrops drip down my cheeks.

I can't think of anything, apart from getting to my husband.

57

Sophia

The familiar smell of hospitals hits me the moment I race to find the right ward. I rush down endless corridors in a total daze, as if trapped in a nightmare.

'I've already been handed the details of a "no win, no fee" personal injury lawyer,' Mark says after I've fussed over him.

I'm grateful to hear him joking. He's broken a leg, fractured some ribs and suffered a concussion. There are deep cuts to his hands and a minor head injury that I'm assured looks worse than it is. A nurse tells me they still need to run some tests for internal injuries and to make sure his spine isn't damaged, but initial examinations seem to be positive. Shock and heavy painkillers are keeping the worst of the pain at bay, for now. He was lucky. It doesn't bear thinking about, what would have happened if he'd struck his head or landed slightly differently. He might not even be here now. I blink the thought away. In all these years of covering accidents and call-outs, I never imagined it would be my husband as the victim.

'What do you remember about the crash?' I ask, refilling his plastic cup of water.

He yawns. 'I've already told you and the police.'

'I know, but tell me again. Please.'

'Is this an official interview with a hit-and-run victim?' he says, deadpan. 'If so, then I want a flattering photo to be used.'

I reassure him that this is his concerned wife, not a journalist trying to get to the bottom of a story. He sighs deeply, wincing as he does. That will be the pain from the fractured rib that smashed into the tarmac.

'I tried to call you to see what you wanted to do for lunch. When you didn't answer, I presumed work was busy so thought I'd bring food to you.'

'So you were in Tesco? Where's your shopping?'

'The police must have taken it. Maybe it rolled away. I dunno. Anyway, I was crossing the road when out of nowhere I heard a screech of tyres. I didn't even have time to look up from my phone to see where the noise was coming from. The next thing my legs go out from under me as the car hits me, as if a ton of bricks were dropped from the heavens. I honestly don't remember a thing apart from the noise and then it all goes blank.'

I shiver, despite the stuffy warmth of the hospital ward.

'I spoke to a bus driver – he was just behind you when it happened,' I say, brushing down his bedsheet.

'Oh, yeah? What did he say?'

'He's shaken up. Thankfully he has inbuilt cameras on his bus, so whoever did this won't stay hidden for long.' I pause. 'He said he thought it might have been a woman that hit you.'

'A woman?' Mark's eyebrows knot in confusion. 'No, I'm sure it was a man.'

'Really? But you just said you can't remember anything. You didn't even have a good look at the driver.'

'I know.' He moves slightly, wincing in pain at the effort. 'But that doesn't feel right. I dunno, perhaps something went in somewhere.' He raises a hand to tap against his temple then looks as if he regrets the sudden movement. There's a pause. 'So . . . I've been thinking – after I'm discharged, I'm going to stay at my sister's place for a bit.'

'Sorry?' I'm sure I misheard him.

There is a deep sigh. He looks exhausted. 'Soph, this has made my mind up over something. We need to move. I'm not happy here. I don't feel OK in London any more. I need to get out of the city and clear my head. And I want you to come with me.'

'Come with you?'

'You can't stay here on your own. It's not safe.'

'It is safe. We've got the alarm and CCTV and—'

'It's clearly not enough! I'm saying that it's not safe for you here any more. Someone literally tried to run me over, Sophia.'

'We're going to find out who's behind this,' I reply, my jaw tense.

I've seen the footage that Amira managed to locate of the silver hatchback from Twitter. It's grainy, but the police should be able to enhance it for the appeal they're going to be putting out. ANPR around the city will have caught their plates. Surely.

'Don't cry,' Mark says, lifting a bruised arm to touch my face.

'Sorry. It's just . . .' I sniff the tears away '. . . who could *do* something like this? How could you hit someone and not stop to see if they're OK?'

There's a clatter of crockery from outside his cubicle. The
grating squeak of a tea trolley being wheeled down the ward.
A woman, who sounds as though she smokes sixty a day, is
calling out for everyone's orders. Every conversation filters
through the thin curtains around Mark's bed. I hear her loudly
complain about the weather. Apparently the next few days are
going to be terrible. A storm is rolling in.

Another patient lets out a hacking cough. I don't envy
Mark having to sleep here tonight.

I wait until the ward quietens slightly again, then clear my
throat.

'Anyway, this could have happened anywhere, not just in
London . . .'

'What do you mean?'

'Well, I don't think this was a random accident. I think you
might have been targeted on purpose.' I rub my face, a wave
of exhaustion hitting me. 'At first, I thought it had to be connected to Rupert's gang. Not that there's a reason they would
be after you. And I've dropped the Lou stuff. I've dropped all
of it.' I press my fingers to the bridge of my nose. 'But, do you
know who else could have done this? And yes, I know you
don't want to hear it. Erin and Jamie.'

'What? No!'

'I know it's a bit "out there", but listen! He must know I've
been doing some digging into them. This could very easily be
a warning.'

'Why does everything have to go back to this bloody story?'

'What else is it connected to, then?'

His eyes shoot away. A sort of funny, itchy feeling washes
over me. Something isn't right.

'Mark?' I push.

He takes a deep breath and gives a slow shake of his head. My stomach drops at the look he's giving me.

'They've got nothing to do with it.'

'But how do you know? Surely everyone could be a suspect right now!'

He avoids my gaze. I notice his hands trembling as he pulls the blanket over him.

'I just do.'

I'm unable to ask him anything else, as the curtain is pulled back and a nurse explains that he needs to have his next dose of painkillers. Reluctantly I tell him I'll go and grab a coffee. This conversation isn't over. I see Mark's wallet in a plastic bag that the police gave him. My heart aches at the sight of it and my anger subsides. Whoever is behind this, he really was very lucky to escape unharmed. And the police will track whichever scumbag is responsible.

I forgot my purse when we rushed out of the office, so I take his wallet, knowing he won't mind if I use his card for a coffee, and head to the on-site café. I'd prefer a strong drink – my nerves are still shot to pieces – but I settle for an oat milk cappuccino. How can he be so sure this isn't to do with Erin and Jamie? Surely all the signs point to them – a way of shutting us up, hoping I'll drop this story. It can't be such a coincidence that I go round to speak to Erin and then the next day this happens.

I go to pay, but, as I open Mark's wallet, some receipts flutter to the floor. Someone behind me picks up the pieces of paper and hands them to me.

'Thanks.'

I tap his card against the card reader.

Transaction declined.

I tap the card against the machine again. I can sense the queue building behind me. It still says declined. My cheeks flush with heat. I give the debit card a wipe on the hem of my jumper.

'Do you want to try another card, or pay with cash?' the guy serving asks. Mark doesn't have any banknotes in here and I don't know his PIN to try that way, so I shake my head.

I mumble an apology. 'I'll have to leave it on the side and come back.' Perhaps their machine isn't working.

I hurry out of there, nearly bumping into a guy on crutches while I put Mark's card back into his wallet along with the receipts, glancing at them as I do.

Saliva rushes to my mouth.

I shoot out a hand against the wall to steady myself.

They're not receipts. They're betting slips.

A coldness creeps across me despite the heat in the hospital corridor. I step to one side to let an elderly man in a wheelchair move past and quickly log into my banking app. My vision blurs as I take in what's on the screen. Surely this can't be right.

I twist on my heels and run back to the ward.

58

Erin

There's been another power cut. Blackness wraps itself inside the house. The suddenness of it makes me jump. I try to act braver than I am, being plunged into darkness all alone.

The glow of my broken phone screen is the only light to guide my way. Instinctively I go to call Jamie's number, to tell him what's happened, to see if he knows how I can get the power back on. I have no idea where the fuse box is. But I stall, my fingers hovering above his name in my contacts.

I change my mind. Instead, I slowly feel my way up the stairs, taking great care to watch myself over the destroyed top step, and shuffle towards the study.

Goosebumps break out across my arms as I rest a hand on the doorframe. There is the smallest moment of hesitation, quickly overtaken by courage.

I push open the door and step inside.

Without the whir of the washing machine or the hum of the dishwasher, the house is completely silent. The only thing I can hear is my own shallow breath and thumping heart. Why does it still feel as if I'm being watched? As if I'm trespassing in my own home?

Wooden floorboards creak under my weight. The sound crawls into my bones.

A thick honey-coloured oak desk is pushed against the wall opposite the window. There's a couple of blank notebooks, a stationery holder with biros and a half-drunk bottle of mineral water. Surrounding the desk are unpacked cardboard boxes that I told the delivery men to stack in here until we decided where they'd go.

I suddenly feel silly creeping about like this. I don't even know what I'm looking for. Perhaps I'm being paranoid.

Then I remember. He lied about the flowers and, if Sophia's telling the truth, about her coming on to him. It isn't just the lies; it's the change in mood, his sudden violent temper, the creepy way he seems to know my every movement. Sophia has a point – it is strange how we don't have any form of surveillance on this house.

A shiver runs through me. What if we do? What if I'm right about this place being bugged? I glance up at the smoke alarm. There's no red light flashing now the power has been cut.

Has my own husband been watching me?

The thought makes me dizzy. I blink, my eyes still adjusting to the semi-darkness.

I have to move as fast as I can. The power could come back on at any time. I keep expecting my phone to ring with a concerned call from Jamie.

It's hard to make out shapes beyond the bright light of my torch. I catch my hand on the edge of a thick plastic storage box and swear. It's taken off a patch of skin.

I start tugging at the drawers in the desk. The wood creaks with resistance and there's a whine from the bloated oak drawer as it reluctantly opens. Inside is a collection of paperwork tucked into a plastic A4 wallet, a stapler, a key, a couple of leaking biros and an empty, puckered paracetamol packet. I drop the key into the pocket of my dressing gown, where it rests beside the business card Sophia gave me the other day.

I open up the wallet, casting the phone light on what's inside.

My cold fingers flick through what looks like a contract printed on his company headed paper. Many of the acronyms and descriptions go over my head. Something about changes to the camera sizes being disallowed. I put it to one side, worried that I'm being overly dramatic because I'm pregnant and hormonal.

I should be planning an incredible pregnancy reveal, not snooping around in Jamie's private paperwork. But right now I don't trust the father of my child, so, despite these seeds of self-doubt, I carry on searching.

Below this document is another piece of paper. A sense of unease grows as I hold my phone over the text to read it. I hunch closer under the glowing artificial light.

This one looks eerily familiar. There's the ominous logo at the top which I know I've seen before – once you see it you can't unsee it. It's not every day I've received correspondence from this address.

I swear under my breath then dash to the chest of drawers in our bedroom to find the tin where I keep my own paperwork. Inside are our marriage certificate and some private letters and mementos. I rustle through to find what I'm searching for, praying with every second that passes that I'm wrong.

My fingers pull out the official Metropolitan Police 'Notice of Harassment' that was addressed to me. The complaint from Claire, claiming that I'd stalked her. A powerful piece of paper that could be used against me if anyone discovered that I'd been at her apartment on the day she died. One that suggests that, somehow, I tipped her over the edge. I told Jamie I'd shredded it. Instead, I'd tucked it inside an interior design magazine and put it in this tin. I'm not sure why. It felt like something that shouldn't be thrown away, discarded.

I am so relieved that I kept it.

A rush of coldness washes over me. I place the two forms side by side on our crumpled duvet and hold the phone higher, hovering the ghostly light between both pieces of paper. I swallow, needing to oxygenate my brain so it can make sense of what I'm staring at right now, come up with some reason for what's going on.

Nothing concrete rushes to the surface. No explanations. No solutions. There's no way I can be seeing things clearly. I blink. Cough away the sudden scratchiness in my throat. But no, it's very, very clear. In the days after Claire died, I remember the constant panic that I would be arrested, that they would believe I had something to do with her unexpected death. My innocence would be questioned because I'd crossed a line. I was there that day! I could only breathe again when Jamie showed me the CCTV, a copy of which he'd handed to the police. Somehow, he had spliced the footage and deleted my entire presence.

I look down at the papers I've placed on my bed.

On one side is the notice the police sent me, the 'cease and desist' document.

On the other is the folded piece of paper I've just found in Jamie's desk drawer. The exact same logo, layout and design, but this one is blank. A template that anyone could use to make it look like an official form.

I start to shake, the light from my phone dancing erratically in the dark room. Seeing this self-designed 'official' document more clearly, it suddenly all falls into place. The form I was sent by the Metropolitan Police Force wasn't real.

Jamie comforted me after I received that scary letter full of criminal jargon and confusing language. But seeing it again clearly, it's terrifyingly obvious. He was the one who sent it.

59

Sophia

The nurse on Mark's ward looks up as I race past.

'Where the hell is our money?' I demand.

The colour drains from my husband's face, drops of water jumping from the plastic cup as he places it back on the side table with a shaking hand.

'Soph, I can explain.'

I think back to the final demand for an unpaid bill that I opened. He told me that it was a mix-up, a banking error. He lied.

'*Where is our money?*' I repeat through gritted teeth, trying to keep a lid on the boiling anger coursing through me. As soon as I found those betting slips, I tapped open the banking app on my phone, staring at my screen in utter disbelief. I was grateful to be propped up against the wall outside the hospital coffee shop.

Our savings have been wiped out. The joint account is at zero.

'Sit down, please. Let me try and explain.' He darts his eyes to the thin curtain separating us from the rest of the ward. I drop into the hard-backed plastic chair.

'I'm so sorry,' he says, chewing his lip, looking as if he might cry. 'It all got out of hand.'

'Mark . . . Where is our money?' My heart is pounding in my chest.

There's a tiny, hopeful part of me that thinks he will be able to explain this away – perhaps he's transferred it all to a high-interest account or done some really savvy saving trick – but as the seconds tick on, I know I'm clutching at straws.

His voice is so small I think I've misheard him.

'Sorry? What did you say?'

'. . . I've gambled it away.'

The cubicle tips around us.

I think of the eye-witness who said she saw a man leaving the betting shop. He wasn't in Tesco buying us lunch to bring to my desk like a dutiful husband. He was gambling away our money.

'I got into a bit of a sticky place. I borrowed some money and I couldn't pay it back. Then I borrowed some more, and, well, it's all gone . . .'

Tears are dripping down his ashen cheeks now. I blink and steady myself on the frame of his bed. How did I not know what dire financial straits we were in? How could I have been so distracted trying to defend my career that I didn't see any of this?

'How have we been paying for things, then?' I think of the extravagant honeymoon, the carefree lifestyle we've been living.

He winces. 'Payday loans.'

'Fuck!' I feel I'm in a nightmare that I can't seem to wake from. I rub my eyes roughly, as if it will help.

'How long has this been going on?'

'A while. At first, it was manageable but then I took a bad hit.' He swallows. 'That week, the week from hell, well, I must have been followed, and somehow Rupert and his gang knew about my problems. They offered me some cash. And . . .'

I already know what he's going to say. I want him to clamp his lips shut. I don't need to hear this next part; I don't want to be somehow culpable.

'They paid me to make the story go away. I'm so sorry, I was desperate. I needed the money!'

'The damaged recording. That was you . . .'

Pieces finally fall into place. It was no accident. Mark moved my work laptop and let go of the bottle of red wine on purpose, which then smashed, ruining the contents.

He gives the slightest of nods.

'You sabotaged my career. That was my chance to make a difference!' My words are tangled up as I try and speak. There's a strange sort of buzzing in my head, a migraine coming on.

'Soph.' He shifts under the thin hospital blanket, sweat beading his forehead, and lowers his voice. 'I did it for you too. I watched the video. I saw you holding that bag.'

My head twists. 'I had no idea it had petrol in it!'

'But if the police had found the unedited version, then you would have been pulled in too.'

I can't believe what I'm hearing.

'I didn't install the cameras just because of what happened with your job. I was terrified they would come and demand the money back. I thought if I bought some time, opened up some equity in the house, then . . .' He trails off, tears in his

320

eyes. 'But by then I had developed a problem, I was gambling more and more.'

A red-hot rage descends. 'You never thought to tell me the real reason why you wanted to sell our home? Or were you worried you might gamble that away too?'

'Right, I'm going to have to cut this short,' a nurse huffs as she tugs back the thin curtain of Mark's cubicle that scrapes on the metal rings. 'I will not have my other patients disturbed by your noise!'

'It's fine. We're done.' I turn on my heel. I can't bear to look at my husband's face any longer.

'Soph, please! I love you. Don't go!' Mark calls after me, but I ignore him. I am shaking all over. I need to just focus on putting one foot in front of the other.

It's true when they say that every marriage has secrets. I just had no idea ours would be so earth-shattering.

60

Erin

There's a sudden bang from downstairs. I almost leap out of my skin. I was too distracted discovering the fake police stalking forms that I didn't see the headlights from Jamie's car sweep the drive. I hear him call my name; he sounds out of breath. I quickly place the document back in the drawer and push it shut, trying to be as quiet as possible. My heart races. I can't let him know that I'm on to him. I have to remain calm and figure out how to call for help. Who knows what he's capable of?

I stumble out into the dark landing. The bright light from the torch on his phone darts about downstairs.

'There's been a power cut!' I call. Fear cracks in my voice.

'How long has it been like this? Why didn't you call me?' he shouts up the stairs, flashing his phone light.

I blink. 'It's literally only just happened—'

He cuts me off. 'Bloody hell. What have you been doing!'

I freeze. Can he see that the door to the study is open from down there?

'The stairs, Erin?'

I exhale. The broken top step.

'Thank God I came back when I did – you could have broken your neck tripping on that!'

He turns and walks into the kitchen, grumbling about being the only one to know where the fuse box is. I pull the door to the study shut as gently as I can. I swiftly move downstairs, being ever so careful, and into the kitchen, where the dim light is now back on over the table. My underarms are damp with sweat.

'I'll have to call someone out to fix that crack.' He finally turns to look at me and grimaces. 'Shit. What's happened to your face?'

'I tripped over the step. I told you it was rotten.'

He winces. 'It looks sore. Make sure those cuts don't get infected. Could turn nasty.'

Something shifts in my mind. If Sophia was right, that he's been watching me, then he would have seen me fall down the stairs. I can't help but glance up at the smoke alarm. The red light is back on, flashing again. If there were a camera in there, then he would have seen my accident, but his reaction seems genuine. Doesn't it? I can't trust my own judgement any more. He might be dishonest about some things but surely he would never want to hurt me.

Apart from when he pinned me against the wall, my subconscious reminds me. Did he damage the top step on purpose? I think of Claire. Of George. No, surely not; they were accidents, just like me tripping over. This is an old house, of course things could easily be rotten under the surface.

I need to come out and ask him about the flowers, why he lied about when he ordered them, and what really happened when he was alone with Sophia in the car when he told me she tried it on with him. It's her word against his.

However, now he's back, moving around the kitchen to find me some antiseptic wipes that he thinks are in a first aid kit at the back of the larder, I'm doubting myself. What if there's an innocent answer behind it all?

I do have a habit of jumping the gun sometimes.

But there's one thing that can't be easily explained away – the fact that he created a fake police form accusing me of stalking Claire. As hard as I try, I can't figure out why he would have done that.

'Stick the kettle on, will you?' he asks.

I move around the kitchen, filling the kettle and getting two mugs out, on autopilot, hoping he doesn't see the tremble in my hand. My head is too full to think properly. I rinse my grazed knuckles under the tap, wincing as the water hits the broken skin. It's a short-lived relief to feel something other than fear and confusion.

'Sorry, nothing in here. I'll pop to the chemist later.' He closes the door to the larder. 'So, have you missed me?' he asks.

'Course!' My voice is two octaves higher than normal. I cough. 'I didn't expect you back so soon.'

'I told you I was back today.'

No. He definitely said four nights and it's only been three. I'm sure of it.

'So, how did the meeting go?' I ask, finally turning to face him and hoping my clammy face isn't giving anything away.

'Great!' He smiles, baring his perfect straight white teeth. 'Great. We're back on track. Anyway, what about you? Have you been up to anything exciting since I've been away?'

I wave a hand. 'No, nothing. Just the same as usual . . .' I take a teaspoon out of the cutlery drawer.

'So . . . nothing out of the ordinary happened?' he asks slowly.

'No. Why?' I close the drawer, the rattle of silver jangling inside.

'No reason.' There's a moment where he starts to say something but stops himself.

'Jamie? I need to ask you something.' I take a deep breath. 'Where were you on the day that Claire died?'

The police never asked for alibis as they clearly had enough evidence that it was a tragic accident. But what if it wasn't? I'm quickly learning what a master manipulator my husband is. He has the skills to make things look different to how they really are.

'I was in work, then I came over to your flat for dinner. Then the coppers turned up. Why? Where has this come from? Is this to do with why Sophia was snooping around?'

The spoon drops out of my fingers at the tone of his voice, clattering on to the worktop. Coldness grips the base of my throat. This simple question reveals so much.

Sophia was right. He has been watching me.

'S-s-sorry?' I stutter.

'When were you going to tell me that she visited you?' he asks, matter-of-factly.

I try to swallow but my mouth is completely dry.

'Er, I forgot,' I say, distracted with the rush of confusing thoughts. 'I mean, she was literally here for five minutes, if that. How did—'

'What did you talk about?' he interrupts me.

'She wanted to know about Claire,' I reply as calmly as I can. If he needs to know what she said, then that must mean he didn't hear our conversation. I'm praying that's because the cameras can't detect audio.

'Claire?'

'That's all she said.' *And for me not to trust you.* 'I told her she had to leave.'

He keeps his eyes fixed on mine. 'So you didn't say anything else?'

I shake my head.

He's silent for a few seconds. A sudden gust of wind makes the windowpanes shudder.

'Come on,' he says firmly, snatching up his car keys from the side. 'We need to go and get something to clean you up. We don't want that to get infected. Hurry up and get dressed.'

Blood rushes from my legs. A wave of anxiety overwhelms me. I don't want to get in the car with him. I manage to shake my head slightly. 'I'm fine. Please don't worry.'

He looks at me, eyebrows knotted. 'Of course I worry about you, Erin. Now come on, don't be silly, we need to get you properly cleaned up. That cut looks nasty.'

I try to find my voice but my throat has clogged up.

'I promised to look after you in sickness and in health, remember?' He breaks into a cold smile, which doesn't meet his darkened eyes.

61

Erin

Jamie is speeding down dark, winding country lanes. I sink my nails into the leather seat cushion with every sharp turn. The roar of the engine and the chatter from the radio station fill the car. I can't think straight. We shoot past empty ploughed fields, startling birds resting in the bushes lining the road. There's a flap of wings as they take flight.

'W-w-where are we going?'

'I told you.' He thrusts the gearstick. A crunch of metal. 'To get you something for the cuts on your face.'

I don't believe him. Where is he really taking me? My stomach churns with nausea as he follows signs to the main road, overtaking other cars with wild abandon. A stream of angry drivers beep their horns behind us. The car jolts to the left. I shoot out a hand against the dashboard. Jamie's sitting slightly forward in his seat, his neck pulled taut, his arms locked tightly holding the steering wheel. A man on a mission.

Suddenly there's a lit-up sign in the dark night sky. We pull up outside the shopping precinct on the edge of the town centre. *Open till late.*

Despite the hour, it's surprisingly busy. There's a tightness in my chest as I follow Jamie in a daze. We move past packs of teenagers bent over screens, loitering on benches. Hand-holding couples peering into brightly lit shop windows. A squeal from an overtired toddler. Smells of salty fast food and roasted coffee waft over me.

I don't want to be here. I need to be at home looking for more evidence. The smoke alarms that are actually cameras, the fake police notice, the flower delivery, the lies, the violent side. My husband has changed beyond belief and I've only just scratched the surface.

He hands me a bag from the chemist with a tube of antiseptic cream, a pack of wipes and some gauze. 'Coffee?' he suggests. 'I need to work late, so I could do with a pick-me-up.'

I don't want to sit opposite him with an overpriced latte. How the hell can I pretend everything is OK? Everything is far from OK. But I can't find my voice.

As he's at the counter ordering, my mind is running wild. Does he know I'm on to him? No, there was a complete power cut. There's no way he saw me snooping. But I need to come up with a plan. There's only so long I will be able to get away with trying to stay calm in front of him. Every time he takes my hand or touches me, I freeze. He's going to catch on sooner rather than later that something is up.

My fingers tremble over my cracked phone screen. I could run to the toilets, call the police, but what would I even tell them? What I need is more time – another power cut, a way to work things out.

A cup of coffee is placed in front of me.

'Decaf. Don't want you to be up all night.' He winks.

Ironically, I need to cut back on caffeine now I'm pregnant. Not that I can even begin to wrap my head around the fact that I'm growing his baby inside me. This man feels like a complete stranger. I try and push the panic down. I have to keep my wits about me.

Jamie rummages in his jacket pocket and pulls out some folded pieces of paper. 'I hope you haven't got any plans this weekend.'

'W-w-why?'

'I wanted it to be a surprise but you know I'm terrible at keeping secrets,' he says, taking a sip of his drink. 'I'm taking you away.'

I blink. 'What?'

'You said we haven't spent much time together recently. So, how does a long weekend in Venice sound?'

'Jamie, we can't go away now.' A coldness creeps inside me.

'Why not? I'm my own boss, remember? I set my own rules.' A flash of irritation appears for a microsecond on his face. 'Anyway, isn't a man allowed to surprise his new wife with a romantic city break without being interrogated?'

I want to say that I'm hardly interrogating but I stay quiet. He slides a slim brochure across the table. The front cover has an image of rustic gondolas on a turquoise-coloured canal that I'm certain has been Photoshopped. I pick it up and open it with trembling fingers.

'I know you've always wanted to go. It will be out of season so it should be quiet – fewer tourists getting in the way.' He clears his throat. 'I've been working loads and, well, the honeymoon didn't quite go as planned, so . . .'

He's waiting for me to say something.

All I can think is that he's done this in public so I can't create a scene.

I force myself to get to my feet, my legs like lead, and wrap my arms around him. The smell of his aftershave catches in the back of my throat. 'I'm sorry. Thank you. I guess I'm just a bit on edge, especially after what happened last time we went away,' I mumble.

'Exactly. That's another reason why it'll be good for us to get away for a bit. Have a change of scene. It's time to look to our future.'

'When do we leave?' I try to hide the apprehension in my voice.

'Tomorrow afternoon. I had hoped to wake you up and whisk you away, but there's a few things I need to see to first.' He glances at my cup. 'Ah, you've finished your coffee. Here's some money to treat yourself to some new holiday clothes. Some sexy lingerie, perhaps?' My stomach turns. A wad of cash lands in my hands. 'I've also found a place to fix your phone screen. I can drop it off after this if you like,' he says with a smile.

There is a brief flash of the man that I married sitting opposite me once again. What am I supposed to say to avoid letting him know that I can see what he's doing? Everything is screaming at me not to hand my broken phone over, but I can't think quickly enough.

'Thank you.'

'My pleasure.' He pauses. 'You know, Erin, you could try and look a bit more excited.'

'I'm sorry,' I say quickly. 'It's just the last time—'

He holds up a hand. 'I promise you it'll be better than our honeymoon. Right, off you go, darling. The parking will run out soon.'

I scrape my chair back against the tiles. The sound shoots through me.

62

Erin

Friday 30 September

Heavy grey clouds drag themselves past the bedroom window. The dark skies and brewing rain warn of the storm that's predicted to hit at some point. It looks as though it's going to be the type of day where there's no point getting out of bed. I don't know what time it is as I don't have my phone. The man in the repair shop needed to keep it overnight. Jamie told me he'd go and pick it up in his lunch break if he had time.

I shrug on my dressing gown and pad downstairs, needing a strong coffee after tossing and turning all night. I didn't hear Jamie leave this morning. His car isn't here and his work bag has gone.

It's eerie to be suddenly left alone. I don't know what time he is planning to be home or what exactly is happening later with this surprise Venice trip. I need to go along with things and try to stay calm as I figure out a plan to escape. Jamie watched me like a hawk at the shopping centre. The only time he let me out of his sight was when he encouraged me to go into a fancy boutique, the money he'd given me sweating in my palm. I caught sight of him pacing outside, his phone pressed to his ear, an unreadable expression on his face.

I thought about running away, nervously glancing around for a fire exit. But where would I go? At the till I handed over the clothes I didn't want, screaming with my eyes that I needed help. The shop assistant scanned the items and asked if I was interested in signing up for a store card. I heard Jamie call my name before I could reply.

Once we were back in his car, he tenderly applied the strong-smelling antiseptic cream to my head wound. Before he started the engine, he tipped my chin to kiss me, telling me that he loved me. I don't know how I mustered the words to say it back, but I did.

A shiver passes through me as I walk into the kitchen. He's left breakfast out for me. I must be doing a good enough job of acting as though everything is normal. I pour out a cup of coffee from the pot that's still warm and add some milk. It tastes funny. I should eat something for the baby's sake, I think, so I spoon up a couple of mouthfuls of cornflakes, which also taste different. Perhaps the milk is going off.

As I'm chewing I spot a brown envelope on the worktop. Inside, along with a wad of euros, is a piece of paper with our flight details. I scan the information and go cold. Underneath the times of departure is a section for passenger details.

Only one seat selected. One name printed.

My married name.

The kitchen swells around me. Why hasn't Jamie booked a ticket? Why has he arranged for me to go alone? My scalp prickles. If I go on this trip then I know I won't be coming back. I'm sure of it. What was the reason he made me go to the shops to buy holiday clothes alone? So I'm the only one on their CCTV. A sweat breaks out at the thought. He's smarter than me. He always has been.

I tell myself to stay calm. He could be watching my every move right now. I daren't look up at the smoke alarm. Instead, I put my empty bowl in the sink. It clatters against the ceramic.

Before I do anything, I need to be certain he's not in the house.

Fear threatens to overwhelm me.

Has he been here the entire time? Hiding in these four walls, watching me as I naïvely move around? I bet there are hidden passageways or stairwells I have no idea about. The dripping sound . . . was that him all along? My mind is awash with spine-chilling thoughts, each one wilder and scarier than the last.

With a deep breath, I walk towards the larder, coming up with a plan. This is where we keep the cleaning products. My eyes dart over the antiseptic spray, scourers and plastic bottles of bleach. My trembling hands pick up a can of furniture polish and a yellow dust cloth. I have to be clever. If he's watching me then I need to look as if I'm innocently cleaning.

My heart is in my mouth; I'm convinced he will suddenly leap out of somewhere as I wipe the cloth over the banister while I trudge up the stairs. I start in our bedroom, swallowing the fear that accompanies me when I peer inside the wardrobe doors.

I drop to my knees and check under the bed frame, half expecting to be met with his eyes in the darkness.

Suddenly, I hear a noise coming from the bathroom. Fear flutters in my stomach; it's like a kick from the baby, willing me to do something. Everything tingles with adrenaline. I walk towards the closed bathroom door, sweat prickling across my back.

I reach for the handle, trying to push away thoughts about what might be on the other side.

With a deep breath I thrust it open.

It's just the shower head dripping.

I exhale and rub my face with my hands. Buoyed by the shot of adrenaline, I quickly check the other rooms upstairs. All lie eerily empty and still.

The only door I haven't looked behind is the airing cupboard. I press the handle down firmly but nothing happens. It refuses to open. Jamie told me I just had to give it a shove but he was lying. I can see now that there's the slit of a keyhole inside the handle, easily missed if you weren't looking for it.

Why would the airing cupboard be locked?

I want to press myself against the wood, see if I can hear anything from inside, but something catches my eye. The blinking light of the smoke alarm on the landing just above me.

Jamie's not in the house, but that doesn't mean he's not watching me.

I remember the key I found in his office desk. It's still in my dressing gown pocket. Even if it fits, I can't just unlock the door and go inside. Not yet. I hurry downstairs, as casually as I can, to put the furniture polish back in the larder. I need to cut the power. But where is the fuse box? I still have no idea where it is and I'm running out of time to start looking properly. Jamie could return home at any minute.

Hanging on a hook, beside the shelves holding Kilner jars of flour and tins of soup, is a wooden broom. I pull it free then drag the hard bristles across the cold kitchen tiles. The painful scratching sound runs through me.

With both hands on the broom, I raise it high in the air and, using all my strength, whack it against the smoke alarm in the kitchen. I'm overwhelmed with an urge to put my middle finger up just before it crashes to the floor.

The clock is ticking.

I leave a satisfying path of destruction as I make my way upstairs, smashing the hallway and landing smoke alarms, accidentally taking out the gilt-framed mirror too, in my haste. A hidden strength blossoms from deep inside, as if the baby is spurring me on.

Once outside the locked airing cupboard, I drop the broom and scrabble a hand inside the deep pockets of my dressing gown. I've done all I can to make sure my husband isn't watching me. I place the key in the lock, my fingers trembling with anticipation and fear as I turn it and push open the door.

I scream as Jamie's face stares back at me.

63

Erin

The airing cupboard isn't a cupboard at all. It's a small storage room filled with things I've never seen before, including a large canvas print of Jamie's face, directly in my eyeline, resting on a bookcase in front of me. The way the light hits it from the tiny window makes it look as if he's here, hiding and waiting for me to find this secret den.

My heart is about to leap from my chest. I momentarily close my eyes, forcing myself to slow my breathing. It's only a photograph. The fear of coming face to face with my husband has sent my brain into overdrive.

He's not here. But he might be, as soon as he discovers that I've smashed up his hidden cameras.

I take another look at the print. It's from his wedding day to Claire. Tiny flakes of confetti flutter around their beaming faces as they exit the church. Why is this on display in a secret room?

With my heart rate returning to normal, I scan around the rest of the small space. It's no bigger than a walk-in wardrobe. There's a desktop computer resting on an antique dressing table. Jamie has been in here recently, by the looks of things. A couple of crushed lager cans, an empty crisp packet and a sludgy brown banana skin sit beside the mouse mat, the cloying smell at odds with the damp odour of the room. Is this where he goes when he tells me he's working? A coldness spreads through me.

Piles of boxes are awkwardly placed on top of one another. Are these mementos from their life before? Trinkets he's held on to as a reminder of their marriage?

There's a small, sealed cardboard box that looks out of place next to the other ones. I need something sharp to open it. In the stationery holder is a letter-opener. I lean across the mystery box and press the blade into the thick brown tape. As I do, the edge slips and I nick the side of my thumb. Crimson drops of blood fall on the brown cardboard lid.

'Ow.'

I stick my finger in my mouth and suck the blood, wincing at the metallic taste on my tongue, while I use the other hand to look at what's inside the box. It smells of faded, musty perfume. There's a couple of woollen jumpers – women's clothes, judging by the labels of high street brands I recognise. Are these Claire's?

My hand hits something hard against all the softness. An Apple iPhone. It's out of charge so I can't turn it on. I frown. Jamie hates Apple products. Tucked beside it is a leather wallet containing several bank cards – none of them are in Jamie's name. There is also a pouch with a bundle of folded euros bound by a thick elastic band.

A strange buzzing begins in my head; my fingertips prickle with pins and needles. I can't think straight, my mind suddenly cloudy as if trapped in heavy fog.

I hear something. My whole body freezes with fear. The windows rattle in their frames as the wind picks up outside. The storm is coming. There's a sudden gust of icy-cold air. The house creaks in resistance.

Wait, is that the sound of a car?

I stop breathing and rush across to the nearest window, splattered with raindrops in the dirty grey light. No. There are no headlights approaching. However, I can hear the warning caw of a gull circling overhead, as if telling me I need to get out of here.

My feet move as fast as they can downstairs. I turn the handle on the front door. It's locked.

It's never locked.

Trying not to give in to the panic that's creeping up my shaking legs, I carefully move through the kitchen, stepping over broken bits of plastic, and push the handle on the back door. Another wave of adrenaline courses through me. It won't budge. My mouth runs dry as I try the handle once more.

Jamie has locked me in the house.

There's no point shouting; there's no one outside to hear. I force myself to take deep breaths.

I can't get out but I can call for help.

I run upstairs and connect the iPhone to the charger that's plugged into the wall, my fingers trembling. The screen stays black. It's a few painful seconds before the lightning symbol flashes up. It works, at least. Suddenly I have a lifeline.

I have to concentrate on not dropping the phone. My finger presses hard on the power button. It feels like a lifetime but, finally, there is the Apple symbol. It doesn't ask me for a passcode. I quickly jab 999. My numb fingers hover over the dial button.

They will come after me too. For my part in George's death. For tampering with Claire's CCTV. I can't have my baby born in prison. Escaping is my only option but I can't get out.

I don't know Kat's number off by heart. I only have one other person I can call. My hands roam the pockets of my dirty dressing gown. I half expect it not to be here, but it is. Air escapes my lips as I pull out the business card, and cross everything that she picks up.

64

Sophia

Friday 30 September

I think the reason I offered to drive Mark to his sister's house after he was discharged was because I needed to know he had gone. The only sound on the entire journey was the rain hammering against the windscreen. I couldn't bear to look at him. His confession has been turning over and over on a loop in my shattered mind.

'Are you not going to stay for a bit?' he asks when we arrive, looking up at me with huge watery eyes.

Jules's house is eerily silent. She's gone to pick the kids up from their various after-school clubs and childminders but left a key for us.

I shake my head. The weather is bad and the traffic is only going to get worse. I want to get back to my own bed. Alone. I need some time by myself to work through it all.

'I've got to get ready for work tomorrow.'

It's a lie. Claudia has put me on compassionate leave. When she discovered my husband was the victim of the hit-and-run, she immediately softened, making sure to splash the front page with the police appeal for witnesses. Amira has sent me some lovely messages checking I'm OK.

Everyone thinks I'm by my innocent husband's bedside. No one would believe that this may have been a targeted incident – that, because he borrowed money off some truly awful men, he has put his own life at risk. The menacing dogs, the terrifying man in the alleyway, the hit-and-run. Mark might be right. These are the actions of Rupert's gang, but my husband's secret gambling, not my investigation, is behind it all.

Amira also wanted to know if she should pick up the George Kingsley investigation in my abscence. I haven't replied yet, but it's time I dropped it and admitted that there isn't enough proof that would stand up in a court of law. Technically, the Instagram reel capturing Erin and Jamie heading to the cliffs doesn't prove anything. They might have turned around and gone in a completely different direction when the camera was off. I have no other evidence that they have anything to do with George's death.

I've also come to a dead end with what might have happened to Claire. My gut tells me Jamie had something to do with her death, but the police clearly didn't think there was anything untoward, and I don't know what else to do to hunt for clues. I don't trust them, not after everything I've learned from Erin's suspicious stalking tendencies and the fact that Jamie lied to me about his wife having bipolar disorder and telling her I tried it on with him. They might be a fucked-up couple but it doesn't mean either of them is a killer.

I drag myself back to the present. 'Jules won't be long.' I shrug on my coat, avoiding Mark's gaze.

'I really am sorry, you know,' he says, his voice small.

I have to bite my lip to stop myself from bursting into tears. 'Have you seen my phone?' I ask instead.

'It's over here,' Mark says, stretching an arm to the coffee table to pass it to me. 'Looks like you've got a message from Angie.'

I take my phone and frown at the screen. Why's Angie messaging me? I tap it open.

Have you seen the news? I can't believe it!!

She's sent me a screen grab from a private Bali Facebook group that she's a member of. According to an ex-pat named Jackie, a man has been arrested in connection with the murder of George Kingsley. I frown, staring at the mugshot supplied by the police.

'Everything OK?' Mark asks.

I ignore him. My fingers can barely move fast enough to type.

Is this a joke?

No!!!

I blink again at the face I recognise. My insides run cold. I try to focus my eyes to read the text. It's been roughly translated but the gist of it is clear. The person they've arrested, the one looking up at me from my screen with a haunting expression, is Ketut, the hotel barman.

Mark is waiting for me to explain what's going on.

'Ketut's been arrested for George's murder! I've just had this message from Angie.'

I show him my screen. He scrolls in silence.

This doesn't feel real. How have I got this so wrong? I start to pace around the lounge. 'Can you believe it? He served us drinks every single day! You went to that market with him!'

Mark's muted reaction fills me with creeping dread. All the colour has drained from his cheeks.

'What's going on?' I ask, taking my phone back. He presses the heel of his palm to his eyes. I catch sight of the bruised puncture marks from the IV line.

'It wasn't actually a proper market, it was a . . . cockfight.'

I blink, convinced I've misheard him. He was gambling on our honeymoon.

Of course he was.

'And George was there too.'

The floor rises up to meet me. My legs almost give way as I sink to the armchair opposite.

'What? You knew George Kingsley?' I shriek.

Mark gives an awkward shake of his head. Eyes wide and bloodshot. 'I didn't *know* him. We had one quick chat at the fight. He was showing me the ropes. That was it!'

My head pulsates with tension. 'Then what?'

'He was betting big – a few of the local lads were watching him pull out large wads of cash. He wasn't being subtle at all.' He coughs, wincing. 'However, I was on bad form and kept losing. Gambling is illegal in Bali so there was this police raid at the end. Nothing like you see in the films, but it meant it was over before it began.'

Before he could win our money back. There was no confusion over currency at an innocent street market, as he told me.

Mark rubs his pale face. 'George must have recognised me in the Blue Fin after Erin accidentally spilt that drink over him. I couldn't believe the chances. I was terrified he was going to say something to you about me being at the cockfight when I'd told you I was at a market. Just before we left the restaurant, I bumped into him by the toilets and he told me there was another fight planned for that night. He asked if I wanted to go with him.'

I can't believe what I'm hearing.

Mark swallows. 'These fights don't last long. I knew I could be there and back before you went to bed, especially as you told me you were staying out for a drink at the hotel bar. I needed to try and win our cash back.'

So that was why he looked so ill and unsettled and wanted to leave the meal early.

I swallow. 'So you went to this other fight when you told me you were locked out . . . Trapped on a fire escape . . .'

It's all starting to make horrific sense. How foolish can I have been? He wasn't coming to find his terrified wife who has a phobia of storms. Instead, he was gambling with strangers at a macabre illegal blood sport. For the second time on our honeymoon.

And one of those other gamblers ended up murdered.

'No!' He firmly shakes his head, seeing my face. 'It wasn't like that! When we got back to the hotel, I was going to find Ketut. To see if he could arrange a lift to the fight. But you went to the bar and I couldn't risk coming there and you spotting me. I knew I should have gone to bed like I'd told you but I tried to walk to find a taxi instead. It began to absolutely chuck it down, so as soon as I realised how stupid the idea was, I turned around and came back. I thought you'd still be in the bar, I didn't expect you to be back in the room.'

'Why didn't you tell me this before?' I stutter.

'Because of how bad it looks! But I swear I had nothing to do with George's death.' Silent tears drip down his cheeks. 'Imagine if I'd gone to meet him – who knows what could have happened? I could have been killed too!' Mark roughly wipes his eyes with the sleeve of his hoodie, trying to compose himself again.

My head is pounding. My phone buzzes in my hands. Angie's sent another message.

Isn't it extraordinary? Ketut seemed so nice! But I guess you don't ever really know someone . . .

No, I think, looking over at Mark. You don't.

65

Sophia

The engine is running but I can't move. I sit staring out of the windscreen, my jagged breath fogging up the glass. The wind has picked up and rain pounds the roof of the car. Mark begged me to stay and listen to more of his apologies but I had to get out. I twist my wedding ring around my finger and try to make sense of the past twenty-four hours.

It pains me to believe a word of his confession, yet things have started to fit into place. I can't stop going over and over the events of the last night of our honeymoon in my tired mind.

I remember leaping out of my skin when he turned up at the bedroom door, after I presumed he was asleep under the covers. I thought he was sweating with a breaking fever but he must have been flushed from running back to the room once he realised how stupid it was to go and meet George. Despite everything, I can't help but thank God he did turn back.

My stomach lurches thinking how close Mark could have been to getting caught up in what happened to George. I slam my palm against the steering wheel. How stupid he's been! I'm furious, not only with him, but with myself too. How blind I've been to miss all of this.

I'm about to reverse off Jules's drive when my phone rings with an unknown number.

'Hello?' My voice cracks.

There is a drawn-out pause down the line.

'Oh, my God, Sophia! You have to help me.'

I sit bolt upright. 'Erin?'

'Jamie is a monster. I think he killed his ex-wife and now he's going to kill me!'

Her words come out in one continuous stream. It takes me a second to work out what she's saying.

'Sophia, he's trapped me in the house. I can't escape. He knows that I'm on to him! You have to help me!'

Goosebumps break out across my arms at the fear in her voice.

'I can't leave.' Her voice is painfully tight, clogged by tears. 'I don't know where he is and I don't—'

'I'm coming over. I'm at Mark's sister's, so I won't be long. If he's locked you in then break a door down. I promise, I—'

'I can't leave him because I'm pregnant.'

I close my eyes.

'Sophia?'

'I'm still here.'

She's sobbing.

I take a deep breath. 'I know this isn't what you want to hear, but you and your baby are in danger. Please, Erin. You need to think of your child now.' Jamie may not have killed George, but who knows what this man is capable of? 'I'm on my way. Try and get yourself to safety and call me again.'

A fire is lit inside me as I screech off the drive.

66

Erin

As darkness falls, the storm worsens and a bolt of lightning suddenly splits the murky black sky. The house seems to be holding its breath. I pray that Sophia will get here before Jamie does. I've tried to find other ways to open the front and back doors but there are no spare keys anywhere. He's locked all the windows too. I'm completely trapped. The realisation swirls in my chaotic mind.

Hurry up, hurry up.

I'm shaking in fear at what my husband has planned for me. There's too much adrenaline zipping through my body to allow me to sit still. My head is pounding.

Suddenly I hear a scraping of tyres against gravel. Surely Sophia can't have made it here that quickly?

There's a scratch of a key in the lock.

It's not Sophia.

'Erin!' Jamie slams the front door behind him and thunders through the hallway and into the kitchen. 'Are you all packed and ready for Veni—?' He swears. 'What the hell has gone on here? What the fuck have you done to the smoke alarms? Why have you smashed them into a million pieces? Have you lost your mind?'

Can the baby hear my heartbeat quickening? Does the pulse of my blood carry through my veins and feed into this tiny thing? Do they know how scared I am?

'I know you've been watching me,' I pant. 'They're not smoke alarms, they're cameras. Following my every movement.'

Why does my head hurt so much? The buzzing noise is only getting louder.

He goes to say something, deny it, but catches himself and lowers his voice. 'It's for your own good, Erin.'

'What?' I stutter.

'You're not well. You've not been well for a long time and I just wanted to keep you safe.'

'No! You're a liar.'

'What did you call me?'

I don't get the chance to repeat myself as he picks up a mug from the draining board and launches it at the stone wall. It shatters across the floor.

'Say that again!'

Strands of spittle spray from his lips, his eyes wild and terrifyingly dark. It hits me that I have no idea who this man really is.

Something else is thrown – a wine glass this time. My breath is trapped in my chest. I'm growing light-headed. The corner of my vision starts to blur, a sudden wave of heat washes over me and my legs slump to the cold tiles.

I think of the coffee and the cereal he left out: they both tasted funny. I thought the milk was off, or that maybe it was a change in my taste buds because of the pregnancy hormones, but I was wrong. He's drugged me.

The dim kitchen light seems to glow and fade. I blink. I'm still on the floor in a crumpled heap. I have a throbbing headache and a ringing in my ears. The room sways even though I'm not moving.

Is this what he did to Claire? Drugged her so she fell down the stairs? Made it look as if it was self-inflicted? An accident?

Jamie's voice somehow continues to pierce through the high-pitched buzzing. I shut my eyes to concentrate. Rain is pounding against the patio doors. There's a flash of lightning. The sound of a phone ringing. It's impossible to know what's real and what's in my head.

'You have to believe me that I never wanted it to get like this,' Jamie says, as if he is at the other end of an echoey tunnel. 'If I could change what happened on that night by the cliffs then I would. Of course, if you hadn't put your foot out . . .'

'What?' I gasp.

'I know what you did, Erin,' he says matter-of-factly. 'George fell because you tripped him. You didn't even check he was dead. You just assumed he was! You left him lying there. What sort of person can walk away like that?'

It's as though he's taken a plank of wood to my chest.

I try to protest. Words gurgle in my throat, unable to reach the surface.

He speaks over me. 'You think you're so innocent in all of this. I shouldn't have punched him, but at least I didn't kill him. That was you.'

I blink. My eyelids are too heavy to hold up. The muscles in my face seem to be melting.

There's one final realisation before the blurriness in my head threatens to take over. Sophia isn't coming.

67

Sophia

The windscreen wipers are no match for the heavy rain that's pounding against the glass. I'm tearing down the country road, hands gripping the steering wheel. My mind is struggling to process everything I've learned in the past forty-eight hours.

I should probably slow down a little, take more care on these unlit lanes, but I have to get to Erin. I round the corner and begin the approach up to their house at the top of the hill, flicking my lights to full beam in an attempt to see through the darkness of the woods. Every so often there's a fork of lightning in the distance. I bite down the voice that's telling me to turn around and run to safety. Hide.

I need to get to Erin. I've never heard anyone sound so scared in my life.

A loud ringing sound startles me. I peel my eyes from the road to see Amira's number flashing up on my screen. I frown and accept the call. 'Amira, is everything OK?' I have to shout over the sound of the rain. 'I'm driving.'

'Sophia, I just had to call you!' She sounds as if she's out of breath. There is a click-clacking of her fingers speeding over a keyboard. 'I'll be quick. I've been thinking about Erin and Jamie.'

I'm about to tell her that it's over, Ketut has been arrested, we got it wrong, but she speaks over me.

The signal dips in and out. I'm only able to catch certain words.

'I didn't catch that. Amira?'

'I said . . . George's autopsy report . . . not what we expected.'

There's something about her frantic breathlessness that sends a shiver up my spine.

'Say that again?'

'I . . . another look at George Kingsley's autopsy report. It mentions . . . rash . . . neck.'

'Yeah?' I try and remember. There was something in the report about this. 'A rash on George's neck? A shaving rash or—'

There's a delay on the line and she talks over me.

'George was . . .'

'What?' Goosebumps spread across my tense body. 'Amira, I really can't hear you. Try again. What did you say?'

'George was strangled . . .'

This time I catch what she's trying to say, but then there's a crackle and a loud beep. The call cuts out.

Shit.

He was strangled? The police definitely didn't mention it in their report.

My mind is too clouded. The answer feels as though it's staring me in the face, but I can't find a way to see it clearly.

A sudden corner appears. My breath is trapped in my throat as I press hard on the brakes. Spindly birch trees sway ominously before me, lit by my rain-splattered headlights. There's no way I want to go down into the thorny ditches. I drop down a gear. I need to take these unfamiliar bends slowly.

Amira's number appears on the in-car system once more, and I jab to accept the call.

'Hi. Are you there? Did you say George was strangled?' I say hurriedly, in case I lose her again. 'Listen, I've just found out that a barman from the hotel, a guy called Ketut, has been arrested. Do you think he strangled him?'

She's not listening to me. Her voice talks over mine. 'I can't really hear you either. If it cuts out again then I'll text you what I've found.' Another gap of static. 'But – hang on, where are you anyway?'

'I'm—' There's a beep. No signal whatsoever. I must be in the deepest part of the woods now, exactly where Jamie stopped the car and told me to stay away from his wife. The place where he lied to my face that Erin suffered from a serious mental illness, blaming her changed behaviour on something that doesn't exist.

I stab at the phone screen but it won't reconnect the call. Just then another car speeds past, its headlights dazzling me.

'Shit.' My hands fly to the wheel, gripping it tightly, a sweat breaking out at the back of my neck.

Amira said she'd text me. I can't risk trying to call her back; I need to concentrate on not getting myself killed. I shiver, despite the warm air blowing out of the heaters.

Hang on, Erin. I'm almost there.

68

Erin

I don't know how long I blacked out for, but it's clear that Sophia isn't coming; she would have been here by now. If I'm to escape from this man, this monster, then I need to stay lucid. But the more time that passes, the harder it is to focus. With all my might I try to summon the energy to pick myself up off the floor. A constant thud pounds at the back of my head. I blink rapidly, praying my eyes will focus on the familiar shapes in the cold kitchen.

Jamie's taken out a wine glass – just one – and is lining up painkillers and sleeping pills beside a bottle of vodka. The easy motion of his movements chills me. It's growing more and more obvious that this isn't the first time he's performed this set-up – making it look like an overdose.

I have to get out of here alive. My baby depends on me. Being strong is the only way I can save us both.

My stomach flips as he speaks. 'At first, I liked how possessive you were, taking such an interest in my ex-wife. Found it kinky, if I'm honest. It was proof of how much you truly loved me.'

The walls are closing in. He sounds as if he's being interviewed but there's no one else here. I push my hands on to the
tiles and try to lift myself up. I'm fighting against the wooziness
in my mind. I have to stay focused, stay calm, work out what
to do next.

'It took Claire a while but eventually she was on to you.
When she worked out that her "stalker" was actually my
fiancée, I had to swoop in and clear up your mess.'

'You killed her!'

'What are you talking about? I wasn't there. *You* were the
one caught on the CCTV at her apartment – well, you would
have been if I hadn't worked my editing magic on the footage.
You're welcome, by the way. I wish I hadn't bothered now.
The things you do for love!' He sniffs. 'I suppose that meant
you needed someone else to obsess over, and then in walks
Sophia. Perfect Sophia. I knew the moment I saw her that you
would want to be her best friend. See, I know you better than
you think I do.'

I clench my jaw. With my fingernails digging into the wood
of the dining table I'm able to hoist myself to my wobbling
feet. My whole body starts to shake now that I'm upright. I'm
terrified the blackness will pull me under once more.

'You killed an innocent man,' I splutter. My tongue feels
too big in my dry mouth. 'I didn't trip George. You punched
him!'

He finally looks over at me, disgust on his face.

'No, *you* killed George. What have I said to you about
getting things confused in your head?'

I see him walk towards the kitchen knife block, the jet-
black handles jutting from the wood just inches away. The air

has been sucked from the room. What about the pills? Have I got this wrong?

'I took my vows seriously. In sickness and in health.' He taps the side of his head. 'I would have done anything for you, Erin. Well, at the beginning. Then you kept going on and on about that final night of our honeymoon. Reframing the story in your mind, forgetting things. With your history, I doubt anyone would ever believe you anyway.'

'Y-y-you made me run away that night. I would have stayed and called an ambulance.' It doesn't sound like my voice at all.

He throws his head back and lets out a laugh so deep it makes me jump.

'Yeah, right. Course you would have! Don't make me laugh. You've never faced up to anything that's gone wrong in your life.'

I ignore him and concentrate on forming words in my mouth, stumbling over them like a drunk. 'You ran because you knew the police would find out about Claire and lock you up for her death too!' Every time I swallow, I feel a sharp dart of pain.

Jamie turns away. My eyes widen in pure horror as his hand slowly and calmly pulls out a carving knife.

Time seems to slow down. Surely this can't be happening.

'Erin. I did this for you.'

The room spins. A wave of icy fear darts through me.

He doesn't expand any more. No, no, no. I can see it clearly. He's going to slit my wrists. The pills, the booze, the self-inflicted injuries – he's staging this to look as if I've done it to myself.

'I'm pregnant!' I manage to spit out.

His hand freezes mid-air. Light glints off the blade of the knife. 'What?'

He begins to pace, crunching over shards of glass and jagged pieces of plastic from the smoke alarms. The knife is still in his fist. I swallow the rush of saliva in my mouth. I can tell this has completely thrown him.

There's a flutter in my stomach, as if the baby's kicking me for being so stupid, for telling anyone our secret.

'I thought you'd be happy.'

'No.' He blinks rapidly. 'You're lying.'

Before I can say another word, his whole body snaps alert.

'What the fuck was that?' He darts his head to the side.

A bright light sweeps the room, illuminating the chaos. It's the headlights of a car.

Sophia is here.

69

Sophia

A torrent of rain drenches me the moment I step out of the car. There's an ominous howl from the wind rushing across the exposed fields. The solitary grey house looks even more sinister in this ghostly light.

I'm terrified I'm too late.

Jamie's car is already here, parked beside another car I've not seen before. My body tenses. He's back. I don't have time to think about my own safety. My hair is whipped by the thrashing wind, my face pelted with ice-cold raindrops.

I try the front door but it's locked. No lights on. I shoot around the back of the house then freeze. They're in there. Jamie is standing in the kitchen with his back to me. Erin looks terrible, her face all blotchy and bloated, skin covered in angry spots and hair pulled into a greasy ponytail. My knees are shaking in fear. I force myself to be brave and try to open the back door.

A loud creak heralds my arrival.

'Erin, get your things,' I say with an authority I don't possess.

'Sophia?' Jamie spins to face me. 'Thank God! Maybe you can talk some sense into her. She's completely lost it!'

'Don't you even think about coming closer.' My voice trembles in his presence.

'Sophia, please. She won't talk to me. I'm terrified she's having some sort of psychotic episode. I mean, just look at the place,' Jamie pleads. 'I rushed back as quickly as I could to see if she was OK. She's in a really bad way, not making any sense at all. You have to help!'

There's broken plastic all across the floor. Exposed wires hang from the ceiling where a smoke alarm used to be.

'He's lying, Sophia,' Erin gasps. Her nose glistens with snot. Mascara is smudged around her wide, reddened eyes. 'He's been watching the house. The smoke alarms are cameras!'

'She's talking gibberish. The last time she got this upset it was bad, trust me,' he adds. His attention is focused on me alone. He looks alarmingly pale.

'Trust you?' I shout. Fear zips down my trembling legs. I look past him, at Erin. 'Are you OK? Please try and stay calm, think of the baby.'

'She told you that too?' Jamie says. 'Sophia, Erin's not pregnant.'

I watch as her hand goes straight to her stomach, eyes wide as if he's just slapped her.

'What?'

'She's convinced herself she is but it's just another delusion, like the smoke alarms.'

'No! He's lying!' Her face crumples in on itself. 'Why would you say that? I've done the tests! It's true.'

'Sophia.' He turns to me, hands held up high.

362

'Don't come any closer. I don't know what the hell is going on right now—'

They try to talk over one another. Erin is louder. 'He had a fucking knife in my face and—' She stops and turns her head to the knife block in the kitchen. Five black handles point in the air like dog tails. 'He must have put it back when you came in . . .'

Jamie takes this as a cue to grab my attention. 'Sophia, you have to believe me. Erin's really not well!'

I make myself stand a little taller. 'You said she has bipolar disorder but that's a lie, isn't it?'

'No! It's true. She gets worked up like this. Obsesses over things. Look.' He points to a handbag that's on the worktop, identical to my Chanel one that my parents bought me for my thirtieth. 'Her wardrobe is full of clothes exactly like yours, all new with tags on. She's trying to become you.' He tries to calm his breathing down. 'The only crime I've ever committed is keeping her secret. Claire would be alive if it weren't for Erin.'

'What?'

The rain lashes against the windows and a sudden draught runs through the kitchen. It's only then that I realise Erin isn't in the room any more.

'Erin killed Claire?' I repeat slowly, my eyes darting around, trying to see where she's gone.

'Claire would still be here if it weren't for Erin stalking her, trolling her, pushing her over the edge. She was obsessed with her, even killed her cat. Claire drank and mixed her medications because she was afraid of what Erin would do next.'

Erin was Claire's stalker? The one Marie told me about? No one believed her, but what if she was right? What if he's telling the truth?

'I'm calling the police.' I pull my phone out.

Jamie doesn't try to stop me but there's something on the screen before I can dial 999. A message from Amira. I need to know what she so desperately wanted to tell me.

She's attached a photo from George's autopsy, and has written notes to go with it.

These are petechiae, sort of pinpoint reddish spots that appear in clusters. It looks like a rash but it's actually the result of bleeding from broken capillaries. I've seen these marks before on other court cases I've covered as a reporter. Victims of strangulation or smothering. The marks are only faint. I don't know if the Indonesian pathologist picked up on it or if it has been lost in translation in the report you received. Basically, it's highly unlikely that Jamie did it. George's killer was someone with smaller hands or a lighter touch . . .

I swallow, feeling Jamie's eyes on me. Ketut is a small guy. Perhaps this is proof that he murdered George.

BUT GUESS WHAT?! And this can't just be a coincidence . . .

A chill runs through me as I read on.

I've managed to find out why Erin was sent to Red Bees. There was a nasty fight in her previous school. Thankfully, a teacher managed to intervene just in time but the other student still ended up in hos-pital. She was being strangled . . . by Erin.

I look up. Jamie is waiting for me to do something. His hands are clasped, pleading for my help. My heartbeat quickens as the scene before me becomes clear. This is a trap.

I'm not here to save Erin from this evil monster.

She *is* the evil monster.

70

Sophia

Erin rushes back into the room. Gone is the meek, beaten-down wife; instead a warrior stands panting before us. 'Here! The doctor gave me this.' She waves a piece of paper in the air. It's a leaflet about antenatal care.

'That doesn't prove anything, my love,' Jamie says slowly. 'I think I would know if you were pregnant.'

Her wide eyes dart to mine. 'Sophia, we have to go. I don't know why he doesn't believe me. The doctor did the tests at the surgery! I just haven't told him before now because I don't trust him!'

Jamie speaks again. His voice is calm and low. 'You're not pregnant, you're just very unwell, Erin.'

'He's twisting everything. Don't fall for it, please, I'm begging you.'

My head is spinning. There's an ominous creak from outside. The storm is really picking up now.

Amira's words ring in my mind about Erin's hushed-up past. She tried to strangle someone once before; who says she couldn't have done it again?

'Erin,' I take a shaky breath. Thoughts are tripping over themselves as I try and make sense of things but I have to choose my words carefully. 'You need to be honest now. We can't go until—'

'Sophia, I wouldn't leave with her if I were you . . .' Jamie says, cutting me off. He's weirdly calm, dejected even. 'It's not just because she's got herself in this state. If you get into the car with her, you'll regret it. Trust me, please.'

'What are you talking about?' Erin shrieks.

My heartbeat is in my ears. Wind howls through the house.

'I'm sorry. You know I love you but I can't keep this secret any longer.' Jamie looks pained. He turns to me. 'Sophia, I told you she gets obsessed. She tried to kill Mark.'

Erin gasps. There is a boom of thunder. I feel the ice-cold hand of genuine fear grip my neck as I realise that no one knows I'm here.

'Sophia, come on. We have to go!' Erin is suddenly in front of me, pushing me. Gone is the woman I met on our honeymoon: the warmth, the cute laugh, the generous nature. In its place is a wild woman with fire in her eyes.

My feet remain planted.

I knew there was something I'd not yet pieced together.

Until now.

Jamie's right. That's why the car outside looked so familiar. It's the same size and colour as the car in the footage released by the police. I was in too much of a rush to see if Erin was OK and too soaked by the rain to stop and take a closer look. But somewhere in the back of my mind, something went in.

A witness said it was a female driver.

'You . . . It was you.' I stumble backwards, away from Erin. 'You hit Mark!'

'I don't know what you're talking about.' Erin raises her hands in defence, her eyes wide, darting around the room. 'My car's in the garage!' She clamps her hands over her ears, making a high-pitched whining noise as if to drown me out.

'Now will you believe me, Sophia? She's not well.' Jamie has to shout over her to be heard. 'Like this "pregnancy" – she believes things that aren't real. She gets obsessed very easily. It happened with Claire and now it's happened with you.'

Erin has stopped making that terrible noise.

'Sophia, we need to go!' she screams. 'Ignore everything he's saying!'

They're both talking over the other. My head snaps back and forth between the pair of them. The house seems to shake. The lights flicker and a gust of ice-cold air whooshes through the kitchen.

'Sophia, please. He's the insane one,' Erin pleads, tears rolling down her flushed cheeks. 'He's planning on taking me away but making it look like I chose to leave him. There's a one-way ticket with just my name on it.'

Jamie shakes his head in disbelief. 'What?' He grabs some papers from the side, near the kettle. I see a logo of a travel company on the envelope. 'You mean this? This printout I left you so you'd know what time to be ready for? It's not the actual ticket, Erin, they're in my emails. Return ones. Not that it matters now. The flight left hours ago.'

'W-what? No . . .' she stutters.

'Erin, my darling.' His voice is slightly softer now. 'You're not well. You haven't been well for a long time.' He turns his back on her. 'Sophia, I've been so worried about her. I thought coming here would be a fresh start. A project for her to throw herself into. I wanted to keep her safe for her own protection—'

As if in slow motion, woken from a sort of trance, I hear a primal scream. Erin suddenly launches herself forwards. Something catches the light in her right hand, something jagged. It looks like the blade of a knife. A sharp cry lodges in my mouth.

Then it all goes black.

71

Erin

Tuesday 15 November
HMP Broadfield, London

Today is the day.

I've been trying not to get myself too worked up in case it falls through at the last moment. It's all I've been able to think about from the moment I heard that the governor had given it the OK. I've tried to do my hair as nicely as possible. There's no chance of something decent to wear but I was able to trade a Pot Noodle for a clumpy mascara and tinted lipgloss, so that will have to do.

I take a deep breath. I need to stay calm, that's what my counsellor says. She's not actually a counsellor, she's a middle-aged woman with severe dandruff called Trudy who is trying to get us all to convert to Christianity, but I like sitting in the circle and feeling part of the group. They have to listen to me when it's my turn. I like that bit the best. Sometimes they nod, some yawn, some even snore, but Trudy always listens. When I told her about today, she placed two fat hands on my shoulders and told me to take lots of deep breaths and remember that God is by my side.

Until my visitor is sitting opposite me then I won't believe it's actually happening.

I can't help but smile watching her enter the room, filing in behind other people's visitors. There's a wariness in her pretty eyes.

I straighten out my smile and drop my eyes to the table. This is serious.

I know she will have been taken from the reception down the many corridors, all identical, designed to confuse you even more, before she reached this room. She would probably have heard the zoo animals all screeching and wailing and falling into hysterical fits of laughter from behind closed doors. At first, these noises scared me – I was used to living with the weight of silence, so it took a lot of adjustment – but slowly I've got used to them.

Sophia isn't here just for some sort of closure, restorative justice, or anything like that. Visits by the media are only allowed in exceptional circumstances. I specifically requested her. I need her to challenge my conviction. And I'm not sure how many strings were pulled, but she's here. It's incredible, really – not just the fact that she's here but more generally speaking. If I'd got the knife in a couple of inches lower, then she wouldn't be sitting opposite me now.

Jamie's lawyers claim I knew exactly what I was doing that stormy night.

They played the voicemail he'd saved on his phone, the one where I'm shrieking about being sent flowers, complaining to my kind husband for the unexpected gift. They also took my phone – supposedly a rich source of evidence to prove my guilt. The photos of Sophia I'd absently saved to my camera roll all those months ago came back to haunt me, to make me out as an obsessed stalker. Everything correlated with this behaviour ending in a jealous rage where I tried to stab Sophia to death.

Or so they allege.

At one point I gave up hope when they tried to pin the hit-and-run on me too. My weak alibi – home alone with no witnesses – didn't help my case. My car was picked up on a number of ANPR systems but they couldn't prove I was the one driving. I was so relieved when the court dropped it. Not enough evidence.

My defence team argued that I was 'mentally unwell' thanks to being a 'victim of coercion'. I was supposed to stab Jamie, after all. Sophia simply got in the way. I willingly admitted to that.

Wounding with intent, that's what they banged me away for. As soon as I was arrested, I asked the police officers if she was OK – I told them how I didn't mean to hurt her. I'd wanted to stay to make sure she was OK, that she was alive. But I couldn't; I had to flee before Jamie came after me. Who stabs their best friend on purpose?

Sophia's smile when she's escorted into the room and sees me for the first time looks pained. I rub the sleeves of my grey sweatshirt; there are tiny bobbles on the cuffs where it's been washed too many times. She's wearing smart black trousers that fit her perfectly and a pretty azure-blue jumper which reminds me of a tropical sea. I wonder if that's on purpose. Her hair is tied back into a low ponytail, with two grips on either side.

The room is cold. A window's been left ajar, just like at home.

She places her slim arms on the scuffed plastic table that sits as a barrier between us. The table reminds me of one you'd find on holiday. Once upon a time we were seated around one just like this. Well, perhaps a little more upmarket. The honeymoon was such a long time ago. A lifetime, in fact. It was the trip that changed everything, for all of us.

I know this table hasn't been placed here just to elicit something from the recesses of my mind. They're not that clever. They have plastic ones so no one gets hurt if it suddenly flips. I learned that the hard way. Still, it brings forth a comforting rush of nostalgia that I wasn't expecting. But it's sitting opposite her that's doing this, not the items in this horrible room.

'Sorry I'm late. I got a little lost on the way here.'

This forced politeness between us is strange. I bite down the annoyance that's nipping at me, overtaking the wistfulness that was there just a second ago.

'You're here now.' I clear my throat then pointlessly pat down my hair. There's a baby crying in the far corner of the friends and family room. I had hoped to be somewhere private.

'How's Mark?' I ask.

She isn't wearing a wedding ring. There's not even a faint tan line at the base of her ring finger to suggest one had ever been placed there. It's as if Mark, the honeymoon, us, didn't exist.

She ignores the question. 'Shall we get started?'

72

Erin

Sophia was there that night, yet she wants me to tell her exactly what happened. So I do. I tell her how I found a sharp piece of plastic which had broken off the smoke alarm and used it as a weapon. Granted, I only meant to hurt Jamie, but he moved and I ended up accidentally stabbing her. I learned later that he was the one to call 999. He waited with her, trying to stem the bleeding, as I was arrested up the country lane not far from the farmers' fields, looking like a drowned rat, blood all over my trembling hands.

I don't know how he was able to tend to Sophia's wound while, at the same time, he managed to get rid of the evidence before the house was sealed off as a crime scene.

Because I smashed the smoke alarms around our house into tiny pieces there was no way of knowing if they ever contained recording devices, as I maintained. In a way, I'm relieved that no footage has ever been released from that night. Imagine a courtroom seeing what happened – the final moments, before the cameras went off, would be my face in clear HD, a broom held aloft and eyes wild with intent. The prosecution would have used this to pinpoint the exact moment that I 'lost my mind'.

When they learned I had access to a phone I was asked why I didn't call the police if I truly feared for my life. If the doors were locked, as I claimed, then why didn't I break a window to escape? they asked. Clearly, my inability to do any of these things proved that I wasn't ever in danger of being harmed by my husband, as I continually repeated to anyone who would listen.

The police didn't find the alleged fake stalking notice documents or the phone I'd used to call Sophia. I still don't know who that phone belonged to or if it was a burner that Jamie used. As I said, he cleaned up good.

I guess it doesn't matter. It won't change the outcome of that night.

Kat sold her story, interviewed by our very own Sophia. I don't know how much for, but I bet it's a lot, judging by the photos of her kitchen renovation that has somehow magically appeared. They think we don't have access to phones and Facebook here, but we do. We just need to be careful about it. Kat said that she 'should have seen the signs all along'. Apparently it was all linked to my childhood trauma. She went on about how I strangled some girl at my high school. That rumour has followed me around like a bad smell.

They used such an awful photo of me in the newspaper. The one Sophia took of us on our honeymoon, a split second before George entered our world. I'd lifted my hand to brush my hair back; the motion is blurred and my eyes captured in a way that makes me look crazed. Of course the press were always going to use that picture.

I can tell that Sophia still believes I drove into her husband and left him for dead. As if I could do something like that! I'm not sure how Jamie got away with that one.

I underestimated him. We all did.

When I heard that Ketut, the hotel barman, had been arrested for murdering George, and that the fall didn't kill him, he'd been strangled, I allowed myself to breathe a sigh of relief. I always knew someone else was there that night. He was the one who killed George. Neither Jamie nor I have publicly spoken out about George's murder. We both know we're each as guilty as the other for our actions – the moment we decided to flee instead of call for help.

Jamie was the one who thought George was dead and I took his word for it. Why didn't I properly try and find a pulse? I don't know if Jamie just panicked, but the truth is that we maybe could have saved his life.

I don't think I'll ever understand why I ran away. The shame will be with me until the day I die. I was a coward. Too scared to speak up. I'm not running away any longer.

Perhaps if we had gone to find help then George would still be alive. Or perhaps Ketut would have killed us instead. I still don't really understand what George had on Ketut that could have led to his murder. There's no clear motive, regardless of the wild rumours on the Bali Facebook page that I still occasionally check.

Despite everything, the hardest part wasn't being abandoned by everyone I loved or thought I loved, but the fact that I lost the baby. For a short time I was pregnant – the tests I did at the GP are proof of that – but when I fell down the stairs, it proved too catastrophic and what I thought was spotting was actually my worst fears coming true. There wasn't enough of the pregnancy hormone to show up on a requested urine sample at the police station. My heart is still in pieces.

Of course, Jamie denied ever drugging me, saying it was just another of my 'delusions'. He was too clever. Whatever he used went under the radar of the blood and urine tests I took. He made sure to cover his back with everything.

Another female prisoner with terrible bleached roots, sitting on the table nearest to us, lets out a machine-gun cackle, jolting me back to the present. I sit up a little straighter.

Sophia crosses her arms. 'In your letter you said you had something new to tell me. The reason you got me here?'

I clear my dry throat. I want this to come out just as I rehearsed. 'I really want to say sorry. As I've said a thousand times, I never meant to hurt you.'

I flick my eyes over to the guard slowly walking around the room. He drags his feet the closer he gets to us. Listening in. Watching us intently.

'That's it?' Sophia lets out a sigh.

'No.' I shake my head.

'Erin, I gave you a chance. I took a gamble because you sounded so desperate in your letter, but you've not told me anything I don't already know.'

She is getting to her feet.

She can't go, not yet.

'Please, wait,' I say. 'Here.' I twist my wedding ring. The skin around my knuckles resists but after a firm tug the ring comes off. I place it on the table in front of Sophia. 'To say sorry. You can pawn it. Jamie told me it belonged to his grandmother. It's an antique.'

'I can't take this, Erin.' She pushes the ring back towards me with an outstretched finger. It scrapes across the scuffed tabletop.

'I insist. I don't want it. I only kept it because it might be worth something.'

'Erin, take it back.' She nervously glances around to see if anyone is watching us. The guard has walked on by.

'No. Sophia. I *need* you to take it.' I hope she picks up on the emphasis. If there wasn't a no-touching rule I would lean over and shove the bloody thing on her finger.

Her nose twitches as if she needs to blow it. There's an awkward pause.

'Come on. Stop being silly.' With a heavy sigh, she picks the ring up and goes to hand it back to me.

Then something crosses her face. She holds the gold band closer to her eye and twirls it up to the light. I hear her swear under her breath, colour rushing to her cheeks.

Finally, I think. Finally she can see what it is I'm trying to tell her. I can't say it out loud because I will sound crazy, and Lord knows I've been tarnished with that brush enough times.

She slips the ring on to her little finger and slowly shakes her head. And then she sits back down.

73

Jamie

I answer the call on the third ring. Not wanting to appear too keen.

'Hey, you.' I hold the phone closer to my ear. 'Did she say anything new?'

'No,' Sophia replies with a sigh.

When she first told me she was going into prison to interview Erin, I'd been nervous, just in case something came out. Some small thing I might have overlooked. I've been restless all day waiting to hear how it went. There was a slim chance that Erin might somehow fool Sophia and twist things so she'd feel sorry for her. However, deep down, I know Sophia is too intelligent to fall for something like that.

'It didn't go how I expected at all.'

I can hear the disappointment in her voice.

'How did it feel, seeing her again?' As soon as I ask her, I wish I hadn't. It's a bit of a stupid question: how do I expect her to feel, being face to face with the woman who tried to kill her?

'Weird. Sad. I don't know what I expected,' Sophia says. There's another sigh. 'Are you at home?'

'Yeah.' I sit back on my sofa. A noisy bike speeds past, the rattle of a motor cutting her off from whatever she was about to say. 'Sorry? You broke up,' I say, irritated at the interruption.

'I said she's dyed her hair blonde. It was quite unnerving, to be honest, walking in and seeing her sitting there looking like me.'

'She doesn't look anything like you.'

I glance at the time. She must have gone back to work after she left that awful place, so Erin can't have said anything to upset her too much. The thought cheers me. Now I've heard from her, I can relax.

'Well, anyway, I had to tell my editor that Erin hasn't budged a bit from her testimony. If anything, I'm impressed with how rigidly she's stuck to her story.'

'She's always been that way. Stubborn,' I reply.

I can hear London life buzzing around her. A car horn beeping and the faint sound of music.

'Anyway,' I say, 'enough about her. Are you still coming round later? Is seven OK? Thought we'd eat about eight-ish.'

I've offered to cook dinner, a thank you for sticking by me throughout all of this.

'Yeah, sounds great.'

I don't mind that it took Sophia so long to see sense. It was a traumatic time for us all. It was only when she officially split from Mark and the press attention had died away that we began to hang out more. It happened organically. When you've been through something like this it creates a bond.

My biggest concern with Sophia visiting the prison was that Erin would start mouthing off about Claire again.

An unwritten part of the divorce agreement was that Claire would continue to keep her mouth shut about some of the 'legalities' she'd discovered about my business. But this silence came at a price. For a while it was fine, but then the odd favour turned into regular, needy demands to be paid. A cheeky fucking hefty sum at that too! Of course, unhelpfully, that was when Erin decided to start showing an interest in Claire, obsessing over her social media, sending cryptic messages that could easily be read another way.

I didn't want my old wife telling my new wife how the company snooped on its customers. That's when I sent that stupid fake stalking notice. I couldn't let her get any closer to Claire, in case she also discovered the truth about what I'd done.

The notice worked: Erin backed off. Everything was good for a time.

And then Claire lost her job. She upped her figure. If I didn't pay then she would take it to the police, make it public, which, in turn, would have quickly reached the investors. Not that she knew even half of it. The secrets I'd heard, the lives I'd been given access to with the touch of a button and a wifi camera. People are blind to how vulnerable security makes them. It worked to my advantage – anonymous bribes, even the odd burglary on their street when I heard them speaking about changing supplier or getting rid of their security. I have a team beneath me who are only too happy to do the dirty work, for the right price.

I tried to shut Claire up by killing Pepper. She loved that mangy cat. I saw her on the phone to her mum in hysterics, thanks to the camera I'd hidden earlier. Smoke alarms are great hiding places – everyone has one and they rarely, if ever, get properly checked.

It wasn't enough. I needed to shut her up. For good.

I was given a master key when my company won the security contract for the apartment block. I'd pulled some strings to move Claire in after we separated and sold our previous flat. I could keep an eye on her there. She never questioned my kindness – vanity and wanting to live at a fancy address took care of that.

She thought it was someone from maintenance at the door so was more than a little surprised to see me standing there.

She was a mess. I could already smell the booze on her breath, despite 'working from home'. Her blouse had a stain on it. Her tights were snagged on the calves, and threads were hanging from her tight skirt.

She started crying over Pepper the minute she saw me, snot sliding down her nose. God, she was repulsive.

After some stilted condolences, she pulled herself together and checked the clock. She told me she was leaving for a meeting in ten minutes but I managed to persuade her to rearrange. Told her she needed to be kind to herself, especially after what she'd been through with the poor cat. She pulled a sickie and, after some painful small talk, I encouraged her to have a drink. A toast to Pepper. She hesitated for a microsecond but the cold white wine – her favourite brand – I had brought was too tempting. I watched her drink from her drug-laced glass, identical to one she owned. When she was out cold, I went into the bathroom to run her a bath.

The plan was to make it look as if she'd taken an overdose and drowned, but somehow she came to and was halfway out of the door, stumbling towards the stairwell, before I realised. She saw me coming after her and panicked. All I could do was watch as she fell down the metal steps, bones snapping along the way.

I couldn't believe it when I pulled up the CCTV to splice the footage and saw my own fucking fiancée there just a few hours earlier! I'd already tampered with the tapes before the police rocked up and Erin confessed about her visit, beside herself with panic.

I hear the sound of a reversing lorry at Sophia's end of the phone line. The methodical beeps jolt me back to the present.

'Do you fancy chilli con carne or enchiladas for dinner?' I ask Sophia, wandering into the kitchen.

'I'm easy. You choose.'

I smile down the line, glancing up at the smoke alarm fixed to the ceiling. No more cameras. I never discovered how Erin sussed that one out.

The irony is, because of all this negative press with my mental wife, all the investors pulled out ahead of the launch date anyway. But I try not to dwell on what I've lost. I'm planning on taking my product abroad instead, somewhere where the laws aren't as strict or there aren't as many hoops to jump through.

'Oh, I forgot to tell you something,' Sophia says.

'Hmm?' I tip the phone against my chin and open the fridge, checking I've got everything I need.

'The Balinese man who killed George Kingsley has started an appeal process.'

I almost drop a jar of chopped garlic. 'Oh, yeah?'

'Mmm. Ketut. I'm not sure if you remember him? Well, he's always maintained his innocence and campaigners have been trying for months to get him in front of the court of appeal and it's finally worked. They claim there wasn't enough evidence to lock him up in the first place.'

I let this sink in. I rub a hand against my chin, still getting used to the clean-shaven look that I've gone back to.

'That's mad.'

I hear someone wolf-whistle in the background and a dart of jealousy slices through me.

Sophia coughs. 'I know. I mean, who knows what the judge will say. But, if Ketut gets released, then you know what that means. George's killer is still out there.'

74

Jamie

I grit my teeth at the mention of George Kingsley. In an instant I'm back in Bali on the last night of our honeymoon. The whole reason we're in this mess is because of that drunk filming us. I couldn't risk a sex tape getting out – not to mention the possibility of the Balinese police arresting us for shagging on the cliffs. If the investors ever found out about that, it would be career suicide. But it was clear that George was never going to just hand over his phone and walk away.

So I took matters into my own hands.

A foot out, a slight nudge, that was all it took. The slippery steps did the rest. I remember watching George fall, his body tumbling and a helpless cry escaping from his lips. Then the sickening crack as his skull kissed the wet concrete. It was pretty grim to watch, but I couldn't take my eyes off him.

I never found out why this George fella was even there that night. Turns out he was waiting around looking for Mark. You couldn't make it up! Later, when Sophia told me that in confidence, I had to excuse myself to go to the bathroom, emerging only when I was sure my face didn't give away how fucking ironic it all was. Turns out that Mark – Mr Plain, Mr Nice Guy – had secrets of his own. Debts, gambling, loan sharks, you name it. I have to admit this confession made me look at him in a different light. I'd never have thought he'd have the balls.

And then, to top it all off, some barman turned up after me and Erin left, to deliver the final blow. This Ketut guy strangled the old man, no doubt about it, appeal process or not. In fact, I wish I could shake his hand. I thought I'd killed George. At least now I can sleep easy knowing I'll never be linked to the crime.

To be honest, now I think about it, Sophia kept me on my toes for far too long. She certainly put up a good fight – I was exhausted trying to put her off the scent that we played a part in George's death. But then, just as I finished fighting that fire, she started banging on about Claire.

I watched as she paid a visit to Claire's parents, boring Marie and even more boring Richard. I could only imagine what dirt she was trying to dig up. That was when I knew I needed her to back off.

I had a real stroke of luck during that D.R.U.M. gig where, after a few too many beers, I got Mark to share the reason why he'd had CCTV installed. I listened to him harp on about some fella called Rupert. He even told me about this bloke's dogs, some breed I'd never heard of. It was a no-brainer, but sending a thug and the same kind of dog to scare Sophia on her run was clearly too subtle. Or she was stronger and more determined than I'd expected.

The trip to London in Erin's car after I picked it up from the garage was a last-minute decision. I needed to ramp things up, make them realise the lengths I would go to, to stop her snooping around in my life. A wig and good fortune were all it took. I followed Mark from his office then took my shot, just as I'd done to Pepper the cat. With Erin already clearly losing her mind, she was the obvious fall guy. Or girl.

God, she was tricky to manage after George's fall. I tried to hold my temper but there were times she simply pushed me over the edge with her endless questions and paranoia.

Once I came up with a plan, she was like putty in my hands. I knew the only way to save myself was to discredit her. Everything about her. After all, no one listens to the crazies. The voicemail of her screaming about those flowers I sent was the perfect proof of her deteriorating sanity – I was the victim having to live with someone so unstable.

Then it was a case of getting rid of her – in the least obvious way – but the loose top step didn't do the job well enough. I watched in fury as she picked herself up from the pile at the bottom of the stairs. I wasn't planning on staging an overdose, instead we were supposed to go to Venice where she would have 'accidentally' drowned, but she went on her little power cut spree and discovered too much too soon. I like to think I'm nothing if not adaptable.

Even I have to say that her pregnancy lies took me by surprise, but I guess at that point her mind wasn't her own. I mean, I knew what my wife was up to 24/7, I'd have known if she was pregnant. The thought of having a baby with that woman sickens me.

That stormy night in our kitchen, it couldn't have been more perfect when Erin properly lost it and stabbed Sophia herself. She pleaded guilty, and Sophia readily bought the story I'd fed her that night. And, with no evidence placing me or Erin at the scene, Claire's death was never mentioned again. Sophia apologised for ever doubting me. I got off on that . . .

'Do you want me to bring anything for tonight?' Sophia asks, pulling me back to the present. Her voice is like warm honey.

'No, just yourself.'

'I thought you might say that.'

See! We're practically finishing each other's sentences. I laugh.

'You're not planning on driving, are you?' I ask. I want to fast-forward time so she'll be here, beside me.

Sophia coughs. 'No, I'll get a taxi over. But I won't be able to stay too late as I've got work tomorrow.'

Just then the doorbell goes. Developers have taken over some of the farmland; it's probably one of them coming to inform me of a planning application or some bollocks. So much for my slice of peace and quiet up here. Soon there will be a whole host of new homes, but I'll be long gone before they lay a single foundation. It's too risky sticking around – they might find something I've overlooked.

'Hang on. That's the door,' I say. 'Shall I call you back, or . . .'

'No, I'll wait. There's something else I wanted to ask you.'

I like the sound of that.

'Oh, really?' I smile to myself as I jump to my feet, tucking my phone between my shoulder and my ear as I open the front door.

'Mr James Steele?' a police officer asks. Behind him are two more officers, all wearing the same tight expression.

A ripple of panic tears through my chest. 'Yes. What is this about?'

'I'm arresting you on suspicion of the murder of Claire Connelly and the attempted murder of Mark Spencer. You do not have to say anything, but anything you do say may harm your defence . . .'

The police officer's voice fades out as he reads me my rights. The mobile phone falls to the ground as they roughly tug my arms into handcuffs.

I swear I can hear Sophia laughing down the receiver.

75

Sophia

'They've done it. They've arrested him!' I tell Amira, tears of relief filling my eyes.

I hear Jamie swear and then the thud of his phone dropping to the floor, then a policewoman confirming that he is being taken into custody.

'Incredible work.' Amira lifts her coffee cup to mine. 'I knew you'd get him in the end.'

This has been the hardest undercover operation I've ever done. It's almost killed me, trying to keep Jamie onside.

'Hang on, let me call Peter just to confirm. I wouldn't put it past Jamie to slip out of this one.'

Peter tells me a snapper was waiting in the bushes to capture the whole thing. It's official. I swallow and turn slightly away from Amira, needing to pull myself together. This sudden rush of emotion is embarrassing, but it's been overwhelming at times.

A Costa napkin is pushed in front of my flushed face.

'It's OK to cry. You've been through a hell of a lot!'

I take the napkin and dab it against my eyes, smiling at her. The past few months of holding it together in front of Jamie, acting as a shoulder to cry on, while recovering from being stabbed, has taken its toll. I sniff. 'Yep.'

Jamie painted the picture of Erin being the villain so perfectly. However, something told me that it wasn't as clear-cut as that. That was when I offered to go undercover – keep your friends close but your enemies closer. I was sure that if I gained Jamie's trust then he would open up, or at least drop a clue about what really happened.

Jamie insisted that Erin was never pregnant but, according to sources in the prison, she was adamant that she was – and that it was his fault she lost the baby. I'm not able to access her medical records so, to this day, I don't know the full truth.

For weeks, I've been waiting for the missing piece of the puzzle.

There was always something off about how Jamie had seemed to know everything. He had bragged about it the first time we met: how his company was working on something so small, tiny cameras, the size of pinheads. I was sure he'd used cameras to follow Erin around the house – in the smoke alarms, as she said – but investigators found no evidence of them – if they were ever there, he did a good job of getting rid of them all. And it wasn't enough: he also seemed to know where she was when she was out of the house.

Something didn't add up.

Ironically, it was Erin who helped me figure it out. Or, rather, it was her wedding ring.

'There was a hairline crack inside the ring that you would miss if you weren't looking. I cracked it open like an Easter egg and inside was what looked like a tiny black chip,' I tell

Amira, remembering how my breath caught in my throat at the grim discovery. 'He had been tracking her all along.'

'No way! When did she discover this?'

'She said she found it recently and that's when she wrote to me, begging for a visit, wanting to show me in person. She seemed genuinely spooked by it. She had no idea what the microchip contained: whether it was purely a GPS location tracker or if it recorded conversations. Either way, that's when the floodgates opened and everything rushed out. She admitted she'd been there on the day Claire died, how Jamie had tampered with the CCTV to make it look as though she wasn't.'

As soon as I left the prison this morning, I contacted the police, and they were able to use sophisticated software to enhance the footage Jamie had given them from Claire's apartment. It didn't take them more than a couple of hours to see how it had been cut and spliced together, knitted to look like the same day when it wasn't. They're reopening the investigation into Claire's death. A source told me, off the record, that apparently a neighbour at the time mentioned hearing raised voices but presumed it was the television blaring. Officers didn't follow this up. And, on the back of the coroner's verdict of accidental death, the case was closed.

'I called Marie and asked her to check Claire's wedding ring to see if it was the same,' I say. 'Another tiny microchip. They couldn't believe it – he'd told Claire the ring was his grandmother's, a family heirloom, just as he'd told Erin – probably to explain why he didn't ask her to help choose it. He was able to track his wife's every move.' The thought chills me. 'I think the hit-and-run was unplanned, to try and put me off looking into his background. Because it was so rushed, he got sloppy. Erin's GPS wedding ring placed her at home – not in London – add this to the fact his DNA was in her car and, well, I just hope the police can get this evidence to stick.'

Amira visibly shivers. 'What a creep.'

'I know.' I sip my cappuccino. 'So then all I had to do was call Jamie and keep up the lie that I was going round for dinner.'

I can still taste the overriding nausea at having to act so normally around him.

A message from the snapper at the scene buzzes through. 'Check this out!' I say, turning my phone screen towards Amira.

When they arrested him, officers found a brand new jewellery box. Inside was a necklace with a location tracker – surely intended for Sophia. Jamie was alleging that he installed the microchip as a way to track the expensive piece of jewellery, in case it got lost or stolen.

I can't help but roll my eyes. 'An extreme version of "Find My iPhone". What bullshit.'

'"They also discovered two forged passports in his name . . ."' She continues, passing my phone back. 'Whoa. I mean, who knows how long he's got away with it? You told me he'd planned a romantic break to Venice – he was definitely going to bump Erin off there. I just can't believe it! There's no doubt Claire wasn't his first victim. It was all too slick for a beginner.'

'Who knows? Personally, I still think the pair of them were there that night in Bali. They killed George, not Ketut. But neither of them will admit to anything. If they do, then they'll both face the consequences,' I say, finishing my coffee. 'It depends on how sophisticated the GPS location tracker is in her wedding ring, whether the data will be found to exactly pinpoint them at the cliffs. In wanting to know exactly where she was all the time, he might have set them both up for a fall. I literally have no idea! I don't think you can predict anything about a couple like that.'

'Yeah, they were definitely both there. But . . .' Amira shakes her head. 'My money's on Erin still.'

She's convinced that Erin was the one to try to strangle George but gave up, or didn't have the strength to apply as much pressure as was needed. She likes to regularly remind me how Mark and I went for dinner on our honeymoon with a pair of psychopaths.

I'm not sure. I believe Erin needs a lot of help, but she isn't insane – and this is coming from the woman she stabbed. What happened to me wasn't premeditated. I simply got in the way. I tried to change my statement but it was too late. The police didn't want to know – their job was done.

'Right, I think we deserve a slice of cake. What do you reckon?' Amira asks, breaking into my thoughts.

'Sorry, I can't, I'm meeting Mark. Oops, that reminds me.' I pull out my purse. Tucked into the inner compartment is my wedding ring. I've not been wearing it for the past few months. Subconsciously, it was to help me stay in the zone, but also just in case Jamie was watching. I pull it out and marvel at how shiny it still is as it slips comfortably down my ring finger.

Mark wants to give me an apology letter that his counsellor asked him to write – part of his ongoing process in Gamblers

Anonymous. I've heard all his apologies; writing it down is just another step in his recovery. I'm proud of him for sticking with it.

After being released from the hospital, he got a nasty infection which blighted his recovery. He leans a little to the left now, still limping from the hit-and-run. I get a pang of sadness whenever I think of all the activities he once adored that he can no longer do. The hiking, jet-skiing and rock-climbing. Our honeymoon was packed full of them. A cold chill runs through me. *Don't think about that trip.* For so long I lay in bed blaming myself. I was the one who wanted to go to Hotel Asmara. What if we'd chosen a different place? Our paths would never have crossed with Erin and Jamie's.

It's too late to think of alternatives; what has happened has happened and I can't change it. That's what my therapist says. They would have latched on to someone else if it wasn't us. My scars are healing nicely and everyone says I'm coping with the events remarkably. That tough terrapin skin does come in handy.

But it's been far from easy. There were so many times I considered getting a divorce and starting afresh, unsure if I could trust Mark again. He has moved in with his sister for our trial separation, which has helped give me time to think. I've realised that I can't give up on what we had that easily. He needs help; this addiction is an illness. As long as he's working hard on getting better, then I will support him. I took my vows seriously: in sickness and in health.

'Say hello to him from me. And well done again, I always knew you could do it.' Amira smiles.

I give her a hug before waving goodbye, pulling my coat around myself. I need to hurry. I pick up my pace, excited to be able to tell Mark that we got Jamie.

Finally, we can turn a page. Everything is going to be OK.

76

Mark

I'm sitting in the library as it's the only place where I can access a printer. I choose a table tucked away in the theology section, surrounded by maroon hardbacks and gilded pages. It all seems a bit over the top, writing Sophia a letter and printing it off, but it's necessary. I could handwrite it but she probably wouldn't be able to read my messy scrawl. I can't leave any room for error. The quietness makes this feel even more like a confessional.

I run my fingers across my chin. I've grown a beard – Sophia says it suits me; it's like being married to a new man. I pull my gaze away from the books and try to concentrate on what I have to say to my amazing wife. My sponsor tells me how important it is to be real and honest. If I'm to get my marriage back on track, then we have to have everything out in the open. Sophia has been an angel. I know how much I hurt her, and this is one of the ways I can prove that I'm a changed man.

This might just be a letter, but it is so much more than that.

I start to type.

Dear Sophia,

I need to explain some things. Bear with me as this might take a while. To start with, I never should have gambled on our honeymoon. The reason I'd tried to encourage us not to be on our phones while we were away was because of the temptation of online casinos. I'd already lost so much money . . .

It's bad enough that I let myself get swayed by Rupert and took his money in return for a 'favour'. But to lie to my new wife about going to a market when I was at an illegal cockfight was a new low. And then it got worse.

It feels as if there's a rock on my chest, but I must take myself back.

Back to that night at the Blue Fin. I haven't been completely honest before. Yes, I went to the cockfight with Ketut. Yes, George was there trying to show me how it all worked. But I didn't lose my money. It was stolen by George.

It was incredible really, when I saw him at the Blue Fin, that I was able to carry on a conversation with him. This retired butcher was as corrupt as they come.

I needed to get my money back but I didn't know how. It was only after bumping into George accidentally by the gents' toilets in the Blue Fin that I came up with a plan.

I went along with the pretence of meeting George for another fight that evening, after the meal was over, but really I vowed to get my money back.

As the storm drew in, I snuck out of the hotel and went to the steps by the cliffs, the prearranged meeting place.

I couldn't have imagined in my worst nightmares what I'd see when I got there.

At first, it was too dark to make out the body, the rain dripping in my eyes making it harder to see. I tentatively approached the figure lying broken and bloodied at the bottom of the steps, legs and arms flailed out, a crimson stain puddling around his beaten head. It was only as I got closer that I realised I was looking at George.

I froze, my mouth rushing with saliva, spots appearing at the edges of my eyes. I'd never seen a dead body before. As horrifying as it was, I'd come all this way, I couldn't leave empty-handed. I had to get the cash that was rightfully mine and then race back to the hotel before Sophia discovered I was gone.

I needed to be quick; I couldn't hang around in case anyone happened to walk past, although that was unlikely given the weather. But, as I thrust my trembling hands in the pocket of another man's jeans to search for a wallet containing my rightful cash, trying to block out the absurdity of it all, there was a choking sort of sound.

I shot back in horror.

George wasn't dead.

His chest quivered; the slightest gasp of air left his parted bloodied lips. Whoever had done this to him hadn't finished the job.

I moved closer.

It was a split-second decision.

It wasn't just because it was the humane thing to do. If George had somehow recovered then he could have easily told Sophia the truth, ruined everything.

I found myself reaching out and wrapping my trembling, damp hands around George's throat. Unable to look, my stomach lurching at the spongy flesh between my fingers. Then the unmistakable crunch. I hadn't expected that. My eyes were anywhere but on George. Tears ran down my cheeks, mixing with the rain that was falling. Once it was done and I was sure he was definitely dead, I pulled out his wallet and took the wad of cash, careful not to touch anything else.

I was about to put the wallet back in his pocket when I realised my fingerprints would be all over the faded leather. Did rainwater wash off DNA? I had no bloody clue. But I needed to make a decision, and fast. I stumbled away from the body and cast a shaking arm back, tossing the wallet over the cliff edge and out into the inky black ocean with as much force as I could muster.

There was no thrill or pleasure at taking a man's life. Nothing else crossed my mind as I performed the final act. It was only afterwards, in the isolated madness that followed, that I thought about George and his family on a terrible loop. I had killed him to save my own marriage. I did it so Sophia would never know of the depths I was in. What sort of person does that? I didn't think I could stoop so low.

Then came the paranoia. I was certain that Sophia would know something terrible had happened. How I'd managed to act normal at a fucking floating reed breakfast the next day was beyond me. I was walking a tightrope and could fall off at any moment. So many times, I would run a shower or blast music just to drown out the catastrophising voices in my head, or go for late-night runs to try to burn myself out so I could sleep. I was trapped in hell.

When Sophia started to do more and more digging into George's death, I could barely keep it together.

I made some really stupid decisions. Like when I got way too drunk at the D.R.U.M. gig, desperate just to cut loose and act 'normal' without the weight of the world on my shoulders. How fucking foolish! The night is a blur. I don't remember Jamie specifically asking questions about what had happened with Sophia that made us step up our security, but I must have told him everything.

However, when she said she was meeting Peter in person the next day I knew I had to try and sober up. I switched her phone charger off at the wall once she was asleep, so the alarm wouldn't go off. Not that my plan worked. This story just seemed to consume her!

The night Sophia asked me to my face about Angie's accusation, I had to go to bed early. I laughed it off but inside I was terrified what else might crop up and disgusted at myself for looking my wife in the eye and lying to her. The CCTV I had installed soon became invaluable for keeping track of whether the police were on to me. Of course, I had no idea I'd been conned into upgrading it by such a psycho. When Sophia suggested getting rid of it, I knew I couldn't let her. But, back then, I had no idea I'd let Jamie into our lives.

Living with this terrible secret was my penance. So was being hit by that car. It felt like fate that it happened coming out of the bookies'. Despite promising myself that I would stop gambling, it was a sickness inside me. Having to confess everything to Sophia in the hospital, and seeing the look of hurt on her horrified face, was the wake-up call I needed to sort my life out.

When my sponsor suggested I explain to Sophia how it had all begun, I'd struggled to answer. At first, it was innocent, a tip-off on the horses that came good. Then, a short lucky streak at the bookies'. Soon, I was congratulating myself for increasing our savings pot. But then it spiralled. The buzz got harder to chase. I lost more than I won. I emptied our savings, spent all the cash wedding gifts, even used her bank card to withdraw cash once or twice. Reclaiming the money that George stole was my opportunity to fight back and stand up for myself.

With a deep sigh, I write my name at the bottom of the letter. I press print, making sure to snatch the piece of paper before any librarians cast their eyes over my confession. With a lick, I seal the envelope and scribble Sophia's name on the front.

'Hey,' I say when I see Sophia waiting for me outside.

'Hey.'

I lean over and kiss her tentatively on her cheek. Baby steps.

'How did it go?' I ask, stuffing my hands into my coat pockets.

'We got him! The police will be calling you soon about the hit-and-run. Jamie was behind it all.'

The look on her face makes my spirit soar. Finally, I can breathe. 'Are you . . . crying?' Sophia asks, looking puzzled.

I swipe my eyes and let out a laugh. 'No! It's just the wind.'

I'm lying. I want to drop to my knees and weep with happiness. Hold my arms outstretched to the sky and thank whoever has helped me get away with this. With Jamie arrested and Erin inside, that means there are no more links to our Balinese honeymoon. The nightmare is finally over.

'Now what?' I ask.

'What do you mean?' A breath of cold air escapes her perfect lips. 'Now we go and get on with our lives.'

It's time.

I hand over the sealed letter. One page of A4, explaining how sorry I am for putting us both through this. My gambling addiction almost ruined our lives, but I am determined to keep that in the past. We have a bright future ahead.

It is all true, but it's not the whole truth.

I think of the deleted text. The version of my confession that will never see the light of day. I will protect this secret for the rest of my life.

After all, I made a vow to my wife, and I intend to honour it.

In sickness and health, for better or worse, till death us do part.

ACKNOWLEDGEMENTS

The idea for *The Honeymoon* came from a nightmare but, since then, everything else has been a dream.

I'll be forever grateful to Welbeck for taking a chance on me. From the moment we met, I knew you meant business. I trust your wonderful vision in making this book the best it can be.

Shout out to the talented folks in sales, design, marketing, PR, production and editorial for all your hard work: Jon Elek, Rachel Hart, Jennifer Edgecombe, Simon Michele, James Horobin, Nico Poilblanc, Carrie-Ann Pitt, Sophie Leeds, Lizzie Ferenczy, Annabel Robinson, Rob Cox, Margarida Ribeiro, Arlene Lestrade and the team Down Under at Welbeck Australia.

Special thanks to everyone who has helped shape this book, including copywriter extraordinaire Linda McQueen, Jenny Page for the proof-reading magic, and especially my editor Rosa Schierenberg – beautiful inside and out – who has been the most wonderful support.

I still pinch myself that I'm represented by the best in the biz at Mushens Entertainment: my agent Juliet Mushens, and her wonderful team Rachel Neely, Liza DeBlock and Kiya Evans. Thank you for all you do behind the scenes, especially for reading early drafts of *The Honeymoon* and offering such valuable feedback.

To my incredible family at home and overseas, and especially to our new family members – Anastasiia Kozmina and Oleksii Danko. We're so grateful that you chose us when you were forced to flee.

My everlasting love and thanks to my husband, John, and my children, E and A, for bringing such joy to my world.

To my friends for putting up with me talking about imaginary characters as if they were real people. In particular Jen Atkinson, Claire Birch, Jo Huggins, Laura Hughes, Emma Lord and Jenna Tester.

Thanks to Jenny and Chris Higham for always making me feel welcome when I need to get away and focus. Time spent at Top End Cottage makes me so happy.

Thanks to my talented author friends, especially Cesca Major, Kirsty Greenwood, Isabelle Broom, Katie Marsh, Emylia Hall, Katie Khan and the team at The Novelry, and to Claire Douglas for the motivating word races. Your support and encouragement is priceless.

Finally, thank you for picking up this book. I really appreciate your support. You can get in touch with me: kate@kategrayauthor.com, send me a tweet: @KateGrayAuthor, or tag me on Instagram @kate_gray_author, where I'll be following the hashtag #thehoneymoonbook.

ABOUT THE AUTHOR

© Johnny Ring

Kate Gray lives in Yorkshire, England.
She juggles her love of writing around her
two young children. *The Honeymoon* is
her first psychological thriller – she has also
written six commercial women's fiction
novels as Katy Colins.